Chloe Baker's Lost Date

Also by Katie Wicks

Hazel Fine Sings Along

Chloe Baker's Lost Date

Katie Wicks

 by **wattpad** books

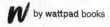 by wattpad books

An imprint of Wattpad WEBTOON Book Group

Copyright © 2024 Catherine McKenzie

Published in Canada by Wattpad WEBTOON Book Group, a division of Wattpad WEBTOON Studios, Inc.

36 Wellington Street E., Suite 200, Toronto, ON M5E 1C7 Canada

www.wattpad.com

First W by Wattpad Books edition: May 2024

ISBN 978-1-99077-860-5 (Trade Paper original)
ISBN 978-1-99077-861-2 (eBook edition)

Library and Archives Canada Cataloguing in Publication information is available upon request.

Printed and bound in Canada

1 3 5 7 9 10 8 6 4 2

Cover design by Laura Eckes
Typesetting by Delaney Anderson

Chloe Baker's Lost Date

Chapter One

He was late. Late for our date.

Five minutes, seven, ten.

I sat at a table covered with a red-checkered tablecloth in the crowded brunch place on Columbus Avenue where we'd agreed to meet, clutching my phone, waiting for an explanation for his tardiness.

Twelve minutes, sixteen, twenty.

I sipped slowly at the freshly squeezed orange juice I'd ordered and read the pun-filled menu for the tenth time, full of items like *You're bacon me crazy* and *I like you a waffle lot*. I smiled nervously at the waitress, a pretty Black woman who looked like she was in her early twenties and whose name tag said JANIE. She was starting to look at me with pity. How many times had she seen someone stood up by a blind date?

Judging from her expression, I wasn't the first.

The restaurant was full of couples—laughing, enjoying the lazy

Sunday ritual. As I watched them with envy, I wondered: What was the reasonable cutoff time for me to leave? Half an hour, right? Any longer would be ridiculous.

I crossed my legs nervously, tapping my light-gray Vans against the black and white tiled floor. My faded-wash jeans felt too tight, and I was regretting the thin blue shirt I'd chosen last night. It matched my eyes, but I was worried it was see-through in the sunlight that poured through the window.

This is why I hate dating. It turns me into a questioning mess. I can't help second-guessing every decision and criticizing myself for each one.

It was my best friend, Kit, who'd insisted I go on a date with Jack Dunne, the tech guy from her office.

"You need to go out with him, Chloe Baker," Kit had said, her thick black hair swinging around her face as she moved her hands for emphasis. "And get back out there. Your dry season has gone on way too long."

That's what she'd taken to calling the two years since I'd broken up with Christian and replaced him with Netflix binges of *Love Is Blind*.

"No need to be so smug, Katherine Wang. Not all of us were lucky enough to be set up with the perfect guy by our *mother*."

Kit made a face, but it was true. Her mother, Lian—who'd refused to call Kit by the nickname I'd given her in second grade—had set her up with Theo the Vet after he'd treated Lian's sadly cancerous Maltipoo.

"When was the last date you went on?"

"In Ohio or New York?"

"Have you *been* on a date in New York?"

"Maybe?"

"Feels like something we would have talked about," she said.

"I haven't met anyone yet."

"How could you have? It's only been a *year* since you moved here."

"I'm settling in."

The truth was New York guys intimidated me. Every time I dipped a toe into one of those dating sites after moving here, it felt like I was bombarded by dick pics and guys who only wanted to hook up. I've never been into hookup culture, and I've yet to meet a girl who was happy to receive an unsolicited dick pic.

"Will you think about it, at least?" Kit had asked, texting me Jack's number and a screenshot of his picture from their company directory, in which he did, admittedly, look hot. Dark curly hair, a slim build, and eyes that could be brown or hazel. Kit promised he was twenty-eight, stable, and interested in a relationship. He was the New York equivalent of a unicorn.

Twenty-three minutes, twenty-seven, thirty.

I had to face it: there was no way he was coming. But I couldn't face the humiliation of walking to the front door alone, convinced that everyone in the restaurant knew exactly what had happened.

I opened our short text thread. He preferred to meet in person, he'd said, rather than text, and that was the first thing I liked about him. Texting with a stranger made me sweat. The silences and pauses provided too many chances to worry about what I'd written or how it was being perceived. In person, I had facial expressions to gauge. In person, I was funny. In person was better. Theoretically, anyway. If the guy actually showed.

Are you on your way? I wrote, feeling stupid. He was obviously not on his way. If he was running late, he'd have let me know.

I waited for his bubble of reply, but nothing.

He's thirty minutes late! I texted Kit. *I ducking knew this would happen.* Kit and I never bothered to correct our phones when they censored us. We'd met at age seven and had been friends for almost twenty years. We knew what the other meant.

Oh shot, Kit wrote. *Maybe he's stuck at work? The company's server is down.*

TECH HUNK GOES DOWN, I wrote reflexively. Kit and I had this thing where we turned random phrases into porny movie titles.

Not your best work.

I never should've agreed to this. I blame you!

She sent me a kiss-off emoji and I put down my phone.

I'd been waiting for thirty-five minutes, and that was enough. It didn't matter what the restaurant patrons thought. The Upper West Side wasn't even my neighborhood. I'd never see any of these people again. I'd only agreed to meet him here because Jack said the eggs Benny were amazing. I didn't need amazing eggs Benny, though. The coffee shop down the street from my apartment in Bushwick sold great breakfast sandwiches. I just had to signal the waitress and get the duck out of here.

As I lifted my hand to get Janie's attention, my body flooded with relief. Jack was walking through the door. He looked tired and stressed, his eyes darting around nervously like he wasn't quite sure where he was, but it was him. I waved enthusiastically to get his attention. After a moment's hesitation, he walked toward me.

I stood as he approached the table. "You made it, finally," I said in a voice that was too loud. "You got the servers working again?"

Before he could say anything, I drew him into a friendly hug. "Go with it, okay?" I said into his ear. "Think of it as your punishment."

He pulled away with a nervous laugh. "My *what*?"

"For almost standing me up," I said in a low voice. "For being thirty-five minutes late for our blind date and making everyone in the restaurant think I'm a loser."

"Ah." Jack stepped back and cleared his throat. "I was stuck in the subway. I'm sorry," he said, his voice booming, then pulled me back into the hug. "That do the trick?"

His breath tickled my ear and sent a shiver down my neck. "Perfect."

"I'm glad you made it," I said ten minutes later, after we'd both gotten coffee and put in our orders. *Friends with eggs Benedict* for me and *I hope our paths croissant again* for him. "I was about to give up."

"I'm sorry," Jack said, fiddling with his fork.

Up close, he was different from his photo. Not in a bad way, but his face was broader, his hair shorter, and he had ten pounds more muscle. His eyes were hazel, and there were a few flecks of early gray in his dark-brown hair. He was wearing a forest-green checked shirt that made his eyes pop, and had an almost beard.

The deviation from his photo didn't bother me. In my experience, only 10 percent of people have profile pictures that accurately reflected what they looked like IRL. Mine, unfortunately, was devastatingly accurate, right down to the curl in my strawberry-blond hair that I could never get straight no matter how expensive the flat iron.

"What happened? Were the servers down?"

Jack gave me a crooked smile. "Do you mind trying something with me?" His voice was clear and deep over the restaurant clatter. Our original meeting time had been ten. It was close to eleven now and a line was forming outside and trailing along the sidewalk.

"What's that?"

"Let's not talk about work. You know, all that usual conversation— *what do you do?* and *where are you from?*"

"Small talk?"

He pointed his fork at me. "Exactly. Small talk. Let's not do that."

"What should we talk about?"

"Hmm." He rested his hand on his chin. "I've put us in a box, haven't I?"

"I like boxes."

"You do? Why?"

"That would violate the whole we can't talk about work rule."

Janie arrived with our food. As she put my eggs down, she mouthed, *He's cute.* I blushed and glanced at my plate. She put the rest of our things on the table and left us alone.

"She thinks I'm cute, huh?"

I met Jack's eyes with a challenge. "You want to get her number?"

"Nope, I'm good." He reached for his croissant, which was flaky and too dark. "Your eggs look fantastic."

"Right?" I cut a bite and tasted it. The sauce was thick and the egg was cooked perfectly. "Thanks for the recommendation."

He bit into his croissant and made a face.

"Not good?"

"A bit stale." He reached toward my plate. "You don't mind, do you?"

"I probably should, but I don't. Take a whole muffin. It's very rich, I'll never finish all of it."

"Thank you." He moved the egg I hadn't touched onto his plate and cut into it. He put a bite in his mouth. "It's really good." He took another bite. "So, I know I put the rule in place, but am I allowed to try to guess what you do for a living?"

"Sure, go ahead."

"Something with boxes . . . Amazon fulfiller?"

"Ha, no."

"Mover?"

"Wrong again." I doubted he'd be able to guess.

I'm a book curator at BookBox, a book of the month club where I'm in charge of the rom-com selection. I'd worked for a competitor in Cincinnati for five years and had applied for the job here on a whim one night when I was feeling sorry for myself and missing Kit, who'd moved to New York with Theo shortly after my breakup with Christian.

Rom-coms weren't a genre I'd read much before, and some days the contrast between them and the reality of my dating life was too stark. But I knew a book was good if I could still root for that happily ever after ending regardless of how many "Hey, babys" I'd received in my Insta DMs that day.

"No one ever gets it right."

"Now you're challenging me to a duel."

"You forget I know what you do." I picked up my phone. "Which reminds me, I should let Kit know you arrived." I tapped out a quick text. *He showed.*

And? she wrote back. *Was I right?*

We'll see!

The servers are still down! He's going to be in the doghouse.

DOWNWARD DOGGIE STYLE.

"Are you telling Kit I'm cute?" Jack tipped my phone toward him, trying to read what I'd written. His eyebrows rose as he caught sight of my last text.

"I can explain."

"You don't have to."

"It's this thing Kit and I do, turn ordinary words into porny titles."

He snapped his fingers. "Like Pulp Friction?"

"Yes."

"Game of Bones."

I suppressed a laugh. "You got it."

"Horny Potter."

"You're a natural." I put my phone away. "Probably shouldn't be the only thing we talk about, though."

"I agree."

My mind whirred. How had this conversation gotten so off track? "How about . . . what's the worst date *you've* ever been on?"

Jack frowned. "Is that your way of saying this is the worst date you've ever been on?"

"Far from it."

"Oh?"

"It's hard to pick just one, but if I put the guys who exposed themselves aside, top honors probably goes to—"

"Wait, you're putting the flashers *aside*?"

I shrugged. "A girl has to, these days. Have you not been online for the last ten years?"

"Not so much. But also, I don't think guys mind getting flashed. Not that I'd know." Jack stopped, flustered. "This happens to you? Like regularly?"

"Sadly, yes."

He shook his head. "Men kind of suck, huh."

"A lot of them."

"I'm sorry."

"You don't have to apologize for your gender. But I appreciate the sentiment." I took a sip of my coffee but it had gone cold. "Your turn. Worst date ever."

Jack cocked his head to the side. "Names changed to protect the guilty?"

"Of course."

"Hmmm. It was a long time ago, but probably the one where the girl—let's call her Debbie—brought her mom along."

"No."

"Yes."

I tried to imagine it and couldn't. "Wait, wait, wait. How old were you when this happened?"

His mouth twisted. "Fifteen."

"That puts a different spin on it."

"You've never been a fifteen-year-old boy."

"And thank god for that." He touched my hand then pulled back quickly, but it was long enough to register.

I cleared my throat. "So, things didn't work out with Debbie?"

"No, they did."

"No way this counts, then."

Janie slapped the bill down next to me. "Sorry, but I need the table."

"We just got here," Jack said.

"*You* just got here."

"Ah, right. We'll pay up."

She tapped her foot impatiently. I could see the people who had the eleven-thirty reservation glaring at us from the doorway.

"Let's split it," I said.

"No, let me." Jack patted himself down, looking for his wallet, which he located in his front pocket. He pulled it out, then hesitated. "Remember how you said I wasn't the worst date?"

"Um, yes?"

"Someone charged a bunch of stuff on my card last week, and I'm waiting for a replacement. I have enough cash to cover the meal but not the tip."

"Why don't you give me the cash and I'll put it on my card so I can tip?" I said.

"That'd be great." He handed me forty bucks and I gave Janie my card. I completed the transaction quickly, making sure to tip her generously.

She checked the receipt as it came out and smiled. "Thank you, Chloe. *You* have a good day, now."

I put my card away and we stood up.

"Thank you, Chloe," Jack said. "I feel like an idiot."

"I don't think Janie wants to see you back here again, but it's fine."

I didn't care who paid for breakfast. He'd shown up, we'd had a nice conversation, he hadn't talked about his needs as a lover (true story) or been on his phone the whole time (also true, twice). It was enough.

As we walked to the exit, Jack placed his hand on the small of my back. It was a gesture I normally hated, but it felt comfortable with him. Part of it might've been that I haven't been with anyone since Christian and I broke up and I was missing a man's touch. But it wasn't only that. Something about Jack felt different, and that was a pleasant surprise.

Outside, I turned my face up to the sun. It was a beautiful day. The cherry blossoms were in bloom and the sky was deep blue and cloudless. It had been a cold, wet spring, and it was nice to feel the sunshine. I decided to fight the temptation to return to my apartment and hermit inside for the rest of the day. Central Park wasn't far. I should walk around. Maybe Kit would meet me.

"You find something you like up there?" Jack asked.

I brought my chin down. "A beautiful day. I'm always looking for a beautiful day."

Our eyes met. He gave me a look that felt appreciative, as if he understood me. "I like that."

"Thank you for brunch, it was nice, if brief."

He touched his chest above his heart. "Ouch. I'll have to make it up to you."

"I'd like that, Jack."

A shadow passed over his face, then lifted. "This has been great, Chloe. I was having a crappy morning and . . . let's just leave it at that."

"Sure." I extended my hand and he took it, then pulled me in for a hug.

I hadn't had time during our theatrical greeting to appreciate how well we fit together, but we did. I breathed in his smell of soap and the light spice of his aftershave as his arms tightened around me. I leaned against him, then came to my senses and pulled away.

My dry season *had* gone on way too long.

We parted and I turned and walked away with a skip in my step. I was proud of myself for not trying to prolong the date. I felt pretty sure Jack would reach out soon, but if he didn't, that was okay. He was a good icebreaker, and proof that dating wasn't futile.

He was the start of something, and I was excited to find out what.

Chapter Two

Kit called me a block later, as if she had some sixth sense that my date was over.

"So? How was it?"

"How do you know I'm not still with him?"

"Are you?"

"No, but I could be." The light changed and I stopped at the corner, standing too close to the curb, which is a habit I've had trouble breaking since I moved to New York. In Cincinnati, it had never been a problem. But the crazy drivers in this city make getting too close to an intersection life threatening. "Wait, did he call you?"

"Nope."

"You're clairvoyant?"

"Potentially."

"Pretty sure I'd know this by now."

She laughed. "How about I tell you where you are?"

The light changed and I crossed the street. "I don't even know where I am."

It was partly true. I've never been great at directions, and I still had no sense of the points on the compass in New York, despite it being on a grid that was supposed to be easy to learn. It was embarrassing how many times I took out my phone to figure out if I should turn left or right, particularly when I was in Manhattan. I didn't like looking like a tourist in the city I lived in.

"You're about to hit Central Park West."

I checked the street sign ahead of me. "How did you know that?"

"We have Find My Friends on our iPhones, remember?"

"Oh right." Kit had insisted I install it when I moved to New York because she was, rightly, worried I'd get lost. "But that's kind of creepy that you're checking on me."

"Well . . ."

"What?"

"I might have an alert set up that tells me every time you're on the move."

This stopped me in my tracks. A man slammed into me, then cursed me out as he hurried away. "What?"

"I never told you?"

"Um, no."

"It was a precautionary measure until you settled in."

"And the reason you never turned it off is?"

"I got used to the reminders of where you were. It was out of love, I promise."

Kit's always been a bit overprotective of me, like she's my big sister instead of us both being twenty-six. Was it that big a deal, though? It wasn't as if I didn't tell Kit everything that was going on in my life anyway. "Okay, but turn it off now, all right?"

"I will. Hey, you know what? You're close to the Met. You should go."

"We were supposed to go together."

"I'm tied up with Theo today, and it's like fate that you're right there after talking about it so much."

I gazed into Central Park, thinking about the Met sitting across the lawn from where I was standing. At least, I thought that was where it was. I'd check the minute we got off the phone. "It's nice out. I was going to hang in the park."

"Do that after. Go to the museum, already. You won't regret it."

"Why do you care?"

"Because it was on your top five things to do when you got here and you haven't done it yet. I want you to finally start exploring this place."

"You're worried I'm going to move back to Ohio."

"Obvi. But also: do something unexpected, for once. You know, live a little."

"Love you, Kit."

"Love you too."

I put my phone away after verifying that yes, in fact, I could go straight through the park and get to the Met. I resolved to make it without checking my phone for directions as I set out, taking in the park, the cool of the trees, the people buzzing along the paths, pushing carriages, riding scooters, or jogging on the internal road.

As I walked past the Jackie O. Reservoir, I watched the sunlight glint off the water and listened to the happy shouts of children running across the fresh green grass. Kit was right to worry I might leave. My apartment was small, everything was expensive, and I often felt anonymous and overwhelmed.

But right now, I only saw the positives, and the city felt like a place I'd be happy to stay in forever.

It didn't take long to get to the Met. I stopped to admire the building, taking in the impressive triple porticos and the wide sandstone stairs.

"Pretty nice, right?"

I turned toward the familiar voice with my heart hammering. "Jack? What are you doing here?"

"Going to the Met?"

I tried to steady my heart. Was Jack following me? How many people did I have on my tail? "Odd coincidence."

"We were close by, and it's one of my favorite places. I try to get here three or four times a year. You?"

"It's my first time."

"How is that possible?"

"I only moved to New York a year ago."

A large family made their way up the stairs, the mother anxious, the father holding one little girl on either side of him. The girls were wearing bright floral dresses that matched their mother's, and when they got to the top of the stairs one of them stopped and executed a perfect pirouette.

"That settles it then," Jack said. "I'll be your tour guide."

"You don't have to do that."

"Trust me, you want this tour."

I was amused by his earnestness. "Okay, you convinced me. Lead the way."

We walked up the steps and I resisted the urge to execute my own (bad) pirouette at the top. Kit was right. The Met had been on my top five places to visit when I came to New York along with the High Line, Coney Island, and Central Park. So far, I'd only made it to the park for a few runs with Kit. I was glad she'd pushed me to come here today.

We went inside and stepped up to the ticket window. While we were able to get in for free as New York residents, Jack insisted on paying for our tickets. He said he'd gone to the ATM after we'd separated and now had enough cash.

"We should pay for the arts," he said. "They're important."

"I agree. But you don't have to buy my ticket."

"It's the least I can do after this morning. Besides, I need to earn back your goodwill."

"Good Will Humping," I blurted.

"A Few Hard Men," Jack replied without missing a beat.

"Buffy the Vampire Layer."

Jack took our tickets and a museum map from the woman behind the counter, who was now giving us a funny look. "Impressive."

"I've had a lot of practice."

We walked away from the ticket window. "We're in one of my favorite places and I get to show it to you for the first time." Jack rolled up the map and tapped me on the arm excitedly. "Look at this place. Isn't it great?"

We were in the main hall, a vast expanse of white marble and soaring pillars. Light flowed in from the glass rosettes in the coffered ceiling and the arched windows below them. Families with excited children and older couples wearing serious walking shoes were milling around us, the children's pitter-patter echoing off the walls. It was a happy space.

"It's beautiful."

"Right? Designed in 1902 by Richard Morris Hunt in the neo-classical style—"

"Wait, wait, wait. You *were* a tour guide? I thought that was a figure of speech."

He clasped his hands behind his back. "I guided a few summers when I was a teenager. My mom worked here and kind of insisted I do it. College applications, blah, blah, blah. But to be honest, I ended up loving it."

"That's adorkable."

He didn't look so sure. "My ex thought it was lame."

And there she was. His ex. I wanted to ask a million questions—who she was, how long they'd dated, when had they broken up, and why?—but I squashed it. I didn't want to ruin the moment.

"It's good she's your ex, then."

Jack nodded, but some of his enthusiasm had seeped away.

"Where should we go?" I asked. "What are your favorite spaces? Tour guide me."

"You sure?"

"One hundred percent."

"Okay, we need to see the temple. And the armor is cool."

"Those sound great. But I have one request. Can we see the bed where Claudia slept? You know, *From the M—*"

"Oh, you're one of those!"

"What?"

"A *Mixed-Up Files* girl."

He was right. *From the Mixed-Up Files of Mrs. Basil E. Frankweiler* was one of my favorite books. That book saved me. It was the first book I'd read after my sister died, and I'd tell myself that she'd gone to the museum like Claudia and Jamie had. That she'd be back. That my life didn't have to go on with a Sara-sized hole in it.

"Is that a bad thing?"

"Depends. How do you take disappointment?"

I scrunched up my face. "I can't see the bed?"

"Dismantled, I'm afraid."

"The chapel where she prayed?"

"Closed in 2001."

"You seem to know a lot about it."

He lifted his left shoulder. "Girls used to come in all the time with their favorite passages marked and it was my job to tell them

17

that the museum was a lot different than when the book was written."

"Ten-year-old girls came into the Met alone?"

"They were usually with their parents. Sometimes an older sister."

"Ah. And you were how old? Seventeen, eighteen?"

"Where are you going with this?"

I tapped him on the chest with my index finger. "I bet the big sisters found you pretty irresistible."

Jack pulled a face. "Seventeen-year-old me is feeling judged."

"How different was he from fifteen-year-old you?"

"He of the bad first date? The seventeen-year-old version probably should be judged. He made some stupid decisions. And before you ask, no, I don't want to talk about them."

He said it lightly, and I got it. No way I wanted to tell Jack the stupidest things I'd done at seventeen. Not even the tenth stupidest thing, which had been Gerry Bush, the lead in the school play, who had a way of memorizing swoony speeches from Shakespeare and using them when you were weakened by a few hits from his flask.

"You said something about a temple?"

"The Temple of Dendur!"

"That sounds like something from *Lord of the Rings*."

"Is that bad?"

"Not necessarily."

Jack clicked his map against his palm. "I see . . . likes books, just not *those* kinds of books."

"I've read them."

"And they're awesome?"

"If you're into reading eight hundred–page books."

"With all three volumes it's about twelve hundred pages, but—"

"I rest my case."

"Are we in court?"

I laughed. "We're in the Met."

"You want to see that temple or what?"

I crooked my arm out. "Lead the way."

He put his hand through the space I'd made, forming a link. It felt good to have that point of connection.

"Stick close to me," Jack said. "There are monsters ahead."

The Temple of Dendur was nothing like *Lord of the Rings*. Where Middle-earth was dark, the temple was in a light-filled room, surrounded by a quiet pool. The sunlight streamed in through a wall of slanted windows, reflecting off the gleaming stone. When you walked in, the present fell away. It was easy to imagine yourself two thousand years earlier, in another place, another time.

"Did they sacrifice virgins in here?" I asked.

Jack snorted. "Not to my knowledge."

"Why did they build it?"

"You want the long version or the short version?"

"You still remember the long version?"

"You are going to think I'm a massive dork."

I put my hand on his forearm. "I won't. I'll be impressed."

"That's because you haven't heard it." He touched my hand briefly, trailing his finger along the tendon as our eyes locked.

"Tell me."

He dropped his hand and cleared his throat. "I'll stick to the short version. Basically, it's a shrine to the leader combined with religious and mythological elements."

I knelt and examined a relief of figures on one of the walls to hide my blushing face. "This detail is fantastic."

"You can buy a rubbing in the gift shop."

I stood up. "I might do that. Where to next?"

"Knights in shining armor?"

"That's right up my alley."

We made our way to the Arms and Armor galleries. Once inside, we stood in front of a long procession of knights on horseback and examined their gleaming armor.

"This is one of my favorite rooms," Jack said.

"Why?"

"Because the armor was once worn by real people. Imagine being in battle, how close you had to get to your opponent. You would've been surrounded by smells—horses, sweat, fear, mud. And there would've been so much noise—cries of pain, hoofbeats, the clang of the armor . . ." Jack trailed off, a tinge of red on his cheeks. "Sorry, I get carried away."

"You must've been a great tour guide."

"I enjoyed it. But wait, 'must have'? Am I failing today?"

"Not at all. This is the most fun I've had in a museum in a long time."

"I'm glad."

I turned back to the knights. "And I get it. It's how I felt when I'd read books as a teenager—lost inside them."

"Romance novels?"

"I was more into V. C. Andrews, though I guess you could say that those books had romantic elements if you're completely twisted?"

"I remember my sister reading those. They were awful."

"I would've been better off reading romances."

"I don't get why women want to read books about being saved by a man."

"It's a fantasy. No matter how bad things are in real life, you always know that there's going to be a happy ending."

Jack touched the side of my face, his fingers moving gently on my skin. "That's—"

"Sammy, no!" A harassed-looking mother tried to catch her small child before he climbed onto the plinth that held the soldiers.

Sammy clenched his fists and boosted himself up. He was wearing overalls and yellow rain boots. "Wanna ride the horsies!"

Jack's hand dropped and he bolted after the boy, scooping him up right before his little hand clasped the tip of one of the knight's swords. "No touching, little buddy."

"But I wanna! I wanna ride the horsy!"

Jack jumped off the plinth with Sammy in his arms. He delivered him to his mother, who thanked Jack profusely before she pulled a howling Sammy away from the knights.

"My hero!" I said as he walked back to me, the feel of his touch still lingering.

"All part of the training. I'd like to show you one more place. But it's a surprise."

"Should I close my eyes?"

"Not necessary. Follow me." He turned on his heel with military precision and strode out of the gallery.

I trailed along, wondering where he was leading me. "Wait up," I called.

"Come on now, almost there." He had a laugh in his voice as he turned into the Greek and Roman Art gallery. He moved purposely until he got to a large sarcophagus. He opened his arms. "Ta-da!"

"Is that where—"

"Claudia hides her violin case? Yes!"

I admired its smooth surface. "Thank you, Jack."

"Why do you love that book?"

"I . . . it helped me through a hard time. This was a nice place to escape to."

He points ahead of us. "There used to be a large wishing pool there that had something in it called the Fountain of the Muses."

It was in the book, too, described so vividly that it was easy to conjure a large fountain with bronze sculptures rising out of it. Visitors grasping pennies, warm in their hands, taking an important moment to wish for something.

Love, happiness, a dream come true.

"Do you have something you wish for, Chloe?" Jack said beside me, standing close, his tone intimate.

"Doesn't everyone?" Our eyes locked again. "Do you?"

"I do."

I felt the heat of his gaze and my hands started to tingle. Something was happening between us—but, wait. We'd only met a few hours ago. I was getting carried away by nostalgia and the novelty of being on a real date.

"It's a shame the pool's not here anymore, then," I said, breaking eye contact. "But what about the statue? Where's that?" The statue had fascinated Claudia and her brother while they hid in the museum.

"It's always surrounded by a million people, but we can go see it if you like. Or—" He checked his watch.

"You have somewhere you need to be?" I said as gently as possible, masking my disappointment.

"You promise not to laugh?"

"How can I promise when I have no idea what you're about to say?"

"How do you feel about boats?"

"What do you mean?"

"It's not far, over in the park, but it'll be easier to take you there than to describe it."

The ground felt uneven beneath me. It wasn't a rational response to what he was saying, but I couldn't control how my body reacted. "What am I getting myself into?"

"It'll be fun, I promise."

"And if it isn't?"

"Then your next meal is on me."

Chapter Three

We left the museum and walked south on Fifth Avenue. He seemed excited, and I couldn't imagine where we were headed. I only hoped it wasn't something that would expose my worst fears.

"You have to tell me where we're going," I said after a few minutes of fretting. *Boat* was a scary word in my life, and though I knew that there was nothing to fear in Central Park, I couldn't shake the feeling of dread.

Jack looked shy. "More fodder for the Jack is a complete dork file."

"The tour was great." I shook my fears away. "I'm glad my first time was with you."

"So, it was good for you?"

I swatted his arm. "Quit it. Where are we going?"

"Somewhere for my nephew."

"It's a *bit* early to introduce me to the family."

"Ha. No, he won't be attending today. Patience. We're almost there."

He directed us back into the park at East Seventy-Second. There was a pond up ahead with a small crowd gathered in front of a brick structure.

"Are those remote-controlled sailboats?"

"Yep."

Relief washed over me as I watched the colorful boats sailing around the pond. "Thank goodness."

"What is it?"

"I thought it had something to do with actual boats. You know, human sized, not for Stuart Little."

"Are you afraid of boats?"

"Yeah."

"Why?"

"I . . . it's not really first date material."

"Moving on," Jack said. "I present you the Central Park Model Yacht Club and one of their weekly regattas." He swept his arms wide, taking in the pond and the delighted faces of those watching.

There were twenty boats in the water, each about two feet high. A line of adults and their children stood on the side of the pond, behind a small rope.

"How do the remotes work?"

"They're wind powered. They can adjust the trim of the sail and the rudder's direction. Many of the boats are handmade."

"You seem to know a lot about it."

"My nephew, he's six and obsessed with sailboats. He's wanted to come here since he heard about it, and we've spent hours researching it together. I'm going to surprise him for his birthday."

"This is a reconnaissance mission?"

"You could say that. I want to make sure it's safe for him. He's on the spectrum and there are lots of places that trigger him. Before I bring him anywhere new, I check it out first, look for warning signs, where the exits are, that sort of thing."

How cute was this man? "You're a great uncle."

"It's a lot on my sister and her wife, especially recently, and . . . anyway, you want to watch the regatta?"

"Definitely."

We walked closer and watched as the boats lined up at the starting line, a rainbow of primary blue, red, and yellow, with white sails trimmed in matching colors. There were several buoys in the water, and as far as I could tell, the boats had to do some sort of lap between them.

The starter's gun went off, and there was a lot of excited yelling from the contestants, some of whom were controlling their boats more accurately than others. The race ended with much cheering, and the boats were retrieved by their owners.

"You want to take a turn?" Jack said. "It's an open competition now. Anyone can enter. We just have to rent a boat."

I scanned the boat club building. There was a line of people at the rental window. "What if they're sold out?"

"I'm willing to chance it if you are."

I smiled. "Sure."

Jack pointed to a roped-off area where the previous group of captains had been standing. "Why don't you go over there and hold our place by the starting line, and I'll get the boat?"

"Sounds good."

We parted and I walked to where the competitors were gathering.

"Only participants, miss," an older man who looked like he was in his seventies said to me in a gruff voice. He had a whistle around his neck like a referee and was wearing a white polo shirt with a yacht club logo on it. All he was missing was the captain's hat.

"Oh, my, uh, friend, is getting our boat."

"All right, miss. You stand over there."

I moved to where he was pointing, quickly realizing that the other participants were all kids with a max age of ten and their parents. One of them, a boy of about eight with black hair and pale skin, gave me an intense look as I stood next to him. He was dressed like one of the royal children, in short pants with socks pulled up to his knees and a cream-colored crewneck sweater.

I scanned the line for Jack. He'd gotten a boat and a controller and was walking back to me.

"Looks like we're a bit older than the competition," I said when he was by my side.

"I did tell you it was for my nephew."

"I guess we have to let the kids win?"

"We do." Jack bent down and put the boat in the water. It was painted a dark blue and had white sails with matching trim. He gave it a little shove to get it going, then stood up.

"Cheating!" the black-haired child said, pointing at Jack. "Daddy, he's cheating!"

A larger and older version of the kid appeared from behind him and put his hand on the little yeller's shoulder. The dad was wearing a matching outfit, though he'd tied an ascot around his neck and his pants reached his ankles. "Now, *Kenny*, the race hasn't even started yet."

"He pushed his boat!"

Jack gave them a wide smile. "I was getting it into position."

"Kenny here is very particular about the rules being followed."

"As you said, the race hasn't started yet, and it's my first time doing this."

Kenny glared at Jack.

"Can you tell us what the rules are, Kenny?" I said, stooping down so my eyes were level with his. "So we don't make a mistake again?"

Kenny scowled and held his remote control tightly to his chest.

"Come on, son." His dad encouraged him. "Tell the nice lady how it works."

"You can only use the *wind*!"

"Okay, sport, we got that," Jack said. "Won't happen again."

Kenny didn't look like he believed him, but his dad turned him away gently. I walked back to Jack. He had a remote in his hands. "You know how to work that thing?"

"They gave me a short demo at the booth, but I figure if a kid can do it, then how hard can it be?"

"Kenny seems pretty sure of himself," I whispered.

"Eh. I can take him." He fiddled with the remote and the boat started moving as it caught a small breeze. With some grunting and a lot of frustrated expressions, he got the boat to go to the rough approximation of the starting line, though it took tacking back and forth a couple of times to get there. By that time Jack was red in the face. "Don't laugh."

"I'm admiring your dedication to giving your nephew a good time."

"Thank you. You have any nieces or nephews?"

I watched the water dance in the sunlight. "No. I'm kind of an only child. I had a sister, but she died when I was eight."

"I'm sorry, Chloe."

"It was a long time ago."

"How did she—" Jack stopped himself. "Sorry, I shouldn't pry, it's just, my mom is sick, and she's in the hospital, and . . ."

The starter made his way into the crowd. "Two-minute warning! Two minutes to get into position."

"Shit," Jack muttered. "How am I supposed to keep the boat here for two minutes?"

"Put it into the wind and let the sails go."

"You a sailor?"

"I was. I—god, I never talk about this."

"You don't have to."

"No, it's okay. It's what I was saying before—my sister and I, growing up in Ohio, we spent our summers at a sailing camp in Kentucky. But that's how she died, and I haven't been sailing since."

Jack's hands dropped and he almost let go of the remote. "You should've said something."

"It's fine."

"It's not fine. This must bring it all back, and then I go prying and—"

I touched his hand. "It was a long time ago, and this is an innocent activity on a beautiful day."

"You sure?"

"One hundred percent. And I'm sorry about your mom too. That must be a lot."

"It is." A cloud raced across his face. "Look, I should've said something before, and I don't know why I didn't, but—"

"We're starting in ten seconds! Boats in position!" The starter bellowed next to us, then raised his arm above his head with his starter's gun. "Five, four, three, two . . ." *Boom!* The gun went off and the boats started moving slowly past the starting line.

"Come on, Jack, catch the wind!"

Jack was momentarily stunned, then concentrated on the controller and got the boat going slowly.

"Open up the mainsail some more," I said, long-buried knowledge coming back to me. "Let it go out as far as you can."

Jack fiddled with the controls and the sail went into position. "This is much harder than it looks."

"It's easy!" Kenny said, a smirk on his face. "You're bad at it."

"Kenny," his father warned, then gave us a bemused expression. "Kids."

"Right," I said, then muttered to Jack, "That's not a kid. He's the devil."

"I'm glad Tyler's not here."

Jack's boat gained some speed as a gust of wind spread across the pond. He was still pretty far behind the other boats.

"Aim for that red buoy," I said. "Then you'll want to try to tack around it and get going back in the other direction."

"In English, please."

"Try to turn the boat around that buoy and get going in the other direction. Like the other boats are doing."

He tried to hand me the remote. "You should do it."

"No, you're doing great. Besides, you wanted to impress your nephew. He'll be excited when you win next time."

"Good point." Jack fiddled with the controls again. He gained on two of the other boats that were having a harder time with the maneuver. Once he was around the buoy, he opened his sail and caught a good wind, picking up speed.

"That's great! Keep trying to stay straight and you should overtake that other boat." I pointed to a red sailboat that was a few feet in front of him.

He held the remote tightly as he approached the other boat. "I can't believe how stressed I am."

I giggled. "You're in a full sweat. What about letting the kids win?"

"It's silly. I have this competitive streak—"

"Watch out!"

The red boat swerved to the left and rammed into ours, knocking it almost over onto its side. The offending boat didn't seem to be affected and sailed away quickly as ours started spinning in a circle.

"What the hell?" Jack said. "What happened?"

I searched for the culprit and made eye contact with Kenny. He was grinning like a maniac.

"I thought you were against cheating, Kenny?" I said gently.

"I didn't cheat! Daddy! She accused me! She made an accusation!"

"He rammed our boat," I said to Kenny's father.

"He's just a kid!" Kenny's father said.

"It's fine, forget it," I said.

"She has to apologize!" Kenny said.

Jack was shaking with laughter. It was contagious, and I started laughing too. Meanwhile, our boat looked like it might go down the drain.

"Daddy! They're laughing at me! Daddy!"

I turned away from Kenny and his dad and bent down to take off my shoes.

"What are you doing?" Jack asked.

"Rescuing our boat."

I pulled off my shoes and socks, then rolled up my jeans. I hopped over the small concrete wall and waded into the water. I could hear the shouts of others telling me to get out, but I ignored them. Then the referee started blowing his whistle at me like I was a kid at the community pool who'd broken the rules. I reached our boat, picked it up, and carried it back to the side of the pond. The water was deeper than I'd thought and my jeans were soaked to the knees.

"You're disqualified!" Kenny said, pointing at me.

"No shit, kid."

"She sweared! Daddy!"

Jack was hovering at the edge and held out his hand. He helped me out, and I handed him the boat. Jack shook his head but his grin was wide, his eyes dancing. "We're out of the race."

"Probably."

"I'm sorry, Chloe."

"What are you apologizing for? This was the most fun I've had in a long time."

"Really?"

"Honestly."

"I'm glad to hear that."

"Why don't we get that boat back and find somewhere where I can dry off?"

"Sounds like a plan."

Jack quickly returned the boat and came back with a towel.

"Where did that come from?" I asked.

"The gift shop." He handed it to me. It was white and had a sailing logo on it.

"Thank you."

Jack pointed to a picnic table not far away. "Why don't we go sit there?"

"Good idea." I slipped my feet into my shoes, and we walked to the table, my wet jeans tugging on my legs. I took a seat and used the towel to dry off. "I'm glad we did that."

Jack sat next to me. "It didn't bring up too many bad memories of your sister?"

I put my legs out in front of me, letting the sun dry them, and kicked off my shoes. "No. Honestly, I mostly only have good memories of her."

"We don't have to talk about it."

"I don't usually." I glanced at Jack. "I'm surprised I told you." I kicked myself for saying that last part. "Anyway, it reminded me of how much I used to love sailing. I should go back to it. Conquer my fears and all that."

"It's okay to be afraid. Some things are scary."

"Kenny was scary."

Jack chuckled. "He was. But I guess some people might find Tyler like that too."

"Is he a lot?"

"Sometimes."

"And with your mom . . ." I touched his knee. "I'm sorry about that."

"One day she seems fine, and the next. . . . This has been a great distraction." He stopped and shook his head. "That came out wrong. It's been fun to hang out."

"It has."

He stood up.

My heart sank. "Do you have to go?"

"What? No, no, I'm just hungry. That friends with eggs benefits or whatever was good, but it feels like we ate a thousand years ago."

"A thousand, huh?"

"A hundred at least."

I shaded my eyes from the sun. "I could eat."

"And I do owe you a meal." He pulled out his phone and tapped at it. His eyes lit up. "Perfect."

"What?"

"Do you trust me?"

"Should I?"

"About this, definitely."

"It would help if you told me what *this* is."

"Only the best food truck in New York, which happens to be nearby."

"Oh yeah?"

"Any food allergies I should be aware of?"

"Nope."

"Great. Wait here. I'll be right back."

Jack loped off toward the street. For a day that had started with the near certainty of being stood up, it had taken a fantastic turn. I pulled out my phone and texted Kit.

Thank you.

For what?

Jack. He's great.

Not great for me. Still no email. Wait, you're still with him?

I wasn't but we ran into each other at the Met.

I TOLD YOU TO GO THERE!

Yes, yes.

And yet you doubt my powers.

I don't. Magical Kit. It's your new name forever.

She sent me a praying hands emoji and I tucked my phone away. I knew it was a dangerous thing to think, but I couldn't keep my mind from going there. Everything about this day felt perfect. I couldn't remember the last time I'd felt this connected to someone. Well, that wasn't true. I could—when I met Christian—but given how that relationship had ended, it wasn't something I wanted to remember or compare to.

No. Today was *good*. The connection we had was real. I could already imagine telling the girls at work about it—how it'd gone from almost being stood up to the best date I'd ever had, exactly like the books we curated.

I stopped myself. This wasn't high school, and I didn't need to be mentally writing my name and his in intertwined hearts.

That could wait until the second date at least.

Chapter Four

Jack was gone long enough for my pants to dry in the sun.

As I waited for him to return I watched a couple sitting in the grass. Her back was leaning against a tree, and he was facing her on his knees. Her eyes were closed, as she enjoyed the sun, and he leaned in and kissed her, surprising her.

It made me smile and remember that every first kiss I'd ever received had happened with my eyes closed.

It started when I was fifteen, and the boy had liked me forever and I liked him too. I was in his bedroom, more innocently than that sounds, and at some point, I sat on the floor, leaned back against the wall, and closed my eyes. I don't remember why, but the next thing I knew he'd kissed me.

It was a pattern that would repeat in my life. Something about closing my eyes around a man I wanted to kiss made me kissable.

I tried not to think too much about what that said about me.

Why I waited for him to make the first move. Why I had to hide my desire to get what I wanted.

All I knew was—I never saw a first kiss coming.

But I did see Jack coming.

I watched him walk across the lawn to me. He had an easy, comfortable stride, and was holding a large plastic bag and a couple of take-out boxes that smelled so delicious my mouth started to water before he reached me.

"What'd you get?"

"You'll see." He put the boxes down on the table, pulled out chopsticks, napkins, and paper plates, then made a motion for me to spin around so my back was to the table.

I did as he asked, listening to him bustle around the picnic table while my stomach rumbled.

"Glad to hear you're hungry."

I rubbed my noisy stomach. "You heard that? That's embarrassing."

"Nah."

It growled again. "My stomach would like you to hurry up."

"Hold your horses."

"Can't think of a porny title for that one."

"That's probably best."

"What's the origin of that saying, anyway? Like, stand there and hold a horse so you don't, what? Charge the other side?"

"Mental note," Jack said. "She gets a little loopy when she's hungry."

"That's a good note."

There was the unmistakable pop of a bottle cap being removed, and then something in a glass being put on the table.

"Okay, turn around!"

I spun slowly in my seat, lifting my legs to bring them over the bench. Jack had laid out the plates and utensils and there was an array of dishes. A bottle of Chinese beer sat by each plate, and there was a small bunch of flowers resting on the table.

"Ta-da!"

"This looks great. Thank you." I eyed the flowers. "Are those for me?"

"I thought they'd make the table more festive."

"Good idea. What's this?" I pointed to one of the containers.

"The best bao buns with Peking duck in the city." He opened the other box. "And this is a mix of shrimp toast and scallion pancakes."

"I haven't had shrimp toast in years."

"You've never had shrimp toast until you've had this shrimp toast."

"Can't wait. And the beers? Contraband?"

Jack picked his up and angled it toward me. "Probably, but I don't see any cops around and I'm willing to risk it if you are?"

His look was a challenge, one I wanted to accept. I picked up my bottle and clinked it to his. "Definitely."

Jack served me one of everything and we dug in. I started with a bao bun, a delicious mix of hoisin sauce, scallions, and crispy duck skin in a steamed, fluffy bun. "This is good."

"Try the shrimp toast."

I took a sip of beer and did as he suggested. It was equally fantastic—shrimp and ginger and fat fried together on bread—and I could feel my blood getting sluggish as I ate it.

"Right?" Jack said.

"How did you find the truck?"

"It's the knowledge."

"The knowledge?"

"Native New Yorker knowledge."

"New Yorkers are snobby."

"Oh?"

"It's impossible to be a New Yorker unless your high school had a PS number."

Jack bit into a shrimp toast. "I don't make the rules."

"It's frustrating." I eyed the last bao bun. "You want that?"

"I do, but you can have it."

"Chivalry isn't dead." I scooped up the bun. I was going to have to go for a massive run to work all of this off, but it was worth it.

"Tell me an Ohio thing. It must have things you'd never know if you weren't from there."

I thought about it. "Cincinnati chili is spaghetti with meat sauce and cheese piled on top."

"Interesting."

"The Cincinnati airport isn't even in Ohio. It's in Kentucky."

"Bizarre."

"There's riverboat gambling."

"Like in *Ozark?*"

"Kind of. Though I don't know if they're money laundering operations."

Jack sat back, cradling his beer in his hands. "You miss it?"

"Cincy? Sometimes. The people are nice. They move slower. When you smile at a stranger on the street, they don't assume you're mentally ill. And at least I knew what direction north was there. I never got lost."

"This city is easy to get around; follow the numbers up and down."

"So *you* say."

"What's the thing I'd find weirdest there?"

"Hard to say, but I can tell you about the weirdest thing I ever saw."

He leaned forward. "Please do."

"There's this whole cave system called the Ohio Caverns. It's famous, and at various places you can take a boat into the caves and look at the stalactites."

"Sounds cool."

"I'm sure you'd love it. Anyway, I went with Kit a few years back, and we got into these boats for the tour and the guy sitting across from me had a dummy on his lap."

Jack put his beer down. "A what?"

"A dummy. You know, like a ventriloquist's dummy?"

"You're shitting me."

"Nope."

"Did it talk?"

"The guy holding it talked for it, yeah."

Jack scratched at the back of his neck. "He threw his voice and it seemed as if the dummy was talking?"

"He talked through his lips and it was obvious it *wasn't* the dummy talking."

"Did anyone say anything?"

"Everyone acted like this was perfectly normal. Like it was something they saw every day. Kit and I were dying. But I did manage to get a photo."

I pulled out my phone, brushing away several texts from Kit. I scrolled through my photos until I found it, a blurry shot of a ventriloquist's dummy grinning madly from the lap of a middle-aged man. It still creeped me out to look at it. I passed the phone to Jack.

He started to laugh. "This is outstanding. How did you get the shot? Did he know you were doing it?"

"Don't think so. I took my phone out and held it at hip level. And snapped it quickly. He didn't seem to notice."

He handed the phone back. "That's the best. I feel like this should be one of those things that you see on a viral meme."

"Oh, I tried that. No traction."

"If people did not see the genius of this story, they are idiots." He finished his beer. "I should've gotten two of these."

Mine was empty as well. "This was perfect. Thank you."

"You're welcome." He started to clear the containers and plates away.

It felt like our day was coming to a natural conclusion, but I wasn't ready for it to be over. I searched for something to prolong it. "How are your tour guide skills with the park?"

His eyes widened. "Please tell me you've been to the park before?"

"It was the first place I went when I got here. But I don't *know* it. Not like a 'real' New Yorker."

"Ha! Using my words against me, I see."

"Am I?"

He bit his lip, then checked his watch. "I guess I have a bit of time."

My heart fell. I shouldn't have said anything about a tour because it got him thinking about the time. I was an idiot.

"I don't want to keep you."

"You're not." He sighed. "I'm supposed to go see my mom, and I don't want to miss visiting hours."

I felt awful. I should've known that's what it was. No wonder I was single.

"Of course. Go see your mom."

"I didn't mean . . . I want to show you around." He checked his watch again and thought it over. "You know what? Visiting hours are till eight. I have some time."

"You sure?"

"I am."

I stood and brushed off my legs, kicking myself. Everything had been fine, and I'd gone and made things weird.

"Why's your mom in the hospital? If you want to say."

He tied the top of the plastic bag together, sealing off our trash. "She has MS. She's had it most of my life, but it's been a lot worse these last few years, and when she has a bad flare-up, she has trouble breathing. Hence, the hospital."

"That sucks."

He seemed sad but resigned. "We've all lived with this for a long time and so has she. Honestly, she wants it to be over."

I couldn't imagine what it must be like to deal with that. I understood loss—Sara's death had been devastating and something I still hadn't gotten over—but that had happened in an instant. A long-term illness was something else entirely.

I touched his arm. "That must be hard. I hope it's okay that I asked."

"It's good." He raised his hand to mine and squeezed it. I felt a shiver rush through me. "I don't talk about this, usually, and that's not a good thing. Bottling things up, it's not always the best way."

He let my hand go and it felt like a loss.

"Easier though," I said gently.

He made eye contact, fighting his emotions. "It is. Until it isn't."

I knew what he meant. Sara's death was hard for me to talk about, but for some reason, it felt safe with Jack. Maybe because he was experiencing loss, too, it felt like he could understand in a way most people couldn't.

"For years after my sister, Sara, died no one talked about her. It was like she didn't exist. Like she never had. Kit was the only one I could talk to about her. It's why we're close, even now. Because she didn't pretend I never had a sister. Sometimes my parents will say I'm an only child when they're talking to someone new, just to make things less uncomfortable. I hate it."

My stomach churned with anger and loss. Sometimes the enormity of what my family had been through, what I'd been through, hit me, and I wasn't prepared for it. It's why I didn't talk about it. Better to stuff it down like WASPs had been doing for centuries than let it out.

"I'm sorry if that's dark," I said. "You've got enough to deal with."

"No, I'm glad you told me. And I'm glad you have someone in your life like Kit."

"Me too." I blew out a long breath. "Phew. When you said no small talk . . . we're taking that pretty literally."

"It's nice to have a real conversation."

"Yes, it is."

He touched my hand again, then stepped back. "Okay, time's a-wasting. I can't give you a full tour, but why don't I take you to my favorite bridge."

"You have a favorite bridge? Wait. Of course you do." I folded the towel Jack had bought for me and tucked it into my bag. "Tell me about it."

"It's not far, just over there by the lake." He pointed over my shoulder. "It's called the Bow Bridge."

I scrunched up my face.

"What?" Jack asked.

"I'm trying to get a title from that, but I've got nothing."

"Bridge Over the River KY," Jack said without hesitation, his lips twitching.

I laughed in response and it felt good to let out the tension. "Why's this bridge your favorite?"

"You'll see when you get there."

We threw our trash away, then walked across the lawn toward the lake. The bridge was a low expanse of weathered cast iron that had an intricate railing. I recognized it as soon as I saw it.

"Oh, I've been here." I turned to Jack. "You're not disappointed, are you?"

"Not at all. And do you like it?"

"It's beautiful." I took in the bridge—the blue water to the left, the border of trees along the edge of the park, and the sandstone buildings beyond it on West Eighty-Sixth Street. "I can see why it's your favorite."

"My mom used to bring me here." He stood next to me, his hands on the railing, his left arm brushing my right.

"After work?"

"That's right. We'd get ice cream unless it was freezing out, and then we'd come here. It's her favorite place in the park too. My dad even proposed here."

"Like in a movie."

"Yep. They're cheesy like that."

"Oh?"

He grinned. "Honestly, growing up my sister and I thought they were . . . *disgusting* was the word we used. But now I'm jealous. They're happy. Despite everything."

"That's great."

"What about your parents?"

I watched the water ripple in the breeze. "Mine? They're . . . not great. Losing a kid, it broke them."

"Are they still together?"

"Yes, but not in a good way. More like how you are sometimes with family. Not the people you'd choose to hang out with but you're stuck with them come what may."

"I'm sorry."

"Thank you."

I tried to shake the feeling I always got when I thought about my parents. That it wasn't worth yoking your life to someone else if there was a possibility of ending up like them—hating one another but unable to quit.

"What's the craziest thing you've ever done on a bridge?" I asked, changing the subject.

"What?"

"I'm trying to lighten the mood."

"Ah, okay. Let me think."

"I don't need a sexploits story."

He raised an eyebrow. "No? It's a good one."

"Moving on!"

"I guess that only leaves the famous Steve Mala story."

"Can't be that famous," I said. "I've never heard it."

"No? You're in for a treat. Have you ever been to Oxford?"

"Mississippi or England?"

"England."

"Nope."

"There are a lot of bridges in Oxford," Jack said.

"Because of the Thames?"

"Yes, though it's called the Isis there, don't ask me why."

I laughed. "Go on."

"I'm in Oxford with my friend Steve Mala, and we're in college and we're there for crew."

"Oxford, rowing, Thames. I'm getting a . . . what's that running movie called?"

"*Chariots of Fire?*"

"That's the one. I'm getting strong *Chariots of Fire* vibes."

"If you're imagining us in white short shorts and singlets, then no."

"Damn it."

"Anyway," Jack said, his eyes dancing. "We have our regatta, and we lose pretty badly because our team sucks, and we end up on a pub crawl to commiserate."

"As one does."

"Right? Anyway, it's late at night, superlate, and Mala has had a lot of beers, only they're pints there, which is like two beers per beer."

"Recipe for trouble."

"Exactly. So, we're on some bridge in Oxford, and Mala, who I should've said is a guy who talks with big, sweeping hand gestures, especially when he's drunk, is talking enthusiastically about Gretchen."

Jack's eyes were bright as he mimicked his friend's hand gestures—his hands almost flapping, like he was trying to take off.

"Who's that?"

"Only the love of his life who he met in the pub we just left. Or maybe it was the pub before. It's hazy."

"Did Gretchen like him?"

"Gretchen did not. He's very disappointed, but also kind of delusional, like he's going to get her to like him, he just needs to sober up a bit. That's what he kept repeating, 'sober up a bit,' and he'd wave his arms like this." Jack raised his arms and flapped them like a bird.

A laugh bubbled out of me. "Shocking that Gretchen wasn't into him."

"Indeed. So, he's walking ahead of me on the bridge, his arms going, trying to sober up and then he disappears."

"Like in a magic show?"

"Like in he went right off the side of the bridge."

"Holy shit."

"That's what I said."

"Was he okay?"

"He was. He was lying on the concrete piling that was out of the water because the river was low, and he was laughing. The son of a bitch was laughing so hard."

"How did he survive?"

"The doctor said it was because he was drunk. It made him pliable."

"My god." I leaned into Jack. "How did he go over?"

"It was an old bridge, and the side was much lower than we're used to since it was built before building codes or when people thought about things like a drunk college kid who might simply fall over the side."

"That's a great bridge story."

"It's one of my favorites for sure."

"It's amazing. You're amazing."

Uh-oh.

"Forget I said that."

"Why?"

I tucked my head down. I didn't know what I was doing, and I was scared. "I wasn't supposed to like you."

"No?"

"You were supposed to be my get back out there guy."

"Like a rebound?"

I closed my eyes and inhaled deeply. "Something like that."

"Hey, look at me."

I brought my chin up, but my eyes were closed. And before I could open them, it happened. He kissed me.

I never saw it coming.

Chapter Five

The kiss lasted the right amount of time, and not long enough at all.

My hands made their way around his neck and his settled on my waist, firm and strong. Our mouths parted briefly, his warm breath mingling with mine, his tongue against my teeth, his fingers grazing the patch of skin above the top of my jeans, which was revealed as I rose on my toes.

And then we broke apart, both of us startled that it had happened at all.

"Jack," I said as I opened my eyes.

"Chloe." Jack kept his hands in place on my hips, partially in contact with my skin. "I—I need to tell you something."

A chill went through me though I was still warm from the kiss.

I took a step back. "You have a girlfriend."

"What? No." He ran his hand through his hair. "I don't have a girlfriend."

My heart was thumping against my rib cage. "You're married?"

His eyes went wild. "No."

"What then?"

"I should've told you right away in the diner, but—" Jack's phone rang in his pocket, a snippet of a song I couldn't immediately place. "I'm sorry, I need to get this—that's my mom calling."

"Of course."

I stepped away, my mind whirring. If he wasn't with someone else, what could it possibly be? He was gay? No, that didn't make sense. He was dying? No, that was—

"Mom?"

"Mamma Mia"! That's what the song was.

I walked down the bridge, not wanting to intrude on his privacy. I wanted a moment for myself, too, to collect my thoughts. The water danced in the sunlight. I could still make out the tone of his voice, and it sounded like anguish. His mother was calling with bad news, worse news than Jack already knew.

I had a flashback to that awful moment when I was told Sara was dead, that I was never going to see her again. We weren't going to do any of the things we'd planned, silly and small, big and important. It felt like my own life was being ripped away from me, and I've never felt the same again. It wasn't a feeling I'd wish on anyone.

I shivered in the sunshine and wrapped my arms around myself, a poor substitute for Jack's embrace.

"Chloe," Jack said, coming up behind me moments later. He was pale, his eyes troubled.

"Are you okay?"

"I have to go. My mom, it's bad. She might not . . . that was my dad calling."

"I shouldn't have asked you to show me around the park. I feel terrible."

"It's not your fault, neither of us knew. But I have to go." He reached out and hugged me quickly, then released me. "I have to go."

I met his gaze. "Don't think about me. Go."

Jack bent his head to mine and kissed me, his lips a light brush against mine. "Today has been great," he said, and then he was gone.

After Jack left, I wandered around the park for an hour, thinking over our day together, trying not to linger on whatever it was he wanted to tell me. Mostly, I tried to enjoy the sunshine and the feeling of possibility. Because that's what Jack represented—potential.

I only let it go that far. I wasn't thinking that I'd met my future husband. After my failed relationship, I was too jaded for that, and no matter how many rom-coms I read and recommended, that wasn't going to change. Possibility could easily turn to disappointment, could fade into indifference, could melt into nothing.

That's what happened with Christian. Maybe we hadn't been right from the beginning; how can you ever know? But what I knew for certain was that I didn't deserve what he'd done to me, betraying my trust and falling for some girl at his office. He said nothing had happened while we were still together, but something *had*. Because feelings weren't nothing. They were what we were supposed to have kept for each other.

That was the real reason behind my dry spell. Anytime I'd go on a date or even think about it, I'd rush to the end and see myself hurt and disappointed.

But, oh, the hope that it would be different this time!

That's what love starts with, isn't it? The wish that *this* is your person? Someone to have and to hold through good times and bad, through sickness and health, until death did you part. There's something to those ancient words—a promise, a dream, and maybe, for some people, a reality.

Not for my parents, but for Kit's. For Jack's. I had to hold on to the belief that it could happen for me. Maybe not like in the movies, on a crowded street where we'd run to each other in a moment of realization, but in a series of days like the one we'd had, where I felt a sense of synthesis.

Could Jack turn out to be a worthless jerk? Of course he could. Whatever it was that he hadn't said could reframe the entire day, but it didn't feel that way.

I decided to hold on to that hope and see where it took me.

And then it was late, the sun thinking of setting.

I walked to the subway and when I got off at my stop at Knickerbocker Av my phone was ringing. Kit.

"You haven't turned that tracker thing off, have you?"

"I will, I will."

"Uh-huh." I stopped outside my local bodega on the corner of Schaefer. I was still full from the meal with Jack, but I knew that would wear off in an hour, and I was out of provisions. "How was your day?"

"Eh. We were shopping for furniture."

"For the new apartment?" Kit and Theo were moving to a two-bedroom in Harlem that had me drooling over the massive increase in space. Real estate wasn't the main reason to be with another person, but I'd be lying if I said I didn't sometimes get turned on by Zillow listings.

"Two weeks till moving day."

"You've hired movers, yes?"

"What? You don't want to schlep our stuff up and down a million stairs?"

"I do not. Has he proposed yet?"

"You sound like Lian."

"I assume you're going to tell me *before* Lian when he does."

"Maybe I'll propose to him."

"There's zero chance of that happening."

"Why do you say that?" Kit asked.

"Because you made me enact proposal scenarios a million times when we were kids?"

"You were good at getting down on one knee."

"I had to after Ken's leg snapped off. Anyway, I don't think that's the hard part."

Kit sighed. "Honestly, I'm nervous about it."

I pulled open the door, the bell tinkling above me. I breathed in the musty smell and picked up a rickety basket. The first time I'd come in here, I'd been too scared to buy anything, used to the pristine Kroger near my old apartment in Cincinnati. Kit had told me I was being a snob and to get over myself. She was (mostly) right. Ninety percent of the food was perfectly edible. It was simply a matter of knowing which 90 percent.

"Why are you nervous about Theo proposing? Are you thinking of saying no?"

"No."

"Then what?"

"It's scary to think of something like that being decided. Like, am I never going to fall in love again? Never going to sleep with another person? For the rest of my life?"

"Never have to worry about whether your date is going to show up or if he's going to expect you to split the bill or if he's a serial killer . . ."

"You've never dated a serial killer."

"But I could! That's the point," I said. "Theo's amazing."

"I know."

"So what's the issue?"

"Nerves?"

"You have nothing to be nervous about," I said.

"You only say that because you're single."

"I don't think that's true." I walked down the nearest narrow aisle. This is how I grocery shopped, with no lists or planning, snagging what caught my eye in the moment.

"You're not single?"

"Well . . ."

"Wait, you're not *still* with Jack, are you?"

"No."

"Fill me in."

"It was great."

I told her about the day while I wandered up and down the aisles collecting cereal, milk, and spinach that could potentially have E. coli, but I needed something green. It felt like the conversations Kit and I used to have in high school that would go on for so long my ear would be hot from being pressed against the receiver.

"Sounds like a great day," Kit said when I finished telling her about the kiss and how Jack had to go. "I never thought of Jack as a museum kind of guy. I like it."

I emptied my cart onto the counter at the cash. I felt an annoyed tap on my shoulder. There was a red-faced woman who was probably in her sixties behind me in a ratty fur coat with a ton of yellow gold jewelry clanging on her wrists. "Yes?"

"You cut the line."

"Oh, I'm sorry. I didn't see you there."

Her lips were in a thin red line. "I'm sure you were too distracted recounting the best date ever."

I shrank away from her. "Please, go ahead of me."

"I wouldn't dream of it. Go back to your conversation. We're all riveted." She waved her hands at the two other people in the store, who were doing their best to look anywhere but at us. "What *was* Jack going to tell you?"

"Hold on, Kit," I said into the phone. I pushed my items along the counter to the cashier, who was trying hard not to laugh. He rang my things up quickly and handed me my bag as I paid.

I hustled to the front door. "I'm back."

"What was that all about?"

"My story is amusing to lonely old ladies wearing fur coats in May."

"Whatever, ignore her."

I glanced back at the cash. The woman threw me an angry look over her shoulder.

"What do you think he was about to tell you?"

"No idea." I stepped back onto the street and walked toward my apartment.

"Should I give you a list?"

Kit loved lists, pro-con, to-do, not-to-do. I of the no grocery list ever did not.

"Trust me, I've already thought of everything."

"He's married? If he is, I'm going to HR."

"For what? Dating your friend under false pretenses isn't a work offense."

"It is to me."

"He said he wasn't. No wife. No girlfriend."

I stopped in front of my building, an unremarkable new build that was five stories and had little charm. Generations of TV shows about unrealistic New York apartments had made for a hard let-down when I realized this was the best I could do anywhere near Manhattan. But I felt like I was too old for roommates, even if Kit was available, which she wasn't.

"Maybe he's wanted for a murder." Why didn't Kit sound like she was joking?

I walked up my front steps. "Ha. Ha."

"Sorry. You know my obsession with *Forensic Files*."

"Kit, you work with this guy. Does it seem like he could have a dead body in his freezer?"

She paused. "No. I don't think so."

"That's reassuring. Remember, you were the one who suggested I date him." I got the front door open, then went inside, taking the stairs because the elevator was small and scary.

"Maybe he's about to leave for an around-the-world trip that will separate you for a year? I would love the plant in his cube. He's got one of those moon cactuses, you know those color—"

"Kit."

"Sorry. You seem blasé about it."

"I'm not. But he's at the hospital with his mother and I have to cut him, and me, some slack. Otherwise, I'm going to go crazy."

"You're right. My email came back online. Maybe it was a false alarm?"

I felt queasy. Her email was back up. Jack had gone to work after the hospital but hadn't texted me? No, I was being silly. It had only been a couple of hours since we'd parted. Did I truly expect him to text me already? And maybe the email had gone back online without his intervention. Maybe he was able to work on it from the hospital. There were a million possibilities that weren't an insult.

"I hope so, for his sake and his mom's." I rounded the corner to the final flight to my third-floor apartment, right smack in the middle of the building for maximum noise from all directions.

"It's funny. Jack never talks about that stuff at work. I didn't know his mother was sick."

"It's not work talk."

"Or he likes you."

I unlocked my front door and entered. I put my bag of groceries down on the gray tile floor. "Maybe."

I heard a noise through the phone, a voice in the background, then: "Theo's back from his basketball game. I should go."

"Talk to you tomorrow."

"Of course."

"Turn off that Find My Friends thing!"

"Love you!"

We hung up and I walked into my living room/kitchen/dining room/office. It was tiny but I'd made it feel like home. In the last year I'd done what I could until my apartment felt cozy and maximized every square inch of space, from the two-seater couch in a soft gray chenille to the bookshelves lining the wall of my bedroom, full of the books I couldn't part with. I'd painted the wall the TV was on a bright red and hung flowery curtains on the window.

I put my bags down on the small glass table that sat between my kitchen and living room and checked my phone. Nada from Jack. Should I text him? Surely a short text letting him know that I hoped his mom was okay would be fine? Wasn't it the decent thing to do?

If I thought about it too long, I'd talk myself out of it or do something way stupider like call. I tapped out a text.

Thank you again for today. I hope your mom is okay. Fingers crossed for you and your family.

I reviewed it to make sure there were no typos, then hit Send.

I watched for the delivered sign, and then there was a reply bubble. Three dots moving. I didn't have to wait long for his response.

???

I checked my text thread, assuming I'd texted the wrong person, which happens more times than I can count. But it was the right one for Jack. What could that *???* mean? Was it a typo? Had he already forgotten who I was?

I didn't have to wait long to find out.

I just realized you never got my earlier text canceling, Jack wrote. *Our servers have been down and I've been in the basement all day working to fix the problem without service. I'm sorry I missed our brunch. Can I make it up to you?*

I dropped my phone. *I'm sorry I missed our brunch?* What?

I stooped and picked up my phone. The glass had partially shattered, spiderwebbing over Jack's text.

Is this a joke? I wrote, feeling desperate.

Not sure I get your meaning. I thought I'd written you this a.m. to tell you I couldn't make it, but it seems that text didn't go through. Only realized now. Sorry about that. A pause, then: *Why did you ask about my mother?*

I almost dropped my phone again.

Shit. *Shit.*

This wasn't a joke. Jack hadn't made brunch. I hadn't spent the day with him.

So, then who the hell did I just kiss?

Chapter Six

"That's everything that happened," I say to Kit two hours later. "All five chapters of it."

We're sitting on my couch, surrounded by empty pizza boxes. When I'd recovered from the shock of discovering that I'd spent the day with a strange man who wasn't Jack, I'd summoned her post–furniture shopping to an emergency summit at my apartment. She'd arrived with hot pizza and a tub of ice cream, and I felt like a fool when the sight of our special comfort food combo made me cry. She'd listened to me rehash my story without interruption even though I was sure I'd given her way too much detail.

"So," Kit says thoughtfully, "how do you think you made the mistake in the first place?"

"I was stressed that people in the restaurant were judging me because I was being stood up. That's why I latched onto the first guy who walked through the door who looked like Jack."

"How much did he look like him?"

"A lot at first, I thought. But when he sat down. . . . So many people have pictures that don't look like them, right?"

"For sure, but"—Kit waves her ice-cream spoon around, a dollop of vanilla looking precariously close to sliding onto my couch—"he sat down. He went along with it. Why?"

I explain again about how I'd sort of shamed him into it. That hug. The loud voice I'd used. "I guess he took pity on me."

"Okay, sure, at the beginning. But why keep up the ruse afterward?"

"I don't know."

She tilts her head to the side, her dark-brown eyes considering me. "You think it's because he liked you."

Damn it. That's exactly what I was thinking. "Stop reading my mind."

"Stop being obvious, then."

I made a face at her. "The thing is, I don't think I was making up us getting along. We spent the day together. He kissed me on a bridge. He bought me flowers—"

"Hmm, the kiss." Kit tucks a lock of her thick hair behind her ear. She has a row of studs that goes halfway up her earlobe—she'd almost passed out when she'd gotten them done when we were fifteen, but they look cool now. "Good kiss, bad kiss?"

"A great kiss."

"Like, tongue, teeth, hair pulling?"

"We were outside!"

"What's that got to do with it?"

"I've never had a hair-pulling kiss where someone else could see."

"You should try it sometime."

I start to laugh. "I can see Lian watching you now . . ."

"Not in front of *her*. But come on, details. Give me the heat level at least."

My cheeks are flaming. "A nine, okay." I hug myself, remembering the feel of his hands on the skin at my waist as we were kissing, the press of his lips. "Can you have heat like that with someone if you don't like them?"

"Totally."

"How would you know?"

"Come on. Remember Roger?"

"That gross British guy?"

"He *was* gross, but also kind of hot. And the sex—" She put her fingers to her lips, then flicked them away. "Chef's kiss."

"You never told me you slept with him."

"I don't tell you everything." She digs her spoon into the ice cream. I ate so much pizza, it doesn't even look appetizing. "The point is, heat doesn't mean anything."

"But it was more than that. We connected. We fit. I felt . . . this is going to sound nuts, but I don't think I've ever felt that way with someone before."

"Sure you have."

"No, I . . . forget it."

She licks her spoon. "Question is, can you?"

"Don't know. I wish I understood why he didn't tell me who he was."

I run through the day again. All those moments when he could've said something. But wait, maybe he did try. At the lake? And then again after we kissed.

"He was going to, but then his dad called and he had to go."

"He could've told you after his call."

"It was an emergency. His mother's probably dying."

"Or it was some friend of his and he was using it as an excuse to ghost."

My stomach flips over. Is that possible? No, no. "That's not what happened. You didn't see his face."

"He should call you then."

"But he can't. He only knows my first name. We never traded numbers."

"Why not?"

"Because we were already supposed to have each other's numbers."

"Right. Hmmm. What's the real Jack say about all this?"

"The real Jack?"

She rolls her eyes at me. "The guy you spent the day with is fake Jack, obvi. Real Jack is the guy I was trying to set you up with."

I grimace. "He said he wanted to make it up to me."

"Are you going to let him?"

"I don't know. Wouldn't that be weird?"

"How?"

I look down at the rug I found at a local flea market. It's a mix of blue and green geometric patterns that fits perfectly with the mid-century modern vibe I'm going for. I can tell Kit anything, but how do I say out loud that it would be weird to date Jack because he's someone else in my mind?

"I can't explain it."

"Real Jack is great. Fake Jack sucks."

"Don't call him that."

Kit puts the ice-cream container down on the coffee table. "What am I supposed to call him? I don't know his real name and neither do you."

"You don't have to rub it in."

She considers me as she pushes her oversized glasses up her nose. "This is another way to hide, you know."

"What's that supposed to mean?"

"Don't take that tone with me, Chloe Baker."

"Sorry."

"Look, babes, I get it. You meet this seemingly great guy and then he disappears like a magic trick. But you have to forget him. He lied to you. He took advantage of the situation in a way that's kind of gross. And you have a real guy, a good guy, who wants to take you out. Don't mess it up for some fantasy, okay?"

"You're right."

"I'm always right." She pulls me to her. I lay my head on her shoulder as her arms encircle me. "You'll forget all about him, I promise."

"You say so."

"I do."

I lift my head. "But don't you think—"

"Chloe, no. You've been reading too many rom-coms. It's screwed up your thinking. This isn't the universe telling you this is your guy. If it's talking, which is unlikely, it's telling you he's the person you *weren't* meant to be with. Move on."

"I'll try."

"At the very least eat some of this ice cream so I don't gain a million pounds."

"That I can do."

The next morning, I have trouble doing up my pants and vow not to wallow anymore. Then I stick my tongue out at myself in the mirror because I shouldn't be judging myself so harshly, and make a run for it so I'm not late.

I arrive at BookBox at nine. It's located in an old brownstone in Lower Manhattan in the Bermuda triangle formed by the HarperCollins, Macmillan, and *Fortune* magazine offices. On my first day in the office a year ago, my boss, Tabitha, told me to be careful about what I said outside the office when I was in the area.

You never know who's listening, Tabitha had said, looking around as she said it like even the fact that we needed to be careful needed to be kept a secret.

I'd wanted to ask if I'd accidentally signed up for some CIA operation that was infiltrating the publishing industry, but quashed it. I learned soon enough what she meant. Turns out there are a *lot* of writers, or wannabe writers, out there, all desperate to get attention for their books. And if they find out that you work for BookBox shit can get weird fast.

The few times I'd told someone where I worked, I'd been bombarded with unpublished or self-published manuscripts and emails begging me to consider them for inclusion in that month's box. Those emails had often been followed up numerous times, even when I said I couldn't consider it, demanding to know why.

And it wasn't only the unpublished; publicists and marketing directors were also eager to get our attention. It was an oddly powerful position to be in for someone who was twenty-six and made a mid–five figure income that barely supported me in my five hundred square feet of space.

I arrive at my desk and clear off that morning's deliveries. I love books, but this job could make me hate them. Every day is an avalanche of pastel illustrated covers with women's names in the titles or clever puns. I've had to set up a triaging system that any author would weep to know—if you don't get me with the first chapter, I'm not reading on.

"Mondays, amiright?" Jameela says, looking up from her screen across our shared T-shaped desk. As usual, one of her screens is open to Twitter.

She's obsessed with *Bridgerton*; with Kate and Anthony Bridgerton more specifically, and her screen name is @MayfairIsJustAhead.

"What's up in the ton today?" I ask.

Jameela rolls her eyes. "Someone with ten followers was disrespecting Simone again."

She means Simone Ashley, the actor who plays Kate. Anthony (pronounced An-tuh-nee, if you please) is played by Jonathan Bailey, i.e., Jonny (no *h*!) for those in the know.

I've had to learn these names—and many others—to keep up with her rapid-fire commentary. She spends much of her day making screencaps and refreshing Getty Images obsessively looking for any sighting of #Kanthony out in the real world. It's a miracle she gets any work done, but since she's in charge of our social media, she claims it's crucial to keep plugged in with the fandom. Our BookBox Twitter account has a massive following, so she's probably right.

"I'm sure Cat and the gang will take care of *her*." Cat is one of #Kanthony's greatest online defenders because apparently, fake couples need "gatekeepers" against nobodies to protect them.

Jameela scrunches her button nose. "You know it. Don't come for Simone. Do. Not. Come. For. Her."

"Never."

I pry open the first package and pull out a novel with a pink cover called *Love at First Sight*. There's an illustrated couple standing inside a heart, looking at each other lovingly. "Do you believe in this?"

I tip the cover toward Jameela. She often wears her thick, dark-brown hair in an updo with two small braids woven into it, a look Kate sports. They do bear a passing resemblance to one another, though Jameela is on the shorter side and doesn't have a glam team.

"Anthony loved Kate from their first race in the park."

I smother a laugh. I probably know half the dialogue from *Bridgerton* from Jameela. I watched their season once, and though Jonathan Bailey is superhot and those actors had amazing chemistry, it didn't infect my brain chemistry the way it did hers.

"But for real," I say. "Do you think it's possible to *know* someone's right for you when you meet them? Or is that our memories playing tricks on us if it works out later?"

"Romance books are bullshit," Addison says, arriving with her bike helmet firmly attached under her chin and her fold-up bike under her arm.

She's our third deskmate, in charge of subscriptions, and this is not the first time I've heard her express that sentiment. I'm pretty sure she has an entire set of coffee cups with that exact phrase imprinted on it. Why she works here I'll never know, though it might have something to do with whatever she's writing on Wattpad. I haven't been able to get her to tell me anything about it, but one day I'll crack her screen name and then I'll know.

"This isn't a romance," I say. "It's a rom-com."

"Same, same." Addison peels off her helmet, shaking out her braids. She's wearing a hooded top in a deep purple that suits her. Addison always looks effortlessly cool, even with bike clips on her pants.

"There are two hundred people on Twitter who would kill you for saying that," Jameela says.

"Twitter is also bullshit."

Jameela narrows her eyes and turns back to her screen. She starts typing something and I don't have to see it to know that it's what Addison just said.

Jameela loves stirring up drama on Twitter. I'm convinced half of the someone's saying such and such about Simone posts are made up by her to create content. But her tweets routinely get thousands of likes. Who am I to judge?

"Keep or toss?" I say to Addison, shaking the book at her.

"We already had a book with that same title two years ago. It's a no-go off the bat."

"That memory of yours."

She sighs. "You could check the database."

"And deprive you of the opportunity to show off? Never."

Addison almost smiles. She's a hard-core cynic, and part of my daily work goal is to make her laugh. I give myself half a point for this effort.

"How did that date go?" she asks as she sits at her desk. She has two screens also, something that was offered to me but I declined. Since I spend most of my day reading physical books, I don't see the need.

Jameela's head pops up. "Ooh, spill."

So much for putting him out of my mind. "Eh. He was a no-show."

"Seriously?"

"I can't believe it," Jameela says. "Isn't he friends with Kit?"

"Work colleagues. It's more complicated than that. Their servers crashed, he works in IT, it was a whole thing."

I don't feel like going through it all again with them. I'm supposed to be forgetting about fake Jack anyway. Because Kit is right—I can't trust him regardless of how he made me feel, and I'm never going to see him again.

This makes me sad, though, so I pull the next package over to me and open it. It's a book with a bright-yellow cover called *Second Chance Around*.

I flash it at Addison. "What about this one?"

"Clever," she says.

"Original?"

I flip it over and read the back. *Sometimes love takes more than a meet-cute. When Tanner and Jacob met for the first time, the stars didn't align. But now they have a second chance to make it work. Can they find love the second time around?*

"Worth pursuing?" Jameela asks.

"Hmm?"

"The book."

"Oh right. Yes, I'll give it a read."

I tip the book against my lips like it might impart its secrets through osmosis. The kiss with fake Jack (goddamn you, Kit) flashes through my mind. It was a great kiss, maybe the best first kiss I've ever had.

And, okay, he should've told me who he was. He should've tried harder to do it and not gotten distracted no matter what was going on. But maybe, right now, he's regretting that. Maybe he wishes he had a way to contact me. Maybe it's worth it for me to put a bit of effort into finding him so I can see whether we have something real or whether I should've left well enough alone.

Because if I don't do it, I'll always regret it. I'll always wonder if we could've made it.

And I have enough regrets in my life to know I don't need to add to them.

Chapter Seven

"I can't believe I agreed to do this," Kit says the following Saturday. She's wearing an adorable pink romper, with her hair in braids, and she's already received three "hey, baby" calls from touristy college bros on our way to the brunch place where I met fake Jack last week.

Try as I might, I haven't come up with a better name for him.

"Do what?" I ask as we take our seats, one table over from where I sat with Jack. "Have brunch with me?"

"As if that's all we're doing." She sits back in her chair. "What's the point of this?"

"Maybe we'll find him."

"And then?"

"I don't know. Maybe I'll get answers."

"About?"

"Why are you cross-examining me?"

"Because this is not like you."

I stare down at my hands. She's right. It's *not* like me to obsess over a guy I just met like this. Even with Christian in the beginning, I held him at arm's length. He had to work to make me fall in love with him. When I finally let my guard down it was because I was finally convinced he wouldn't disappoint me. And look where that had gotten me.

"You're right, it's not. Which should tell you something, right?"

"What?"

"That this is different."

"Sounds like magical thinking to me." She picks up her menu. "What's good here?"

"Not the croissant. We ended up sharing my *Friends with eggs benefits*."

Janie walks up with a pencil and ordering pad in her hand. "What can I get you?"

"Janie, hi. Chloe. Remember, I was here last weekend?"

Janie taps her pencil against her pad and looks bored. The restaurant is as full as last week, and I was lucky to get a reservation. The Upper West Side loves its brunch.

"With a guy?" I persist. "He was late? And his credit card had been compromised?"

Her face clears. "Oh, the dude who almost stood you up?"

Oh my god I was right. She *was* thinking that.

"Yes."

"What about him?"

"You ever seen him in here before?"

She cocks her head to the side. "Maybe once or twice. Not a regular."

My stomach twists. "Any chance you know his name?"

"Hmmm. It's something basic."

"Like Jack?" Kit says unhelpfully. I kick her under the table.

"Something like that."

"Okay, um, do you think you could do me a favor?"

"Depends."

"Can I leave you my number? If he comes in again, can you give it to him?" I take out a card I prepared beforehand with my name, number, and a $20 bill.

She eyes the money. "He lose your number or something?"

"It's complicated."

"I don't want to get in trouble."

"You won't, I promise. Give him this. If he doesn't want to talk to me, he doesn't have to take it or call or anything."

"But you want me to tell you if he's been in, right?"

"Only if you're comfortable." I push the twenty and the card toward her. "Please?"

She hesitates for a moment, then takes it.

"Thank you."

She tucks the card and the twenty into the pocket of her apron while Kit laughs at me across the table. "You ordering?"

"Definitely."

Two hours and two thousand calories later, we're walking across the park toward the Met.

"I can't believe I ate all that," I say, holding my belly. We each got the eggs Benedict and ate every last bite, a move I regretted the minute my fork hit the plate for the last time.

"I can't believe we're even doing this after real Jack sent you flowers," Kit says.

"After *you* told him to send me flowers, you mean."

The flowers had shown up at my office on Friday morning, much to the delight of Jameela and the bah humbug of Addison.

They were tulips, my favorite, and the card read: *Sorry to miss our date*. I'd texted him to thank him, and he'd responded immediately, suggesting we get dinner tonight at Lola Taverna, a Greek restaurant I'd been wanting to try for a while. I'd said yes because the man had sent me flowers, but I felt like a jerk. I didn't want to go on a date with him; I wanted to find fake Jack.

"I did no such thing," Kit says, jutting out her chin.

"So he happened to pick my favorite flowers and know my work address?"

"Okay, okay, he consulted me, obvi. But it was his idea."

"I can't believe I agreed to go out with him."

"You'll have a good time if you go in with the right attitude."

"Hmmm. Isn't that what you're always telling me about work?"

Kit twists one of her braids around her finger. "I should take my own advice. Work has sucked recently."

Kit works in consulting and transferred from her company's Cincinnati branch to the Manhattan one three years ago when Theo had a chance to take over his uncle's veterinary practice. She's a wizard at sizing up a company and figuring out how to fix it, a skill she likes to apply to her friends too.

"What's up?"

"Roger's being an asshole."

"I'm sorry."

"Comes with the territory."

"It shouldn't." I stop walking and take in the Met's façade like I did last week. It's hotter today, and there's a small trickle of sweat running down my back.

That might be because of my nerves, though. I'm nervous about what I'm about to do, but also—what if I find Jack, or whoever he is? What then?

"What are we doing here again?" Kit asks.

"Fake Jack's mom worked here." I turn to her. "I can't believe you haven't memorized our entire story by now."

Kit gives me a look. "Uh-huh. And?"

"Maybe someone will remember someone who worked here whose son was a docent."

Kit takes out her phone.

"What are you doing?"

"Filming this for Theo. He won't believe it."

"Stop it, put that away."

"You're no fun."

"That's been obvious since the second grade."

Kit puts her hands on her hips. "You're saying I have bad taste in best friends?"

"Seven-year-old you did for sure."

"Let's get on with it, shall we?"

We walk up the stairs, me searching the crowd for fake Jack's face, my heart pattering at an absurd rate.

"Who are you going to ask?"

"Not sure." We enter the building, the air-conditioning enveloping us, and I search around for somewhere to ask about fake Jack's mom. "Speaking of asking. Any movement on the Theo proposal front?"

A blush creeps up Kit's neck. "Pretty sure he went virtual ring shopping with Lian this week."

"Oh dear."

"Yeah, I can only imagine what that's going to produce."

"Did you do what we talked about?"

"Leave printouts of rings I like around the apartment? I decided against it. Seemed too desperate."

My eyes rove around the marble hall. "What will you do instead?"

"When he shows up with something gold and covered in lapis or some other semiprecious stone that's not an emerald-cut diamond?"

"Yep."

"Take it back and pick out something I like."

"So practical."

"How about there?" She points to the information booth, where there are two mishappen security guards wearing black uniforms with white lettering. The woman looks to be about our age, and the man is much older, past retirement even.

"That might work." I pluck up my courage and go to the booth.

"Can I help you, ma'am?" the woman asks. Her dark-brown hair is pulled back in a severe bun and she's wearing no makeup.

"I'm looking for someone."

Her face creases with concern. "Someone's lost?"

"No, I . . . my friend . . . his mother worked here years ago, and so did he. I was wondering if you'd be able to check in your records for anyone who matched that description? Like, the personnel records?"

"What's the name?"

"Um, I don't know."

"Hey, Mort, getta load a this." She prods the other security guard in the back. "This lady wants me to search for a mother and son who worked here, and she don't even know their names."

Mort turns around and peers at me through dirty Coke-bottle glasses. His faded blue eyes are watery and clouded. "That right?"

"I . . . it's not that weird is it?"

"Ma'am, this is New York City. We get all kinds of weird all day long."

"So you'll help me?"

"No," he says firmly. "We can't be looking in personnel records."

"Even if they're at least ten years old?"

"Even if they're *fifty* years old."

I sigh, sensing Kit's *I told you so* next to me. "Does it ring a bell, though? Dark-brown hair, cute, six feet?"

The woman snorts. "You hear that, Mort? He was cyuu-te."

My cheeks flame. "Forget it."

"Nah, nah, ma'am," Mort says. "Sylvie was only making fun. But I wasn't here back then. I was still walking the beat."

"And I was still in high school," Sylvie adds.

"Okay, this might seem weird, but if you think of anyone? Or maybe ask some of the other people who might've worked here then, can you call me?" I take out another card with my number on it and think about giving money again, but this is getting expensive, and Mort used to be a cop. I don't want to get in trouble. "This is my name and number. If you think of anything, please give me a call."

Mort takes the card and puts it in his shirt pocket. "All right, *little lady*. I'll keep that in mind."

I grind my teeth at the *little lady*. Mort has agreed to help me. Now's not the time to make a feminist point. "Thank you."

Sylvie smothers a smile. "I'll keep my eyes peeled."

I nod to her and back away, feeling stupid.

"We done here?" Kit asks.

"One more stop. One more stop and we'll be done."

My last hope of finding something about fake Jack—or fake Jack himself—is the boat club. There's an open regatta today, like there was last week. I smooth my hair down nervously as we approach.

"You look great," Kit says.

"Thank you." My throat feels dry and my breakfast is doing somersaults in my stomach. I reach for Kit's hand and she squeezes mine.

There's a crowd around the lake of about twenty adults and kids holding controllers and navigating their colorful boats.

"Has this been here the whole time?" Kit asks. "It's awesome."

"Right?"

My eyes dart around, searching for a familiar face. An older man and his granddaughter. A young mother, her blond hair damp against her neck as she tries to help her son. A couple in their forties who're fighting over the controller. A younger man with dark hair—oh!

I take a step forward.

"Is that him?"

"I—"

I watch the back of his head. He's with a young boy and his hand is on the boy's back, guiding him. I'm not sure I saw fake Jack from behind—I'd made it a point of pride *not* to look back at him when we'd separated outside the brunch place.

I inch forward as Kit lets go of my hand. But I'm suddenly calm. This is what I wanted, right? To see him again? To give him a chance to explain why he'd let me believe he was Jack for so long?

Turn around, fake Jack. Turn around.

He doesn't though, so I continue to push my way through the crowd, keeping my eye on the back of fake Jack's head. The crowd is tighter around the water's edge, and I reach it as the starter lets off his pistol.

The man to the left knocks into me, sending me off balance and right into the little lake.

Splash!

It's not deep, but I have a moment of panic as my head ducks under the water and my arms flail around. I'm struggling to find my footing when a set of sure hands pull me up to a standing position.

"Are you all right?"

I push my hair away from my face. It's the man I thought was fake Jack, but it's not him. He's ten years older and is wearing a wedding ring.

"Thanks for jumping in."

"Of course. Here let me help you."

He takes my elbow and helps me get up onto the side of the pond.

"Chloe, babes, are you okay?"

"I'm fine."

"Daddy, Daddy, it's that lady who cheats!"

Oh for the love of Pete. "Hi, Kenny."

"She knows my name. Why does she know my name?"

"Do you have a towel?" Kit asks the man who pulled me out of the water.

"No, sorry."

"They have them in the gift shop," I say.

Kit rushes off as I twist my hair with my hands and wring it out. The crowd that was watching me disperses, but not Kenny or his dad.

"Sorry about that," he says. They're wearing their matching outfits again, and Kenny's dad has a stripe of sunburn across the bridge of his nose. "The horn startled me. I didn't mean to push you in the water."

"*You* knocked me into the water?"

"Not on purpose."

"Don't take that tone with him, young lady," Kenny says.

He looks so serious, his hands on his hips, that it's hard not to laugh.

"It's fine. Don't worry about it."

"Oh good," Kenny's dad says. "I'm glad to see you again."

Um, what?

"Okay."

"I got some good pictures of you last week."

"You were taking pictures of me?"

His cheeks turn red. "Not like that. When you went into the water to get the boat. You do seem to like going into this lake."

"Yes, right."

He holds out his phone. "Would you like to see?"

"I—"

"Look, here you are going into the water. And here you are getting the boat, and here you are handing it back to that guy you were with—"

"Wait. Stop." I take his phone and look at the photo. I'm clear and in focus, fake Jack less so, but he's clear enough to be recognizable. "Can I have this?"

"What? Oh sure."

I reach into my pocket and pull out my amazingly still working phone, even though the screen is half-shattered I guess Apple meant it when they said they'd made them waterproof.

"Here, airdrop it to me."

He transfers the photo to me as Kit comes back. "This is my friend, Kit."

"Bearing a towel," Kit says, holding it out with questions in her eyes.

"Thank you." I take it from her and use it to wipe off my face, then drape it over my shoulders. "Thanks, Kenny's dad."

"My name's Jim."

"Oh, thanks, Jim."

"Will we see you next week?"

"Uh, not sure."

"Right, then."

Kit and I walk away.

"What was *that* about?" Kit asks when we're not nearly far enough away.

"Lonely dad, I guess. Who knows. His kid is a nightmare."

"It was pretty funny when you went in."

"Thanks."

She tugs on the towel. "And you'll never guess what I did for you in the shop."

"What?"

"I remembered that fake Jack bought you a towel last week—see, yes I *do* listen to you—and so I asked to see their records of the towels they'd sold."

"And?"

"They said that they couldn't give me the name of anyone who bought a towel, but then she did look anyway and there were twenty. She couldn't give me the records."

"He probably paid cash."

"Maybe, though I was thinking about that, too, and don't you think he probably said that about his card so you wouldn't see his name when he paid?"

Ugh. "I never even thought of that."

"Anyway, no joy in that department."

"I did get this cool towel, though. I can add it to my collection." I hug her. "Thanks, Kit."

"Hey, you're getting me wet."

I pull away. "The day wasn't a total loss."

I tell her about the picture Jim had, and show it to her.

"Hmm. He does look like Jack. Real Jack."

"See?"

"You're still going to meet him tonight, right?"

"Yes, yes."

She looks at the picture again. "Is this guy worth going down with the ship?" She puts a hand up. "Don't even go there."

"I guess that's it then." I sigh. "Short of stalking the boat club every weekend and making Jim think I'm into him, I'm all out of leads."

"Sorry, babes."

"Me too."

Chapter Eight

When Kit and I separate, I go back to my apartment to change and get ready for my date. I wish I could beg off, but I'd never hear the end of it from Kit. I take a shower and put on a light-green summer dress with ties at the shoulders, then slip on a pair of comfortable sandals. My hair has decided to cooperate, so I leave it loose on my shoulders and apply a bit of makeup.

I'll have to do.

I take the L train toward Eighth Avenue, then change to the C train. As the car rattles around me, I mull over the failure of today. I owe Kit a day for her. It feels gross that we barely spoke about the fact that she's about to get engaged. I take out my phone and text her.

Thanks for today. Next time will be 100% about you.

She sends me back a heart emoji. *Good luck tonight!*

If he proposes call immediately.

You mean if he GOES DOWN ON ME ON ONE KNEE?

Ha!

When I get to my stop, I walk up the stairs and then to the restaurant.

It's seven and the day has cooled off, a gentle breeze in the air. The restaurant is on a street with a string of similar places—smaller, with bistro tables outside and flowers draped over the entrance. The smells coming out of the building are wonderful—garlic, butter, and fried cheese. I haven't had anything to eat since I devoured the eggs Benedict of death, and I'm finally hungry again.

I walk up to the hostess and give her my name. "I'm here for Jack Dunne."

"Yes, he's already seated."

"That's a nice surprise."

Her thin face pinches. "What's that?"

"Nothing."

She gives me the bland smile of a million similar interactions. "Follow me, please."

She picks up a menu and walks around the outside of the building to the last table under the deep-blue awning. A man's sitting there, fiddling nervously with a fork. Jack.

He looks up. "Chloe. Glad you could make it."

He stands and it's a shock. Because he does look superficially like fake Jack—*my* Jack my mind bleats—but also different. His eyes are more brown than hazel, his hair a shade lighter with less curl in it, and his frame is thinner. He's a good-looking guy, and his blue checked shirt and dark blue chinos fit him well.

If he'd shown up last weekend, I would've been pleased. But all I can feel right now is a vague disappointment. Some stupid part of my mind thought that it might be him—fake Jack. That the two Jacks might be the same person, playing a trick on me.

I'm such an idiot.

"Hi," I say, trying to smile.

We stand there for a moment awkwardly, with me wondering if he's going to try to hug me. He doesn't, just comes to my side of the table and pulls my chair out for me.

"Thank you." I sit and take my napkin off the table.

"Have you been here before?" Jack asks.

His voice is medium deep, without any trace of an accent that I can discern. A nice voice for a nice man who so far I'm feeling no chemistry with.

But I'm not being fair.

Did I feel chemistry with fake Jack immediately? Or was it the relief of thinking that I hadn't been stood up when I had?

"No, but I've heard good things."

He nods enthusiastically. "It's great. I live near here. I've been a bunch of times."

"Oh, I thought you lived on the Upper West Side?"

"Not anymore. I grew up there. My parents still have a place on Park Avenue."

"Fancy."

"The apartment's been in the family since before it was that fancy, but yeah."

"Sorry, I didn't mean—"

"It's fine. Everyone always says that."

I look down at my plate. It's white with a blue trim that matches the awning. There's rain forecast for later and I can feel it in the air.

"That's how you knew about the good eggs Benny?"

"Yes."

"It *was* good."

He frowns. "You had food?"

"Oh, Kit didn't tell you—" I stop. How am I supposed to explain fake Jack to him? "Um, we went there today. Kit and I. You'd spoken of it so highly. I was curious."

The lie feels weird in my mouth and like a bad place to start a date.

I search around for some other topic. "And it's near the Met, so we went there also."

"How was it?"

Yikes. This conversation is a minefield. Kit and I hadn't actually walked around the Met, but I can't tell him why. "It was good."

"What was your favorite part?"

"The Temple of Dendur. And all the *Mixed-up Files* stuff."

"Huh?"

A waiter approaches, wearing a white shirt and a black apron. His dark hair is slicked back. "Have you had a chance to look at the menu?"

"Oh, sorry, no," I say.

"Anything to drink?"

Jack gestures to me.

"I'll have a glass of white wine. The pinot gris?"

"Of course. And you, sir?"

"Water for me."

The waiter makes a note on his pad. "I'll be back in a few minutes."

"Do you not drink?" I ask.

"Not really, no."

I bite my lip. I don't want to tread into dangerous waters. There could be any number of reasons why Jack doesn't drink. It doesn't have to be a red flag.

"I don't have to have wine."

"No, go ahead, please." He picks up his menu. "What looks good to you?"

I grab my menu. It's full of delicious-looking items including fried zucchini and grilled octopus.

"I love tzatziki," I say.

It's my favorite condiment. When Kit and I went to Greece on our graduation trip from college, we judged the restaurants in Santorini by the price of their tzatziki. The cheaper it was, the better the food.

"Oh," Jack says. "I, um, don't like creamy foods. But go ahead and get it, of course."

"Creamy foods?"

"You know, that texture." He shudders. "Makes me gag."

"Does that include hummus?"

"It does."

"Okay." I look at the menu again. "What about the octopus?"

"I'm allergic to seafood."

My menu goes limp in my hand. "Why don't you choose some things."

"Lamb chops?"

I don't normally eat lamb but if I say anything we're shortly going to run out of options. "Sure."

"And the fried zucchini is amazing."

"Finally, something we agree on." I smile at him but he doesn't smile back.

"Were we not agreeing?"

"No, I . . . we seem to have different tastes in food."

"My quirks aren't adorable?"

"Oh, um."

"I was joking."

"Right, of course."

He lays his hands flat on the table. "Sorry, my food things can be a pain."

"It's fine."

The waiter returns with my glass of wine, which I'm grateful to see is large, and takes our order. Jack adds a bunch of delicious-sounding things from the menu as the clouds start to darken above us.

I look up at the sky. "Will we be safe, you think?"

"It's not supposed to rain until nine thirty."

"You trust those weather apps?"

"They're pretty on target for bad weather. It's the sunshine they seem to get wrong."

"Totally. Why is that?"

"No idea."

Good lord, we're talking about the *weather*.

"What was it like growing up on the Upper West Side? I'm not from here in case you couldn't tell, and I love hearing authentic New York stories."

"Hmmm. One of the Kennedys lives in our building."

"Ooh!"

"And during the pandemic, she was ratting out everyone who was violating the rules."

"Interesting."

I want to ask *which* Kennedy, but since he hasn't volunteered, it feels rude. I can't help thinking that fake Jack would've told me. But I should stop comparing them. That's not going to get me anywhere good.

Our first plate of food comes out, including the tzatziki, and we dig in. The conversation never sparkles, but it's pleasant, and the food is great. I nurse my large glass of wine, feeling like I can't order another given Jack's not drinking, even though I desperately want one. The waiter brings the bill right as a huge clap of thunder shudders above us.

Jack pays despite my protest, saying it's the least he can do, and then it starts to rain.

"Are you getting wet?" he asks as the drops pelt down next to us and drip off the canopy.

"A bit." I scooch my chair over so it's almost touching the person next to me. "Sorry, you don't mind do you?"

"No," she says, though she does. She and her friend have been talking shit about someone named Tiff all night.

"We'll be leaving in a minute." I turn back to Jack. "I should've brought an umbrella."

He turns and looks at the street. The rain is pounding against the blacktop. Across the street is a Citi Bike rack that's painted in multi-colors. There's a blue restaurant behind it covered in patio lighting.

"That looks like a painting," I say, taking out my phone to snap a picture.

I take it, then check it in my photos. It turned out well, but my eye also drags to the photo next to it—the snap Jim took of fake Jack last weekend. I look happy in this photo, my eyes shining at him. And it looks like he returns my affection . . . god, I sound like Jameela.

Return my affection? This is not an episode of *Bridgerton*.

"Let me see?" I switch to the photo of the building and show Jack. "That's cool," he says. "Should we make a run for it?"

"Sounds like a plan."

We stand and I consider swiping the napkin to cover my head. But the subway stop is only a couple of blocks from here, and I've already been soaked once today. What's once more?

I step toward Jack and we hover under the edge of the awning.

"I had a nice time," he says.

"Me too."

"Which way are you heading?"

"To the subway."

"Ah, I'm going the other way."

"No problem."

"We should say good night here."

I turn toward him and our eyes catch. I can't read his expression, but he might want to kiss me. I'm not ready for that—to be kissed by two Jacks in a week.

I lean forward and give him a quick hug. "Thanks for dinner."

He squeezes me briefly, and it's not unpleasant, but I feel nothing when he lets me go.

"Maybe we could see each other again?" he says hopefully.

"Sure."

"Night, Chloe."

"Night, Jack."

He reaches for my hand, catching the edge of my fingers, but I'm already spinning out into the rain, trying to dodge between the raindrops, feeling like I narrowly avoided something I didn't want to experience.

When I get back to my apartment, soaked, I'm too tired to do anything other than pull off my wet clothes and dress in my comfortable pajamas. I settle in on the couch with my phone to spend an hour scrolling before I go to bed.

How was it? Kit writes.

You didn't turn off Find My Friends did you?

Guilty.

Kit.

Whatever. Tell me everything.

Zero chemistry.

You didn't think he was cute?

He is, but that's not everything.

But he's nice and smart too.

He is.

So what's the problem?

He's not Jack, I want to write, but of course, he is.

I'm broken, I guess.

I'll say.

???

You'd go out with the guy who lied to you in a heartbeat, but this nice guy not so much.

Ugh. She's right.

You should go on a second date, Kit writes.

Assuming he wants one.

Did he say anything?

He said he did but maybe he was being polite. If he thought that was a good first date, I'm going to think less of him.

Jeez. Don't turn him down because you're waiting for someone you're never going to find.

Okay, I write, but then I open a dating app and begin scrolling through potential matches, looking for fake Jack. Because I'm guilty as charged. I *would* rather go out with fake Jack despite the circumstances.

What does that say about me?

I haven't had enough to drink for that kind of introspection, and when he doesn't turn up, I refine my dating parameters to what I guess is his age and his description. There's a bunch of late-twenties guys with dark-brown hair and hazel eyes but none of them are my Jack.

I put my phone down in disgust.

I feel restless, and know I won't be able to sleep. I pull out the book I need to read for work. It's a rom-com set at a murder-mystery conference where everyone dresses up as their favorite detective. It's a zany premise, but I like to shake things up a bit sometimes.

There's an Agatha Christie as rom-com vibe in it, with each of the participants having been lured to the conference by a highly specific personal ad.

I read the first fifty pages, which are addictive, but now my eyes are drooping and I'm half asleep. I fall into a half-dream state, where I'm now in the book, dressed up as Miss Marple, consulting Poirot on how to get fake Jack's attention.

"You have a mass marketing campaign at your disposal," says Poirot, twirling his large moustache between his fingers.

"Excellent suggestion!" Miss Marple says, and then I wake up.

Oh!

BookBox. His photo.

I could use it to do a marketing campaign to have our subscribers help me find him. It could be a fun gimmick. I bet Addison would be all over it, despite her protests against love. Anything that gets the online world talking about BookBox is a good thing because it tends to drive subscriptions. And we could tailor it so that it's only the New York boxes. We've even got a good rom-thriller to tie it to this month—a romance about a man who returns to a small town after he's been missing since he was a child.

My brain is racing, but I'm happy. This is how I'm going to find him.

My phone dings next to me with a notification from the dating app I was surfing. I must've favorited one of the guys who came up in my search by accident because I have a message from him. He also looks superficially like Jack, like both Jacks, but he's wearing a tight-fitting suit that looks suspiciously like it comes from the J.Crew catalog.

I open the message with trepidation. This app doesn't let men send photos to women even after they've matched, but that doesn't stop guys from getting gross in other ways.

Up for a late-night hookup? he asks. His name is Dan and he's thirty.

Are you drunk? I write back.

I might be.

You're drunk texting a girl you don't even know?

I have a thing for redheads. Tell me, are you red all over?

FU.

I wait until he's read my kiss off, then block and report him.

There has to be a better way to meet men.

Chapter Nine

"I can't believe they disrespected Kate like that," Jameela says midmorning on Monday at work. The rain has continued for the last couple of days and they're worried about flooding in Lower Manhattan. I came into work in rain boots and a large umbrella, and resisted the urge to splash in the puddles like I used to do with Sara when I was little.

I look up from my computer screen, where I'm busy making a WANTED poster with the picture of fake Jack on it. I created a whole marketing plan on Sunday and presented it to Addison this morning. She'd shrugged and said it was worth giving it a shot and there was just enough time to get it into that month's boxes, which are going on at EOD on Wednesday, if I was willing to hand stuff them myself.

"Like what?" I say, even though I have little interest in this topic. I've learned better than to express that, though. Jameela can get huffy if you don't love her 'ships.

Jameela shows me the post by turning her screen. I squint to read it. *I still think Anthony should be with Edwina.* I check the date. "This is from March 2022."

"So?" Jameela says. She's wearing a top made out of orange sari fabric, which looks great on her but is a bit fancy for the office on a rainy Monday.

"Why get upset about it now?"

"Because we just found it."

I don't ask who "we" is. It's her and her Twitter cronies who are getting increasingly desperate for content in the lull between seasons and have resorted to googling old Twitter posts to find something to complain about.

"What do you think of this?" I ask, holding up a printout of the poster. I've edited out my face and blown up fake Jack's. The headline says MAN WANTED. A FREE ANNUAL SUBSCRIPTION FOR ANY INFORMATION THAT LEADS TO HIS IDENTITY.

Jameela looks it over. "Did you clear that with Tabitha?"

"She's out this week."

"Not the best shot of the guy."

She's right. Fake Jack is both clearer and blurrier with the blowup, but I feel like if you know him, you'll recognize him. And it's not like I have any choice in the matter. It's the only photo I have. "Would you recognize this person if you knew them?"

"Probably. Who is it, anyway?"

I will my face not to blush. "A friend."

"Who agreed to be in this promo? You got him to sign a waiver?"

My stomach flips. I didn't tell Addison and Jameela that I was using the poster to find an actual person. I pitched it as a fun marketing idea that would help boost interest in BookBox. Clearly, I didn't think this through.

"Um, yeah, I will for sure. Jack won't mind." Or whatever his name is.

Jameela plays with her side braid. "Is this the guy who missed your date?"

"Something like that." My heart is racing now. This is like a rerun of my dinner with the real Jack. Everything I say is a land mine. "Hey, Addison, how many do I need to print up?"

She speaks without lifting her head. Her fingers have been flying over the keyboard for the last half an hour in a way that happens about once a day, which is when I suspect she gets inspired to add to whatever story she's writing on Wattpad. I've tried to pass behind her screen a few times to see if I can see what it is but she always minimizes it if anyone gets near her. "Five thousand."

How am I even going to get to half of those boxes? "Got it."

She stops typing and looks at me. Her large gold hoop earrings are swinging from the typing vibrations. "What other assets are you making?"

"I thought a TikTok video and some Insta graphics?"

"We could do something on Twitter too," Jameela says.

"That'd be great."

"What book does this relate to again?" Addison asks.

"*Most Wanted.*"

"I haven't read that one."

"It's good. *White Lotus* meets *The Kissing Booth.*"

"I can't even visualize what that means."

"It'll do well," I say.

"Let's hope so." Addison's phone rings and she answers it with a frown. She actively discourages anyone from calling her.

Jameela's gone back to her Twitter feud, simultaneously tweeting furiously and DMing with three different people.

I check my subscription numbers. We pick five books a month

plus an add-on, and subscribers can order past books that we still have in stock. Ideally, we want all five picks to sell through evenly, but it rarely works out like that. *Most Wanted* is trending slightly low for the month, which was part of the pitch I put together for this whole thing. Generating buzz for books is what we do. The more we're seen as tastemakers, the more subscriptions we get. And anytime you can get a book to go viral, then that helps subscriptions and sales.

Addison ends her call. "Apparently, my social security number's been compromised."

This happens once a week. Addison does not take shit from scammers.

"Did you make him cry again?" I ask.

"Almost." She scrunches her face. "Those assholes. It's bullshit."

"Agreed. Any chance either of you wants to help stuff boxes tonight? Beer and snacks on me?"

Addison taps her chin. "Tempting, but I have something I need to finish."

I hazard a guess. "A new chapter?"

"What?"

Oops. "In your book . . ."

"How did you know that?"

I raise my hands to ratchet down the tension. "I'm not snooping. We work five feet away from one another."

"Right." She breathes out through her nose. "I write sometimes. No big deal."

"I'd love to take a look."

Addison turns away. "Nah, I'm all set."

"Is it *First Kill* fan fiction?" Jameela asks. She's as curious about what Addison writes as I am, and has even gone so far as to suggest we break into her workstation when Addison is away to see if we can find her profile.

"What? No."

"We'll find out eventually."

"What's that supposed to mean?"

I make a motion to waive Jameela off. "Nothing. Jameela's feeling punchy because someone said something shitty about Kate."

"A daily occurrence."

"Yep. But she's got Jameela and co to defend her so, it's all good."

Addison shrugs and starts to type again, then stops and closes out of something. She stands. "I'm going to go get a coffee. Anyone want?"

"I'm good."

Jameela gives Addison her coffee order. Addison starts to leave, then goes back to her workstation and logs out, shooting us both a look.

"Damn it," I say when she's out of earshot. "Now we're never going to find out what she's up to."

"Patience."

"Not my strong suit. You didn't say if you'd help me tonight?"

"Don't think so."

Shit. It's going to take me forever to do this. Do I want to find Jack that badly? "Can I enlist a friend?"

"Don't see why not. As long as you don't share anything confidential with them."

"'Course."

"Good luck."

"I can't believe I agreed to help you with this stupid project, again," Kit says that night in the break room. I've bribed her with best friend points, Thai food, a six-pack of beer, and a promise to try to show

Theo the ring she wants without it being too obvious that Kit knows he's about to propose.

"You?" Theo says, finishing his beer. He's tall and wiry, with hair close enough to my color that he could be my brother, something I pointed out to Kit when they first started dating. "Imagine me."

"Kit and I come as a boxed set."

"So I've been told."

"Thanks to both of you," I say. "And this is the last time, I promise. If this doesn't work, I'm done."

Kit points her chopsticks at me. "Why don't I believe you?"

"Hush. You finished?"

"Yeah." She pats her stomach. "I couldn't eat one more thing if I tried."

I stand and clear away our things, making sure to rinse out the beer bottles and put the leftovers in the fridge. We have a Friday drinks thing sometimes, and contributing to the fund is considered good form.

"Okay," I say. "Let's get to this."

I lead them down to the storeroom in the basement, where we store the books and where two young guys box them up every month. I've seen them at work a few times, and their dexterity is amazing. There's been talk of making the switch to an automated system, but Tabitha's been resisting because everyone loves the Weasley twins (not their real names, obviously, but they're redheaded twins, so the name was kind of inevitable).

The boxes for this month were already done, but they've segregated the New York boxes for me—after I bribed them with fifty dollars each, dipping into my emergency fund because it felt like an emergency to find fake Jack.

I printed up the flyer earlier and left the copies we'd need down here—a high stack of them on bright fuchsia paper so they can't be missed and they'll photograph well on social.

I turn on the lights in the cavernous room, and they illuminate in a sequence. *Pop, pop, pop.* The room is full of high shelves containing inventory. The rest is taken up with long tables. The boxes are lined up against the wall.

"This room is cool," Kit says, drawn to the shelves and shelves of books. "How come you've never brought me down here before?"

"Because it's classified."

"Seriously?"

"Kind of."

She plucks a book off the shelf, a big seller a few months ago. "Can I take this?"

"I'll get you a copy from upstairs. They need those for the boxes."

"Cool." She puts it back. "Where are these boxes?"

I point to the stack against the wall. It's as tall as we are and ten feet wide.

Kit puts her hands on her hips. "You've got to be shitting me. We have to do all of these?"

"As many as we can, yeah."

"You owe me."

"For life. Both of you."

Theo takes off his glasses and polishes them with the end of his shirt. "Beats being on call for late night pet emergencies."

"Who took your shift?"

"New guy." Theo put his glasses back on and pushes them up the bridge of his nose. "Got to find out if he can handle it."

"You would not believe some of the things people do to their pets in this city," Kit says, shivering.

"Please do not tell me." I walk to the wall, pick up a stack of boxes, and lay them on the table. "We need a system. One person should open the box, then the other person can put the flyer in, and then the third can close them up again."

"I'll open," Theo says.

"I guess that leaves me to stuff the flyer?"

"Yeah, I'll close. Here, let me show you, Theo."

I show him how to open the deep green boxes with the BB motto embossed in gold without damaging them. There's a trick to opening and closing them without screwing up the fold. He picks it up pretty quickly, and in a few minutes, we get an assembly line going—box open, slide down the table to Kit, flyer in, slide to me, box closed, slide down the table so we can stack them again.

"You think this is going to work?" Kit asks, standing next to me.

"No idea."

"You like this guy, huh?" Theo says.

"I thought that was obvious." I tuck in a corner of a box, giving myself a paper cut in the process. "Ouch." I raise my finger to my lips and suck on it. There's a small bloom of blood, and its tang fills my mouth.

"Watch it," Kit says.

"I'll be fine."

"No." Kit has a serious expression on her face. "I meant with fake Jack. This guy could seriously break your heart."

"Yeah."

"Have you thought about what you'll do if he doesn't want to see you again?"

"You mean if I make this grand gesture and after all that he doesn't want to be with me?"

"Yep."

I hadn't let myself think about that. Too depressing. "That would suck."

Kit slides another box my way. "Can you handle it?"

"Of course."

"The move's been hard."

"The move has been fine."

"Deflector Chloe."

I stick my tongue out at her. Even though she's right, like she always is about me, she could cut me some slack given she's all loved up and happy while my dating life's been in the penalty box.

"*You're* the one who insisted I get back out there."

"She has you there, K," Theo says.

Kit shoots him an annoyed glance. "You're supposed to be on my side."

"I'm on the side of facts."

I fold up the next box and slide it down the table. "Don't worry so much, Kit. If I don't find him or if he doesn't want to be with me, it's fine. I promise." I put every ounce of sincerity I have into saying that, and in that moment, I almost believe it.

"Okay."

She's not convincing, but I don't want to fight. And I get what Kit is saying, I do. I even think she's right. But I'm going with my gut, not my brain. Because I can intellectualize why I've been alone so long all I want. It's not going to get me what I want.

I stack up the boxes we've completed. We've only done fifty and it's taken us half an hour. "We need to get a move on if we're ever going to get through half of these tonight."

"Half?" Theo says, his voice small.

"I thought that was reasonable, and then tomorrow—"

"Tomorrow?" Kit says.

"Did I not mention tomorrow?"

"Um, no."

I raise my right hand and place it on my heart. "I solemnly swear that I will never again ask you for a favor."

"All right, let's get on with it."

She spins another box down the table. I take out my phone and photograph it with the flyer in it, careful to get the best composition shot possible. Then I take some other shots of the boxes lined up and create an Instagram story on the BookBox account.

A special surprise coming at you in this month's BookBox! #ManWanted #HelpUsFindThisMan #Giveaway #Win #MostWanted

I make sure that there's a good shot of *Most Wanted* next to the flyer so they get the connection between the two, and let the post go live.

Come what may, I'm in it now.

Chapter Ten

I wake up the next morning to my phone blowing up.

For a minute, I can't figure out why I have this many notifications and alerts. But then I realize that it's the BookBox Insta account that I'm signed into on my phone. I'd checked it for the last time when we'd finished up around midnight, and there hadn't been much traction. But sometime overnight—more people were on social media in the middle of the night than seemed possible—it had gone semiviral.

I open the app and check the post. It has over a thousand likes and almost as many comments. I scan through them quickly, my stomach tumbling with nerves.

Oooh, that guy looks like my ex. TROUBLE.

Promote it on triplehot.xxx

I don't get it, is the guy missing, because this isn't funny.

    —Chill, girl, chill, it's just some marketing thing.

I'm ordering 10 copies of MOST WANTED if I get this guy
with purchase.

    —YAAS!

    —100%

MOST WANTED, indeed.

    —LOL

BookBox getting spicy! I like it.

Couldn't they have used a better photo? This dude is BLURRY.

    —That's kind of what makes it hot, tho?

Is that Central Park?

He's HAWT. JFSKDSKSKSK

He'd know what to do with his hands is all I'm saying.

I continue reading through the comments, which are appearing as fast as I can read them. Most people seem to think he's an actor, hired for the marketing campaign and potentially available for special appearances. Which was so not the point. I'm probably going to have to edit to clarify, but at least it's getting some attention.

I go back to the first comment and click through to the page of the poster who said fake Jack looks like her ex. She's solo in the first twenty photos, but after searching through her posts, I find the guy she must be referring to. He has brown hair and greenish eyes, but he's also fifty pounds heavier than either of the Jacks and at least five inches shorter. Definitely not him.

I put my phone down and get ready for work. When I get out of the shower there are a hundred new comments, with one or two people claiming to know him. But when I check the links they put in, neither looks anything like him. One guy is in California and another in Canada. I should've clarified that he lived in Manhattan.

Even after I edit the post (**Looking for a man in Manhattan***; ***Man does not come with purchase***), the potential leads that appear on the thread are useless.

My BookBox DMs are no better. It's full of people wanting to know what they get if they identify him—a free subscription, I keep writing—and then producing nothing. I quickly realize that my edits are not helping things. The way people will twist anything you say into something sexual is truly amazing. And this from someone who has spent years coming up with porny movie titles!

I clarify *again* that the contest is to find the specific man in the photo who is *not* missing, just a date who got away; other people feel the need to tell me about the men that ghosted *them*, a collection of sad stories that makes me wonder why I want to find fake Jack in the first place. I answer those messages with as much empathy as I can. I still feel hopeful, but overwhelmed too.

When I'm finally done and about to leave for work, my phone pings again, but this time with a text. From Jack. Real Jack.

Hi, Chloe, how are you? I had a great time the other night and would love to take you out again. Maybe you choose the restaurant this time? I'd love to explore Bushwick. XO Jack

XO Jack?

We didn't even kiss. Our date was pleasant but boring. And, okay, I'm not the ugliest person, but is the New York dating scene so desperate that he wants to have another experience like that?

Jack wants another date, I text to Kit.

Fake Jack??

No, real Jack.

Oh. I got excited there for a minute.

Ha! Nothing on that front other than a bunch of sad stories about guys disappearing after a couple of dates and why do I want to find him again?

I'm supposed to be convincing you? Kit writes. *I told you to forget about it.*

Yeah.

So what are you going to do?

About what?

The date with real Jack.

Oh! I forgot. Ugh.

Not a good sign.

I've been saying . . .

Wouldn't hurt to give him a second chance tho.

You sound like my mom.

You told Carol about this?

Ugh, no. You know we only speak on national holidays.

This is sadly true. My family sort of kept it together while I was still living at home, but after I went to college the pretense that we were a normal, happy family fell apart.

It didn't help that they used my first time away from home to clear out Sara's room and remove the rest of the photos of her that were in the house. Like they needed to erase her from our lives and pretend she never existed. When I confronted them about it when I came home that first Christmas, they told me it was too painful to remember her, and that I'd never understand what it was like to lose a child, they hoped.

And what could I say to that?

I hadn't wanted to know what it was like to lose a sister, but I didn't get that choice. And I didn't get the choice about how to mourn her. I wasn't in control of my life. My parents were.

But they'd been peeling her away from me for years, and that was the final straw. I knew they were grieving but I couldn't forgive them for not even giving me a chance to choose some mementos for myself from among her things.

I found a job on campus that summer, and when I went back to Cincy after graduation I moved into an apartment and saw them as little as possible. They could control Sara's life, the lack of it, but not me. And ever since I moved to New York it had gotten worse. I couldn't remember the last time we'd spoken.

I just mean, I write to Kit, *that Carol always said you should give someone three chances to impress you before you write them off.*

Seems like good advice.

Maybe.

So Jack has two more chances?

Nope. He stood me up, remember? So that was chance one. He's got one more chance, if I decide to give it to him.

Will you?

Not sure. Mulling. And am about to miss my train. Got to go.

I stuff my phone into my purse and locate my keys. I won't say no to Jack immediately. I've got the rest of the day to respond to him. And maybe in the meantime fake Jack will appear and solve the problem for me.

A week later, subscriptions are up 20 percent, I've been through more Insta DMs than I ever want to again, and there's no sign of Jack.

What there is, is a very angry boss standing over me with a copy of the flyer I put in the boxes clutched in her hand.

"Who authorized this?" Tabitha asks. She's got bright red–almost purple dyed hair that she wears short and spiky, but the rest of her is ultraconservative. Addison calls it her boomer librarian look, though if Tabitha heard that she'd give us a twenty-minute lecture on the difference between boomers and Generation X. "Chloe? Jameela? Addison?"

Jameela and Addison both accuse me with their eyes.

I raise my hand. "It was my idea."

Tabitha crosses her arms over her chest. She's wearing a white button-down tucked into a khaki skirt, and her glasses are hanging around her neck on a chain. Now's probably not the best time to ask why a forty-five-year-old woman wants to look like a sixty-year-old one. "You didn't think you needed to run this by me?"

My throat goes dry. "You were on vacation and it was time limited. It fit perfectly with *Most Wanted* but there were only a few days to get it into the box. And you said to only send you emails if there was an emergency."

Tabitha's not impressed. "Let me get this straight. You're using the book box to find a guy?"

"Not exactly?"

"How, not exactly? Is this a real man?"

"Yes."

"Do you know him?"

"I do."

"Is he missing?"

"No. I can't find him, but I'm sure he's perfectly okay." My eyes go to Jameela's then Addison's. They're watching intently while pretending not to. "Could we, maybe, go to your office to discuss this?"

"I see no need for that."

"Okay." I take a deep breath. My hands are shaking. "I'm sorry, Tabitha, I should've talked to you before doing this. I went on an accidental date with this guy, and it was great, but I didn't have his number and I was trying to find him, and I was thinking of ways to maybe do that, and it occurred to me that there was a good tie-in with this month's box, that it could be this cool marketing thing for the book."

"Did you at least get the author's permission? Or talk to the publisher?"

Shit, shit, *shit*. I didn't do either of those things.

"No, I didn't have time—"

She raises a hand. "Stop. This is a romantic thing between you and this guy?"

"I'm hoping it is."

"You used company time and property for a personal reason."

Oh, no, no, no. I'm about to get fired. "In part, yes."

She taps her chin, considering. "Subscriptions are up?"

"Yes, twenty percent over this time last year. And we've sold out of *Most Wanted* when it was trending behind the other titles. We're going to do a second printing. So I'm sure the publisher's okay with it."

"Hmm. And any results?"

"You mean, have I found him?"

"Yes."

"No."

"That works, then."

"That works, for what?"

She gives me a fake smile. "I've been contacted by BuzzFeed. They're doing an article—well, you're going to be doing an article."

My throat goes dry. "About?"

"The ten most desperate things you've done to find a man."

"Wait, what?"

"That's the title."

"Which I have to write?"

"No, no. You'll be a subject. They want to interview you."

"The article is about me? I'm the desperate person looking for a man?"

"Aren't you?"

Addison sniggers and then lowers her head when I glare at her.

"Yes, but they don't know that," I say.

"They asked to speak to the person who came up with the marketing campaign."

"We don't have to tell them who it is. Maybe if we don't, it would be even better—"

"Chloe, do you want to keep working here?"

"Of course."

"Then you'll do the article." She puts her hands on the desk and leans toward me, her grandma-like perfume cloying in my nostrils. "Are we clear?"

"Yes."

"The reporter will be in touch."

"Got it."

"And, Chloe? Don't ever do something like this again."

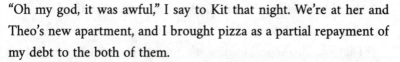

"Oh my god, it was awful," I say to Kit that night. We're at her and Theo's new apartment, and I brought pizza as a partial repayment of my debt to the both of them.

"Talking to you in front of your colleagues was a violation of your privacy," Theo says stiffly.

I like the guy, but he can be a bit formal sometimes.

"They already knew the whole story. Most of it, anyway," I say. I hadn't told Jameela and Addison why I'd been looking for Jack, something they both grilled me about once Tabitha stalked away.

"A BuzzFeed article!" Kit says. "Cool, though."

"I'm so embarrassed."

"Eh, don't worry about it."

"Have you *been* on Twitter, like ever?"

She makes a dismissive gesture with her hand. "You know I'm not into it. Too angry."

"I hear about it all day long from Jameela and I've been on it enough myself to know. Some people will threaten to cut you if you say an outfit their favorite character wore is ugly. They call themselves gatekeepers and they're vicious."

"You didn't disrespect a Bridgerton or anything."

"No, I did something worse."

"What?" Theo asks, taking a third piece of pizza from the box.

"I disrespected Romancelandia."

"Duh, duh, duh."

"What is that, even?" Theo says.

"They're the online gatekeepers of romance books. People always shit on romance novels, rom-coms, rom-com movies, et cetera. They're, like, these intense fans who feel the need to defend anything they see as an attack on that."

Kit frowns. "And you doing this thing to find Jack violates that how?"

"Hard to predict at this point, but I have a bad feeling."

"But what if it works?"

That was the hope, but now it's a week later and I've fucked up at work and I'm about to have to reveal my desperation to the world . . . and there's no sign of him.

I lean back in my chair. "I don't think it will make a difference. I didn't think it was going to be big like this. I thought a few thousand book obsessives would see it, and that would be enough. New York is a small place. Not in the number of people, but it's usually pretty easy to find a connection with someone when you meet someone new."

"Totally," Kit says. "When I first got here, I thought no one knew anyone, but then I found out that Theo is Dave's vet."

Dave is a mutual friend from college we reconnected with when Kit moved to New York.

"That's what I'm talking about."

"Speaking of which, are you going to his party?"

"Don't think so. I can't stand his girlfriend. Kristal?"

"Krista," Kit says. "Yeah, we have a thing so we can't make it."

"I'm her vet too," Theo says.

"That's weird."

"I'm a connector," Theo says, pointing to himself for emphasis.

"What's that?"

"One of those people who knows lots of other people because of my practice. I'm like the center part of a Venn diagram."

Kit pats him on the hand. "That's cute."

"What? It's true."

I watch them, jealousy blooming in my chest. I try to quash it because I *am* happy for them. But I can't ignore the fact that I don't have what they have, even though it's something I want, and right now, it feels like I'm never going to get it.

"Anyway," I say, pushing these thoughts aside. "That's what I was counting on. That a big enough vector of people would see the photo and send in a clue to help me find him. But instead, it's thousands of people thirsting after him or telling me guys suck. That's only going to get worse once this article drops."

"Is it really that big?" Theo asks.

"The Instagram post has over two hundred and fifty thousand engagements. We can't even keep up with the comments. That's how BuzzFeed heard about it."

"So it's already out there."

"Not my involvement, though. Right now everyone thinks it's a marketing gimmick. Now I'm going to be the story."

Kit nibbles on the end of a piece of pizza. "Maybe it's a story with a happy ending?"

I slump in my chair, the hope draining out of me. "It's too late for that."

Chapter Eleven

The Buzzfeed article comes out a few days later, and it's like I predicted. Suddenly, I'm the villain of the day in Romancelandia because I used someone else's book to try to find a guy.

Before all this, I had seventy-five Twitter followers and I'd get a like maybe once a week. Now I have over two thousand and my mentions are insane.

> @ChloeBakerCincy *Don't use authors to advance your personal life.*
>
> @ChloeBakerCincy *It's hard enough to try to sell books these days without some desperate millennial using you for clout.*
>
> *This girl should get Fi-red. #cancelchloebaker*
>
> @ChloeBakerCincy *Bitch, bye.*

Etc. No matter that the author of *Most Wanted* was happy with the publicity and tried to defend me. No matter that it was getting more people checking out BookBox, which meant more book sales, which was good for romance writers in general.

Oh no. *Chloe* was *trending*. My name!

It wasn't only my name. That's the problem with trends on Twitter. Sometimes it's a lot of people tweeting about a bunch of different people with the same name. And there are more people named Chloe out there than I thought. But at least half of the tweets are about me and how I should be canceled, and even though I should be happy about that because it's increasing my chances of finding fake Jack, I'm not.

No one likes to be a villain.

It doesn't work, anyway. Fake Jack doesn't appear. No one identifies him. The Venn diagram theory is all for nothing. I almost lost my job, I earned the disdain of thousands of people, I've even got my mother calling because some friend of hers read the article and told her all about it.

"Why didn't you tell us you were going to be in the paper?" she says after I let the phone ring three times and consider letting it go to voice mail.

"It's not the paper. It's some stupid online article."

"About you dating a boy?"

"No." I sigh. I haven't spoken to my mother since Christmas and *this* is what finally makes her call me? Not that she was ever interested in my dating life. She met Christian once, and when I told her that we'd broken up, she'd said "That's too bad," in this vague way and then switched the subject to what we were going to eat for my father's birthday, which was three weeks away.

"What about this other man?" she asks.

"Real Jack?"

"What?"

"Jack Dunne. The man I was supposed to go out with."

"Yes, that's right. Where is he?"

I turn my desk chair around from Jameela and Addison's prying eyes. "I've been on a date with him."

"And?"

"It was fine, Mother. What's it to you?"

"Can't I call my daughter and inquire about her life?"

"Yes, of course." I take a deep breath. I'm on edge, near tears, something I haven't let my mother do to me in a long time. I was used to her disinterest in my life. Her prying feels oddly intimate, like a hug from a stranger that you didn't know you needed. "It's embarrassing. Everyone's talking about this stupid thing I did."

"I'm sure it will blow over soon. Will you go on another date with this Jack?"

"I dunno. He wants to."

"Why not go then? You know I always said—"

"Three chances. I remember. But if I don't like him, should I waste his time?"

"How can you know if you like him or not if you don't spend time with him?"

I want to say that when you know, you know, but I stop myself. That's the way it's been with everyone else I've dated, including fake Jack, but where did it get me? Two high-school boyfriends, one who'd broken my heart and one that had fizzled out, and Christian, the guy I thought was it who hadn't guarded his heart against falling for someone else.

So maybe that was my problem. Maybe my gut attraction was leading me down the wrong path.

"Maybe," I say, and when we get off this conversation, I decide to give Jack another chance.

112

So here we are, back on the Upper West Side at the breakfast place, sitting at Janie's table on a sunny Sunday morning.

She gives me a quizzical look when I come in, and I try to give her a reassuring smile like everything is okay and I'm not a total crazy person who dates men who have a superficial resemblance to one another every week. It's a lot to get across in a look.

"You want the eggs Benny again?" she says, tapping her pencil on her pad.

"Again?" Jack says with a hint of amusement. "You have a good memory."

"Don't remember you, though."

"Oh, ah, Janie, this is Jack."

He frowns. "I used to come in here all the time."

"That's nice," Janie says. "I haven't seen him if that's what you're wondering," she says to me.

"No, no, thank you. Can we get a few minutes to look at the menu?"

"Sure."

She leaves as my face burns, and I curse myself for another stupid maneuver.

"Hey, Chloe?"

"Yeah?"

"I read the article."

I look up slowly. Jack has a half grin on his face, a friendly expression meant to put me at ease. "You did?"

"I did."

"Why didn't you say?"

"I didn't want to embarrass you."

"I've done a pretty good job of that myself."

"No, don't worry. I get it."

"You do?"

"I dated someone for a couple of years. We broke up last year. I thought that was it. And then . . ."

"It didn't work out."

He rubs his hands together. "When you're with someone for a long time, even if it's not the right person, you get comfortable. You're not thinking should I call her, or how long should I wait to reach out, or does she like me—all the stupid things that go through your head at the beginning."

"Guys think like that?"

"Yeah, of course."

"Huh."

He laughs. "What did you think guys thought about?"

"Is she going to sleep with me tonight or not?"

"We think about that too." He laughs again. "But not exclusively."

"Good to know." I hold the edges of the menu; I'm not sure why. "I'm sorry I didn't tell you about him."

"It's fine. Weird situation, I'm sure."

"Yeah."

"But he hasn't reappeared, right?"

"No."

"And I *am* here."

"You are."

He touches my hand briefly. "I like you, Chloe. I don't know where this is going, or if it's got legs, but I'd like to find out."

"That's a really sweet thing to say."

"But?"

"No but. That was the end of my thought."

He runs his hand across his chin. "Did you want to come here today because you might see him?"

Why lie? "That was part of the reason. But I did want to see you again. I wanted to spend more time with you, to see if there's something here."

"And?"

"I don't know, yet, Jack. But I'm willing to spend a bit of time to find out."

"That's good."

I smile. "Should we order?"

"Eggs Benny again?"

"Um, no. I'll try something that is less likely to give me a heart attack."

"Bit young to worry about that, no?"

"It's never too young to think about protecting your heart."

We have a pleasant brunch, and when it's over, we make vague plans to see each other again. He says he'll text me in a couple of days and I know he will. Jack's a man of his word, despite the disaster of our non–first date. I already know this about him, and it's a good thing to know. We hug briefly and then separate, he to his parents, me to the park.

Then, against my better judgment, I do the loop I did with fake Jack. First to the Met, only this time I don't go in; I stare at the façade and curse my life choices, feeling stupid and sorry for myself. Even that doesn't deter me from going back to the pond, where I watch the boats and don't fall in the water, and try to connect to the fun atmosphere around me, but fail.

Jim and Kenny are there again, and Jim waves to me from a distance. I wave back but don't approach. I have to stop coming here or Jim is going to think I'm stalking him.

I go to the picnic table where Jack and I had our lunch and sit down. It's hot, the humidity building and curling my hair. I remember this weather from last year—the air thickening through the day until there were thunderstorms most afternoons. It made it hard to plan outdoor events, but it was helpful for sleeping. I suffered through a few nights in the heat then bought an air conditioner for my bedroom. Now I sleep with it on each night, creating white noise, blotting out the city sounds. When it turns cold in the fall, I miss it.

The park is full of couples, kids, young and old people walking solo. The table is shaded and it feels peaceful. I need to let that peace steep into me. To throw away my romantic notions about finding fake Jack, about us being perfect for one another, meant to be.

Because the funny thing is, I never thought I believed in that. But I have to ask myself why I'm going to all this effort. Why I'm *still* trying to find him despite my efforts failing to produce any results.

Why do I care so much about this guy I spent six hours with?

The only answer I can come up with is that I must believe, deep down somewhere I didn't know I had, that he's the guy for me.

It feels stupid to admit that, even to myself, but given that I work in an entire industry built around that idea, I shouldn't be so surprised. I've been acting like I'm in the middle of some rom-com, and who can blame me?

But those stories are so popular because they're fantasies. And yeah, sure, maybe that happens for some people, not only in books but in life, but it didn't mean it was going to happen to me.

Or maybe real Jack is my guy, and this rocky beginning is just a hiccup. I won't know unless I put the time in.

I take out my phone to send Jack a thank you text. The furor about me on Twitter has died down, but my screen is full of Facebook notifications. Good lord, what now?

I open the app and follow the link. I breathe a sigh of relief. My friend Dave, whose party I missed last night, has gotten engaged. Looks like I missed a good time. Dave and Krista are standing in the middle of a crowd with confetti and balloons streaming down around them. They must've gotten a professional photographer— totally something Krista would do. I recognize some of the faces, but then my stomach plummets.

Because, standing off to the side, on the edge, with his arm around another woman that I don't recognize, is fake Jack.

I use my shaking thumb to hover over the photo. Dave's tagged everyone in the post including fake Jack. Only his name is Ben Hamilton.

He was right there all along. In the middle of the Venn diagram.

Chapter Twelve

"He knows Dave," I say to Kit over the phone two hours later, still in a state of shock. "Can you believe it?"

"I guess New York *is* a small town."

"Beyond."

"What are you going to do?"

Hide on my couch under a blanket forever? "I'm not sure. I've been gathering intel."

"Do tell."

I adjust my laptop on my legs. I've spent the last hour cyberstalking fake Jack. Ben. Ben. His name is Ben, because of course it is. Only my favorite boy name ever. Damn it.

"His name is Ben Hamilton. He's twenty-nine and runs an indie record label."

"Interesting."

"He's from New York, but we knew that already."

"Right."

"And get this—he *does* have a girlfriend."

"What?"

"Maybe they're broken up, it's not entirely clear. Her name is Rachel Wise and she's beautiful."

I toggle to a photograph of Rachel I found on her Facebook page, which isn't set to private. She smiles at me through the camera, her head slightly tilted back and laughing. She's everything I always wished I was—two inches taller, hair that keeps its style in all weathers, a better sense of style.

Looking at her felt like I'd been put through some Instagram filter that shows you an idealized version of yourself.

She seems much nicer than me also. She volunteers as a Big Sister, loves hiking on the weekend, and is a freakin' *kindergarten teacher*. She also hangs out with her parents regularly and probably never had a serious fight with them. She also has a younger sister—dark haired, luminous, *alive*.

She doesn't have her relationship status set but there are plenty of pictures of Ben on her feed, none of them that old. There are a few of her on his page, too, but he doesn't post that often. They look happy in those photos, the way Jack—Ben—looked when we were sailing the boat or having lunch. The way he looked right before he kissed me.

"We hate Rachel, obvi," Kit says.

I do kind of hate her, which is stupid. She hasn't done anything to me other than get to Ben first. "She seems nice. She, like, volunteers for things."

"You could do that."

I grab the mohair throw from the back of the couch and wrap it around my shoulders. It's hot out, but I feel cold, chilled, like I'll never warm up. "I don't though."

"True. So, what now?"

"Can you imagine if I'd gone to that party at Dave's? I would've *died*."

"Or maybe you'd be dating him by now."

I try to imagine it. Us running into each other in the small kitchen in Dave's apartment, each of us looking for a drink. Would he have smiled or looked horrified? I want to think smile, but I keep seeing his face fall in a way that breaks my heart. "Do you think it's significant that I didn't go to the party?"

Kit laughs. "The universe again?"

"Maybe."

"Nah. You found him didn't you?"

"Basically when I'd stopped looking."

"That's the way it is. It doesn't have to mean anything. But you *did* find him, so if you want meaning, there it is."

I expand a picture of Ben from a year ago, and my heart gives a strange beat. He's wearing a polo shirt with the collar open and his face is tanned. His eyes are hidden behind sunglasses, but they're crinkled around the edges, a wide smile on his face. He looks happy and free; attractive and open. And he does look like Jack, real Jack, but something about him is more appealing to me. I don't know why; relationship alchemy is an odd thing.

And what about Ben? Rachel and I could be sisters. Should I read anything into that? It's okay to have a type. Maybe I do, too, though I've never thought about it. But maybe he wasn't into me, exactly, but a memory of Rachel. Maybe I was a way to start over with her again, with a clean slate.

Maybe I'm reading way too much into this as always.

"What do you think I should do?" I ask Kit.

"Reach out."

"What, through Facebook?"

"Why not?"

I shiver under my blanket. I'd thought of doing that but then realized it was a terrible idea. "Ugh, no. Facebook Messenger is the worst. You can tell when someone's read your message."

"So?"

"What if I message him and he reads it and doesn't respond?"

"You'd have your answer, then."

"Only about whether he was interested. Not about the rest of it."

"What's the rest of it?"

"Why he pretended to be Jack. Why he didn't tell me the truth over the course of a whole day. What he wanted from me."

Why he kissed me. That's what I wanted to know most of all.

Why'd he have to go and kiss me?

"That's a lot of questions. He might not answer any of them even if you met him in person."

"You're right."

"You want to, don't you?"

I close my laptop screen. Staring at Ben isn't helping. "In my head again?"

"It's an interesting place."

"Ha. Am I crazy?"

"For wanting to see him? No. But are you ready for that, Chlo?"

"For face-to-face rejection? Probably not. But look at all the trouble I went to to find him. I can't turn away now."

"There's your answer, then."

"Right."

I put the laptop aside and stand up. I'm stiff from sitting in the same position for so long. I raise my hands above my head, then bend to touch my toes. I've always been flexible, and I stretch out my back, placing my hands flat on the floor, the phone tucked under my chin.

"What are you going to do if not a message?" Kit asks.

"Not sure."

"You could ask Dave for his number."

"And then Dave would know I was interested. No."

"Who cares?"

"I do."

"You could make up some story."

I stand up. "I've made up enough stories."

"True."

"But you've given me an idea."

"What?"

"I'll tell you if it works out. Thanks for the pep talk."

"Anytime."

"Things any better at work, by the way?" I ask.

"I don't want to talk about it."

"That bad?"

"I was bending Theo's ear all day. I'm sick of talking about it."

"I'm here for you if you change your mind."

"Thank you."

We hang up and I text Dave. *Hey, so sorry to miss the party, congratulations on getting engaged! Great photos on FB. Let me know where you're registered so I can get you a gift.*

Dave answers almost immediately, which I knew he would. He's always on his phone.

Hey, hey. We missed you!

Couldn't be avoided!

We should get dinner soon, all three of us.

Ugh. The last time we'd done that Krista had glared at me across the table all night, clearly worried that something had happened between me and Dave in college, though nothing ever had.

Yeah, for sure! Hey, I didn't know you knew Rachel.

Rachel?

Rachel Wise? She's dating Ben Hamilton? I bite my lip nervously. There are so many ways that this can go wrong.

Oh, right. You know Ben?

We've met.

Small town.

Right? I wait for him to write more but he doesn't. *So, Rachel?*

Oh, yeah. Nice girl.

Are she and Ben dating, goddammit??

Where did you meet them? Dave writes.

Ugh. *Them.* They are together. Despite what Ben said. Dammit, dammit, dammit.

My fingers fumble as I text. *I met Ben a couple of weeks back. NBD. Anyway, got to run, but let's hang soon!*

Most def.

I throw my phone down, wanting to scream. This is what everyone warned me about, but did I listen?

Nope. Not one little bit.

I spend the next day at work going back and forth on what I should do, while I sort through a pile of books to try to triage down the selections for our next picks.

We pick the books four months before they're announced so we have time to print our special editions and the publishers have time to adjust their sales in other channels. BookBox can make a book successful, and when we pick one, it's good for everyone.

Right now I'm picking for October, and that's when Christmas books start to appear. I've got three of them in front of me, with nearly identical plots and covers.

I hold them up. *"All I Want for Christmas? Starry Night? Or Jingle Bell Rocked?"*

Addison scowls. She hates Christmas almost as much as she hates romance. "Let me guess, a twenty-something who's just broken up with her boyfriend goes home for Christmas and reconnects with her high-school boyfriend who's hotter and nicer than he was ten years ago?"

"Ding, ding, ding."

"Dysfunctional families and snarky sisters/hometown best friends."

"Of course! Bonus question: Which one of these features a same-sex couple?"

She squints. The books usually have the couples drawn on the cover so that question is easy to answer. But none of these do. Instead, each of them has some version of a Nancy Meyers house with a wreath on the door.

"None of them?"

"No, they all do!"

Addison scowls. "They trying to hide that with those covers?"

"Unclear."

Jameela pops her head up. She's been deep in some drama involving the #Polin stans (the couple name for Colin and Penelope, the love story from the fourth book but the third season—long story). "If they aren't out and proud, then I say ditch them."

"I agree," Addison says.

"But the covers aren't the author's fault," I say. "Should we ditch them for that?"

"Are these books good?" Jameela asks.

"They're so similar it's hard to tell."

"Next!"

I laugh because they're right. Rom-coms follow a formula, but that doesn't mean they can't be original within it.

I put them aside to put in our discard pile and pull the next three toward me. I need to have one holiday book in the selection, and it's dispiriting to have to start over.

"Chloe," Tabitha says in a sharp voice, startling me from behind. "Have you found him yet?"

I turn around slowly. She's been asking me this every day since the BuzzFeed article dropped. I briefly consider lying to her, but that's a bad idea. "I did actually."

Jameela and Addison look at one another. I'm going to get it from them later for keeping this information to myself all day.

"Through the ad?"

"No, uh, he was tagged in a friend's photo on Facebook."

Jameela barks out a laugh, then covers it. "Sorry."

"It's fine," I say. "It is kind of funny when you think about it."

"What now?" Tabitha asks.

"Not sure. He might have a girlfriend."

"Plot twist," Addison says. "Didn't see that coming!"

"Hmmm," Tabitha says. "You have to meet him."

"What? Why?"

"BuzzFeed wants a follow-up."

I'd stopped looking at the Instagram account after the Buzzfeed article had come out. It was too much. "So I have to go humiliate myself again?"

"You've come this far."

"Ouch."

Tabitha softens. "It will complete the story. You can't leave everyone hanging like that."

"Is my job on the line?"

"I wouldn't go that far."

This time. "So it's up to me?"

"Yes, though we do have to give some update."

"Don't you want to meet him?" Jameela asks.

"Don't be silly, of course, she does," Addison says. "She's been obsessing about him for *weeks*. She's scared."

Three pairs of eyes look at me. So that's what that knot in my stomach means. "Wouldn't you be?"

Addison lifts a shoulder. "Can't get anything if you don't take risks."

"You also can't get hurt."

"Not sure about that. You haven't seemed very happy since this happened."

That clocked. I wasn't happy. But whose fault was that? My own, obviously, because I was an idiot for giving a man I barely knew so much power in my life. What I felt that day was real, though. Am I wrong to try to get it back?

"I guess."

"Why not meet him?"

"What do you care, Addison?" I say more aggressively than I mean to. "You don't believe in love."

"Hey, now," Tabitha says. "No need to get personal."

"Sorry," I murmur and Addison does the same.

"Look, Chloe, this is your show. You want to meet him, great. You don't, that's fine too. You decide."

Tabitha walks away and I count down in my head to when Jameela and Addison are going to start peppering me with questions. Three, two, one.

"Oh my god," Jameela says. "I need a photo pronto."

I pull him up on my phone and show it to her. "He's no Jonathan Bailey, but cute, right?"

"Très cute."

Addison holds out her hand. "Gimme."

I pass her my phone. She looks at him, blowing him up and peering close, then passes it back.

"What?" I say.

"Checking I didn't know him. He kind of looks like my cousin."

Oh god no. "But he's not your cousin, right?"

"Nope."

"Phew."

"I'll say. That guy is a total beta male."

"No, thank you."

"You're meeting him, yes?" Addison says.

"I'm still on the fence."

"I'd do it if I were you."

"Why?"

"Because he strung you along all day and made you think he liked you and he had a girlfriend the whole time when he told you he didn't. He needs a piece of your mind."

"Or yours?" I ask hopefully.

"No, no, no, I am *not* doing that."

"I wasn't seriously asking."

"Hmmm."

"Maybe it was a misunderstanding?" Jameela says. "And he's not dating her anymore."

"It's possible."

"You'll never find out if you don't try."

"Are you about to quote that line about living in regret from season two?"

"Maybe."

"How about we not."

"You don't have to be a b-i-t-c-h about it." She turns back to her screen, her cheeks deepening in color.

"Sorry, Jameela, I'm stressed. This has all been a lot."

She talks to me without taking her eyes off her screen. "If you don't want our advice, you shouldn't ask for it."

"You're right. But I do, I promise."

Her shoulders soften. "If you don't talk to him you'll never know."

"Yeah. That might be a good thing."

"But then," Addison says, "you'll—"

"—never know."

"We're like an old married couple."

I laugh. "Who's going to die first?"

"You, clearly."

"That tracks."

Chapter Thirteen

I do it. After dithering between anger at myself and fear of finding out that Ben is out of my reach forever all afternoon, I decide I have nothing left to lose except for some dignity. I do a bit more Google snooping to find out where his office is, and then I chart a course to it in the five o'clock rush hour.

It's in the Village, and I set off without knowing if he's going to be there but with the quiet certainty that he will. Because he has to be. After all this.

The universe owes me that, at least.

That certainty evaporates when I get there. His office is a number on a bright-yellow door in a narrow, brick walk-up with a small sign, and that door is locked.

I press the bell as my heart squeezes in regret. I can hear it echo in the space above the coffee shop below it, but no one answers.

Goddammit.

I can't believe I was stupid enough to come here and get let down by him again.

But this is it. I can't go through this once more.

This is the end of our story.

"Chloe?"

I turn and it's him. Ben, though the name *Jack* still leaps to mind. Here in front of me, wearing a midnight-blue shirt with khaki shorts, his hair a bit longer, flopping onto his forehead. He's got a pair of classic Wayfarers on, the tortoiseshell ones with dark lenses, but they don't cover enough of his face to hide his shock.

"What are you doing here?" he asks.

And what can I say?

What *am* I doing here? That's the question of the hour, isn't it?

"I was looking for you."

"How did you find me?"

Is that disappointment in his voice? This was a terrible, terrible idea.

"We have a mutual friend. Dave? You were at his engagement party. I saw the photos on Facebook."

"Oh, wow. Small world."

"I was supposed to be at that party."

He pushes his sunglasses up onto his head. His eyes look confused. "You were?"

"Yeah, I . . . you're not Jack. Your name is Ben." As the words leave my mouth, I feel stupid. Of course he's not Jack. He knows that.

"I . . ."

There's a massive crack above us, the sound of close thunder. The sky has turned dark the way it does sometimes, almost instantly, and the air smells like rain, that mix of moisture and grass, even though there's no grass in sight.

"We should go—"

"—okay, I'll go," I say.

"Wait, no, Chloe. Will you come inside with me? This is my office. We can go up there?"

I agree and he steps ahead of me and takes out a large set of keys. He finds the right one and opens the lock, then a second lock. "I look like a janitor, but we have expensive equipment in here."

"It's fine." A drop of rain hits the top of my head, and then my hand. It doesn't feel real, standing here with Ja— . . . Ben. I'm close enough to smell him, and between that and all the tension, I feel a bit dizzy.

He pushes open the door. "Come in, you don't want to get wet."

I dart through the door, wondering how long I'm going to be trapped here, with him. These sudden heavy storms don't usually last long, but sometimes they do.

"Hold on," Ben says. "Let me get the light." He reaches past me, and I catch another whiff of his scent—soap and something earthier, almost a heat. He catches the light switch with his fingers and flicks it up. The atrium fills with harsh light as Ben stares down at me. "Hi."

"Hello."

There's a beat as we stare at one another, but then Ben says, "Should we go up?"

"Sure."

He tugs on the edge of my shirt and I follow him up a narrow staircase. The air is full of the smell of roasting coffee and butter croissants.

"It smells amazing in here," I say, feeling awkward and stupid. The last time we met, the conversation flowed. But then, I thought he was someone else.

"It can be distracting sometimes. Almost there." He gets to the top of the stairs and takes out his keys again. Two more locks, heavy and serious. "We got robbed once, right after we got this space. Thank god I was insured."

He opens the door and puts his keys away. "Come in?"

I follow him through the door and suck in my breath. I'm not sure what I expected, but it's not this—a massive open room with high ceilings and tall windows and old wooden floors that look like they come from the early 1900s. One corner of the space is cordoned off as a sound booth, presumably to record in. There's a small kitchen in the other corner, a brown leather sofa, and framed albums on the walls. "This is amazing, Ben."

"Thanks."

"How long have you had this space?"

"Couple of years now. It belonged to another label that went under, so we were able to pick up the lease for something reasonable."

"That's lucky."

"Yeah." He looks at me, and the look isn't a happy one. "Look, Chloe—"

"You have a girlfriend."

"What? No."

"I saw you together. Rachel."

He runs his hands through his hair. "She was at the party, yes. She's friends with Krista, but we're not together anymore. We haven't been for a while."

"But she's still in your life?"

"Can we sit?" He motions to the couch, and I follow. He puts his hands on his knees. "You want something to drink?"

The suspense is killing me. "Just tell me, Ben."

"I'm sorry for what happened. I didn't mean . . . when I went into the restaurant, I wanted to get some coffee. I'd been at the hospital with my mom and I hadn't really slept. Anyway, that's what was on my mind. And then you called out to me, you were so happy to see me, and then you sort of begged me to go along with it."

"I wasn't begging."

"No, sorry that's the wrong word. You told me to go along with it."

"I did."

"So I did. I sat down and you smiled at me and I felt . . . at peace. I felt like I could help you not feel so bad for being stood up on your date. I didn't expect—I didn't expect to like you so much."

My stomach flutters at those words, but I can't lose focus. "Why didn't you tell me who you were, then?"

"I wanted to, but my life is a mess right now, Chloe. I'm not looking for a relationship. I thought we'd have a nice breakfast and then I'd go on my way and you'd go on yours."

"And that I'd find out afterward who you weren't?"

"I didn't get that far in my head. We launched into conversation, and then that waitress was there, with her accusing eyes, looking at me like I was an asshole."

"Which you kind of were."

"Which I was." He smiles, then it drops.

"Oh," I say. "Is that—was your card really hacked?"

"No."

"You didn't want me to see your real name."

"I couldn't risk it. I didn't want you to find out like that, in front of everyone."

"You didn't want to be embarrassed."

"I didn't want *you* to be embarrassed."

I pull in a long breath. I feel like there's not enough air in the room, like I'm at altitude. "And then?"

"I thought that would be it, but then we ran into each other at the Met."

"You couldn't pretend you didn't see me?"

"I didn't want that. I thought, I'll take her around the museum and I'll find a way to tell her. I was waiting for the right moment."

"Which never came?"

"I tried to tell you at the lake, but then we got interrupted."

I turn to him. "And then you kissed me."

His face falls. "I didn't plan it, Chloe. I didn't mean for it to happen. I couldn't help myself."

He couldn't help himself from kissing me. Part of me loves how that sounds, and the other part is clanging like a warning. "But you still didn't tell me."

"I was doing it. I was in the middle of doing it when—"

"—your dad called?"

"Yes. And he told me that my mom—" His voice breaks. "My mom . . . that she might not make it through the night. She'd been having trouble breathing and—"

"Is she . . . did she . . ."

"No, she survived that crisis, thank god, but it's only a matter of time."

"I'm so sorry, Ben."

He rubs his hands over his face. "Anyway, the next day I wanted to call you, to tell you what had happened, but I realized I didn't have your number. That I didn't even know your last name."

"Yeah, I figured."

"When did you find out?"

"That night. I texted you to see how your mom was doing."

"That was nice of you."

"Only it wasn't you who answered. It was Jack."

"The one who stood you up."

I feel the need to defend him. "He didn't. I mean, he did, but it wasn't his fault. He got pulled into a work thing and he thought he'd texted me, but it didn't go through and . . . anyway, he's nice."

"You've met him?"

My face starts to burn. "Yeah, I— When you turned out not to be him, we went on a date. Two, actually."

"Ah."

"Are you mad?"

"No, of course not. I— It doesn't matter."

"Ben," I say. "Tell me."

He gives me a sad smile. "I thought we had a connection, that's all."

I start to laugh, slowly at first, but then harder.

"What?"

"You don't even know what I've been through, trying to find you."

"You were trying to find me?"

"I've been looking for you ever since I found out you weren't Jack."

I tell him what I did. How Kit and I retraced our steps. How I thought of the Missing poster for the book box, and how it almost got me fired. How it turned up nothing and I'd finally given up hope, and then there he was on Facebook.

"Wow," Ben says. "And all I did was some Facebook and Google searches."

He looked for me too! I'm an idiot for how happy this makes me.

"What did you search for on Google?"

"*Chloe* plus *boxes*."

"I guess that's all you knew, huh?"

"Yeah."

"It was your idea, not going over the normal details." I sigh. "But I guess that was because you didn't want me to figure it out."

Ben looks unhappy. "You make me sound like a villain."

"I don't mean to."

"It's fine. It's my own stupid fault."

I squeeze my hands, then ask what I really want to know. "What about Rachel?"

"We are broken up."

"Why? She seems great."

"You've met her?"

Oh god. Me and my stupid mouth.

"Once I saw that post on Dave's Facebook page, I kind of . . . I couldn't help snooping."

"I get it."

"So, Rachel?"

"Rachel is great. For someone else."

"Why?"

He looks away. "That's a long story. But since I spent several years dating her, you'll just have to trust me on that one."

"Who broke up with who?"

"That's a bit personal, isn't it?"

"Seriously? After all you put me through?"

"Okay, okay. If I tell you it was a mutual decision, will you believe me?"

I cock my head to the side. "Breakups are never mutual."

"I guess I did it, then."

"And she still has feelings?"

"I don't know," Ben says. "Maybe."

"And you?"

"No," he says firmly, and I feel relieved.

Okay, more than relieved. I'm not sure what this feeling is, but I feel lighter, like I might float up to the ceiling like a balloon that's been released.

"Why hang out with her still?"

"Because we've been friends for a million years, and we're in the same friend group and I wasn't entirely sure that if I asked them to choose that they'd choose me."

"Oh."

He smiles briefly. "And my mom was invested in our relationship."

"She doesn't know."

"She has enough to deal with."

"I get it." I put my hands on my thighs, my heart sinking. "Where does that leave us?"

"Remember when I said before that I wasn't in the right frame of mind for a relationship?"

"I've been trying to forget you said that."

He smiles briefly. "The thing is, it's still true. I wish I'd met you at literally any other time in my life, Chloe, I do."

"When you were still dating Rachel?"

"Not going to cut me any slack, huh?"

"Again, after everything I've been through to find you?"

"I get it. I do. I'm disappointed too. But it wouldn't be fair to you and it wouldn't be fair to me to start anything right now. I don't want to hurt you. And to be frank, I don't want to lose the possibility of you."

My throat goes dry. "The possibility of me?"

"It's been nice, these last couple of weeks, thinking about the fact that you were out there somewhere. That maybe, when all of this is settled, maybe then we can be together."

"If you found me."

"Yeah. But it was a fantasy, Chloe. So that part was assured."

"And in reality? You want me to, what . . . wait for you?"

"I'm not asking you to do that, no."

"What if I want to?"

He takes my hands in his. His touch is a shock. "I can't let you do that. I don't know when—if—I'll be ready. I can't think that far ahead. If I do, I have to think about my mother not being here anymore and I can't do that. I can't. Do you understand?"

"I'm trying to."

His eyes lock with mine and I can't help but stare back. And there he is, the man I spent the day with, the man who kissed me, who *couldn't help himself*, whose face is coming closer, closer, closer to mine. I keep my eyes open this time, I want to see it coming, but then he stops.

"I can't. I can't, Chloe, I'm sorry." He lets my hands go and pulls back.

And now I'm crashing back to earth, feeling desperate for something to hold on to.

"It doesn't have to be serious. We could hang out and see what happens."

"You think we could do that? Not be serious? That's why you went to all those lengths to find me. To be casual?"

"No, you're right."

"Maybe we can be friends."

I laugh but it feels bitter. "I have enough friends."

"Okay."

"I'm sorry, Ben, but I can't. That would be too hard for me."

"I understand."

"You've got friends, though, yes? People who can support you?"

He nods slowly. "Yes."

"Your sister? I remember you mentioned her."

"She's been great. And other people too."

"Dave?"

"Dave's all right."

"Krista kind of sucks, though."

He laughs. "She does, doesn't she?"

I stand. "I should go."

We hug, and he holds me close. It feels great, but this hug was a bad idea, because I don't want to let go. I want to sink into it and never leave.

I pull away. "Nice to meet you, Ben."

"Nice to meet you, Chloe."

I walk to the door. I want to stay. To talk to Ben until the rain stops. To beg him to change his mind, but I'm not going to do any of those things.

Because it feels like my heart is breaking, right now, right here, and I don't want him to be able to see me break. He knows too much about me already.

I do say one last thing, though. "You know how rare this is, right? That this might not happen again, for either of us?"

"I hope that's not true."

"Me too."

And then I do leave, holding back my tears until I'm out on the street, where the rain covers them.

Chapter Fourteen

"No, no, put that back," I say to Theo. "She doesn't want gold."

He looks at the gold ring with the plain solitaire in his hand. It reminds me of my mother's engagement ring, the gold almost gaudy, a blinking light with "'80s" emanating from it. "Doesn't she wear gold?"

"Sometimes, but not for this. Trust me. She wants a platinum band with a cushion cut."

Theo's forehead creases. I swear he started to sweat before we even came into the jewelry store. There's nothing about this softly cushioned and over-air-conditioned fancy environment that says "man," and his white dock shoes and khaki shorts don't help matters.

"What is that?" he asks.

"It's why I'm here." The assistant behind the counter is a woman in her forties in the best-tailored suit I've ever seen. She makes me wish I'd put on something other than this slightly oversized flowered summer dress and that my ponytail wasn't quite so casually messy. "You understand."

"Certainly, miss. If you could give me an idea of the price range, I'll bring out some selections."

"That's his department." I point to Theo.

He puts down the gold band. "It's supposed to be a percentage of my salary, right? Or something like that?"

"It's not the 1950s," I say.

"What do you suggest?"

I mention a figure that's the amount Kit and I agreed on. Enough for it to be nice and tasteful while not bankrupting Theo in the process. Kit handles their finances, and, frankly, most of the other things in their relationship because Theo's a great vet but a little scatterbrained otherwise.

Theo doesn't react when I say the number, which is good of him. My dad always does a spit take whenever he gets a bill in a restaurant. I can only imagine what he did when he went ring shopping.

And now that's two times I've thought of my parents today in quick succession. I haven't heard from my mother since the phone call a couple of weeks ago about me trying to find Ben, but her sudden interest in my life has stirred something up. Regret maybe, but also sadness.

I have enough emotions in my life right now, though, so I shove my parents down and turn back to the moment in front of me.

"I'll be back in a minute," the assistant says, then ducks into the back room.

"Do you think she's judging us?" Theo asks.

"For what?"

"Our price range?"

"Nah. And if she does, who cares?"

He rubs his hands together nervously. "Thank you for coming with me."

"Of course."

"I don't want Kit to do that thing with her face when I ask her." He makes a face remarkably like the one Kit makes whenever she sees something she doesn't like.

I start to laugh. "That's uncanny. Don't worry, she won't make that face."

"I hope not." He blows out his breath. "Do you think she'll say yes?"

"Of course she will." I pat him on the back. "Why did you ask that?"

"She's been preoccupied lately."

"About work?"

He fiddles with the ring in the tray. "She says that's all it is. But that's what you'd say if there *was* something wrong but you didn't want to talk about it."

"It's also what you'd say if there wasn't something wrong."

He looks at me. He's worried about this, not the usual guy about to be engaged nervous. "She hasn't said anything to you?"

"No, but I've been monopolizing our friendship."

"Ah. The Jack situation."

"Ben, you mean."

"Right. Though Jack is still in the picture, no?"

I sigh. I don't know what to do about real Jack. I don't think it's fair to keep seeing him when I'm into someone else, even if it's never going to work with Ben. But Jack isn't taking no for an answer. Not in a bad way. He's persistent, wanting to go on a third date, suggesting fun things to do in the city. But ever since my meetup with Ben a week ago, I haven't been able to plan. I'll get over this in due course, but I need a minute.

"Unclear," I say.

Theo raises his fists. "I can beat Ben up if you want."

I smile. "What? No, that's not necessary."

The assistant comes back with a small tray and puts it down on the counter in front of us. There are three rings on it. I reach for the one in the middle—a cushion cut diamond on a platinum band. It's exactly like what Kit's always described (and, frankly, texted me photos of).

"This one," I say.

Theo takes it and holds it in the palm of his hand. "It does remind me of Kit."

"Right?"

"I'll take it," he says to the assistant.

"Are you sure, sir?" *Don't you even want to know what it costs*, her expression says.

"Yes." He turns to me. "When you know, you know, right?"

"I agree." I hug him impulsively, holding his thin frame to mine.

"What was that for?"

"You're getting married."

He pulls away, his face full of happiness. "I'm getting married."

⛵

Theo and I part outside the ring store, he with his purchase secured in his inner pocket, me with no fixed plans. I'm near the High Line (yet another New York landmark that I've somehow managed not to visit), so I decide to go for a walk before heading back to Brooklyn. It's a bit chilly today, the previous ridge of high pressure moving out and leaving a crisper New York in its place. It won't last long, but I'll enjoy the cooler weather while I can.

Back in the winter, Kit and I had talked briefly about getting a summer share somewhere—not the Hamptons, we couldn't afford that—but someplace upstate on a lake where we could laze away the days and start drinking at noon. I wasn't sure when the planning had stopped. It was usually Kit who planned those kinds of things for us.

Maybe Theo is right. Kit has been a bit distracted.

I'm a terrible best friend.

I call her as I walk toward the High Line, putting in my AirPods so I can walk with my phone in my purse.

"How did it go?" she asks.

"Perfect. You're going to be very happy."

"Great."

"Everything okay with you?"

"Why do you ask?"

Uh-oh. "That doesn't mean yes."

"It's nothing."

"Tell me."

She lets out a long sigh. "I'm probably about to get let go."

"What?"

"My boss left, I told you that? She went on maternity leave. And the guy who replaced her is an asshole."

"You mentioned."

"He hates me. And I fucked something up for him a while back. I'm not even sure that I want to stay there, you know? But I can't face looking for another job. You know how much I hate interviews."

"Is there a way you can transfer to a different supervisor?"

"I asked, which only made things worse."

"I'm sorry, Kit."

"Thanks."

"You should tell Theo that's what it is."

"He knows all about it."

"No." I stop at a light, watching people weave through traffic. "He's worried about you. He thinks you're about to turn down his proposal."

"What?"

"That's what he said."

"Oh god, men are idiots."

"Truly."

I cross the road when the light changes and reach the entrance to the High Line. I climb up the stairs and assess. It's semicrowded, a mix of families and couples, and I'm immediately charmed. Built on an old elevated railbed, it's got a gravel path and is lined with trees. Why did I put this off for so long?

"He really said he thought I'd turn him down?"

"Yep."

"I guess I've been ranting about work in general, but I haven't told him about the being let go part."

"How come?"

"I knew he was stressed about the proposal. I didn't want to add to that."

"Hmmm."

"What?"

"Look, I'm no expert about relationships, but it seems to me that to make them work you need to be honest with each other. You need to be able to rely on him when you're stressed. Even if he's stressed."

"You're right."

"Theo's a big boy. A doctor even."

"An animal doctor."

"Same difference. He can be there for you. He *wants* to be there for you. Give him a chance to be supportive."

"You're right. I'll tell him when he gets home."

"Good."

"Where are you right now?"

"I think you know where I am," I say.

"High Line, huh? Doing all the tourist things."

I step out of the way of a gaggle of teenagers, eating ice cream despite the cooler temperature, and talking loudly, the way you do in your late teens, when you don't realize that other people exist.

They pass me and I stop in my tracks. "Oh, no, no, no."

"What?"

"Ben."

"What about him?"

"He's walking right toward me. Shit, I have to go."

I hang up and try to compose my face because it *is* Ben.

Ben, and a little boy of about eight, who must be his nephew. He spots me before I can decide how I want to react.

Instead, I stop walking, my heart pounding, my face hot.

He stops, too, raising his hand in a wave. I wave back. Then the boy waves at me, too, emphatically. He's adorable, with dark curly hair and a compact, sturdy body. A mini Ben.

"Hi," Ben says as they reach me.

"Hi." I pull my AirPods from my ears, slipping them back into their case so I don't look like a complete dork.

"What are the chances?"

"Probably higher than you think."

"What?"

"Never mind."

It gives me a bit of pleasure to see that he seems to be as discomfited as I am. He's wearing a dark-blue T-shirt and dark-gray shorts. His feet are in sandals, and god—even his toes are cute.

Look away, Chloe, look away.

"Hi, lady!" the boy says.

"Hi. You must be Tyler?"

He grins at me. "I am Tyler!"

I crouch down so I'm face to face with him. "I hear you like boats."

"I do! We went to the boats today!"

"Was it fun?"

"It was fun!"

I stand back up. "Glad it worked out," I say to Ben.

"It was good I had the practice session."

"Was the little terror there again? And Jim?"

Ben's confused. "Who?"

"That kid who was terrorizing us and his dad. You know Kenny?" I realize too late that I'm going to have to confess that I went back there and met them not once but twice. Me and my stupid mouth. "Um, when I was looking for you, I met them again. That's where I got the photo of you."

"What photo?"

This keeps getting better and better. "I didn't tell you about the photo?"

"Nope."

"Damn."

"That's a bad word!"

I laugh. "I keep getting busted by kids for language."

"Hazard of hanging out with them," Ben says.

"Right."

"Where is my ice cream?" Tyler asks.

Ben meets my eyes. "We were supposed to be going for ice cream."

"Don't let me keep you."

"Lady should come for ice cream!"

"Her name is Chloe, buddy."

"I like Chloe!"

Ben winces, and it breaks my heart a little. If there's any heart left to break.

"I like you, too, Tyler."

"Do you like ice cream?"

"Who doesn't like ice cream?"

"So the answer to my question is yes?"

Ben puts his hand on Tyler's head. "One of his moms is a lawyer."

"Ah, that's cute."

"You say that until you've been cross-examined by an eight-year-old."

"Don't talk about me like I am not here," Tyler says.

"Sorry, bud. Do you want to come for ice cream, Chloe?"

I don't, I emphatically don't, but it seems rude to say that. Rude, and like I can't handle it, which I don't want Ben to know. "Sure."

He points ahead of him. "If we go down those stairs, there's a place."

Tyler looks up at me. "Are you coming?"

"Yes."

"Good!" He holds out his hand, and when I don't react, he puts his hand against mine. "You're supposed to hold it. I don't like it when people hold my hand, but I'm not good on stairs."

I open my fingers and take Tyler's little hand in mine. It's hot and sweaty. He tugs on it—he knows where the ice cream is apparently.

"Let's go!"

I let him lead me, throwing a glance at Ben over my shoulder. I don't know him well enough to read his expression. I'm sure today's not going the way he thought it was going to go.

Tyler pulls me down the stairs and Ben is right, there's an ice-cream shop across the street.

"Can you stay out here with him?" Ben asks.

"Of course."

"What do you want?"

"Oh, vanilla on a waffle cone."

"That's what I'm having!" Tyler says.

"Vanilla is the best."

Tyler cocks his head to the side. "Chocolate is the best, actually, but my moms say I have enough energy as it is and that I have a bad reaction to chocolate, and so I have to have vanilla."

"Your moms sound cool."

"They are. It's okay to have two moms!"

"It definitely is."

Ben walks across the street and disappears into the ice-cream shop.

"Your uncle Ben is pretty cool, too, right?"

"He is also the best. He took me to the boats!"

"He took me there too."

"It was so fun, right?"

"So fun."

Tyler nods once, twice, three times. "I'm still holding your hand because New York is a big city and I don't want to get lost. Not because I like it."

"You hold it as long as you like."

"Until the ice cream gets here."

"Sounds like a plan."

"Did you have a red boat?"

"It was blue."

"Mine was red, and we didn't win, and Uncle Ben said a few bad words, but it was a lot of fun."

Ben emerges from the ice-cream shop with three cones in a carrier. He looks both ways before crossing the street and bringing them back. He hands me and Tyler our identical cones. Ben's is chocolate dipped in chocolate.

"Oh my god, Tyler," I say. "Do you see what Uncle Ben has?"

Tyle licks his cone but stares at Ben's. "That seems like a bad idea."

"Right?"

"Uncle Ben is going to be very hyper," Tyler says.

Ben puts up his hands in surrender. "Don't both of you go in on me at once."

"You make your choices, you live with them."

His face clouds momentarily. "True."

"If you don't eat your ice cream it is going to melt!"

"You're right, Tyler."

"I am often right."

I start to lick my cone. The ice cream is the perfect amount of creaminess and that real vanilla with flecks in it. "This is good. Thank you, Ben."

He gives me a chocolate grin. "No sweat."

"How's your mom doing?"

His eyes go from mine to Tyler's. I keep stepping in it today.

"She's fine."

"Is something wrong with Grandma?"

"No, Tyler, she's all good."

"My friend Scott's grandma died! He was very sad."

"That does happen sometimes," I say. "And we do get sad. But I bet Uncle Ben would be there to help you, and your moms too."

"Uncle Ben says he will always help me!"

"Then that's okay, right?"

"Yes, I'm not worried anymore."

I meet Ben's eyes and he mouths *Thank you.*

"Where are we going now?" Tyler asks between licks. "We're on a schedule."

"We are?"

"It's something my sister says a lot," Ben says.

"Ah. Tyler, what do you want to do?"

He cocks his head to the side like no one's asked him that in a while. "I get to decide?"

"Yes."

"I want to see Aunt Rachel."

Ben nearly drops his cone but recovers it at the last minute. "Sorry, buddy, I don't think so."

"Why not?"

"I'm sure she's busy."

"No, we text. She always answers. She told me she is never too busy for Tyler."

I meet Ben's panicked eyes. "He texts?"

"He got a phone for his seventh birthday."

"So I can stay in touch with my moms! I can text her now!" He holds his cone out to me and I take it. He's made a bit of a mess of it, and the ice cream drips onto my hand. He takes out his phone. "My fingers are too sticky! Can you do it, Uncle Ben?"

"Not right now, buddy."

"But you said I could do whatever I want and this is what I want."

"It's okay, Ben," I say. "Go ahead." I stoop down again. "Hey, Tyler, why don't you put that phone in your pocket. Uncle Ben will send the text."

"Okay." He does what I say and I hand him back his cone.

"I'm going to go," I say.

"You're not coming to Aunt Rachel's?"

Oh, no, no, no. "I don't know her."

"She's nice!"

"I'm sure she is. Maybe I'll meet her next time?"

"Okay, I'll text you!"

"Okay, Tyler."

"But I don't have your number."

"Uncle Ben has it." I stand up and mouth a quick good-bye to Ben. "Bye, Tyler!"

"Bye, lady!"

I turn and walk away, my cone dripping now, my hands sticky, my throat dry. And it's only a quick block later that I realize that Uncle Ben doesn't have my number, and there's never going to be a text from Tyler, or anything else between us.

Turns out my heart did have some more breaking room, after all.

Chapter Fifteen

When I get to work on Monday, Jameela is crying quietly at her desk. Her dark braids are twisted around her head, and I'm not sure if it's an ode to Leia Organa or Kate Bridgerton.

"What's going on?"

She doesn't look up from her screens, one open to her Twitter feed and the other to Instagram. Twitter is on her curated feed of *Bridgerton* fans, which is a long list of *WHERE ARE THEY*? posts, and people using crying-on-desk emojis. "They didn't go together."

"Who?" I ask though I know the answer.

"Jonny and Simone. They didn't go to Wimbledon together."

"So?"

"I thought they would. We all thought they would." She wipes at her eyes, which are red and rimmed with tears.

"He's gay, isn't he?"

"So?"

"And isn't she dating someone?"

"What's your point?"

"Why would they go together?"

Her shoulders slump. "To promote the show."

"But their season was over a long time ago."

"They're still Lord and Lady Bridgerton."

I sigh as I sit down at my desk, pushing the day's accumulation of new titles off to the left.

"It's time you let them go," I say as gently as I can.

She finally turns away from her screens. "What do you mean?"

"They're going to do other projects. They *are* doing other projects. And they don't have to hang out all the time."

Her mouth opens in shock. "But they're best friends."

"Are they?"

"They said so during promotion for the show. What little promotion they were given because they were totally sidelined in promo, but still."

"Then it must be true."

"You don't know what you're talking about," Jameela says.

"I'm just saying if you build up all this stuff in your mind—"

"It's not in my mind. It's a fact."

"Jameela, you're crying over two people you don't know not going to a tennis match together, so . . ."

She crosses her arms over her chest. "And you constructed some whole fantasy in *your* mind that you'd end up with the creeper that pretended to be some other guy."

Ouch. "At least I'd met him in person."

"That makes it worse. Besides, *everyone* says Jonny's the nicest guy they ever met. Like *everyone*. A ray of actual light. Pure sunshine."

"Okay."

"That Jack or Ben or whatever his name is, is a jerk."

My stomach turns. Maybe because I know on some level she's right. Which makes me an idiot for wanting to be with him, but I don't seem to be able to quash that impulse. Instead, I've been replaying our meeting on the weekend over and over in my mind. Every look, every word. It hasn't helped me want him less, but I do understand where he's coming from.

He wants me but he's afraid.

And that makes sense to me because I am too.

"You don't know him," I say.

"He blew you off, didn't he?"

I clench my fists under the desk. "His mom is dying, and I spent the day with him and his nephew yesterday."

"He's using his nephew as a beard?"

"What? No. It wasn't like that. We ran into each other, and his nephew was there. It wasn't anything bad."

"Uh-huh."

"You don't know him."

"You said."

"Forget it."

Jameela huffs her shoulders. "I will."

She turns her back to me. My thoughts are racing with regret that I engaged with her at all. At the same time, I can't believe she's judging Ben while she lives in this complete fantasyland of fan art and screencaps and 'ships that are never going to sail because, hello, your main character is a gay man no matter how well he plays it straight for the show.

And okay, okay, I'm already halfway to being in love with a guy who isn't available. But at least he's real. I've met him. I don't have unreasonable expectations about who he should hang out with. Well, not Rachel. Maybe Tyler wasn't trying to play matchmaker, but everyone knows continuing to hang out with your ex is not the way to get over her. If she needs getting over. I don't know. I should stop thinking about this.

I should stop.

I must stop.

Crap, no, that's a line from *Bridgerton*. Okay, okay, something else.

I will conquer this.

Ah shit, that's Mr. Darcy's line.

I'm thinking in romance hero even when I'm trying to leave them behind.

I need help. Or at the very least, a new leading man.

I look at Jameela again, now typing furiously into her chat group with her *Bridgerton* stans. I don't have to see what she's writing to know that she's transcribing our conversation, full of exclamation marks and *jsfskfsdks* and worse. I'm canceled in that group, for sure, not that I ever belonged to it.

But that's okay. I don't need them. I'll apologize to Jameela later, because I didn't need to be so harsh with her, even if it was for her own good.

In the meantime, I have someone waiting to be the leading man in my life. Someone who wants to be with me.

I pick up my phone and go through my texts. Jack ("real Jack" in my phone, even though I still don't have Ben's number) wrote to me last night, asking me how my weekend had gone. Like a nice guy. Like a good guy. I'd written something vague that I now regretted.

Hey, Jack, sorry about yesterday, it was a weird day. Anyway, I'd love to go out with you again. How about this weekend?

. . .

How do you feel about bagels?

I meet Jack on Saturday at Scream Cheese, a new bagel shop on the Upper West Side that's as punny as our original breakfast place.

"Tell me," I say, as we wait in line for our order. The inside of the shop has cartoon bagels all over the walls, with jokes like *A bagel calls its grandfather what? Poppy*! written in a loopy script. "Do you only know punny breakfast places or what?"

Jack puts up his hands. He's gotten a haircut since the last time I saw him, and the shorter hair suits him. It also makes him look more like Ben. "The bagels are good here, though."

"Why are breakfast foods considered funny?"

"I'm not sure. Maybe it's the—" Jack scrunches up his face in concentration. "Ugh, sorry, I can't come up with anything."

"The bacon me crazy? I like you a waffle lot? Don't go bacon my heart?"

He laughs. "Yeah, exactly. How did you do that?"

I consider telling him about the porny movie titles but quash it. I don't need to be talking about porn at ten in the morning on the Upper West Side. "I've had a lot of practice. Kit and I constantly make up funny titles for things."

"Oh yeah? Like what?"

"Silly movie titles."

The couple in front of us places their order and we step to the cash. I order an everything bagel with lox and cream cheese, and he does the same. He pays and we take our number and stand to the side to wait for our order to be made. There are a few tables in the shop, but we're going to take ours to the park and eat there. I'll steer us free and clear of any place that has Ben memories attached.

"I like Kit," Jack says. "Only at work we call her Katherine."

"Hmm. Only her mother calls her that."

He shrugs. "It happens."

"It's funny thinking of her as Katherine. Like maybe she has a whole different work personality that I know nothing about."

"How did you two meet?"

"First grade. She came to my defense on the first day of school and the rest is history."

"Who was she defending you from?"

"I believe the bully's name was Jack."

His eyes go wide. "What? No, no, that can't be."

"It's a common name."

"Yours is less common."

"True. Not sure how my parents picked it, honestly. They were never those parents who were big on sharing that kind of detail, or maybe they were, and then . . ."

"What?" Jack asks.

"My sister died when I was eight. Things were different after that."

"I'm so sorry, Chloe."

"Thank you. And don't worry, it happened a long time ago."

"But it must still affect your life? It would if I lost my brother."

I feel a moment of resistance. Other than with Ben, I haven't talked about this in so long that I've forgotten how. That's what happens when you stuff your emotions down for long enough. You lose the ability to speak about them.

"It's hard to separate my feelings about it from how it affected my parents, to be honest."

"I get that. But if you want to talk about it, I'm here." Jack puts his hand on my shoulder and looks into my eyes.

They're a nice shade of brown, clear and direct. I'm not sure what he wants to convey with this look, but it's so solemn it almost makes me laugh. Thankfully, I'm spared that embarrassing reaction by our number being called. Jack goes to the counter to pick our order up, and walks it back to me.

"That smells delicious."

He holds the bag to his nose. "Agree. Where should we go to eat it?"

"How about around the Jackie O. Reservoir? There are some picnic tables along there, right?"

"Think so. Let's go."

I follow him outside. I get in front of him to hold open the door because his hands are full. He smiles at me as he passes, and I follow him through, then let the door go.

And then it happens. I'm not looking where I'm going and I smack into someone trying to get inside the restaurant.

"Chloe?"

Oh no, oh shit. I knew it was a bad idea to come to the Upper West Side.

"Hi, Ben."

We step in unison out of the way of the door while I sense Jack tensing up behind me. And it's then that I notice that Ben's not alone. He's with a woman. Rachel.

"What are you doing here?" I ask.

"Getting bagels."

"Ah." I finally look him in the eye, but I can't do it for long. Instead, I stare at Rachel, who's looking at me with an open, sunny expression. "Us too."

"Us?"

"Oh, me and Jack." I turn sideways to indicate Jack.

He's trying to look friendly, but he's having a harder time of it. Because he knows who Ben is. Rachel has no idea about me at all.

"Ben, this is Jack."

Ben reaches out his hand to shake, but Jack's hands are full, so they end up doing this odd, awkward finger brush.

Rachel laughs. "Ben, who is this? Your brother from another mother?"

My face burns into flame as Ben tries to sound casual. "No, um, Rachel, this is Chloe and Jack."

Now it's Rachel's turn to hold out her hand. Her shake is firm, her hand dry, her nails manicured. She smells like lemons and her hair is that perfect tennis hair, a glossy ponytail, blond, and sun kissed.

What does she see when she looks at me? My hair is okay today because I made an effort for Jack, and I'm wearing something cute, a romper that looks good with tennies. But now I'm feeling like I look like a ten-year-old. What adult wears a *romper*? I've also been shaking her hand for a long time. I drop it.

"How do you know Ben?" she asks.

"Oh, um, we went on an accidental date once."

"What?"

"It's a long story. Not a real date, though, don't worry."

Ben shoots me a look but it's too late now. Me and my big mouth. I guess he'll be explaining me to Rachel once we escape from here.

"When was this?"

"In May."

"She was supposed to be going on a date with me," Jack says. "But I didn't show."

Rachel looks back and forth between Ben and Jack. "I don't get it."

"I'm sure Ben can explain."

"We're going to visit my mom in the hospital," Ben says to me, and I get what he's doing. He's trying to tell me that he and Rachel are not together, that I don't need to take this for anything other than what it is. But he doesn't owe me any explanations, and I don't owe him any either. We're both free to do what we want because that's the way Ben wanted it.

"I hope she's okay," I say.

"Stable."

"That's good."

Rachel's sunny disposition has fallen away entirely now, and I don't want to be in the middle of the fight that's about to happen. Ben might be over her, but she's obviously not over him, and this odd exchange has gone on long enough.

"Nice to meet you, Rachel. We should be going." I grab Jack's elbow and nearly drag him down the street. I want to look back, but I don't.

"Hey, hey, hold up," Jack says.

I stop, a little out of breath. "Sorry, I needed to get away from the awkward."

"That was *the* Ben, I presume?"

"Yes."

"And who was the girl?"

"His girlfriend. Or ex. He says ex."

"Didn't seem that ex."

"Right?"

"Chloe?"

I look at him. He's holding our bagel bags, sweat forming on his brow. "Yeah?"

"You want to cancel our brunch?"

"No, I don't. Forget them. Forget *him*."

"You sure about that?"

"Yes. Emphatically yes."

He furrows his brow. "We do look an awful lot alike."

"Only on the outside."

"Okay, thanks for that. Where to?"

"Anywhere but here."

Chapter Sixteen

It's a week later, July swamping the city like only July in New York can. Sometimes it feels like there's no air. Other times, like the sun is licking my skin. I've taken to spending as long as I can at the office because of the air-conditioning, waiting until it's almost dark to go home so I don't have to get on the sweaty subway. Instead, I take a Citi Bike, enjoying the feel of the wind on my face and the odd thrill I get almost dying every day as a car swerves unexpectedly.

My new, longer hours come with benefits. Tabitha is happy with me, pushing me to come up with stunts for other books, watching our subscriber numbers climb as the WANTED promo seems to have taken on a life of its own on TikTok, even though we've moved on to other titles. I even got a large bouquet of flowers from the author of *Most Wanted* after her book landed on the bestseller list.

But there are downsides too. I'm still getting tons of mail, clues, questions, and stories about Ben—their version, anyway. And even though I posted that I found him, I've been barraged with questions about who he is.

My new office hours have also meant that I haven't had much time for Jack. Despite the rocky start, we had a nice time at the park after the run-in with Ben and Rachel. I did my best to be present, to focus on Jack, to not parse every word and look that had passed between me and Ben.

At the end of the afternoon Jack tried to kiss me and I let him. It was a chaste peck, and all it did was remind me of what had happened with Ben on *our* date in the park. But that wasn't Jack's fault. I'm not in the business of taking advice from my absent mother, but I do feel like I need to give Jack a real chance. One untainted by Ben.

So I make a plan to see him on Saturday night.

"Working late again?" Jameela asks. Addison left a while ago, and despite my attempts to apologize, Jameela and I haven't been speaking since *Bridgerton*-gate.

"Can I tell you a secret?" I say.

"Sure."

"It's for the air-conditioning. Mostly I find this place *dreadfully boring*."

She laughs. "You said it like Anthony."

"I am sorry, Jameela. I shouldn't have taken my shit out on you."

"It's okay."

"It's not, though. Everything okay in the ton?"

"It's been superquiet. It's depressing."

"They're filming, right? Season four?"

"But there hasn't been any promo or anything. Why does the show hate them so much?"

I stifle my internal sigh. "Who knows. But maybe, in the meantime, we can find another 'ship?" I point to the stack of books on my desk. "I could use some help. I've got four books with the same plot *again* and I can't decide which one to pick. Would you mind reading them and telling me which couple gives you all the feels?"

"For real?"

I hand her the novels. They're all set around Valentine's Day. A girl with a broken heart trying to avoid the holiday. The girl always lives in New York but is from a small town in the Midwest where, miraculously, no one ever talks politics. Two of those towns are named Madison, without saying which state. Two of them even have characters with the same name—both the woman and the guy are named Cassidy and Carter. "You'd be doing me a massive favor."

She takes them and hugs them to her chest. "Thank you."

"Anytime."

"I applied for your job, you know."

"You did?"

"Before you got it. I want to move into curation."

"That's cool. Why don't you write up a paragraph about what you like about each book and if there's anything problematic in it? I can share it with Tabitha. Maybe this can be a regular thing."

"That'd be awesome."

I close down my computer and stand up. I do love the air-conditioning but it leaves me feeling cold all the time, like the chill gets into my bones and won't leave. It usually takes my whole bike ride home for it to seep out. "What are you up to tonight?"

"Reading these. Oh! I keep forgetting to tell you. I might have a lead on Addison's Wattpad handle."

"Really? What makes you think it's her?"

"Some of her turns of phrase. I've been reading some fan fiction on there and then I came across this romance novel and—"

"Wait, wait, wait. You think she's writing *romance*?"

"Pretty sure."

"Wow. I was sure it was horror."

"I was a bit surprised. And I might be wrong. I'm doing some more investigating."

"You're the one who figured out who the new cast members were in season three before they were announced by tracking down Insta follows, so I have confidence in you."

She grins. "My proudest moment."

We walk together toward the exit. I put on the alarm and turn off the lights. We wait for the elevator.

"What about you?" Jameela asks. "You have plans with Jack?"

"On the weekend."

"And Ben?"

"Nothing there. It was a fantasy, like you said."

"His loss."

"Thanks."

"Maybe it will work out with Jack?"

"Maybe."

She surprises me by pulling me into a hug. I hug her back, feeling emotional. "Thanks, Jameela."

The elevator dings. "No problem. It infects us."

"What?"

We step into the elevator.

"What we do. Reading all this romance all the time, being surrounded by it. We expect grand gestures and problems and like, love shouldn't be so complicated, you know? It should be easy."

"So no enemies to lovers?"

"In a book or TV show, it's hot. Not gonna lie. But in real life, I'd rather leave the drama on the screen, you know?"

"I do. Good advice."

The doors open and we walk through the lobby, waving good night to the security guard. We part outside and I watch her walk for a minute before I go and find my Citi Bike. Behind all the fan worship and shipping, Jameela is wise beyond her years. I laugh at myself—I sound like I'm forty, not twenty-six, surprised at the wisdom of a twenty-two-year-old. Gah.

Begone, Ben. I don't need a romantic hero. I need a real man who wants to be with me.

And even though I've said this to myself before, I mean it this time.

I swear.

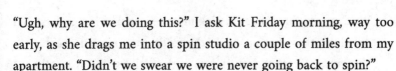

"Ugh, why are we doing this?" I ask Kit Friday morning, way too early, as she drags me into a spin studio a couple of miles from my apartment. "Didn't we swear we were never going back to spin?"

Kit tosses her head the way she always does when she's lying. "Did we?"

"We definitely did."

"That was before I got engaged." She wiggles her finger at me.

She loved the ring, like I knew she would. And she said yes, of course; silly Theo. He surprised her by proposing with breakfast in bed on a morning when he'd cleared her schedule for her at work by pretending to be a new client who needed a consult out of the office. They'd also had a long talk about what was going on at work. Theo was fine with her resigning if she needed to. His practice was going well and he could handle their finances for a while until she got her footing back.

It wasn't lost on me that Kit had her romantic hero with her all along. Low on drama, big on support. A nice guy who wanted to be with her.

"What does being engaged have to do with it?" I ask.

She adjusts the sweatband she insists on wearing at spin class, one of the many reasons why I swore I'd never take spin with her again. "I need to be wedding dress ready."

"Kit, you weigh like ninety pounds."

"Excuse me, no, I do not."

"You know what I mean." Kit's always been birdlike even though she eats like a regular person.

"I want to look good in my dress."

"You will."

"And you're my bridesmaid, so you have to do it too."

"No one's going to be paying attention to what I look like on your wedding day."

We'd agreed that I'd get to pick my dress, something understated that wouldn't show her up, as if I'd ever do that or even could.

We pay at the front desk and go to the lockers, which are, thankfully, not unisex like the last spin studio we went to. I strip off the top layer I wore here, knowing I need to be in the least amount of clothing possible in the class. Which means I'm wearing a sports bra and short bike shorts and not much else.

Will there ever be a time when I'm not comparing myself to other women? God, I hope so.

"You'll love it, you'll see."

"I highly doubt that."

We put on our bike shoes and walk to the classroom, the clips clacking against the floor. We find two bikes in the back row and adjust them. I sit on the uncomfortable seat, clip in, and start to move my legs slowly. The spin room is dark; it's one of those places that will start playing disco music and lights once the instructor gets going. There are two large TV screens at the front and there my name is—ChloeSpinsIGuess—at the bottom of the leaderboard.

"I'm already last," I say to Kit.

"It's random. Stop stressing."

I start to move my legs a bit faster, hoping to move up the board and it works. I jump over a few names, including IamKit, and land steady under RachelSpinsforWine. I appreciate the sentiment and look around for someone who has the same approach as I do. There's a woman ahead of me with a blond ponytail and strong shoulders who looks vaguely familiar.

Oh shit. What the hell is it with this town?

"Kit!"

"What?"

I point to Rachel's back. *That's Rachel*, I mouth.

"I can't hear you."

I give her a dagger look and try to spell out Rachel's name with sign language like we used to do in school when we didn't want the teacher to know what we were saying. Kit watches my fingers move over and over again, R-A-C-H-E-L and then B-E-N, and finally she gets it.

Her eyes widen. "Oh."

"Yeah, oh."

"What do you want to do?"

"Oh hi! It's Chloe, right?" Rachel's looking at me over her tanned and perfect shoulder.

"Rachel, hi. This is my friend, Kit."

Kit waves and Rachel smiles at her. I can't decide whether it's friendly or fake. Maybe a bit of both.

"Okay, people! Let's get this show on the road." A buff-looking woman in her thirties with a microphone leading to her mouth is now on the instructor's cycle at the front of the class. "This is our forty-five minute hill climb. That's right, my friends, we're going up, up, up. Since it's the Tour de France right now, I take my inspiration from that. Today we're climbing Mont Ventoux. Nine miles, eight point five percent of gradient. Are you ready?"

"Ready!" the class roars. Rachel gives me a shrug and turns toward her handlebars.

I glare at Kit. "You didn't tell me it was hills."

"Too late now!"

"Let's get our bikes to a resistance of fifteen and hit that eight-five rotation, shall we?"

Everyone reaches down and adjusts the tension on their bikes. I set mine at ten and move my feet as fast as I can. I quickly fall down the rankings as my watts are the worst in the class. Damn it. I turn the dial up to fifteen, which is supposed to be a "flat hill" according to the instructor, whatever that means, but feels to me like I'm going straight up. I inch up the standings though, so it's almost worth it.

Rachel, of course, is near the top, a single bead of sweat rolling between her perfect shoulder blades. I have a terrifying image of Ben running his finger down that trail, then push it away.

The music transitions to Glass Animals' "Heat Waves," and I push myself further at the instructor's urging. I have forty minutes left to get to Rachel on this leaderboard and I'm going to do it if it kills me.

"Your face is very red!" Kit pants next to me.

"I'll be okay!"

Rachel looks back at me and starts to laugh. I glare at her and she turns away. She might have Ben, but I don't need her judgment. I turn up the dial another notch and rise out of the saddle, even though the instructor hasn't told us to do that yet. But my calves are killing and so is my butt, and I need a bit of relief.

"Let's follow Chloe's lead, shall we, class?" the instructor says, rising in her saddle. "You can take this hill, team! You got this! Hear the crowd cheering you on! Lean into it!"

Everyone follows her instructions, and I fall into a sort of haze for the rest of the class. Each song is a mix of more hills and short flat sections. We rise, we sit, we lean forward, we dig in, we ease off, we go to the hydration station, and all the time my eyes are fixated on Rachel's name on the leaderboard. I inch closer to her with each song. Now there are ten people between us, now nine. One more song and it's eight. I'm running out of time, so I take a bit off the resistance and ramp up my speed and now I'm five behind her. Kit tries to talk to me but I wave her off, leaning low over my handlebars, my eyes fixed on the space between Rachel's shoulders. Four, three, two. Only two dudes are between us, the only two guys in the class.

"Last song, kids! Let's keep up the intensity, you can do it!"

I'm not sure I can, but then Rachel makes a mistake. She sits back in her seat to take some water and wipe her face with a towel. I see my chance and I peddle with all my might, faster than I ever have before even though I'm having trouble breathing.

"Thirty seconds!"

I pump my legs, eyes fixed on the board as I reach level with Rachel. I'm not going to get Ben as a prize if I beat her, but I want to win this imaginary competition nonetheless.

"And time!"

I sit back, gasping for air. I'm not sure I'm going to be able to walk out of here. But at least I did it. My name is level with Rachel's but because the board is alphabetical, I'm ahead of her.

"What got into you?" Kit says. "You don't look too good."

"I'll be fine." I reach for my water bottle and suck as much of it as I can down. Then I wipe my face with my towel while Rachel dismounts gracefully from her bike.

She walks toward me. She barely looks like she's been exercising, with only two bright spots of color on her cheeks. "That was fun!"

"Uh, yeah."

"You hear about this place from Ben?" she says, resting her arms on my handlebars. "We come here a lot."

Well played, Rachel. Well played.

"Oh, um, no, I didn't know that."

Kit hobbles over. "I got a coupon."

"Ah."

"It's a bit out of our way, really," Kit says. "How about you?"

"It's near his place."

I bite my tongue, not wanting to ask if she means his music studio or his apartment. At least she didn't say "our studio." But then I remember that his recording studio is in the Village, not Brooklyn.

"So, you going to join here?" Rachel asks, trying to be casual but not quite making it.

"I'm not sure I can ever walk again, but if I can, maybe."

Kit bites her tongue, for which I'm grateful.

"Ok-ay," Rachel says. "I wouldn't want things to be, you know, awk-ward. If Ben and I come here together."

So she knows. Fantastic. But what has Ben told her? That I'm some crazed stalker that he took pity on and now can't get rid of? Or the truth?

Whatever that is.

"Thanks." I unclip my shoes finally and pull myself off the bike. I try not to think about her looking at my ass in these shorts. I wish I didn't have to think about her at all. "Nice to see you," I say.

"Sure, see you around."

Maybe it's a question, but I don't answer it. Instead, I loop my arm through Kit's and let her help me out of the studio.

I don't look back.

"I might need to move," I say when we're far enough away from her. "New York is way too small a town."

Chapter Seventeen

After the class at the spin studio, I hobble into work, barely able to walk. I don't care what Kit wants us to look like on her wedding day, there's no way I can do this again. I thought I was in shape, but that was a fantasy. Like my life ever since I met Ben—full of the dream that things might be different if I wished hard enough. That hasn't worked, and I'm not magically going to suddenly be some amazing athlete either.

When I finally hobble up to my desk, Tabitha is there, waiting for me.

"Contest day, Chloe," she says, her eyes sparkling with mischief. She's wearing a kaftan made out of some vibrant material, and I can't believe she isn't sweating profusely under it, no matter how cold they keep the temperature in the office.

"What's that?" I say with a sinking feeling.

"We need to tell our readers who came closest to providing information on our missing man."

I lower myself gingerly into my desk chair. I feel like I'm a hundred years old. "We're still doing that?"

"Yes, of course, why not?"

"I thought when I found him another way—"

"Oh, no. We have to keep our promises."

"I don't think anyone identified him." I'm not sure this is true. I stopped checking the emails and messages on social when I found Ben for real.

"Then pick someone. But make sure you go through all the entries first. You know what happened last time."

I sigh as I try to find a comfortable position in my chair. My quads are on fire, my butt a bruise. Six months ago we'd run a contest and got lazy going through the entries. Someone who lost took it badly and ended up figuring out that the winner didn't meet the criteria. There'd been a threat of a lawsuit, and our Instagram got suspended for a week. That one wasn't my fault, but that girl wasn't working here anymore, so I most definitely didn't want to make that mistake.

"I'll check them now."

She nods and walks away. Creating this contest was a personal mistake, no matter how good it was for the subscription base. But I don't seem to be able to move on from it in more ways than one, so I open my computer and go to the email address I was using for the contest. There are at least a hundred emails I haven't checked. Fantastic.

I start to open them, scanning through the included pictures and names, which are not Ben. Another collection of sad missing man stories—this is a popular MO these days, a few dates and then *poof*!

It's depressing and I want to delete the rest of the emails. But then I see one from someone named Kaitlin Hamilton. That's Ben's last name. There are two emails from her stacked on top of one another in a thread. I open the first—it's dated a week before I figured out who Ben was.

Hi, I saw your contest on Insta and I'm almost certain that's a picture of my brother, Ben Hamilton. I've attached a picture so you can confirm. Do I win?

I open the picture she's attached, a sweet shot of Ben a bit younger, on a beach, his hands on his hips, staring at the camera with a laugh. He's tanned and relaxed and happy, and I can't help it, I start to smile, too, wishing I could know what made him laugh like that. What is it about this guy that gets to me so much? Ugh.

I close out of the photo and read her second email.

Hi again,

I never heard back on this, but Ben told me that you've figured out who he was. I'm Tyler's mom. Thanks so much for being so great to him the other day. He's still talking about it.

I check the date. It's two days after the ice-cream incident. It reminds me of Tyler and his exclamation marks. He's a cute kid, and his mom seems nice. Besides, I have to contact her; Tabitha said. There's a phone number under her name. I call it.

"This is Kaitlin."

"Hi, this is Chloe Baker. From BookBox. Calling about Ben?" My voice is rising with each half sentence. I sound like an idiot.

"Oh, Chloe. Hi!" her voice is warm, a nice alto phone voice.

"I'm calling to let you know that you've won our grand prize. A year's subscription to the book box and a signed copy of *Most Wanted.*"

"Thank you. Wow, Chloe. We're talking in real life."

I lean back slowly in my chair and try not to scream out in pain. "That's a surprise?"

"I've been hearing about you on both ends for a while."

"Both ends?"

"Tyler and Ben."

"Oh." Ben talked about me to his sister. I wish I knew what that meant. "Tyler is adorable."

"He's a handful, but thank you for being so kind to him."

"My pleasure."

"Ben told me about the whole accidental date thing."

I close my eyes. Even that hurts, but that might not be the spin class. "Yeah."

"He meant well."

"He said." I tuck my phone under my chin and switch my position so I can google Kaitlin. I like having a visual when I speak to someone. She looks a lot like Ben, with shoulder-length brown hair and the same easy smile.

"I'm sorry it didn't work out," she says.

Me, too, Kaitlin. Me too.

"It happens. I'm sorry about your mom."

"Thank you." Kaitlin sighs. "It's been hard. We don't know how long she's going to have."

"Is she still in the hospital? I ran into Ben and Rachel a couple of weeks ago, bringing her bagels."

"I heard."

"You did?"

"From Ben *and* Rachel that time. That was an epic fight."

My toes curl in my shoes. Ouch! I need to stop moving. "I didn't mean to cause tension between them."

"It's not your fault. And they're not together in case you were wondering. Not that Rachel acts like it." There's a bitterness in her tone that surprises me. From everything I've seen of Rachel, despite her dislike of me, she's well liked. "Probably shouldn't say anything. I'm always saying too much and getting in trouble."

"Yes, of course. And, ha, me too."

"That breakup was a long time coming, and it was a hard decision for Ben, but it was the right one, you know? And then our mom got sick and he felt like he couldn't tell her about the breakup because Mom loves Rachel and—I told him he should tell her. It's not like our mom is some delicate flower. But Ben's protective."

"That's a good quality."

"Yes, usually. But not at the expense of his happiness."

As much as part of me wants to know all of this, another part of me is screaming to make it stop. I cannot be the confidant of Ben's sister about his relationship problems.

"I'm not sure Ben would want you telling me any of this."

"You're right. He just gives so much to us. I want him to be happy."

"That might not be me, though."

"True. But it feels different when he talks about you."

Another ouch, but it's internal this time. "Amendment. I'm not sure it's good for *me* to hear about this."

"Oh, Chloe, I'm so sorry. Of course. I didn't think."

"It's fine."

"No, no, it isn't. You called about the contest. Do I need to do anything for that?"

"Can you send me your mailing address and a photo? And do you mind if we do a post about it with the other photo you sent of Ben?"

"Sure."

"Can you ask Ben?"

"Yes, okay."

"Great. Anyway, I should be going." I'm about to hang up, but something holds me back. "Can I ask you one thing?"

"Of course."

"Why did you enter the contest? You knew what it was about, right? You knew why I was asking because Ben had told you?"

For the first time, she's guarded. "Are you asking whether Ben mentioned you to me before I saw the contest?"

"Yes."

"Yes."

My heart skips a beat. And then another.

There it is. External confirmation that it wasn't all in my head with Ben. Not that I truly thought that. He told me it wasn't, but he's not the most trustworthy source. But if he'd talked about me to Kaitlin, then that had to mean something. On the other hand . . .

Oh shit. Oh no.

"But when you saw the contest, why didn't you tell him? Or did you?" Now my heart's in my throat. Because if she did tell him and he didn't reach out, then he's a liar and there's no sugarcoating it.

"I meant to, but you didn't answer me and then our mom got sicker and he didn't mention you again so it slipped my mind. Then when he told me he'd found you, I remembered."

"You were trying to play matchmaker?"

"Maybe. He told me about the date and then said he couldn't find you. Then a few weeks later I saw someone who looked an awful lot like him—"

I stop her. "Kaitlin."

"Yeah?"

"You don't have to cover for him. I can take it."

"I'm sorry, Chloe."

Somehow I knew this is where this conversation was headed. "You *did* tell him?"

"Yes. But it's not like you think. He was going to reach out when things calmed down with our mom. That's real. She's sick. Dying. None of us are thinking clearly."

Later, when I'm alone, I'm going to parse our conversation at his music studio to see where the lies are. How bad they are. If they can match up, somehow.

But no. There's no getting past this, no matter how much I want to.

I don't have to think about it later. He acted like the contest was a surprise. He didn't tell me he knew about it. He didn't want to find me, not really. He could've easily. He could've emailed me anytime and he didn't.

That's that. Whatever Kaitlin thinks. That's enough.

Fuck.

"Thanks for being honest with me," I say, my throat tight and on the precipice of tears.

"I'm sorry."

"No, it's fine. Anyway, congratulations. You'll be getting some great reads this year."

"Thanks, Chloe, and good luck to you."

I hang up and stare at the phone, blinking my tears away. The call lasted ten minutes. That's how long it took to kill any lingering dream I had about Ben.

That seems like a short time.

But the first death only took a couple of seconds—those texts with Jack, real Jack, when I found out Ben had been lying to me. That he was another man in my life I couldn't trust.

You'd think I'd know by now that people don't change. Once a liar . . .

I don't know how to complete that thought. All I know is that my body hurts. My heart hurts. It all hurts and this sucks.

Love sucks.

I'm not in the best frame of mind to go on a date with Jack, but I made the date and I'm going to keep it.

Jack isn't the problem. Ben is.

I'm the problem for wanting anything with him in the first place, or the second, or the third. I don't know why it's taking me so long to come to terms with that.

I'm going to have to figure it out soon, but not tonight. I slap on a pretty dress and a smile and some lipstick, and I meet Jack at an Italian restaurant in Bed-Stuy and try not to think about the fact that this is Ben's neighborhood, and that the way my luck is going, I'm bound to run into him any minute.

"Would you like something to drink while you wait, miss?"

"God, yes."

The waiter smiles at me. In his fifties, he's wearing a white shirt and black pants, an apron tied around his waist, and a white cloth over his arm. Very old school. The tables have white and red checkered cloth on them, and the air smells like olive oil and tomato sauce. I've been seated near the back, with a romantic candle on the table and easy listening playing on a speaker above me. The restaurant is half full, mostly families and older couples, and I wonder how Jack found this place.

"I have a very nice chianti on special."

"That sounds lovely."

"Shall I wait for your dinner companion to arrive?"

"No, that's fine, he'll be here soon, I'm sure."

The waiter leaves while I peruse the menu. It's as old school as the surroundings—carbonara, amatriciana, classic Bolognese. The idea of hot pasta on a summer night is a little off-putting, but it's cool in here and it's been a while since I've had a good pasta.

The waiter comes back with my wine. A generous glass. "I brought you the eight ounce."

"Looked like I needed it?"

"Call it a waiter's intuition. It's a curse and a tool."

"How so?"

He shrugs. "I make snap judgments about people based on other people I've met over the years they remind me of. It's surprisingly accurate but sometimes I can be way off."

"What about me? Do I remind you of anyone?"

"Sure. There have been lots of pretty girls with sad eyes over the years."

"Are my eyes so sad?"

He gestures to my wine glass. I take the hint and take a sip. It is surprisingly good for the house special. "That's delicious."

"It is. I'll bring you some bread and olive oil while you wait. And might I suggest the stuffed zucchini blossoms? They're divine."

"Please. And thank you—" I pause to look at his name tag. Giuseppe. "Thank you, Giuseppe."

"You can call me G."

"I'm sure that will be much easier once I have a second one of these."

He laughs and leaves. I pick up my phone to check the time. I was a few minutes early, but now it's been at least ten minutes, and it's not like Jack to be late. It rings in my hand. Jack.

"Hey."

"Chloe, I'm sorry—"

I release a slow breath. "You have to cancel?"

"It's a shit show at work. I thought I'd be able to get away, but they're in the middle of firing a hundred people and I have to cut off their internet access tonight or *I'm* going to get fired."

"What is that place, the CIA?"

"You'd think the way they're acting. Anyway, they sprang this on me at five as I was on my way out the door. I thought I'd be able to get it done in time, but clearly not."

"It's okay."

"Are you already at the restaurant?"

"I am."

"Please order on me. I'll call and give them my card."

"That's sweet of you."

"The least I could do. Can we reschedule?"

"Call me tomorrow when the dust settles."

"I will."

"Oh, and I bought concert tickets to surprise you with. This new band I think you'll like. My Mom's Garage."

"I love them."

"I'll send you the tickets. Go. Maybe Kit can go with you. I'm sure she could use the distraction after—"

I put my glass down. "Wait, did Kit get fired?"

"I can't tell you that, Chloe."

"I understand. I'll take the tickets, thank you."

"No sweat."

"Have a good night."

"You too."

We hang up and I start to text Kit, then stop myself. She'll tell me this news in her own time and I don't want to get Jack in trouble for letting it slip. And she and Theo have something planned tonight with his parents to celebrate the engagement.

My phone pings. Jack's emailed me the tickets. The concert's a few blocks away at a local bar. I can go on my own. I used to do that all the time after my breakup with Christian. I don't know why I stopped doing it when I moved to New York, and I'm glad in a way that I've gotten an opportunity to get back to that part of myself. The one who was fine without a man.

So that's what I'm going to do. I'll have a couple of glasses of wine and eat some delicious food then go listen to a good band.

Then I'll tuck this day away and sleep through the weekend.

Maybe on Monday things will finally start to change.

Chapter Eighteen

Of course, it doesn't work out like that. Instead, when I float into the Corner Stop, the local bar where the band is playing, still buzzed from my three glasses of excellent wine, I run smack into Ben.

Not literally this time, but figuratively. He's at the door taking tickets. Because of course he is. Brooklyn is even smaller than New York. I should've known better than to go anywhere on my own.

I have a moment of thinking that I can turn around and leave before he notices me, but I can't pull it off.

"Chloe!" he says with more enthusiasm than I feel. He's wearing dark jeans and a casual cotton blazer with the band's T-shirt underneath. He looks too good to ignore.

Shit, shit, shit.

Okay, okay, calm down. He's just a guy. You're going to be okay.

I tuck my hair behind my ears because I need something to do with my hands. "Hi, Ben."

"What are you doing here?"

"I have tickets." I wave my phone at him and he scans it.

"Two tickets."

"Yes."

He keeps his features neutral but his voice doesn't quite make it. "Ah."

"He's not coming," I blurt. "He got stuck at work."

Shut up, Chloe. Stop talking.

"I assume you mean Jack?"

"Yes."

A hint of a smile. "Again?"

"It happens."

Someone bumps me from behind, wanting to get in. I step out of the way and Ben scans the guy's ticket.

"What are you doing here?" I ask, not really looking at him because looking at him is dangerous.

"Scanning tickets."

"You know what I mean."

He points to the logo on his T-shirt. "It's my band."

"You're in the band?"

"No, they're on my label."

I feel like a moron, but I can't seem to help myself from prolonging this conversation. "And you're taking tickets?"

"I sweep the floors too."

"Right."

"You seem angry."

I catch his eyes. Are we going to do this here? I guess so. "I spoke to your sister today."

His eyebrows rise as he scans the ticket of the next person in line. "Kaitlin?"

"Do you have another sister?"

"No, I . . . can you give me a minute?"

"I guess."

He points to a small, round table near the stage. "I have that reserved. Take a seat and I'll be with you in a minute."

I cross my arms, not sure I'm going to comply. I don't owe him any explanations and what can he say to me that is going to make this better?

"Please?"

I go to the table he indicated. There's a small RESERVED sign on it. I wonder who he was planning on sitting here with. If it's Rachel, I'm out of here. I might be out of here anyway, but I guess I can stick around and see what he has to say for himself.

Curiosity killed the Chloe.

I take a seat and look around. There's a stage in front of me with some instruments on it—a drum kit behind a series of plastic screens, a keyboard, some guitars. The backdrop is matte black and the air smells like beer and cheap disinfectant. It invokes sense memories of my favorite dive bar back home, where Kit and I used to go watch up-and-coming bands once a week.

A waiter comes over with a glass of white wine on a tray. His hair is in a pompadour and he has an over-the-top moustache.

"I didn't order this."

"Ben ordered it for you. Did you want something else?"

"No, it's fine, thank you."

I take the glass and sip. It's dry and crisp and the kind of white wine I'd order for myself. I try not to see this as some kind of sign that Ben knows me even though he doesn't while I watch him gesticulate to one of the people who works in the bar to explain how to take over what he's doing. Or that's what I assume he's doing, anyway.

When I've finished half the glass, Ben slips into the chair across from me, looking slightly frazzled, but still handsome. The bar isn't full, but I can see a line forming at the door. It's nine—the show starts in an hour.

"You can take care of business," I say. "I don't mind."

"No, this is important." He places his hands on the table. "Why—how—did you talk to Kaitlin?"

I hold the stem of my glass. I should've thanked him for it, but oh well. Here we go. "She won the contest you pretended not to know anything about at your office."

"Oh." Ben winces. "Hold on." He turns and signals to the bartender who's standing in front of a shelf of bottles and two beer taps. He holds up two fingers, then turns back to me. "You were saying?"

"You need reinforcements?"

"It might be a good idea for both of us."

"Can't face me sober?"

"It's not that. I . . . can I start at the beginning?"

The waiter comes over with two glasses of whiskey and puts them down in front of Ben. Ben thanks him and offers one to me.

"I don't usually," I say. "Plus I still have this." I point to my wine glass.

"It's good. And one of the perks of being the band's label."

"Free alcohol?"

"Free good alcohol."

"Isn't that how everyone in the music business ends up with a drinking problem?"

Ben picks up his drink and drains it. "Maybe. Which is why I limit myself to two drinks under any situation."

My throat feels dry and I keep clenching and unclenching my hands. We slip so easily into our banter it would be easy to ignore our problems and talk all night.

I take another sip of my wine, then tug the whiskey glass closer to me. Red wine, plus white wine, plus this whiskey might equal blackout, but since I'm not in the music business, I'm willing to risk it. "Is this a situation?"

"I deserve that."

"As you were saying?"

"I had a great time on our date," he says. "I meant that."

"Our fake date."

"Yes. But everything I said about it was true. And my mom. And I did try to find you after. I even talked to Kaitlin about you, which if you knew me better, you'd know I don't do often."

"Why not?"

"Because she's my older sister. It's like her personal mission for me to be happy. And she never liked Rachel. I got in the habit of not discussing that sort of stuff with her. But with you, it was different."

"Okay." That word feels weird in my mouth. But what else is there to say? Nothing, that's what.

"And then she told me that maybe she'd found you. She showed me this Instagram post with a picture of me and your contest. I couldn't believe it. You were looking for me."

"I was."

"I was excited. I was going to reach out. But then my mom had another really bad night. We weren't sure if she was going to make it, and . . . I'm sorry to say this because it sounds terrible, but reaching out to a girl seemed . . ."

"Petty."

"Not the word I'd use, but sort of. Something that wasn't a priority, anyway. Because it was when I realized that you were a real person that it got real. Like if I reached out and you were as great as I remembered, then what? I can't be a boyfriend right now."

I lean back in my seat. I feel a bit strange, not quite the spins, but like I might be getting there. His words are swirling around in my brain, too, and I'm not sure if they're making me less angry or it's the alcohol talking.

"You keep saying that," I say, "but what does that mean?"

"It means I can't be there for anyone else right now. I can barely be there for myself, my business. And I don't want to do that. One of the things that broke me and Rachel up was that she thought I was too focused on other things. That I didn't prioritize our relationship."

"I'm not Rachel."

"I know."

"We kind of look alike, though, right? I'm the less good-looking version, but—"

"No, stop. That's not true at all."

"You don't have to say that."

"I mean it." He runs his hands through his hair and eyes my untouched drink.

I push it toward him. "You want this?"

"Yes, but no. Let me finish. Anyway, I told Kaitlin I wasn't going to reach out. I didn't know she wrote to you anyway. She didn't tell me that part. And then, suddenly, there you were outside my office."

"And we had version one of this conversation."

His forehead creases. "We did. And I wanted to tell you the truth, I did, but it seemed cruel. I could tell you already felt rejected. I didn't want to add to that. Because nothing had changed. I don't know how much longer my mom has, and I'm not ready to be in a relationship."

I breathe in and out slowly but it doesn't seem to help my heart rate. "That's a lot of pressure you're putting on yourself. On me."

"What do you mean?"

"All I wanted was a second date. I never asked you to be my boyfriend."

Now he reaches for my glass and drains it. "You went to an awful lot of trouble to find me for a second date."

"I did."

He puts the glass down slowly. "Come on, Chloe, you know it wouldn't be like that between us."

"I don't know that."

I wish that was true. That counts, right?

"Okay," Ben says. "*I* know. If we were together, for me it would be serious."

I look down at my empty glass. There's a bit of white wine in the bottom, not even a sip, but enough that it will annoy me if the waiter takes it away. And it doesn't make sense, but that's how I feel now. Like something unfinished is being taken away from me.

And it hurts. It *hurts*.

Ben was right. I didn't want to know this. He did me a service when he withheld this information. How does he know me so well?

"Chloe?"

"Yeah?"

"Can you forgive me?"

I look up slowly. He looks hopeful. "Does it matter?"

"It does. It does to me."

"Why?"

"Because I can't . . . I don't like the thought of you out there in the world, hating me."

"I don't hate you."

That small smile again. It's kind of killing me.

"That's something, anyway."

The waiter comes over with another glass of white wine and a whiskey for Ben. "That's above his limit," I say, taking my glass.

"She's right."

"What do you want me to do with it, then?"

"You can leave it," I say as Ben laughs. "What? I don't have a two-drink rule."

"Enjoy it, then."

"I will." I say this with confidence, though taking that drink is a mistake. The hangover won't be worth it.

The bar has filled up around us. Ben moves his chair closer to me. "This okay? It's about to get loud in here." He points to the stage where the stagehands are bringing out more instruments.

"How did you find these guys?"

"I go to a lot of shows, trying to discover people before they're signed. And I listen to a lot of YouTube, TikTok, Spotify. What about you?"

"Jack picked."

"Ah."

"But I knew them already. I heard one of their songs in a TV show?"

"'Live it Up,' that was their big break earlier this year."

Ben's leg touches mine under the table, and maybe it's the drinks, but I'm acutely aware of it. And now that he's closer to me, I can smell his aftershave, something musky that I like. I should move away but I don't.

"They should be big," Ben says. "I'm hoping they blow up."

"It's a tough business, yes?"

"Very tough. Probably not unlike the book business. Everyone thinks music should be free."

"Yeah, that's the problem with our generation."

He laughs. "Aren't we supposed to be blaming the boomers?"

"Nah, it's Gen X's fault. They always get mad when we forget them."

"Totally." He taps my knee with his. "So, you and Jack . . ."

Oh boy. I did not plan for this.

I didn't plan for any of it.

"We've been on some dates."

"Some dates, but not dating."

"I guess that's accurate."

"Good."

"What's that mean?"

He shrugs, then puts his hand on my arm. "Wait here."

His eyes lock with mine for a minute, then his hand drops and he rises then pops up onto the stage in a graceful move. He walks to the mic stand in the middle of the stage and taps it. "Hello, hello!"

"Hello!" some of the room say back along with a few cheers.

"Thank you for coming out tonight to see my new favorite band and yours, I hope, *My Mom's Garage!*"

More cheering now. "There are vinyl and merch to purchase at the back and yes, you can also stream them everywhere you usually stream music! This is, however, my usual plug for paying artists what they're worth."

"Bring on the band, Dad!"

Ben cringes and raises his hands in surrender. "Okay, okay, I had to try! One more thing, though. My good friend Chloe is here tonight. If the usual bozos could behave themselves I'd appreciate it."

A group of bros in the back start catcalling and whistling.

"Thanks, dudes. Exactly what I wanted. All right, enough of me! I give you—*My Mom's Garage!*"

Ben jumps off the stage and sits back down next to me, dragging his chair even closer, by accident or by mistake I'm not sure, but our whole sides are touching now like we're sitting on a bench, and I want to lean into it, to rest my head on his shoulder, to have his arm around my neck, to be *together*. But we aren't, and we aren't going to be.

God, I want to kiss him so bad.

The band comes on stage to more cheering—four guys who look like they belong in a band, with shaggy hair and jeans and skinny bones. They take up their instruments, and the drummer counts them in and they go immediately into their big hit, the one Ben mentioned earlier. Everyone around us stands up to dance, and Ben pulls me up, too, my hand hot in his, my body responding to his touch.

I shuffle awkwardly, but Ben is a surprisingly good dancer, moving his head and shoulders in time to the music. He's still got a hold of my hand, and I'm not sure what it means, that he hasn't let it go, only I've had enough wine that I don't care. With my free hand, I reach to the table and pick up the whiskey glass. I toss it back, then shudder.

"What was that for?" Ben asks in my ear, sending shivers down my neck.

"Courage."

"For what?"

"We'll see!"

Ben spins me and when I finish the spin I'm so close to him that I'm almost in his arms.

I could back up, break the connection, leave.

But instead, I lean into it and let momentum bring us together in a kiss.

Because we keep being brought together by fate, this city, this small town.

And I for one am sick of fighting it.

Chapter Nineteen

When we break apart, we're both out of breath and the lead singer is glaring at us because we're kind of stealing his spotlight.

Ben mouths *Sorry* and the singer flips him off and goes back to singing to the very young girls who are crowding the front of the stage. I didn't get carded to get in here, and I doubt they would've been admitted if the guys at the door bothered checking IDs.

Ben speaks into my ear. "I'd like to get out of here."

My whole body is vibrating. "Okay."

"I can't, though. Not until the concert's over."

"Okay," I say again, a creep of disappointment setting in. This is work, and I've thrown a wrench in it. We both have. But my lips are still tingling and my hands are kind of numb, and I'm one big nerve all over. I want to kiss him again, badly, but that seems unwise.

"Will you stay?" Ben asks.

I shouldn't, but . . . "Yes."

"Good."

He takes my hand and kisses it, then twines our fingers together and we turn back to the stage, our hands locked, our bodies touching along the side, a promise of more things to come, later, when the concert's over.

The music washes over me, that base-note feeling deep in my soul. I steal glances at Ben, who's sometimes stealing glances at me too. I feel happy, like a buoy on the water on a sunny day, but there's a dark cloud on the horizon because: Ben. Ben!

I should ask a million questions. I should leave this place though the music is good, that pop-y, singer/songwriter mix I've always loved. The lights are crisscrossing above the band on the stage, purple and blue, and their energy is infectious. The band should blow up—I hope they do—but what the hell am I doing here? Ben said we couldn't be together; he said that an hour ago, and yet he didn't pull back when our mouths met. Instead he deepened the kiss, all tongue and soft lips until I felt weak in the knees; weak in the heart.

I don't do that, though. Instead, I keep looking at him as the music plays, and he's looking at me too. The night is soft, fuzzy from the drinks and the kiss, and the feeling of his hand in mine. I haven't felt this woozy in years. I've never felt anything like this at all.

I'm not going to run.

I'm going to see what happens next.

When the concert's over, encores sung and hands clapped until numb, Ben tells me he wants to leave but he needs ten minutes. He says this against my ear, his lips touching my flesh.

I shiver and wonder what he needs to do. I watch him, feeling hot and sweaty, as he talks to someone who must be the bar's manager and gets handed a wad of cash. He counts it out quickly, then divides it up and pays the band, pocketing something for himself. It all happens so quickly, with fist bumps and back slaps, that it looks like a drug transaction. He finishes up and gets handed a drink. He takes it, finishes that, too, then comes back to me.

"I thought you had a two-drink limit?" I say, tilting my head to the side.

He checks his watch, then angles it toward me. It's 12:02 a.m. "It's a new day."

"Ah."

"You disapprove?"

I circle his wrist above his watch with my thumb and index finger. They don't make it around, but almost. "Depends."

He gives me a lopsided grin. "On?"

"Why you had it? For courage?"

"Maybe."

"Hmmm."

He takes my hand off his wrist, tracing the flesh between my thumb and forefinger. "Is that a good answer or a bad one?"

"We'll see."

"You want to get out of here?"

"Yes."

He tugs on my hand, leading me out of the building to the sidewalk. I take one breath of the cooler night, enjoying the fresh air on my face, and then Ben's pressing me up against the building, his mouth on mine, his hands on my collarbones, the naked flesh not covered by my dress.

I kiss him back with everything I've been holding in since I met him. All the want, all the need, all the missed chances and disappointments. It feels like we might be saying good-bye with this kiss, like we know it's the only chance we'll have, but I don't care. My body's on fire, a wet heat between my legs, and I can't help from pressing against him, wanting nothing between us, not even air.

I love his tongue and his taste and the way his hands are holding my face. I love the way he whispers my name against my lips, *Chloe*, like he's asking me a question, not stating a fact.

"Chloe."

"Yes?" I say, breathless. I look up at him; his eyes are so close to mine that it's hard to focus. His nose isn't quite straight. It bends right at the end.

"Give me your phone?"

"What? Why?"

He leans back and holds out his hand. I fumble in my bag and pull it out, resting it gently in his hand. He leans toward it, concentrating, and *taps, taps, taps*.

"What are you doing?"

"I'm creating a contact. For me."

"Oh."

My heart thrills. All this time, and I've never had his number, even after I knew how to get in touch with him. A warning bell sounds in my mind.

It sounds like Kit, but I shoo her away.

"There," he says, handing it back to me.

I look at the contact he's created. Ben Mystery Man Hamilton, and his digits.

I laugh. "Mystery man, huh?"

"I thought it fitting."

I smile and start to send him a message.

"What are you doing?" he asks.

"Texting a mystery man."

He stops me. "I have a better idea."

"Oh?"

"Let's go to my place."

I slip my phone into my purse. "Okay."

"You sure?"

"Yes, Ben. I'm sure."

He smiles and it's a flash of white against the night, and now we're kissing again, all tongues and wet mouths and his hands roaming down my sides. If we keep this up much longer, we're going to be having sex on a street corner.

"Ben," I say into his mouth.

"Yeah?"

"Maybe we should take this inside?"

"Mmmhmmm." He kisses me again then pulls away. "Too public?"

"Probably?"

He laughs and takes my hand. Then he walks away and I follow him, our hands linked together, our shoulders touching. The night is dark, and the air feels fresh, like rain might be coming. I feel fresh, too, like a brand-new person in a way that doesn't entirely make sense, but I'm all about going with it tonight. Going for it.

A few blocks later Ben stops in front of a building that doesn't look too different from mine. A newer build, stairs out front, a glass entrance door.

"This is me. You want to come up?"

"Isn't that what we're doing?"

"Just checking."

"That drink starting to wear off?"

"What?" He laughs. "Oh, maybe, yeah. You?"

"I'm sober enough."

"I have wine."

"I don't need wine."

"What do you need?"

"Take me inside and I'll show you."

He grins, and then we run up the stairs together, laughing. His apartment's on the third floor, like mine, but I keep thinking about that old song, about living on the second floor. I don't know what's going through my brain. Not much. Just feelings. Just right now, the key in the lock, the smell of Ben's apartment, like him, only gentler, the hardwood floors, the light walls, the instruments hanging on the wall above the couch.

"Do you want a drink?" Ben asks.

"I want . . . something."

He smiles at me again, slow and wonderful. "Oh yeah?"

I loop my arms around his neck and pull him to me and there's nothing to say after that. We let our bodies talk for us, our clothes falling to the floor in what seems like minutes but is longer because, by the time he slips the straps of my dress off my shoulders, I want to scream for it.

I almost do scream when Ben moves to my breast, taking it into his mouth, using his tongue on my nipple. Things speed up after that. We leave a trail of clothes across the floor as we stumble to the bedroom. And then we're standing by his bed, both of us naked, and it's amazing how his hands feel, how comfortable I am, how very, very wet.

Ben's bed is made like a grown-up, unlike my tangled mess and we fall onto it together, laughing, happy, then serious, exploring. His mouth is everywhere, on my breasts, my neck, my stomach, between my legs, and I arch up to meet him.

I want this, I want all of him. My brain is confused by sensation, by how natural this feels, how right, how it's like we've done it before but it's all new too.

We say all the things we need to, the words of consent, a brief discussion about birth control, and it's not awkward, just part of what's leading us to this moment—his quiet eyes above me in the dark as he penetrates me slowly, moving in and out in a rhythm that brings us closer and closer and closer until there's only us, one body moving in unison, our arms locked around each other until there's nowhere left to go but fall apart.

Later, under the covers, Ben makes a little fort for us. He's tracing small circles on my back, slow, slow, slow, and it feels like his fingers are fire on my skin. That's what we felt like together—fire. Combustible, but maybe also dangerous.

"What are you thinking about?" I ask.

"That I'm glad we did this."

I smile. "You don't mind that I asked that?"

"No, why would I?"

"The last guy did."

His mouth turns down. "Ugh, do not tell me about him."

"Jealous?"

"Obviously. Plus, I met him."

"Wait, wait, wait. I did not mean *Jack*. I didn't sleep with him."

He leans forward and kisses me. "Good."

"What kind of girl do you think I am?"

"A very attractive girl I'm sure most guys want to sleep with."

"Oh, ha."

"You thought I'd say something else?"

I kiss him for an answer. "No, that's the perfect thing to say."

"Mama didn't raise no dummy."

I laugh but he frowns. "What is it?"

"I forgot to check in with my mom tonight. I'm sure it's fine."

"Is she still in the hospital?"

"No."

"That's good."

He winces. "Palliative care."

"Oh, Ben. I'm sorry."

"It's okay." He kisses me on the forehead. "It's what she wants and she still has time. But let's not worry about that right now, okay?"

I tighten my arms around him. "We can, though. If you need to."

"I appreciate that. But it's the middle of the night and there's nothing I can do about it right now." He pulls me closer. "I can, however, do something about what's right in front of me."

"Such as?"

"What's one of those movie titles you're always perverting? Downward Doggie Style was it?"

I crinkle my nose. "No, thank you."

"I wasn't being serious."

"That's good, because if you were then I'd have to rethink this whole thing."

I kiss him to show I'm joking too; there's no rethinking going on on my side of things, no sir, but something falls out of the ether that is my brain.

"You know the only reason we ever ended up meeting was because my vibrator shipment went missing."

He pulls back, laughing. "What?"

I've never admitted this to myself before, but it's true. "I was about to have to place a *very embarrassing* call to Amazon customer service—"

"You can't even call them, you have to text a bot."

"Even worse. Anyway, it was missing and I was lonely and Kit had been bugging me."

He nudges my nose with his. "To date Jack."

"Yes, but let's not let that little detail get in our way, right?"

"The little detail you were supposed to be on a date with tonight?"

"Hey, now. Hey. You should be happy about that."

"How?"

I kiss his lips briefly. "Seems like every time he doesn't show up, there you are."

"Lucky me."

He brings his mouth to mine and his lips are soft and firm and wet, his mouth warm and slippery, and it's hard not to keep my brain from slipping into the language of all of the rom-coms I read.

How it's never felt this right (it hasn't).

How it's never felt this good (that either).

How I never want it to stop (who would?).

How his hands are everything and everywhere.

My brain is on overload, too much happening in one day to process. I do my best to quiet it, and give in, give in, give in.

Chapter Twenty

"Good morning," Ben says to me hours later, after we've melded and melted together again, and then eventually fallen into a deep sleep.

Now the light is flooding in through the large windows in his bedroom, which are only covered by white sheers.

"What time is it?" I ask, feeling groggy and thick in the head. My body feels sore, like I've had a good workout, which I guess isn't far from the truth.

"Early, sorry, I have some stuff to do this morning."

I peek at my watch. It's 7:45. "Is this your usual hour for waking up on the weekend after a night of drinking and sex?"

He laughs. I like the way the skin crinkles around his eyes. "I only had two drinks."

"Two plus one today."

"Right. I forgot."

"I wasn't counting."

"It's fine if you were. I'm the one with the silly rule."

"Not very rock and roll of you."

He kisses the bridge of my nose. "And that's the point."

I open my eyes past the slits I've been peering out of. Ben is rumpled in a good way, his hair sticking up a bit, his stubble thicker than usual. I didn't get much chance to examine him naked last night, but now I can admire his lean torso, muscles like a swimmer has—long and stretched out—and the freckles across his shoulders.

"You checking me out?"

I look up. His eyes are dancing.

"That a problem?"

"Not at all. I only wish I had more time to linger."

"I can get ready in ten."

"No, no. You stay."

"Here?"

"I'll be back in a couple of hours. I'll bring breakfast. Sound good?"

I glance around his room. It's spartan, with only a few band posters on the white walls, a dresser I recognize from Ikea, his closet door closed.

"You can go back to sleep or spend your time snooping. Up to you?"

I take a swat at him. "I wasn't going to snoop."

"'Course you were. I would too."

"Okay, forewarned."

He leans in and kisses me. "Why don't you try to go back to sleep? I'll be back before you know it."

He stands and I lean back against the pillows. His bed is comfortable, the pillows the right firmness for sleeping. The sheets are good too. I try not to think too hard about what that means; if it's because they were picked by Rachel and he got them in the breakup.

I pull the sheets up over my eyes as I listen to him in the bathroom. I'm still tired and a bit hungover—sexed-over—and I could use some more sleep. I start to count down from ten slowly, Ben's movements a background noise.

And whether it's the lack of sleep or the lingering alcohol or our hours of exertion, it works. I fall easily back to sleep and don't even notice when he's gone.

I'm awoken two hours later by the insistent sound of texts coming from my phone. Or someone's phone. Mine probably. It stops then starts again, the angry double pinging of a series of texts. I stand up and riffle through my things until I find my purse and my phone.

I have multiple messages from Kit.

How was your date?

Hello, are you dead?

Are you headless in Jack's freezer?

This isn't funny. I'm getting worried now.

If you don't text me back in ten minutes, I'm calling Jack.

That was the last text, a few minutes ago. I also have two missed calls from her.

I call her, standing there in my underwear in Ben's room while I search for a T-shirt.

"You're alive," she says.

"What the hell, Kit? I can't go silent for a couple of hours?"

"Normally, yes, but then I saw your phone was in a location I didn't recognize."

"I told you to turn that off."

"I worry about you."

"I'm a big girl."

"Big enough for sleepovers, anyway." She giggles. "How was it?"

I locate a T-shirt of Ben's in the top drawer. I slip it on, breathing in his scent.

"It was good."

"So, Jack lives in Brooklyn?"

"Um, what?"

"Jack. You're at Jack's?"

"No. I'm at Ben's."

"Whoa. I did not see that coming."

"Yeah, me neither." I fill her in on what happened. How Jack canceled and I went to the concert and there Ben was. "Like fate, or something."

"I thought we agreed that fate was a dumbass."

"But we kept getting thrown back together. That has to mean something."

"It means that Theo's theory about New York is right. The Venn diagram. Remember?"

"I don't want to reduce my love life to math."

"You're in love now?"

"It's an expression."

"What about his mother?" Kit says. "What about what he said about not being able to be in a relationship?"

"I shouldn't have told you that."

"Well, you did."

"I guess it doesn't matter now. He changed his mind."

"Did he *say* that?"

I think back to last night. Our conversations are fuzzy, like there's a filter over them. "Sort of?"

I can almost hear her crossing her arms. "I see."

"It'll work out."

"Will it?"

I suddenly feel like I'm on the edge of tears. "Why are you trying to ruin this for me?"

"I'm not," she says, modifying her tone. "I'm the voice of reason, remember? That's my role in your life."

"I can make my own decisions."

"You absolutely can."

"I really like this guy. It might not make any sense, but I can't seem to help it."

"Just take care of yourself, okay? Take care of your heart," she says.

"I will. Thank you for caring."

"Always."

I sit down on the edge of the bed. "But wait, why were you calling me? It's early."

"Oh," Kit says. "I, um, have news."

My stomach sinks as I remember what Jack told me yesterday, that Kit had been fired. "What is it?"

"I lost my job."

"Oh, Kit. Why didn't you start with that?"

"It doesn't matter."

"Of course it does! Are you going to be okay?"

"They gave me a couple of months of severance. I have time to find something else."

"Was it that guy? That jerky boss?"

"I don't know. They let a bunch of people go. It doesn't have to be about me and him."

"You should negotiate for more."

"I want to move on."

"Okay, I understand," I say. "What can I do to help?"

"Could you take over the organization of the engagement party next week? I don't have the energy to deal with it."

"Of course."

"You can bring Ben if you want."

"We'll see. I'll talk with him when he gets back. See where his head is at."

"Where did he go?"

"He said he had some errands to do." I hear a key in the lock. "Wait, he's coming in now."

"Okay, I'll let you go."

"Let's do something later, okay? Dinner?"

"Yes, I'd like that."

I hear the front door swing open. "Got to go. Love you."

"Love you more."

I smile as I put the phone down, anticipating seeing Ben again even if we maybe have a difficult conversation in front of us. But the footsteps walking across his living room sound too light to be Ben, and I stand there frozen with a premonition of who's about to open the bedroom door, unable to do anything but wish I wasn't only in one of his T-shirts.

The door opens in slow motion and then, there she is.

Rachel, standing in a perfect summer dress, holding a set of keys on her finger. Her mouth sets as she sees me.

"Well, well, well. What do we have here?"

I've never been in a catfight, and I'm not saying that this is what's about to happen, but it kind of feels like it might.

"Hi, Rachel," I say.

"'Hi, Rachel?'"

"Isn't that your name?"

"You know damn well it is, *Chloe*. What are you doing here?"

"Um, looking for my pants."

I turn my back on her and search the room. I see the dress I was wearing last night in the corner. Right. Shit. I was wearing a dress.

Which means I can't just pull on a pair of pants and get the hell out of here.

"Is this a joke?" Rachel says.

"I wish."

"What's that mean?"

"Maybe this isn't top of mind for you, but this is pretty embarrassing for me right now."

"You *should* be embarrassed."

"Hold that thought."

"What?"

I grab my dress. "I'm going to put this on. And I don't feel like doing it in front of you. So, give me a minute, all right?"

I don't give her a chance to say no, just push past her to the bathroom. I take off Ben's T-shirt and look longingly at the shower. I'd give anything to take one, but making her wait for me seems excessive.

Instead, I give myself a quick sponge bath and put on last night's dress. Then I wash my face and do my best to make my hair look normal and not like sex hair, but who am I kidding?

She knows what happened.

I open the door to the bathroom. She's right outside, tapping her foot in impatience.

"Took you long enough."

"I get this might be awkward, but I don't get the hostility."

"You slept with my boyfriend!"

Wait, what? No, no, hold up. They're broken up. Ben told me, and Ben's sister told me, so it's true.

"You broke up."

She rolls her eyes. "That's a technicality. We're always doing that."

"Then he's not your boyfriend."

"We're still together all the time. His mom doesn't even know."

"Because she's dying."

"Because he knows we're meant to be together. We've been together since we were seventeen. Didn't he tell you that?"

No, he did not.

"He didn't, did he? Well, we have. Ever since high school. And yeah, maybe we've broken up once in a while, but it never lasts. *We* last. I'm the *one*." She taps herself in the chest. "You're a distraction."

I feel sick. From the drinks, from her words, from the ring of truth that I can't escape.

Their history.

Those keys she has dangling from her finger. His keys.

If you break up, you get back the keys. You delete your pictures off Facebook. You don't hang out all the time.

"Why are you here?" I ask her.

"Ben texted me last night. I only saw it this morning, and when he didn't answer me back, I thought I'd come over."

Ben texted her *last night*.

Oh no. Oh shit.

I'm going to puke. "Excuse me." I pivot and slam the door and make it to the bowl just in time. I fall to my knees as tears slide down my cheeks. Two hours ago I was happy. And now this is the worst day of my life.

Can it get any more humiliating than this?

I hope I never find out.

I flush the toilet, then splash water on my face.

"Chloe? Are you all right?"

"Go away, Rachel."

"I'm sorry, okay? I wasn't trying to make you— Please open the door."

I dry my face off with a towel and don't even bother looking in the mirror. I open the door and walk past Rachel.

"Chloe, hold on a sec?"

Where is my purse? Right, in the bedroom. I walk down the short hall and find it where I left it. Kit's sent me another text and it almost breaks me.

I'm happy for you, I promise!

I shove my phone in my purse and turn to leave. Rachel's there again. "Will you stop following me?"

"I want to make sure you're all right."

"Sure, right. Whatever. I hope you'll be very happy together."

I wait for her to move out of the way, and, eventually, she does. I get to the front door and wrench it open, and run smack into Ben.

"Hey, whoa. What—"

I put my hands on his chest and shove him away, then bolt for the stairs because there's no way I'm waiting for the elevator.

"Chloe, wait!"

But I don't wait. I just leave.

Chapter Twenty-one

"Chloe! Hold up, please."

I'm twenty feet from Ben's front door, and all I want to do is break into a run. But the street is crowded and Ben could catch me anyway, so I stop.

"What, Ben?"

"Can we please talk about this?"

I can barely catch my breath. "What's there to talk about?"

"Hey," he says, taking hold of my hand. "Hey."

I want to pull away but it's hard to do it when he's looking at me with soft eyes and a contrite expression.

I am an idiot for this man.

"What's going on, Ben? Why was Rachel there?"

He ducks his head. "I don't know why Rachel came over."

"She said you texted her last night."

"I . . . yes, okay, I did do that."

I pull my hand away.

"Not like that. It was before we met at the bar."

"That's supposed to make it better? She didn't text you back and I'm the second choice?" I swallow hard. "You asked to see her?"

"No, I . . . yes, I did."

"Which is it, Ben?"

He stands still for a moment. The crowd swirls around us, people annoyed that we're taking up space on the street.

"My mom was asking about her yesterday. She hasn't seen Rachel in a couple of weeks because I told Rachel that we needed to stop having her around my mom so much."

"When did you tell her this?"

"After I saw you at the bagel shop."

"Weren't you visiting your mom *with* her that day?"

"Yes, but that was the last time."

I can't stand this, having to pull this story from him piece by piece.

"You have to tell me everything, Ben, if you want something with me. There have been too many secrets."

"I know."

"But maybe you don't want something with me and last night was just a thing and that's okay. You know, bygones or whatever." I hold my breath.

"No, that's not what I want."

"What changed?"

"What do you mean?"

"You said you weren't ready for a relationship. That you couldn't be with me because of your mom. And I assume that hasn't changed. So, if last night was something because you were drinking, a moment of weakness, or whatever, I get it, okay?"

I get it because I was weak too. When I saw him at the bar I should've turned and run. I should run away right now but my feet are rooted to the spot.

"I don't want that."

"What, then?"

"Can we go back to my apartment and talk?"

"Is Rachel still there?"

"No, she left. And I took the keys. I'd asked her for them before, and that's what I texted her about yesterday. She doesn't have keys anymore."

"But that's where you lived with her?"

"Yes."

Ugh, I knew it about the sheets. They were way too nice for a guy to pick out.

"Can we talk," Ben says. "Please?"

"Can we go somewhere else? Somewhere where you never went with her?"

"Okay, yes. Let me think for a minute."

Oh god, this whole city is tainted. They've been together so long that there's nowhere we can go without it holding some memory of her.

"Forget it."

"What? No. Come on, follow me." He takes my hand and leads me down a side street.

"Where are we going?"

"Just up here."

Half a block up the street, there's a set of stairs going down to a diner.

"Here?"

"Yes."

"This must be your breakfast place with Rachel. It's so close to your apartment."

"No, it's not."

"How?"

"She wouldn't ever come here. It was my place."

"Promise she's never been here?"

"She popped her head in the door one time and that was it."

We walk down the stairs. It's a kind of speakeasy diner, one that must've been around New York for a long time. Old photos on the walls with a man in a white apron shaking hands with celebrities, a white Formica counter with red puffy bar stools, booths with little jukeboxes in them.

"I love it," I say and Ben gives me a broad grin.

"Right?"

"Hi, Ben," a waitress in her fifties says. "Who's this?"

"This is Chloe. Chloe, this is Miranda."

"Hi, Miranda."

"Usual table?" She points to an empty booth in the back. "I'll bring you menus in a minute."

We walk to the booth and sit across from one another. I fiddle with my fork nervously, then turn to the jukebox while Miranda fills our coffee cups and puts down two menus. My brain feels full—of emotions, and thoughts, and Ben. I can't concentrate on the music selections. I don't even know what I'm doing. Picking a soundtrack for our last conversation?

"There's nothing past 1985 in there," Ben says.

"Perfect." I flip through the songs, names flashing by. WHAM! Tina Turner. Phil Collins.

"Chloe? Will you look at me?"

He's nervous, too, I can tell, and part of me doesn't want to be having this conversation. There seems like too much to overcome. But I said I'd listen, so I will.

"Tell me from the beginning."

"What do you know?"

"Forget what Rachel said. I want to hear your side."

"Rachel and I met in high school, and we were kind of that couple. You know, the one everyone always thought should be dating?"

I know exactly what he means. In my high school, their names were Sam and Alice. Kit and I used to make fun of them, but, really, we were jealous. I still am. I've never been with anyone who made perfect sense on the outside. Or the inside either.

"At some point, we started dating. Even then, we'd get into fights. She thought I was a bit of a dork, but we had the same group of friends and we sort of fit in other ways. We broke up a bunch of times, and when it was time for college, I wanted to break up for good."

"But?"

"But she was accepted to the University of Vermont like me and we ended up there together. And, this sounds terrible, but it was easier to be together. We didn't know anyone else, and so we were hanging out and we fell into old patterns."

"The breakups too?"

"Yeah, those too. But somehow we'd always make up. Then we came back to the city after graduation and it made sense to move in together. It's hard to explain, but it felt like my life was on this track, and I couldn't get off."

"You never dated other people?"

"We did. In college we were broken up for most of junior year, and I had a girlfriend and she dated someone too. But . . . anyway, when our first lease was up, I moved out for a while. I got my own place, the place I'm in now, and we were apart for another year."

"I don't need to hear about the other girls."

"Right. Anyway, my mom got sicker and Rachel was there. She's always been great with my mom, and then, before I knew it, we were back together."

"Ben, come on. 'Before you knew it'?"

"The truth is, it was easier than being apart."

"You loved her."

"I did. She's part of my family, but this last time, I realized that it wasn't like that anymore. Not *love*, love, you know?"

I nod slowly because I do know, but also the thought of him loving someone else makes me feel sick. How *long* he loved her.

He runs his hands through his hair. "I was trying to figure out what to do. End it or not. Seemed like we'd been together so long everyone was expecting us to get married. Like, people were talking about it like it was something we'd already done, or we were already engaged."

"You were scared."

"I was scared of waking up married to someone I wasn't in love with, yeah. For sure."

"You broke it off."

"I did. And it was final this time. I told her that. No getting back together. We had to move on. Both of us."

"But she still had your key."

"She wouldn't give it back. I didn't press it because it didn't seem to matter. I wasn't seeing anyone."

"And you still hung out all the time."

"It's hard to untangle your life from someone after all those years. I don't hate her. She doesn't hate me. We didn't work."

"Did she agree with that?"

"I thought she did."

"She was coming over this morning to return your keys and she found me there in my underwear."

"Is that what happened?"

I blush at the thought of it. "It is."

The waitress arrives to take our orders, but I haven't given any thought to it or even looked at the menu.

"Only coffee for me, please."

"What?" Ben says. "No, you have to get the full ticket here, it's the best."

"What's the full ticket?"

"One of everything."

That does sound good. "Okay, bring it."

Ben asks for the same thing. She fills our coffee cups and leaves.

"That's the story," Ben says. "Are we okay?"

I clear my throat. "Is there a we?"

"I hope so."

"And what about everything before?" I say with Kit's warning in my ears. "What about you not being ready and having family obligations and everything?"

"That's all still true."

My heart squeezes. "What am I doing here, then?"

"I want to try anyway."

"Why?"

"Because I haven't been able to stop thinking about you since we met. Me sitting down like that? That wasn't something I'd normally do. Normal Ben would've corrected your mistake, collected his to-go coffee, and bolted. Normal Ben would've walked in the other direction when he saw you at the Met."

"You weren't acting like yourself?"

"I was drawn to you from the beginning. And after that day, I wanted to find you, but I couldn't. And then there you were again, looking for me through BookBox, and that scared me. It scared me because I wanted to see you so badly I knew I was going to screw it up."

"That doesn't make any sense."

"If you're me, it does. I stayed with someone I wasn't in love with for years because that was the easier thing to do, Chloe. Change is hard for me. Taking a risk is hard for me. Especially now with everything going on with my mom."

"What changed?"

"You kept showing up."

"Like the universe was putting us together?"

"Like it was reminding me that I was a dumbass and I had this great opportunity I was turning away from. That I had a chance to be happy and I didn't want to take it because what would happen if I did?"

"What?"

"I could get hurt."

Our eyes meet and it's like last night. In this downstairs diner, with the clatter of the morning all around us. All those things I've read about—my heart fluttering, my body tingling—it all happens right then and there, and I haven't felt this before. I loved Christian, and he broke my heart, but it was never like this, even when we were at our best.

It's hard to look away but I do. "The thing is, you *have* hurt me."

"I'm sorry about Rachel this morning."

"It's not just that. It's all the times you turned away. That you're scared at all."

"Aren't you?"

"Honestly, I wasn't."

"And now?"

"Now I am."

Ben laughs. "Welcome to my boat."

I shudder. "You know how I feel about boats."

"Ah, Chloe, I'm sorry."

"It's fine. Truly. It's . . . what do you want from me?"

"To date. For today not to be our last breakfast. I want to do all the things."

"Eat all the things."

"That too."

"You're not going to run away from me again?"

"That is not the plan."

"But you can't guarantee it."

"How could I? But I don't want to, Chloe. I like you a waffle lot."

I burst out laughing. "You're using the punny breakfast place against me?"

"I'll take what I can get."

"That was your choice of restaurant."

"It wasn't."

Ugh, right. It was Jack's. Jack. Shit. What am I going to tell him?

"Can we try?"

Can we? After everything that's happened? With all the obstacles in our way? Can I believe in us enough to take the chance?

"Chloe?"

"I'm thinking about how I can trust this."

"Is there something I can do to help?"

I tap the side of my face. "I have an idea."

"What is it?"

"It's not a what. It's a who."

Chapter Twenty-two

"So," Kit says an hour later in her apartment, "who wants to start?"

She looks at me and then at Theo. He shrugs, uncertain about participating in this, a kind of Bro Code thing, I imagine. I can already tell he and Ben are going to get along. If Ben survives the next hour, that is.

"It will be more effective if you do it," I say to Kit. "I've got too much at stake here to make rational decisions, and Theo's a softie."

"That's true," Theo says.

"Fine, though I'm not happy about this."

"Why not? I thought this was your dream assignment."

"Ha, ha. Okay, yes, fine, it is. But still. Where should I start?"

"Do I get a say?" Ben says from the other side of the table. His phone was blowing up with texts from Rachel on the way over here. After checking with me, he told her he'd call her tomorrow, then set his notifications to Do Not Disturb for everyone but his family.

"No," Kit and I say together.

"All right, then." He sits back in his chair and takes a piece of pizza from the box on the table. We'd ordered it soon after we arrived, but my stomach was in knots from the stress of this morning, and Kit and Theo hadn't made much of a dent either.

Only Ben had felt fine eating half the box. Did that mean he was cool as a cucumber? Certain about how this was going to go?

Then again, maybe he was nervous too. He'd agreed, after all, to my plan—come to Kit and Theo's and let Kit decide if I should forgive him—without too much protest. But on the way over here, he'd asked a lot of questions.

Who was Kit, exactly, and why was I giving her this much power over my life? Shouldn't I be the one to decide if we should be together? I'd pushed those questions off and texted to Kit that we were coming. Unlike Ben, she knew me well enough to understand why I needed her input.

"Start, Kit," Theo says. "You know you want to."

I smile at him. He really is perfect for her.

"Okay, fine." She looks at Ben. "You'll answer anything I ask?"

He takes a bite of the pepperoni pizza. "Within reason."

"Hmmm. Limits, okay, noted."

"What does that mean?"

"One point against you, dude," Theo says.

"There are points?"

"Of course there are," Kit says, taking the notebook we use to note our UNO scores off the table. She flips to an empty page and writes his name across the top. Then she draws a line down the middle. And then she writes the name JACK on top of the other column.

"Wait, wait, wait," I say. "This isn't about him."

"You said I get to decide the rules."

"I'm not dating Jack no matter what happens."

219

"We'll see." Kit puts a minus one in Ben's column. "That's for the limits. I'm taking off five more points for the whole original date thing. Agreed?"

"Should I answer?" Ben says.

"Careful," Theo says. "Sarcasm might get you another deduction."

"Totally." Kit puts another -5 in his column. His total now stands at -11.

"I'm competing against Jack?"

"No, you're competing *for* Chloe."

Ben looks at me and I try to keep a straight face. I'm not going to go by these results, obviously, but I am hella curious about his answers.

"Go ahead."

"Scared?"

"Bring it."

I watch their exchange with some satisfaction. The fact that Ben agreed to come here works in his favor. That he's also letting Kit walk all over him makes him that much more appealing, to be honest.

"He should get five points for agreeing to do this," I say.

"All right," Kit says, tapping the pen against her chin after she puts a +5 in his column. "Where did you grow up?"

"Manhattan."

"More precisely?"

"On the Upper East Side." He names a street that I don't know, but Kit seems satisfied.

"School?"

"Public."

"Grade point average?"

"Kit," I say.

"You said I could ask the questions."

"He's not applying for a job."

"Yes, he is."

"I don't mind, Chloe," Ben says. "I had a three point five in high school. My best subjects were history and music."

"Sports?"

"Baseball and tennis."

"Country club?"

"Local courts."

"What instrument?"

"Piano since I was five. Then guitar, trumpet, drums . . ."

"Impressive."

"Let's give him plus five for piano," I say. "That shows dedication."

"Fine," Kit says. Now Ben's at a respectable -1. "University?"

"UVM."

"Major?"

"Music with a minor in teaching."

Kit marks something down on the paper. It looks like a +2. That must be for the teaching. She has a soft spot for people who are willing to work with kids. At least he's in the black now, if only slightly.

"GPA?"

"Four point oh that time."

"Oh?"

His mouth twists. "I found my calling."

"Being in a band?"

"I wish. I tried that, but I realized pretty quickly that my talents were in discovering others, not being the frontman."

"Can't sing?"

"I can. I had some pretty crippling stage fright, though, and I don't have the it factor."

"What's that?"

"You know—that thing that makes you not want to take your

eyes off the person on the stage? That magnetism all lead singers have. I didn't have it."

Kit taps her pen again, then puts down -1.

"I get a minus for that?"

"You think Chloe should be with someone who doesn't have the it factor?"

"I . . . okay, I get it. But there are positives too."

"Such as?"

"Lead singers make terrible boyfriends. Trust me."

"I can see that."

"And as the business guy, I have a much more stable life. I can keep office hours, for the most part."

"Plus the two-drink thing," I add, and Ben gives me a grateful look.

"What's that?"

Ben explains his two-drink rule. Kit approves; she loves when people impose arbitrary restrictions on themselves. She adds +1 to his column.

"What do you do for employment?"

"I own a record label."

"Indie?"

"Yes."

"Do you plan to scale it up?"

"That's the plan," Ben says, leaning back on the couch. "But I never want to be too large. I like being able to give individual attention to my bands. I take a boutique approach."

"Like a clothing store?"

"Like a small business. One that's curated. That way I can keep control of quality and protect my bands."

"And if they make it big?"

"Then we succeed together."

"And if they tank?"

"I'm there for them then too."

"Hmmm." Kit writes something down. It looks like *shady music business* followed by a -5 and now he's in the red again.

"Hey," I say. "That's not fair."

"I thought I was getting or losing points?" Ben says. "Not getting commentary."

"You want me to put down an additional minus one?"

"No, I—"

Kit taps her pen against the page.

"Tell her about your mother," I say.

"She has MS."

"And she's in the hospital?"

"She's in palliative care, now, unfortunately."

"I'm sorry, Ben," Kit says, her voice finally softening.

"How is it manifesting?" Theo asks. He's an animal doctor, but he has more knowledge than your average person.

"It's her breathing that's mainly the issue now." Ben explains some of the technical issues of her MS as Theo nods and asks gentle questions.

"Give him a plus five," Theo says.

"Why?"

"Because he's dealing with a lot. MS is brutal on everyone."

"And he's good with his nephew, Tyler," I add. "He's on the spectrum. Ben should get plus five for that too."

Kit writes down the points. Ben is finally very much in the black.

"What about this Rachel woman?"

Uh-oh.

"That's over."

Kit narrows her eyes at him. "She knows this?"

"I can show you the texts if you'd like."

"You broke up with her in a text?"

I stop Kit from writing -100. "Kit, let him explain."

Ben is almost laughing, but I give him a warning shake of the head and he buries it.

"No, of course not. She's had a bit of trouble adjusting to the new reality between us and I've explained it to her a couple of times in person and a couple of times over text. I'm better at expressing myself that way, sometimes."

"Kind of invasive to show us that, though." Kit writes down -10. "Kit!"

"It's all right, Chloe," Ben says. "Kit's right. I shouldn't show anyone the texts. What happened with Rachel and I should stay that way, between us. But it *is* in the past. Whether Rachel wants it to be or not. I knew that the minute I met Chloe."

I feel a lump form in my throat and Kit puts her pen down.

"Well played, my friend," Theo says.

"How's that?"

"Romance. Kit's always been a sucker for it."

Kit's blushing. "Chloe's the one who works in romance."

"No, rom-com."

"What's the difference?" Theo asks.

"The comedy, for one."

"Plus there's always a breakup, right?" Kit says. "I don't like that."

A chill goes through me like I've been caught in a draft.

Kit's right. Almost all the books I've read have that moment after the couple gets together for the first time. Something comes between them and pulls them apart. And even though you know they'll make it back together in the end, there are fifty to a hundred pages of despair that the main character has to go through first.

They usually learn something about themselves, though. Some truth they've been hiding.

But I shouldn't be thinking about this.

Ben and I haven't even made it to dating yet. I don't need to think about the obstacles ahead.

They'll be here soon enough.

"Do I pass?" Ben asks.

"I'll have to tally the points."

"Kit, come on, let the poor boy off the hook," Theo says. "He's suffered enough."

"Has he, though?"

"Yes," Theo says.

Ben looks at me. His eyes are soft and it feels like I don't have to speak. I don't have to tell him that I've decided it's a yes, whatever the combination of pluses and minuses is on the paper.

"I passed?" Ben says.

"Yes, you passed," I say.

"That's excellent news."

I smile at him, and in an instant, he's next to me and taking my face in his hands. He kisses me, taking me by surprise, but not in a bad way. We break apart, and Kit and Theo are watching us. Theo looks happy for us, but Kit seems a bit wary.

"What was that for?" I say.

"To seal the deal. And express my enthusiasm."

"Consider it expressed."

"Good," he says, his hands dropping to my shoulders. He's looking directly into my eyes and it's like there's no one else in the room. "I didn't want you to have any doubts about it."

"I don't," I say, but something is tingling at the back of my brain. Some feeling I can't get rid of.

And then I remember.

I have to break up with Jack.

Chapter Twenty-three

"I wanted to thank you for the tickets," I say to Jack that night on the phone. I'm at my place, sitting on the couch.

After Ben and I left Kit and Theo's, we went back to my apartment. We spent a couple of hours lounging on my couch. Okay, we were making out. But when Ben's stomach started to rumble (despite all the pizza) I sent him out for takeout. I had a call to make and I wanted to do it alone.

"You enjoyed the show?" Jack's voice is tired, maybe even a bit low. He's been at work since yesterday he told me, going home only briefly to shower and change. Apparently, his company takes security a little too seriously and insists that all access to company email and servers be terminated immediately. An easy task when it's one person being let go. Arduous when it's over a hundred.

I feel like a shit for adding this news to his burdens, but I don't have a choice.

"I did enjoy it, thank you. But also—" I shift uncomfortably. I don't know why this is so difficult. I have zero feelings for Jack, and it's not like we ever really dated. I need to bite the bullet and get this out. "I don't think we should see each other again."

"Oh, I . . . is it because of last night?"

I feel panicky. "Um, it's not that. I don't feel that way about you. I'm sorry."

He sighs. "Does this have anything to do with Ben?"

"Yes."

"Even if you can't be together?"

I believe in honesty, but I don't think I should tell him that we *can* be together. Or probably I should, but I don't feel like it. I have a feeling that Jack won't be too supportive given some of the things he's said in the past. I have enough questions at the back of my own mind; I don't need to hear someone else's.

"I don't think we should be talking about this. I'm sorry."

"It's all right. But I do like you, Chloe. I like you a lot."

"I like you, too, Jack."

"Maybe another time?"

It would be easy to agree to this, to let him hang there, hoping that something might happen. But that would be cruel. Because even if there was no Ben, I wouldn't be attracted to Jack.

"I don't think so. But I hope you find someone."

"You too."

"Thank you. Do you want me to reimburse you for the tickets?"

"No, those were for you. For us."

I feel a stab of guilt. *Us.* It's a figure of speech, but I have to wonder: Did I cheat on Jack? Am I like Christian?

I didn't cheat on Jack technically, like Christian claimed he never did anything physical with the other woman before we broke up. But he was emotionally involved in her and I was too. I was supposed to be on a date with him and instead, I ended up going home with Ben.

Am I a terrible person?

Maybe I'll figure that out eventually. In the meantime, I need to end this conversation.

"Take care of yourself. See you around."

"See you next week," Jack says. "At the engagement party? Kit invited me."

"Oh right." Shit, I still have to find a venue for that. Kit's going to kill me. "See you then, I guess. Bye."

I hang up as I hear a key in my lock. I gave Ben my keys so it would be easier for him to get in and out. But now I'm regretting that. I could've used a moment between the conversation with Jack and Ben coming back.

He walks in with two bags in his hand. It smells delicious, like the meal he served me in the park. His hair is a bit wet—it's been raining off and on all day, the sky alternating between sun and dark clouds in a way that seems to track what I'm going through too.

"You look grim," he says.

"I just finished talking to Jack." I wave my phone, then throw it down.

"That go okay?"

"Sure."

He puts the bags on the table. "You want to talk about it?"

"Not really." I stand. "What you got in there?" I try to reach into one of the bags but Ben stops me.

He places his hands on my shoulders and makes eye contact. I melt in his gaze, but the conversation with Jack lingers like the clouds outside.

"Hey," Ben says. "We don't have to pretend."

"I want to, though."

He gives me a quick kiss. "I've got all the good things." He starts to remove take-out boxes out of the bags and line them up on the table. "Shrimp toast, Peking duck, mixed vegetables—"

"Vegetables?"

"I thought something green might be a good idea. What do you want to start with?"

"One of everything, obvi." I go into the kitchen and pull out some plates and serving things, then bring them back to the table. "Bring on the empty calories."

"Yes, ma'am."

He starts to dish up the food. The smells are overwhelming. I didn't eat much at Kit's, too nervous about that stupid quiz.

I recognize it now for what it was—an attempt to put off the decision. But why did I want to do that? I've wanted to be with Ben since I met him. Look at all of the effort I went to be with him. Why chicken out now?

I didn't even ask Jack for his opinion, but it's in my head anyway.

"I suggest starting with the shrimp toast and then moving to the duck," Ben says.

"Any reason?"

He lifts his shoulder. "I've tried all the combinations and this one is the best."

"And the vegetables?"

"Think of them as palate cleansers."

"Like sorbet?"

"Exactly," he says, handing me a plate full of food. "Only much healthier than ice cream."

"There's no ice cream for dessert?"

He smiles suggestively. "You can have whatever you want for dessert."

A shiver of desire goes through me, and I flash back to the things he was doing with his hands on the couch earlier.

Oh right, that's why I'm with him. Because I can't get enough.

"Good to know." I pull the plate to me and do as he suggests, putting a piece of shrimp toast in my mouth. It's as good as the one from the park, maybe better.

"Well?"

"Hold on." I pick up a piece of the duck with my chopsticks. The skin is burnished and crispy and it crackles in my mouth. Where has this food been all my life? "You're a genius," I say.

"Right?"

"Thank you for getting this."

He touches my hand, letting it linger. "Of course. Happy to. And I know you don't want to talk about it, but you can."

"You're not jealous of another man?"

"I'm superjealous. But I'm trying to be supportive."

"I like that. You being jealous."

"Oh?"

I pick up a piece of broccoli. "Who doesn't like a jealous man?"

"It's a fine line between jealousy and stalker."

"I'm the one who stalked you, though."

He smirks. "Is it weird if I say that I'm happy you did?"

"Probably."

"I am glad."

"Me too."

"Good." He eats a couple of pieces of shrimp toast. "You think Kit is going to get behind this?"

"She's fine. But that reminds me: I have a favor to ask you. Any chance you know of a venue for Kit's engagement party?"

"When is it?"

"Next Friday."

He makes a surprised face.

"She got overwhelmed with work stuff and asked me at the last minute to take over from her."

"How many people?"

"Fifty."

"Hmmm."

I eat the broccoli then cycle back through the shrimp toast and duck. It is the perfect combination. "Where did you get this?"

"Kam Fung."

"Where is that?"

"Three blocks from here?"

"This has been within three blocks of me for a year and I didn't know?"

"New Yorker knowledge."

"Yeah, yeah."

"It's not the best in town," Ben says, "but it's pretty good."

"Pretty good? I'd have sex with this," I say. "If you weren't around."

"Don't let me stop you."

"How about shrimp toast, then sex?"

"Sounds like a plan."

He grabs us a couple of beers from the fridge and we spend a few minutes in companionable silence, eating our way through the order.

It's funny because when it was silent like this with Jack all I could think about was what was I going to ask him next, but I don't feel that way now. It feels easy. Set. Like it's something that's been in place for a long time. I got to that place with Christian, but it took a long time and it always felt fleeting.

"How do you feel about tzatziki?" I ask Ben when we're finished. My stomach is distended in a good way, but I may need a few minutes to digest before anything sexual happens.

"What?"

"The Greek condiment?"

"Why are you asking?"

"Call it part of the test."

"I thought I passed that test."

"You did, but it's still important."

He shakes his head. "For the record, I love it."

"Excellent."

"And I have an idea."

"What?"

"Why don't you have the party at my place."

"Your apartment?"

"No, my studio. It's a fun place for parties and there's the coffee shop downstairs that does catering too. And of course, the music is awesome."

"Really?"

"Why not?"

"You want to come to Kit's engagement party with me? Isn't that a little serious for the first week of dating?"

"That is what we're doing here, right? We're being serious."

My heart picks up the pace. "We said that, but it's only been a day, and—"

He holds up his hand. "And nothing on my side. I'm all in over here."

And now he looks nervous, like he thinks I might not be all in as well.

And maybe it's his fear, but suddenly, the doubts I've been feeling since the conversation with Jack have disappeared. Here he is, this man I've been searching for, feeding me excellent Chinese food in my kitchen, and offering to host Kit's engagement party at his studio.

I stand slowly and walk around the table. Then I plop down into his lap. His arms snake around my waist, and he buries his face in my shoulder.

"Thank you, Ben."

"For what?"

"For all of it. That venue would be perfect. You're perfect."

"Far from it."

"I'm not perfect either. But I'm in this too. I want this to work."

"Good."

"And you want to come to an engagement party?"

"Why not?"

"It's stupid."

He tilts his head up, looking into my eyes. "No, it isn't."

"It's such a change from a couple of days ago."

"I'm sorry about that. But there's something you should know about me."

"What's that?"

"Why I make up my mind, I stick to it."

I rest my forehead against his. "Doesn't that contradict what you just said?"

"How so?"

"You'd made up your mind not to date me. Then you changed it."

He puts his hands on my waist. "My mind wasn't made up. I was trying to make it up. I was telling myself it was, but it wasn't."

"Why not?"

"Because my heart wasn't in it."

"Where was your heart?"

He touches my clavicle, above my own heart. "I think you know."

I reach down and kiss him. We both taste like dinner, and I'm not full anymore. I'm hungry for it, hungry for him. His hands run up my back and pull me closer. Our tongues meet and mix and twist together and I can feel him harden under me.

"New plan," I say, breaking away.

"Oh?"

"Sex then more dinner."

"Is this a test?"

"No, it's a request."

"Then, yes," Ben says. "Yes."

Chapter Twenty-four

Ben stayed over at my place last night without any drama. He even *asked* me if he could stay over. Like there was a chance that when we were postcoital and tangled up together in my bed that I might want him to go.

No, obvi.

He smiled and pulled me close and we fell asleep like that, and now he's in my bed looking crumpled and adorable and there is zero chance that his ex-girlfriend can walk in on us.

Big win.

She can keep texting him, though. He only placed her on Do Not Disturb. He didn't block her entirely. When he checked his phone last night he frowned, then told me she'd texted a bunch of times. He didn't tell me what she said, just the volume. I didn't know if five texts were a little or a lot for Rachel, and I didn't want to know. He said he'd take care of it, and put his phone away.

"Any plans for the day?" I ask Ben, snuggling into his arms.

"I'm supposed to hang out with Tyler," Ben says.

I feel a flutter of disappointment. "Oh, okay."

"You don't want to come?"

He wants me to come! Phew.

"No, I do."

He smiles. "Good. He liked you."

"He's sweet."

"He is."

"What's on the agenda? More boats?"

He nuzzles his lips into my neck. "I thought I'd take him to the natural history museum."

It's a bit hard to concentrate with him doing that. "You do love your museums."

"Yep. And Tyler loves dinosaurs."

"Just Tyler?"

"Maybe Tyler's uncle does too."

"That's cute."

He kisses a tender spot. It's even harder for me to concentrate, now. Maybe he's hard too.

"Adorkable?" he says.

"That too."

"That's what you called me when we were at the Met."

"Did I?"

"Yep."

"You remember?"

He tilts my chin down so we're looking into each other's eyes. "I remember everything."

I just melted a little. "That's good. Though that part where I went in the lake . . . can you delete that?"

"Why?"

"Because I looked like a bozo."

"You were saving the day."

"Saving our boat."

He laughs. "From that kid!"

"Yeah, Kenny. His dad gave me the photo of you."

"I must thank him."

"I've had enough Kenny and Jim in my life."

We lean in and kiss, our tongues and hands exploring. I could get lost in this, but we should get up and face the day—I don't want to meet Tyler again looking like I've been in bed with Ben all day. And how cute is all this time he spends with his nephew? His whole family really—

I pull away. "Wait, you don't need to visit your mom?"

He frowns and takes a moment to respond. "No, there's an outbreak in the facility and they're isolating people. No visits for a week."

"I'm sorry."

"It's okay. This might sound terrible, but I could use the break."

"I understand."

"I still talk to her every day."

"I'm not judging."

He smiles. "I'm kind of judging myself."

"Why?"

"Because there's going to be some relief when it's over."

My throat feels tight. "That's normal."

"It's horrible."

I bring his chin up like he did to me earlier. "No, Ben. Things like this take a lot of you. A lot out of a family." I swallow. "When my sister died it was like someone took a bite out of us, one that wouldn't heal. And then my parents sort of made this collective decision that we were going to 'move on,' and I hated them for it, but if

I'm being honest, part of me was relieved too. Because living in that grief, missing Sara all the time . . . it was too much."

He kisses the tip of my nose. "How do you do that?"

"What?"

"Make me feel better about the parts of me I'm ashamed of."

"I do?"

"Yeah. I meant what I said yesterday."

"Which part."

"The all-in part."

I start to giggle. "Are you a *Gilmore Girls* fan?"

"No, why?"

"First, it's an amazing show. But second, that's what Luke says to Lorelei when they finally get together."

"Am I supposed to know who those people are?"

I pull away. "Um, yeah."

It's his turn to laugh. "Glad to see your naïveté is still in place."

"You know who Luke and Lorelei are?"

"Doesn't everyone?"

"You've watched *Gilmore Girls*?"

"I have a sister, don't I?"

I shake my head in disgust. "I can't believe I fell for that."

"Never change, Chloe Baker."

"Um, thanks, I guess?"

"It was a compliment, I swear." He leans his forehead against mine. "One more thing."

"Sure."

"I want to introduce you to my mom, but I have to find the right time."

"It's okay."

"No, I want to do it. But she—"

"Thinks you're still dating Rachel."

"Yes. But I'm going to tell her that we've broken up as soon as I can see her again. I promise."

"You don't have to do that for me."

"I want to. I don't know how much time she has left and I want her to know that I'm happy."

"She didn't think you were happy before?"

"She knew Rachel and I had problems. But she's not the kind of mom who tells her kids who to date."

"That's lucky."

"Your mom not like that?"

I shrug. "Mostly, she never noticed. But when she did, she had an opinion."

I remember my last phone call with her, how she'd heard about my search for Ben through a friend. How that's what prompted her to call me—being taken by surprise.

"You're not close?"

"No." I kiss him. "And lucky for you my parents live in Cincy, so you don't have to worry about meeting them any time soon."

"I'm happy to."

"Trust me, you won't be."

He reaches his arms out and pulls me closer. "I'm sorry."

"It's life. Not everyone has a happy family."

"Everyone deserves one, though."

He's right, but I never thought about it like that. I don't think life is about getting what you deserve. Sara didn't deserve what happened to her, and my parents didn't either. Most people don't deserve the pain they receive.

But these thoughts are too dark for this Sunday.

Ben squeezes me tighter. "I have one more thing to suggest."

"I thought we were all done?"

"Just the one, I promise."

"Go for it."

"Let's not talk about anything serious for the rest of the day."

I release the breath I've been holding. Ben *gets* me, he does.

"That sounds like an excellent plan. Can I suggest one of my own?"

"Of course."

"What time do we have to meet Tyler and where?"

"At two at the museum. His moms are dropping him off."

"Excellent. That should give us enough time."

"For what?"

I reach my hands down his back and pull him even closer. "For this."

We make it to the natural history museum with a few minutes to spare, but Tyler's already there, holding the hands of two women. One of them—the one who looks like the female version of Ben—is Kaitlin, and the other must be her wife. She's Black and my height, with a strong build, like she might lift. She has kind eyes, though, and gives me a big smile in greeting.

"Uncle Ben!"

"Hi, buddy."

Tyler's wearing khaki shorts and a blue polo shirt that is almost an exact match to Ben's outfit. "You were almost late. And we're on a schedule."

Ben grins at him. "We're five minutes early."

"You know what my moms say . . ."

"If you're five minutes early—"

"—you're basically late," they all say together.

I laugh. "Hi, Tyler."

He looks up at me. "The ice-cream lady!"

"That's me."

"We're going to the museum, though. Ice cream is for after."

"Sounds like a good plan to me."

"Definitely. It's hot as balls out here."

We all burst out laughing and Kaitlin shakes her head. "Tyler, what have we said about repeating grown-up language?"

"Not to do it. But how am I supposed to know, Mom? You say a lot of things."

"I'll make a list," Kaitlin says.

"I like lists."

I hold my hand out to Kaitlin. "Hi, I'm Chloe."

"I figured. This is my wife, Shantaya."

Shantaya waves at me. "Everyone calls me Taya."

I wave back. "Nice to meet you, Taya."

"You were a big hit with Tyler."

"A bit hit!"

"I'm happy to see him again," I say.

"You like the museum, ice-cream lady?"

"Tyler, this is a bit embarrassing but I've never been."

Tyler covers his mouth in a shocked gesture.

"I know, right? But I only moved to New York last year. There are lots of cool places I haven't been yet."

"That's tragic."

This kid needs a stand-up show. "At least we're fixing one of these today."

"That's true. Plus, you *have* seen the boats, right?"

"Yes, your uncle Ben took me."

He nods slowly. "We need to get going." He reaches out his hand and I take it.

I look back over my shoulder at Ben. He's smiling at us. "I think he prefers you to me."

"He likes pretty girls," Taya says.

"Like Rachel! Rachel is pretty."

Ugh.

"Sorry about that," Kaitlin says.

"It's fine. She is pretty."

"I'll put her name on the list too."

"There's no need, truly."

"Okay. Feel free to hand him off to Ben."

"I will."

"What time should we pick you up?" Taya asks.

"We need two hours in the museum plus time for ice cream," Tyler says.

"How about five?"

"That math adds up."

"Great. Have fun with Uncle Ben and Chloe."

"I will be having lots of fun while you are looking at furniture."

Kaitlin shrugs. "He needs a bigger bed."

"A grown-up bed," Tyler says. "The one I will be taking to college."

"Oh yeah?" I say. "Where are you going to go?"

"That hasn't been determined yet, but I have my eye on Harvard."

"Impressive."

"I'm smart."

"Clearly."

Ben's whole body is shaking with laughter and I feel lighter too. There are obvious downsides, but there's something refreshing about thinking about going through the world with Tyler's frankness. No wondering what anyone is thinking, whether they like you or they don't. No time for ambiguity.

I could use some of that in my life.

"What do you want to see first, Tyler?"

"Dinosaurs, obviously."

"I hear there are lots of them here."

"It has one hundred and fifty-seven taxa!"

I glance at Ben. "Am I supposed to know what that means?"

He shrugs.

"It's different types of dinosaurs!"

"Oh, right, that makes sense."

Tyler tips his head back. "Are you smart?"

"About dinosaurs? No."

"I'll teach you."

"Sounds great."

He tugs on my hand, pulling me toward the entrance. "We'll start with the hadrosaurs. They aren't scary."

"No T. rex?"

"You know T. rex?"

"Doesn't everyone?"

"You said you didn't know dinosaurs."

"I've seen *Jurassic Park*."

"There are lots of errors in those movies!"

"I figured."

We enter the museum, which is all white marble, columns, and high ceilings. There's a massive T. rex skeleton to greet us.

"I thought you said no scary dinosaurs right away?"

He grins at me. "I played a trick on you!"

"You did!"

"Aunt Rachel was scared too."

I try not to grit my teeth. "That is one scary dinosaur."

"Tyler, you don't have to tell Chloe so much about Rachel."

Tyler cocks his head to the side. "Why not?"

"Rachel isn't here but Chloe is. Why don't you ask Chloe some questions about her?"

"I did! I asked her if she liked dinosaurs."

"It's okay, Ben, I don't mind."

Ben doesn't believe me, and I've never had a poker face. But he goes to buy our tickets anyway, and comes back quickly while Tyler and I gaze up at the massive dinosaur. Something in the process used to preserve the bones has turned them a dark onyx, which gives the dinosaur an extra level of menace.

"Imagine meeting one of these in real life."

"Impossible," Tyler says. "We were little rodents then."

"Even scarier."

"We could run away. It was the smaller dinosaurs we had to watch out for." He tugs on my hand. "Come on, this way. I'll show you Aunt Rachel's favorite dinosaur."

I look over my shoulder at Ben. He shrugs and smiles to reassure me.

But there's an edge to this day now. Because even though he says it's over between them, Rachel is still here with us, whether we want her to be or not.

Chapter Twenty-five

"Wait, wait, wait," Jameela says. "You're with *Ben* now?"

I dip my head shyly. It's Monday morning, and I told Jameela that I was at the museum with Ben yesterday because she loves dinosaurs. Maybe not as much as she loves Jonathan Bailey, but it's close. "Yep."

"How did that happen?"

I think back to Friday night, which feels like a million years ago now. "Jack didn't show for our date."

"What? Again?"

"He called this time, but he gave me these tickets to a show we were supposed to go to, and then when I went it was Ben's show."

"Ben's in a band?"

"No, he owns a record label."

"Cool. Not as cool as being in the band, but you know, still cool."

"Right. Anyway, he was there, I was there, one thing led to another and . . ."

Her eyes are big. "You went home with him?"

"I did."

"Wow. I'm impressed."

"You are?"

She raises a shoulder. She's wearing a top in a shade of orange that's her favorite "Kate color." It looks great on her and brings some needed light into this dreary office. "Wouldn't have thought you had it in you, to be honest."

"Had *what* in her?" Addison says, arriving with her bike helmet in hand. Her hair is wet from the rain outside, the droplets clinging to her braids, but the rest of her is dry. She has this awesome rain outfit she wears on rainy days—a bright-yellow pant and jacket combination that goes over whatever she's wearing and keeps the elements out.

"She slept with Ben," Jameela says.

"Ben? Not Jack?"

"Yeah, I—"

Jameela smiles wide. "It was superromantic. They met at a concert. Like it was fate."

Addison scowls. "Cheating is not romantic."

That's a punch to the stomach. But before I can defend myself, Jameela interjects.

"She didn't cheat on Jack. They were barely dating."

"Uh-huh, you think Jack agrees with that?"

"It's not up to him," Jameela says.

Addison puts her bike helmet down on her desk. "Come on. This is exactly like that couple in that show you're obsessed with."

Uh-oh.

"What are you talking about?"

"Kate and what's his name. He was engaged to her sister, right? And they kissed in the wedding chapel?"

"Anthony and Edwina had called the wedding off."

"Please. I watched that shit. He was simping for Kate from the get-go. And that scene in the library? And all that nose bumping and almost kissing, and you're the object of all my desires? They were cheating."

Jameela's so angry you can practically see the steam coming out of her ears. "You're one of them, aren't you? All this time, and I never knew it."

"One of who?"

"A Polin!"

Addison sits in her chair. "Is that supposed to be an insult?"

"Guys?" I put up my hands. "Maybe we should change the topic?"

Addison looks at me. "Back to *your* cheating?"

"It wasn't . . . I'm not proud of it, okay, but I broke things off with Jack. I don't think it was cheating. But it wasn't my finest moment for sure."

"You're dating Ben now?" Addison says.

"Yes."

"What about all that shit with his mom? And doesn't he have some ex hanging around?"

Had I told her that? I've spent so much time thinking about Ben since we met that I don't remember how much of it ended up out loud.

"We talked about that."

"And?"

"It's over." I flash back to Rachel in Ben's apartment. How quickly she'd come to see him when he said he wanted to talk. How they'd been together forever. How am I supposed to compete with that? I can't. I know it deep in my bones despite the amazing weekend we just spent together. What's one weekend against the amount of time they've spent together?

"That's what men *always* say."

"Ben's not like that," I say, trying to keep the uncertainty out of my voice.

"You barely know him."

"He has no reason to lie."

"What did he say exactly?"

I'm feeling shaky, my doubts rising to the surface. "Why are you cross-examining me?"

Addison shakes her hair out. Water flies through the air, catching the overhead light. "Because when I see something I say something."

"And what are you seeing?"

"A girl wrapped up in a fantasy." She picks up a book from her desk and flashes the cover at me. It's called *Splintered Heart*. "You're imagining you're a character in one of these books. Like I bet you think it was the universe that brought you back together with him. Like all the shit that happened before was bad timing and now it's right."

This is a shockingly accurate portrayal of what I've been thinking. "So?"

"It's bullshit. That's not how relationships work."

"How do *you* know?"

This is a mean thing to say because Addison hasn't had a boyfriend or a girlfriend or any kind of romantic friend since I've known her. Not that she's told us about, anyway.

"Because I live in the real world," Addison says, and points to Jameela, who's been silent since their last exchange. "Not in some fantasy about what love is supposed to be like because it was on a TV show, which FYI, is not that good."

"That is such a crock of shit," Jameela says. She's seething now, a level of anger I've only seen from her when people online were saying racist things about Kate.

"Sorry if my truth bomb upset you, or whatever."

"That's not it."

"What, then?"

"Come on, you're really going to play that way?"

"What way?"

"I know, Addison. I know all about you."

Addison doesn't look concerned in the least. "What are you talking about?"

"You don't hate romance, you write it. Romance4Ever, that's you. On Wattpad?"

"What did you say?" Addison's voice has gone hoarse, like she's been partying all weekend.

"I saw you. I saw you writing in there. We both did."

Addison stares daggers at me.

I raise my hands like I've been ordered to by the police. "Don't look at me."

"I see the way it is," Jameela says, pouting. "I'm on my own."

I feel bad, like I abandoned her. But she never told me that she'd figured out Addison's Wattpad name. All of this is news to me. "I was curious, sure. We talked about it."

"You tried to break into her computer!"

"Not really?"

Addison slams her hand down on the desk. "What. The. Fuck?"

"You're so secretive," I say. "We wanted to support you."

"Sure, right. How did you figure it out, Jameela? You learn my password?"

"I don't have to tell you anything!"

Addison stands, picking up her bike helmet. "I'm taking a sick day."

"Addison," I say. "Wait."

"Why?"

"Let's talk this out. We've all said things we regret. But we're friends."

"Friends don't spy on one another."

"You're right. They don't. And I'm sorry if I contributed anything to it. I'm sure Jameela is sorry too. Right, Jameela?"

Jameela's arms are crossed over her chest. "I have nothing to be sorry for."

"And I'm out."

Tabitha pokes her head out of her office. "What's going on here?"

"I'm not feeling well. I'm going home," Addison says.

"All right." She looks at me and Jameela. "Anything else?"

"No," I say.

Tabitha looks at Addison like she wants to ask her something more, but instead, she turns to me. "I need some editorial content for the website."

"See you later," Addison says.

"Feel better," I call after her. Then I turn to Tabitha. "What did you need?"

"I was thinking—Ten Rom-Coms We'd Like to See."

"You want me to come up with the plots?"

"No, ten titles."

I feel a bit panicky. I've had to create editorial content before, but that was always about real books that I'd read.

"Um, okay. For when?"

"EOD?"

End of day? Is she kidding me?

"I have those book selections to write up also, could we say the end of the week?"

Tabitha taps her lips with her index finger. "Yes, all right."

"Thanks."

"You sure everything is okay here?"

"Absolutely."

She looks after where Addison walked to the elevator. "She's sick?"

"Yes, of course. She said it right after she came in."

"I don't want personnel issues."

"Understood, Tabitha. We're all friends here."

Tabitha nods and returns to her office.

I slump back in my chair. "What a shit show."

"I blame you," Jameela says. "Denying all that Wattpad shit. What the hell?"

"Okay, that's fair. I'm sorry she was mean about *Bridgerton*."

"It's fine, I'm used to it."

"You found her Wattpad profile?"

"Yeah."

"How?"

Jameela sighs. "Not by spying. I was scrolling the other night, and the story was *there*."

"What story?"

"It's called *The Wrong Man Showed Up*."

"Wait, what? It's about me?"

"Some of the details are changed, but basically."

"Holy shit." My heart is racing. "Is this why you didn't tell me?"

"I was trying to figure out how to do it."

"Jesus."

"What are you going to do?"

"Read it, I guess?"

She shakes her head slowly. "I wouldn't."

The rest of the morning is a weird panicky time during which I try to think of the imaginary book titles that Tabitha wants while using every last piece of willpower I have to avoid going to Wattpad immediately and tracking this story down.

She's writing about me. She's writing about *me*. Why the hell is she writing about me?

But I can't read it at work. There's been enough drama today.

Instead, and in desperation, I turn to an online title generator that churns out the worst titles I've ever heard. Then it occurs to me that this might be cheating—there's that word again—and I close the browser and take out a piece of paper to try to write some potential titles down.

It would help if I knew the setting/topic of these theoretical books that Tabitha wants to title, but here goes nothing.

Not Another Love Story
Don't Go Falling in Love
Don't Go Breaking My Heart
Been Down This Road Before

Gah. Why are all my titles about how love is a bad idea?

My phone beeps. It's Kit.

How's it going?

TBD.

Trouble in paradise?

No. It's a work thing.

Oh.

You don't believe me? I write.

. . .

Kit . . .

I want to make sure you're protecting your heart.

He passed the test, didn't he?

Yeah, but . . .

I close my eyes. All I wanted was a couple of weeks to settle into this thing between Ben and me. But all I'm encountering is noise and resistance. From Rachel. From Addison. From Kit. And from me, too, if I'm being honest. Without the distraction of finding him, all the doubts are crowding in.

I'm being careful, I write. *I promise.*

Okay. Are the invitations out?

Tonight.

But the venue is locked down?

Yes.

You sure Ben is okay with it?

I asked him a million times.

Maybe one more?

There will be a party, don't worry.

Right. Sure. It's only my engagement party. What's to worry about?

It's not like it's the wedding or anything.

Wait till you see how crazy I am then.

I'm not ready.

Ha-ha.

I'll ask him now.

She sends me a praying hands emoji and I go looking for a text thread with Ben and realize that we've never texted. That's odd. Not that odd given the whole way we met, but given that we've slept together a few times (no one's business how many times at this point), it's odd.

I feel a beat of panic and then I remember. He gave me his number on Friday night. All romantic and outside and kissing. He put his digits in my phone personally.

I call up the contact—Ben Mystery Man Hamilton—and start a text.

Hey, it's Chloe!

He answers immediately. *Hi, Chloe.*

Kit's freaking about that invitation so I'm checking with you one last time to make sure it's okay to have the shindig at your place?

I'm happy to have you at my place. I like a forward girl.

Ha-ha. Is this your way of backing out of having Kit's thing at your venue?

I would never "back out" of anything. I prefer the back way in if you know what I mean.

Um, what?

Ahem. Not into that FYI.

Your loss.

What is going on? Something's off.

Everything okay?

Just a little disappointed over here that my new friend Chloe isn't going to let me in the back door.

My hands start to shake, and I have a pit in my stomach.

Oh shit. Oh no.

Ben?

Who's Ben?

I drop my phone. OMG. Who did I text? What is happening??

I pick it up slowly and check that I wasn't texting Kit and she's not fucking with me.

But no. It's the number I had for Ben.

Are you fucking with me? Because if you are, it's not funny.

I'd like to fuck you but I'm not into threesomes. Leave Ben at home.

Shit, shit, shit. Not Ben. Definitely not Ben.

I block the asshole I'm texting with and hope he didn't screenshot my number.

I put my phone down slowly, then lean back in my seat. It feels like my world is unraveling. Because I don't have Ben's number.

Again.

Chapter Twenty-six

"Are you still mad?" Ben asks that night at my apartment.

He came over after work, like we talked about this morning, with more amazing takeout from another Chinese restaurant I didn't know existed in my neighborhood. I buzzed him up, wondering how I was going to handle the whole I still don't have my boyfriend's number thing. Assuming he *is* my boyfriend, which is not that clear to me at this point.

Anyway, the answer is, not that well. It burst out of me as he walked through the door, all attempts at coolness evaporating like the water on the sidewalk after a hot rain.

We talked it out, ate our dinner, and are now ensconced on the couch, our legs tangled together, but with our backs on different ends. Normally, I would be content with this. Ben, here, in my apartment! A great dinner in my belly and the potential for great sex hanging in the air.

But right now, it feels like I have butterflies in my stomach and I'm not sure what to do about it.

"I'm trying to get over it," I say.

"It was an honest mistake." He pulls my legs into his lap and starts to rub my feet. If he's trying to distract me, he's doing a good job. "It could be romantic, though."

"How?"

"It's only one digit." He'd said that when I showed him the number earlier, that it was one digit off. "That's totally findable. You could work it out and have my number in no time."

"Um, no." I take out my phone and google it. "There are ten billion possible combinations for a ten-digit phone number."

"Wow, that's a lot." He thinks about it for a second. "But if you already have nine digits, it must be less."

"Maybe only a million combinations now? But I don't even know which digit is wrong."

Ben's fingers focus on a tender spot on my foot. It makes it hard to concentrate.

"It's not the area code."

"That's brought it down to seven."

"Easy, then."

I cock my head to the side and pull my foot away. I need all my faculties for this conversation. "Why are we talking about this? Are you not going to give me the correct number?"

He smiles seductively. "It could be fun. Like a quest, or that movie, *Serendipity*."

"The one where John Cusack has to find a book and the phone number's inside?"

"Yeah."

"But it's the right phone number."

Plus, I hate that movie. Okay, I don't. If it was on right now, I'd get sucked in like I do every time. But I'd be mad at myself afterward. Because why did they put up such obstacles to being together? If you want to be with someone, just be with them already. Which is totally not the point of these kinds of movies. The couple can't get together until the end or otherwise it would be boring. But here, in the real world, that's what I want.

A boring, nice relationship without any twists in it.

"Where's your sense of adventure?" Ben asks.

"All tapped out at the moment."

He reaches for my foot again and I give in. It feels too good to resist.

"My fault, I suppose," he says.

"Probably."

"How about if I tell you the first three numbers?"

"You already did."

"I meant the next three."

"There'd only be four numbers to figure out?" I google again. "Ten thousand possibilities."

"That sounds reasonable."

I pick up the pillow behind my back and throw it at him. He catches it easily and tosses it back.

"You're joking, right?"

He shrugs. "You can always Facebook message me."

"Are we even friends on Facebook?"

He takes out his phone and my phone pings a moment later. It's a friend request from Ben. I accept it. I'm not going to do this in front of Ben, but later I'm going to go check if he's removed all his photos with Rachel.

Because obviously, right? That's not weird; it's normal.

"You have your Facebook notifications on?" Ben asks.

"Of course. You?"

"No."

I sigh. "It's not really a way to get in touch with you."

"I'd see it eventually."

"Do you check Facebook every day?"

"Not normally."

"Ben."

"Chloe."

I try to keep my voice steady. "Is there some reason you won't give me your phone number?"

"I'll give it to you if you really want it. But—"

"But? How is there a but?"

"It's a bit silly, but it kind of feels like if you figure it out on your own then we'll know that we were meant to be together."

"You don't know that already?"

"I do, yes."

"Didn't we go through this already?"

"How so?"

I nudge him with my foot. "I had to find you once."

"I'm right here."

"You know what I mean. Like today. I wanted to ask you about Kit's party and I couldn't. It didn't feel good."

"I'm sorry. I didn't want that."

I get a sinking feeling in my stomach. "It's not because you have doubts, is it? You don't think we should be together and you want a sign from the universe?"

"No, Chloe, no." He reaches for me, hauling me across the couch so that I'm facing him, and brings his lips to mine swiftly. He kisses me hard, wrapping his arms around me, then pulls back before I can respond. "I'm being stupid. Of course I want you to be able to reach me whenever you want."

He kisses me again and in a moment, my knees are feeling weak.

There's something chemical between us that's been there since the beginning and grows each time we connect. It doesn't take long until his kisses drive every thought and every doubt from my mind. I want to get lost in this kiss forever.

He pulls away. "Give me your phone."

"I thought maybe we should do something else first."

"You sure?"

"Oh yes." I pull him toward me now, holding the sides of his face with my hands.

I love the way his lips feel on mine, the way his mouth tastes. His hands travel along my sides to my hips and now I'm straddling him, his need clear beneath me and mine growing by the moment, and I don't care if I never have this man's phone number, as long as he keeps touching me like this.

Afterward, we're in my bedroom, tangled up in the sheets. Ben strokes my arm and my hand is on his chest. I can feel his heart beating fast against my hand, and I like that I did that to him. Made him out of breath. Made an impression.

It'll fade, but it's there for now.

"The venue is all set for Friday night?" I ask. "I can send out the invitations?"

"Yep."

"Excellent."

He turns his head toward me. "You already did it, didn't you?"

"That's why I was trying to text you. And since I couldn't reach you I figured I'd go ahead."

"I approve."

"Good."

"You distracted me before from giving you my number."

"In the morning. I'm too lazy to get up right now."

"I like that," he says.

"You think it's because of you?"

"I'm hoping."

I kiss him. "Probably."

"I'll take it." He glances at the clock. "It's still early . . ."

"Hmmm."

"What?"

I reach for the remote next to my bed and turn on the TV. It's tuned to the news, but I go to one of the streamers.

"You want to watch TV?" He sounds a bit disappointed.

"I want to watch *Felicity*."

"Why?"

"I want *you* to watch it." He doesn't argue this time. "You're not going to ask why?"

"Nope."

I laugh. "You're a bit strange, you know that?"

"I'll take that as a compliment."

I cue up the show and skip past season one and go right to season two. "Have you ever watched it?"

"Nope."

"You know the premise?"

"Girl's in college? And she got a bad haircut?"

"Ha. Yes, that happens at the beginning of season two after *Ben* breaks up with her because he's not ready for a real relationship."

"Ben, huh?"

"Yep. Felicity and Ben went to high school together. She always had a crush. He writes this awesome note in her high-school year-book and she follows him to New York."

"That's a lot."

"She can be a lot. But they're meant to be together."

"Why'd he break up with her then?"

"Because he's an idiot. He wanted something with her but he was afraid."

Ben tilts his head to the side. "What are you showing me?"

"How he fixed things."

"Why?"

"Because it's good. It's not something magical. It takes work. He lost her trust and he has to work to get it back."

"A message for me?"

I shrug. "A message for everyone. Relationships aren't easy. Not real ones, anyway."

I think but do not say: it's a message for me too.

"But this is a TV show."

I snuggle against him. "We don't have to watch."

"No, I want to. Where do we start?"

"In the middle of the season."

"Why?"

"Because that's when he starts to do it."

"Do what?"

"Win her back."

We watch a couple of episodes and I fill Ben in on the characters and plots, and eventually, we fall asleep with the TV on.

I wake up in the middle of the night at one of my favorite scenes.

Felicity is on a date with another man and Ben interrupts. And he explains that he knows that she feels like she can't trust him but she can. He's changed. She can't hear him at that moment, but later she'll be able to. Eventually, he makes this grand gesture, and finally she sees—he's ready to be with her. He knows what he did wrong and he isn't going to do it again.

I sigh and turn the TV off. Then I watch Ben sleep for a minute. He's on his back with his hands over his head, like he's lounging in the sun.

I turn away. I feel awake, too awake to sleep. It's been a long time since I had insomnia with someone here. Too long. I could try to wake up Ben but that would be cruel. We don't both have to suffer. But I don't need to be alone with my thoughts either. Because everything is worse in the middle of the night.

I need a distraction. I pick up my iPad and try to find a book I've bought that I haven't read.

And then it hits me.

Addison's story. The one on Wattpad. I can read it.

I log into Wattpad and search for the title. I find it quickly. It has thousands and thousands of reads, and she has a big following. She's been posting chapters weekly, sometimes even more often. My god, she's a Wattpad star!

I click on the cover image for the book that's apparently about me. I read the prologue quickly, which introduces us to Zoey (!), Zack (!!), and Ren (OMG!!!), and start to read the first chapter.

Zoey wasn't a patient person. When she wanted something, she wanted it right now. It was hard for her to sit there, waiting for Zack to show up for their blind date. Each minute felt like torture. Zoey had been ten minutes early. Zack was twenty minutes late. That was thirty whole minutes! But she was sure that everyone in the restaurant knew she was being stood up, and if she left, then she'd confirm it. So she sat there, tapping her foot, staring at every brown-haired, brown-eyed man who came into the place.

And then he did.

He didn't quite look like the picture that her best friend, Kat, had shown her, but Zoey didn't notice that, right then. Instead, she found herself standing and waving like a maniac to catch his attention. When he finally saw her, he looked confused for a moment, then approached her cautiously.

"Took you long enough," Zoey said, trying to sound casual but probably blowing it.

"Oh yeah?"

"If you think thirty minutes is on time maybe we should stop this date right now."

He laughed and sat down. "I have an excuse."

"Better be good."

"Stick around and find out."

"Is that a question or a statement?"

"It's both," he said, and now it was her turn to laugh.

She was glad she'd stuck around.

This date was worth a shot.

Chapter Twenty-seven

"This story is about us?"

"Yes," I tell Ben the next morning as we're sitting at my "kitchen" table. It's the only table I have and it's not in the kitchen but you get the idea. "And it's bad."

"How bad?"

"It's readable I guess? I'm biased."

I stayed up until three in the morning reading all of Addison's story, and a bunch of the comments too. A lot of it was encouragement to continue writing, and reactions with GIFs and emojis, but some of the comments have more bite to them. There's #teamZack and #teamRen and everyone pretty much thinks Zoey is a moron. Added to all of that, the latest chapter was posted *after* the fight at the office. Which means that Addison went home and wrote it yesterday. That chapter was the hardest to read. Because, apparently, Zoey's a bit toxic at work, and always making life difficult for this person she works with who's a thinly veiled Addison called *Allison*.

"I guess it's a bit hard to be objective," I say, spearing the last piece of the French toast that Ben made. It's delicious.

"What's there to be objective about?"

"Whether I can sue her."

Ben adds more syrup to his stack. "I doubt that."

"You haven't read what I read."

"How do I come off?"

"Not good."

"How bad?"

"Bad, Ben. Basically, Ren is a sociopath who enjoys toying with Zoey and still has something going on the side with his ex—"

Ben's eyes dance with amusement, not bothered in the least. He wakes up in a good mood, too, or at least he did this morning. I'll have to judge if that's me related or Ben. It's too soon to tell.

"Let me guess," he says. "Her name is Betchel?"

"No."

"I'm blanking."

"It's Rache."

Ben finishes his portion and starts to clear the plates, bringing them to my sink. "That's the same name basically."

"Right?"

"What are you going to do about it? Besides the suing."

"I'm not sure." I lean back in my chair. "Things are already tense at the office, and, shit . . . what time is it?"

Ben checks his watch. "It's eight thirty."

"Fuck, fuck, fuck. I have to go." I jump up and kiss him quickly. He tastes like cinnamon and syrup, which means he tastes like the best combination ever invented. "Meet me here at six thirty?"

"Chinese again?"

"Surprise me."

I kiss him again and bolt for the door.

I need to get to work. I'm already behind on my book writeups and I have that stupid list of titles to work on too. Usually I'm already at my desk by this time, but I was tired from being up late reading and I couldn't pry my eyes open. And then Ben made me breakfast, and gah . . .

It feels like my life is a mess.

I need to slow down and focus.

If I don't, I'm going to screw things up even more badly.

Okay, okay, maybe I'm being too hard on myself. My life isn't falling apart. But something about it feels a bit out of control, which is scary and unsettling.

I spent the last year basically on my own except for Kit, and now there's someone making me breakfast in the morning. Someone I basically jumped into bed with, which is totally not like me.

And what I did to Jack. Not like me either.

Fighting with people at work.

Another one to add to the list of, wait for it, not like me.

So, yeah. I need to slow all this down and be more intentional instead of reacting on instinct and feelings.

I hustle to the subway and wait for my train. When I get on, I text Kit.

You are not going to believe what Addison did.

Wha?

I'll send you the link later.

Tease.

COCK TEASE.

The woman standing next to me starts to cough/choke. I look at her to make sure she's not dying and realize from the guilty expression on her face that she's been reading my texts over my shoulder.

"It's a joke," I say.

"None of my business."

"Why read my texts, then?"

She turns away, affronted. My phone pings in my hand.

TEASE MY COCKLE.

Ha, good one. Remind me to tell you about the rude woman reading my texts on the subway.

TEXT THIS.

That's not even sexual.

It's hard to come up with these on demand.

HARD TO COME. Srly?

Ha-ha. I guess it's not that hard.

NOT THAT HARD.

Bad porn title.

Totally. I smile and look at the judgmental woman who was affronted by my texts. She's clinging to a pole not that far from me, but she doesn't catch my eye. I guess she got all that she could handle today. *Ugh, I have to write all these rom-com titles for my boss. Can you help me?*

Give me some examples.

LOVE IS A HOUSE. BUILD ME A DREAM. SECOND-CHANCE ROMANCE.

Those are terrible.

I KNOW.

What's the book about?

It's a wish list, not based on anything that exists.

On it.

I send her a praying hands emoji. *I confirmed with Jack, by the way, about Friday.*

Jack?

OMG. I mean Ben. BEN.

Interesting slip.

My throat feels tight. *No, I'm just tired.*

You sure?

Yes! And I sent out the invite to your list last night. I had the responses go to a special email I created so that they didn't clutter my inbox. You want the login?

Kit had sent me the list last week. I didn't even check who was on it, just pasted it into an email with the details and hit Send.

More evidence that I need to *slow down*. Normal me would've checked everyone on the list to avoid any surprises. Now I don't even know who's coming to this thing even though I'm organizing it.

Sure, send, thanks.

Will email. How's the job search going?

I'm giving myself a week to mourn. I'll start looking next week after the party.

Good plan. I may have to look for a job myself.

Why?

You'll understand once you read what Addison wrote.

SEND ME THE LINK!

Will do. At my stop, more later.

I'll send some titles.

TY.

I put my phone away and get off my train, then walk up the stairs into the day. It's hot and muggy, a reminder that summer's still here and not going anywhere.

I arrived in September last year, and this is my first real New York summer. I can't say it's my favorite time in this city. The garbage often stinks and it feels like the air gets stuck over Manhattan and never moves.

I sigh as Ben flits through my mind.

I can't believe I called him Jack, even if it was in a text to Kit. What if I'd done that in bed? It's not like Jack and I were ever intimate, but still. I can never make that mistake again.

My phone beeps. It's another text from Kit.

Forgot to ask—have you written your speech yet?

Um, what?

It's traditional for the bridesmaid to give a speech.

Did you ever ask me to be your bridesmaid??

I needed to ask?

I wanted you to GO DOWN ON BENDED KNEE.

Hmm, is that meant to be porny or funny?

Both, obvi.

Failed.

Dammit.

So, the speech?

For reals? You know I hate public speaking.

Yeah for reals. You don't want my mother to do it, do you?

God no. Don't you have any other friends?

'Fraid not.

I'm at the BookBox building. I swipe my key card to get in, feeling an odd beat of panic that it's not going to work. But it beeps the way it always does and I'm inside.

I kind of wish I wasn't, though, because Addison's right in front of me, waiting for the elevator.

"Feeling better?" I ask her.

She glances at me but doesn't say anything. She's dressed much more conservatively than usual, like she's going for a job interview. And maybe she is. Maybe Jameela and I have driven her away. That makes me feel awful.

"I'm sorry about yesterday, Addison."

She doesn't look at me.

"I mean it. And I don't know how Jameela found your Wattpad stuff. It wasn't me, is all I'm trying to say. I was curious but I never did anything about it other than talk to her. And she told me she found it by accident. She was reading other things on there and the story was suggested to her. She only put two and two together because of the subject matter."

Addison glances at me slowly, then away. "Did you read it?"

"I did. Last night, though. Not before."

The elevator door dings open and we enter. She turns her body away from me and now I'm starting to get pissed off. She's been writing about *me*, after all. *My* life. Sharing it with thousands and thousands of people. I never asked her to do that. I would've told her not to do it if she'd bothered asking me.

I open my mouth to say something and then I stop. I don't want another confrontation with Addison. I want to do my work and read my books and go home to Ben.

So, for once in my life, I keep my mouth shut.

The elevator opens on our floor and we go to our respective desks. I say good morning to Jameela but Addison stays silent.

I go to my inbox and work through the fifty emails that have accumulated overnight. So many people begging for their book to get exposure. I get it, but I wish I wasn't exposed to so much desperation.

I get a notification on my phone from Facebook. It's a message from Ben.

Hey, he wrote, *I ALSO don't have your number.*

OMG. We still haven't exchanged numbers. What is wrong with us. *Oh! Ha!*

So . . .

You got a hold of me didn't you?

But maybe you don't always check Facebook.

I smile. *I always check. You're the one who says they don't check all the time.*

True.

What's up?

Wanted to say hey.

Oh.

Bad thing?

No, I like it.

I thought I might mix it up for dinner tonight, Ben writes. *Maybe I'll cook again.*

I thought no one in New York ever cooks?

This is mostly true. But sometimes we do.

Twice in one day?

Are you suggesting something?

I was talking about your cooking but you know I love porny titles.

Horny titles.

Ha-ha.

Dinner?

Yes, I write. *I think my oven works.*

Do you have pots, pans, staples?

Pots & pans, yes. Staples?

Salt, pepper, etc.

Yes.

Excellent. And you like everything?

Pretty much. What are you making?

It's a secret.

Okay.

Everything all right at work? You weren't too late?

I have to write a speech and do all this work stuff. I should probably go.

Understood. See you tonight. XO

My heart starts to pound. XO. That means . . . wait. It means hugs and kisses. My brain is scrambled.

I type *XO* back and then leave Facebook.

I need to slow down and focus on what I *have to* do.

—write a love letter for Kit.

—write a list of book titles.

—fix things with Addison and Jameela.

That's a lot to get done in a couple of days. Especially since all I want to do is message with Ben all day.

I am in so much trouble.

Chapter Twenty-eight

It's Friday afternoon and I'm desperately racing to finish the list of titles for Tabitha along with the speech I have to give tonight.

It's been an up and down week. Ups are definitely the nights with Ben, eating good food and discovering each other in bed, then watching an episode of *Felicity* before falling asleep. The downs are work. Jameela and Addison still aren't talking, which means we're all not talking, and our formerly lively workplace has turned into something cold and antiseptic. I don't know how to fix it, and I'm not even sure it's mine to fix. Maybe it will all blow over in a week or two, but in the meantime, Addison is writing a chapter a day in her novel, and Zoey keeps making terrible choices.

I haven't updated Addison on anything to do with me and Ben since this all blew up, but she has this uncanny knack of writing scenes that are close enough to reality to sting. I should stop reading it but I can't seem to help myself. Of course, Addison knows I'm reading it, so there's this weird thing where it feels like she's communicating with me through the story. Like she's trying to tell me something but I can't quite get the message.

What she's not giving me, though, is what I need.

Rom-com titles.

I have two open documents on my computer. One where I'm putting the titles that Tabitha wants as they occur to me. And the other where I'm putting porny titles because that's all I can think about for some stupid reason. I've been sending them to Kit, too, throughout the day.

PULP FRICTION.

EVERYONE I DID LAST SUMMER.

Ha-ha. Kit writes. *Is this your speech?*

Maybe!

Girl, no.

Don't worry. I wouldn't want to see Lian die.

That would be bad.

I'm screwed.

Nothing coming to you?

OMG YOU DID IT AGAIN!

Your mind is in the gutter.

I'm tired. Not sleeping well.

Because of Ben?

That is definitely part of the reason that I'm low on sleep. *Yes and yes. Also all the work stuff. I don't know.*

Plus the speech.

So much pressure.

Speak from the heart. It should be easy right? Kit writes. *Given that you're in love.*

This pushes me back in my seat. Is Kit right? Am I in love with Ben? I like him a waffle lot . . . ha-ha-ha. My mind is going.

Okay, okay, it *does* feel like love. But it always feels like this in the beginning, doesn't it? All that possibility and hope and good sex? You don't know if it's going to last until later. It's too soon to say love.

Isn't it?

Hello!

Yeah, still here.

You don't love him?

I don't know yet.

Hmmm.

What?

You're scared.

I'm not.

You *are.* You're scared of putting yourself out there. Remember how hard I had to work to get you to even go on that date with Jack?

I'm allowed to be scared. Remember Christian?

Sure. But don't let one bad ending get in the way of what you want.

Were you the one telling me to protect my heart? I write.

You never listen to me. I'm being practical.

What do I want?

Duh. Ben.

Right, right.

You don't want him?

No, I do.

What's going on with u?

I'll be fine.

Sometime in the future?

Tonight. I'll be great tonight. Everything will be amazing, you'll see.

You don't have to give the speech if you don't want.

What? Don't be ridiculous! I'm giving the speech. I'm finishing this list and then going to get changed. Forget about me, I'm being weird.

You sure?

100%.

I love you.

I love you too.

See how easy that is.

SHE'S SO EASY.

Ha-ha-ha.

I go back to my list. It's after lunch and I've got thirty minutes to finish it before I need to leave to get my hair blown out and then change for the party. I'm meeting Ben there because he needs to get things set up.

I hammer out a few more titles for both lists, then organize my thoughts for Kit. About Theo. About love. About what we all wish we want to happen. My heart starts to slow and I calm down. All of this is going to be fine.

It's all going to be great.

My cell rings. It's my mother calling. My shoulders creep up but I try to keep my voice light.

"Hey, Mom."

"Hi, Chloe. I wanted to know what time you wanted to meet."

"Meet? For what?"

"For Kit's engagement party."

"Um, what?"

"You invited us. We're staying at the Comfort Inn."

"You're in New York?"

"I emailed all of this information to you days ago."

"To which email address?"

"The one I always use."

Damn it. I haven't checked my personal email in days. No one emails me, only my parents and the stupid mailing lists I can't get off.

"Dad's here too?"

"Of course your father is here."

"And you're in a hotel?"

"I just said that."

"I'm sorry, Mom. I'm catching up."

"You didn't read my email?"

I tuck the phone under my chin. "I didn't see it, I'm sorry. Can I meet you at the party?"

"I suppose."

"It'll be easier. I have to get my hair done and all these other things."

"All right." She sighs. "Where is this place, anyway?"

"Oh, um . . . it's my friend, Ben's, studio."

"Who is Ben?"

"A man I've been dating."

"The man you were looking for in that BookBox thing?"

"Yes."

"Why didn't you tell me?" Her voice cracks with emotion.

"It's new, Mom. We've only started dating."

"Am I going to meet this man tonight?"

"Yes, obviously. The event is at his studio."

"He's a musician?"

"He owns a record label."

"That doesn't sound very stable."

I close my eyes. "It's not the 1950s, Mom."

"I wasn't even born then."

"You know what I mean."

"You're about to call me a boomer," she huffs.

"Gen X, whatever."

"I'm not allowed to be concerned for my child?"

"Of course you are. His business is good. But I also have my own job and it's not like we're getting married or anything."

"You're not serious about him?"

I cannot win. Why do I even play? "I said we just started dating."

"I knew about your father right away."

And how has that worked out? They're two strangers living in the same house.

"If you're not serious, you should move on."

"Mom, I've got to go. I'll see you tonight."

I hang up without waiting for her to respond and put my phone down. I feel disoriented. I can't believe my parents are here. They must've been on the list I didn't check. As if I don't have enough going on—

And then it starts. The *laughing*. First Addison and then Jameela. I turn my chair and they are both almost in tears they're laughing so hard.

It's contagious. I start laughing too. "You heard that?"

"Clearly," Addison says.

"I am so fucked."

"Are your parents serial killers?"

I'm still laughing but it hurts. "Killers of joy, more like."

"I'm sorry," Jameela says and I can tell that she's apologizing for more than my parents, who she doesn't know and isn't responsible for, obviously.

"Thanks."

"Why don't you get out of here? Don't you have to get prepared for that party?"

"Yeah. I have to finish this list though." I point to my computer screen.

"It's a stupid assignment," Addison says. "Why are you going to be able to do a better job than a bunch of publishers?"

A BETTER BLOW JOB, I think but don't say out loud. "Yeah."

"Go on, we'll cover for you."

I turn back to my computer and add the blow job one to my list for Kit, then send it to her. Then I write a quick email to Tabitha and send her the other list. *I did my best,* I say. *Writing titles is hard.* I listen to the email *whoosh* away, then I close down my system and pack up my things.

"Thanks, guys. And I've missed you."

They both smile at me and it feels like a beginning. Maybe we'll be in a fight on Monday, but for now, it feels like we're back on track.

I guess I'm an optimist.

Lord knows why.

I'll learn my lesson eventually.

Two hours later I've been blown out and I'm wearing a dress that Kit picked out for me weeks ago and had shipped to my house. She might not want to organize the party, but she does want to control what I wear.

I'm happy, though. It's a white dress with pretty flowers all over it, delicate, with spaghetti straps, and it suits me. I wondered at Kit wanting us both in white, but she said that was stupid and it isn't her wedding day and to say thank you. I did and I'm happy I did. This is going to be my first outing with Ben as a couple and I want to look my best.

When I get to his studio half an hour before the party's supposed to start, though, Ben isn't there. Instead, another guy answers the door. My stomach flutters with worry.

"Are you Chloe?"

"Yeah?"

"I'm Brian," he says, and I recognize him from the band Ben manages. He's in his early twenties and wearing pressed jeans and a button-down shirt. "I work with Ben."

"I saw your concert. You're the keyboardist, right?"

"That's right." He runs his hands through his blue hair. He looks stressed. "I'm also Ben's second in command at the label. For now, anyway."

"Oh?"

"Yeah, if I fuck up this party then I'm out."

"Is that what he said?"

"Yep."

"Don't fuck it up then."

"Did you want to come in?"

"Yep."

He laughs, then stands back and tacks a sign to the door as he does so. It tells people to ring the doorbell if they're there for the party. "I'll take the lock off once the party gets going, but for now, they can ring up."

"Sounds good."

He starts to walk up the stairs and I follow him. "You've been here before?"

"Yes."

"Great, great. Hope you like what we did."

We get to the top of the stairs and I stop in wonder. The space is filled with fairy lights on the ceiling and drapes of fabric that soften it and make it seem filled with a pink glow. There are small standing tables with flowers on each of them. Ben really went all out, and it warms my heart to think of him doing this when he barely even knows Kit and Theo. "Wow."

"It turned out good."

"It's great. But, um, where's Ben?"

"Oh right, he told me to give you this." He fishes in his pocket and takes out a folded piece of paper. He hands it to me and I take it, worry nibbling at the back of my neck.

Chloe,

My mom is out of isolation but she's taken a turn for the worse. I have to go see her today. This timing sucks and I wanted to text you to let you know but you STILL haven't given me your number! Okay, bad joke at this time . . . it didn't feel like something to write in a Facebook message. It feels like this might be the last time I'm going to see her.

I'll get to the party when I can—if I can. In the meantime, you're in good hands with Brian. He might have blue hair but he's superresponsible besides being a kick-ass keyboardist. Have fun tonight and I'll do everything in my power to make it for your speech, I promise.

And if I don't, you'll know why.

Love,

Ben

My hands are shaking a bit by the time I finish reading. Whether it's the word *love* or the sadness pouring out of the paper, I'm not sure. Either way, Ben's not going to be here tonight, I know it.

Shit.

I hate myself when I'm selfish.

"Everything okay?"

"Sure," I say, looking up at Brian. He has kind eyes. "Do you need help with anything?"

"Everything's all set, but if you want, you can open a bottle of champagne?"

"Definitely."

He points to the corner where a bar is set up. There's a silver bucket with several bottles of champagne in it. "The guy will be here in a minute to man that, but go ahead in the meantime."

"Great."

"You sure you're okay?"

"Yes, of course." I clear my throat. "Especially after a glass of champagne."

He smiles. "Great."

I guess he's not the lyricist for the band. Not that I'm being articulate today either.

I walk to the bar and pop open the bottle. That noise usually makes me happy, but today it feels like there's a blanket on my happiness. I wanted to share this evening with Ben, but that's not in the cards. He's not abandoning me. Of course his mother comes first.

Why do I feel left behind anyway?

I pour myself a glass and take a sip as the bell rings downstairs.

"I'll get it," Brian says.

I smile at him like I mean it, and try to shove my disappointment down.

Ben is being a good son. I'm being a bad girlfriend, if that's even what I am.

Tonight is about Kit.

And here she is, glowing in a creamy strapless number and looking around the room in amazement. I pour her a glass and take it to her.

"You look amazing," I say, holding it out.

She takes it. "Thank you."

"Where's Theo?"

"Right behind me. Ben?"

"Delayed."

Kit frowns.

"It's okay."

"It's not. It's his mom."

"Oh, I'm sorry."

"Me, too, but tonight is about you."

"Weird."

"Ha-ha." I hug her, champagne glass and all. "I love you, Kit, and I'm glad you're happy."

"Thanks."

The bell rings again. "That must be Theo."

"Let the party begin."

I float through the next couple of hours on a haze of champagne.

The space fills up, the music rocks, and everyone's having a good time. My parents arrive and we have a perfunctory conversation in which my mother acts like she cares that Ben's not there, then spends the rest of the night talking to Kit's parents. Lian hugs me close and tells me how much my friendship has meant to Kit over the years. This almost brings me to tears, because Lian has never said anything like this before, but I hold it in check. I'm going to be crying in a few minutes when I start my speech, and I won't get through it if I start now.

Speaking of which, Brian is approaching. "You ready?"

"I guess so." I hand him my empty glass—is that three or four? Yikes—and walk to the microphone set up in the corner. He cuts the music and I take out the folded piece of paper I'd tucked in my bra like I was a professional dancer.

"Hello, hello," I say, checking for reverb, but the sound is perfect. "Does everyone have a glass?"

"You don't!" Kit calls from Theo's arms.

"You're right, I don't." I look over at the bartender and he brings me another glass of bubbly. Probably not a good idea to drink this. "We're all set."

God, is my voice slurring? No, no, that's nerves. This is why I wrote this down.

"I'm supposed to talk about Kit, right?"

"Yes!" she shouts back.

"Okay! Ahem, well, Katherine Wang was born on . . . kidding, kidding. You know this is hard right? To sum up someone you've known forever in five to ten minutes, throw in a few jokes, and not offend anyone. My parents are here!"

I wave my champagne glass towards my parents, standing together but apart, as always. My dad smiles at me but my mom is frowning, unhappy that attention is being drawn to her. I've avoided any real conversation with them until now, but I won't be able to do that all night.

"And Kit's parents are here!"

Some applause for Lian and Rob.

"And of course, Kit and Theo are here!"

More applause, more cheering. I glance into the crowd, trying to gather my thoughts. I think I see Ben, finally, but I'm not sure.

"Anyway, the speech, speech, speech. Here we go."

I look down at my paper. I can read the words, but they don't seem like enough.

"Sometimes in life you meet someone and you just know they're your person. You can be five or twenty or fifty, age doesn't matter. There's something between you that lets you know that that's it as far as that person is concerned. *They're* it.

"That's how I felt when I met Kit, and she felt the same. It's like we recognized each other. Hey, friend. And here we are twenty years later still texting each other silly things all day and laughing through the bad parts and the good parts.

"And today isn't only a good part. It's a great part." I smile at them. "I remember when she first told me about Theo. As you know, Lian was the one who set them up. And sorry, Lian, but that hasn't always worked out well for Kit. We all remember Connor. And then there was Gerald."

Nervous laughter.

"But Theo was different. I could tell from the way Kit was speaking about him, and I got it the minute I met him. He was her person. And I couldn't be more jealous, I mean happy."

More laughter, genuine this time.

"It feels rare. All the luck required to find someone. It feels like fate has to intervene, like there has to be some bigger plan at work. And whether that's true or not, it's always something to celebrate when two people do find one another and decide to give a life together a go."

I raise my glass. "Let's raise our glasses to Kit and Theo. To finding your person."

Everyone says it with me. "To Kit and Theo!"

Kit and Theo raise their own glasses but kiss instead of taking a drink, and a huge *whoop* goes up.

And I whoop along with them as I search the crowd for Ben.

And then he's walking toward me; only it's not Ben, it's Jack.

Chapter Twenty-nine

"Hey," Jack says. "Great speech."

I look over his shoulder for Ben, but he's not here. It was Jack all along. "Thanks."

"How are you?" He's wearing a suit jacket and chinos and looks oddly formal, but nice.

That's Jack. He's nice. Why can't I be more attracted to nice?

"I'm good." I feel a bit woozy, actually, but he doesn't need to know that. "You?"

"I'm all right. Work has been a bit nuts. How is Kit holding up?"

"She's taking a moment to process, but having fun tonight at least." I glance over at Kit and Theo, who are still wrapped up in each other. Kit is glowing and Theo's almost glowing too. Kit raises her glass at me and mouths *I love you*.

"That's good."

I bring my attention back to Jack. "She'll find something."

"I'm sure. It's hard out there, though."

"She'll be okay. I hope so, anyway."

"I'm sure she will." He looks around the room. "Nice space."

"Yep."

"You organized this?"

"Ben did."

"Oh, where is he tonight?" He searches the room with his eyes.

"He had a family emergency."

"Ah."

"You think it's bullshit?"

"I didn't say that."

"But you thought it."

He cocks his head to the side. "You don't know what I thought."

"You're jealous."

Jack puts his hand on my shoulder. "I care about you, Chloe."

"Ben cares about me."

"You say so."

I shrug his hand off. "You don't know him."

"All I know is what you've told me about him. And based on that, he doesn't sound like someone who can be trusted."

"That's a big leap."

"I don't think he's going to make you happy."

"You've made that clear."

"You're mad?"

I cross my arms. "Wouldn't you be in my situation?"

"I'm looking out for you."

"Don't, okay, Jack? I don't need you to do that." I step away from him. "See you around."

I walk away, not sure where I'm going.

I should go to Kit and Theo and congratulate them again, but instead, I feel aimless. This room is full of land mines—Jack, my parents, even Lian. They all mean well but there's only one person I want to talk to right now.

Ben.

And now, the air in the room feels like it's too much. All the expelled breath of the laughter and talking and congratulations mix with the drinks I had. I need to get out of here.

I put my glass down and head for the exit.

I don't bother saying good-bye to Kit because I'm planning on coming back. I need to be somewhere else for a few minutes.

I stumble down the stairs and into the night. I push open the door at the bottom of the stairs, then let it click shut behind me. It's after nine, and the street is mostly empty. There's a homeless man up the block talking to the sky, and a couple on the other side of the street, walking close together, laughing at some inside joke.

Other than that, I'm alone. And now that I'm out here, I don't know what I'm doing. I should call an Uber and go home. Kit will understand.

But, shit. I forgot my purse upstairs. Fantastic. The thought of going back upstairs and having to go through all the good-byes I want to avoid is exhausting.

I've got my phone in my pocket. That's enough for me to Uber. I even have a spare key hidden in a small, locked box above my door that I can open with my phone. I can get the purse back tomorrow.

I wish I knew where Ben was and if he was coming to the party. It would be like my life for me to leave and for him to arrive moments later.

I take out my phone and go to Facebook, hoping for a message, but there isn't one, which I knew because I didn't have any notifications. He probably won't see this but what do I have to lose at this point?

Hope you're okay.

I wait, watching for the little bubble that shows that he's read it. But nothing appears.

He doesn't have his notifications on. He told me that. And I still don't have his phone number.

I don't even know how that happened. We said we were going to do it the other night, and then we got distracted and somehow it *did* become a joke between us, both of us withholding our numbers for some stupid reason I can't grasp right now.

But I'm sick of this. It's not some fun game anymore. I can't be dating someone I can't get in touch with.

"Fuck!" I smack my hand against the wall and instantly regret it. That shit *hurts*.

"Whoa."

When I turn around, Ben's standing there looking rumpled. He's wearing what he left the apartment in this morning—a pair of blue dockers and a polo shirt, but it looks like he slept in his clothes and his hair is a bit wild.

"Ben. Where *were* you?"

"Didn't Brian give you the note?"

"That was hours ago."

"I should've messaged you."

"You don't have my number," I say, and I start to cry.

Ben takes me in his arms. "Hey, hey. No. I'm sorry. I'm giving it to you right now." He takes my phone out of my hand and opens his contact. He corrects his number and sends himself a message. His phone *pings!* in his pocket. "All fixed."

But it's not. "I . . . how's your mom?"

"She's okay. It was a tough afternoon, but then she bounced back a couple of hours ago. That happens sometimes at the end, apparently."

"I'm sorry."

"It's rough. But I should've messaged you. I'll do better next time." He tightens his arms around me. "I missed your speech."

"You did."

"What are you doing out here?"

"It was . . . too much inside."

He pulls me even closer, and I want to resist, but I can't. It feels too good to have him here, finally, to be in his arms, and my mind is a mess. I can't make any decisions right now.

"I'm sorry I wasn't here. Is your hand okay?"

"It's fine. You had to be with your mom."

"I did."

"So, that's the way it is."

He tucks his chin onto my shoulder. "I'm going to do better."

"Okay."

"Are you mad?"

I take a step back and untangle myself from him. "I'm sad, Ben. This all seems complicated and my best friend is getting married and my ex, not my ex, but someone I dated, thinks I'm acting like an idiot and I don't even have your number."

"Now you do."

"But why the game about it? Why did it have to come to this?"

"I was being stupid. No excuses. It was dumb, and I'm sorry."

I expel a long, slow breath. If I believe in signs from the universe, isn't this one? Am I supposed to be with the man I can't reach? The one who can't show up for me or my friends? The one with the ex hanging around waiting for an opening to get back in there? The one who lied to me from the minute we met?

Kit, Addison, my mom—everyone warned me. But I've been so wrapped up in our connection I couldn't listen.

"I don't know if this is working out."

"No, Chloe, no. It's been a bit rocky, but we can work this out."

"Can we?"

"We can."

"Isn't the beginning supposed to be easy? We already have so many issues."

"That's my fault."

"It might be both our fault."

He puts his hand on my chin to steady me and looks down into my eyes. "Is that what you want?"

I hesitate. It isn't what I want at all. "I don't, Ben. But I don't see any other way."

"Let me persuade you." He starts to kiss me. As he does, that hard heat between us starts up again, like it's consuming everything about me. Every thought, every objection, everything but the feel of his lips, his hands, his body pressing against mine, filled with need, and I'm full too.

He pushes me up against the wall and my hands go to his hair, tangling in the almost curls. He smells a bit antiseptic, reminding me that he's been in a hospital, but something about the sharp tang brings us into sharper focus too. Everything feels heightened, like it all might come to a climax right here on the street corner.

"Let's get out of here," I say.

"What about the party?"

"I'll text her. She'll understand."

"You sure?"

"Yeah. Besides, my parents are in there." I'll ask Kit to tell them an emergency came up. "And Jack. Let's go." I tug on his hand and he follows me down the street.

"We're walking?"

"You want to run?"

He laughs, and it feels great to hear his happiness. But he doesn't want to run. Instead, he puts up his hand and hails a cab, and I'm grateful for that too. I've had too much to drink and I'm not thinking clearly. I'm going with my feelings, which is something that I don't do that often. Except with Ben. It's been all feeling and zero sense here.

But god it feels good.

We spend the rest of the night exploring each other until we fall into a haze of sleep and sex in the early morning.

I wake several hours later to wonderful smells coming from the kitchen. I stretch my arms above my head, feeling my body, remembering what Ben and I did last night. The memories feel good but my head hurts from too much champagne and too little sleep, and good sex has never solved fundamental problems.

I feel nervous and excited all at once, and part of me wants to hide in this bed all day. But I can't do that. I have to face Ben and whatever it is that we have together.

Also, I'm hungry.

I get up and look at my dress from last night in a pile on the floor. Climbing back into it isn't appealing. Instead, I go to Ben's dresser and take out a T-shirt and put it on, fighting back the déjà vu of the last time I did this. Rachel is not going to magically appear again with her judgment and her keys dangling from her finger. Not magically, obviously, but Ben took back her keys, so I'm safe from that humiliation at least.

I run my fingers through my hair and retrieve my phone. There's a text from Kit.

Everything okay?

She'd agreed last night to tell my parents I wasn't feeling well and to grab my purse, but I didn't think she believed my excuses.

Besides, she still has that Find My Friends thing on. Time to fess up.

Hi, sorry. I needed some air and then Ben was there and we ended up leaving.

Ah.

Did you have fun?

Yeah, it was great. Thank you. And thank Ben.

I should've come up to say good-bye.

It's okay. I could see you were struggling.

You could?

Your parents . . .

They must've been mad.

They weren't happy.

They're never happy. I sigh. *Sorry you had to deal with that. I'll call them. Or go see them today. Something.*

Sounds like a good idea. I have your purse by the way.

Oh great, thank you.

Are you okay now?

I'm okay.

So convincing.

Ha-ha. We had a nice night. We'll see. There are . . . I'll come over tomorrow? We'll talk face to face. I feel like texting is not subtle enough for this conversation.

Come whenever.

Thank you. And I'm happy for you.

Your speech was great.

You say so.

Absolutely. I only have a few notes.

Notes?

Room for improvement.

She must be pulling my leg. *Why?*

For when you do it again at my wedding.

Wait, what?

Have you never been to a wedding?

No!

Never seen one in a movie?

I thought the bride talked. And the dad?

You're a nut.

Says the woman who wants to give me notes on my speech. I spoke from the heart.

I know you did.

"Chloe? You up?"

I've got to go. I'll see you tomorrow. And no notes!

She sends an emoji where her bitmoji is blowing a raspberry. I shake my head. "I'm up, hold on a second."

I write a quick text to my mom. *Sorry I left last night without saying good-bye. But I can come see you this afternoon if you like.*

Her response is instantaneous. *We're at the airport.*

Already?

We only came in for the night.

Oh, I'm sorry.

You had too much to drink?

No, I wasn't feeling well.

Your uncle was an alcoholic you know.

Oh my god. *I don't have a drinking problem. It was a party, I had a few glasses of champagne.*

You say so.

"Ben, it's going to be a minute."

"Okay!"

I call my mother's number. She lets it ring three times before she answers, as if she's not certain she's going to.

"Hi, Mom."

I can feel her emotion vibrating down the line. "First, you act like you don't know we're coming to town, then you don't speak to us, and then you leave without saying good-bye?"

"I said I was sorry."

"You should be."

"Seriously, Mom? Why are you like this?"

"What does that mean?"

I crouch down so I'm closer to the floor because my knees feel weak, like someone kicked me in the stomach. "I know I'm a disappointment to you, okay? You probably wish that it was me who died and not Sara. But I'm the one who's here. That's not my fault. And I'm doing the best that I can. I wish you could see that."

"How dare you say something like that to me?"

"I'm allowed to talk about her. We should talk about her. She was my sister. We all lost something that day."

She hangs up.

That tracks.

Fuck.

"Chloe?"

"Yeah."

"Why are you crying?"

"Am I?" I reach up and there they are, tears on my cheeks. "Talking to my mom." I stand and turn toward him. "Always a joyful experience."

"I'm sorry."

"It's all right. It's been a lifetime coming."

"Do you need to go?"

"No, they're at the airport."

"So soon?"

"They only came in for the night. Though who knows if she was telling me the truth."

"You could go out there."

"To the airport? I don't even know which one they're at."

"You could ask."

"No, Ben. There's no point. It's been like this between us since my sister died. There isn't any way to fix it."

"If you're sure . . ."

"I am. Your mom okay?"

"Texted a few minutes ago. She's doing as well as can be expected."

"Good. Now, is that breakfast I smell?"

He smiles. "Yep."

"I could use something greasy and a million pounds of coffee."

"Luckily, that's exactly what I made."

I follow him to the kitchen. There are eggs Benedict sitting on the table and what looks like freshly squeezed orange juice. The air is pregnant with fresh coffee.

"Wow, Ben, this is amazing."

"Hopefully it tastes as good as it looks."

We sit and I cut off a piece of the eggs and put it in my mouth. It's delicious. "It's great, thank you."

"Should we talk about it?"

"Which part?"

"Any of it."

"I'm sure we should. But for right now, I'd rather sit here and enjoy the morning."

"And after?"

"I have no plans."

He looks nervous. "Should I be worried?"

"I did agree to see Kit tomorrow, so maybe?"

He cuts into his breakfast. "More questions?"

"Almost certainly. Plus she has notes on my speech."

"Oh boy. Sorry again about missing it."

"Apparently, you missed nothing."

"I'm sure it was heartfelt."

"Heart something."

My phone pings with an incoming email. I turn it over so I can't see what it is.

"You want to check that?"

"No, whatever it is, it can wait."

I should know better than that by now.

Chapter Thirty

In the end, I don't check my email until the weekend's almost over.

Instead, I spend Saturday with Ben. We eat the eggs Benedict that he made, then take a shower together (ahem!), and then head to my place so I can get some clothes.

I don't check to see if my mother's written me to apologize. And I haven't apologized either. What I said to her was true. For my whole life I've never felt like enough for them. Not enough to heal them. Not enough to make them happy. It wasn't until I got some distance in college that I realized that what happened in our house wasn't normal. The silence. The memories tucked away. The way my parents' smiles rarely reached their eyes.

But I don't have to let Sara's death define me. It's a terrible thing that happened, and I miss her all the time, but I have to live the life she never got. I can't waste it wishing for some different outcome. I need to take my chance at happiness when I have it.

I need to hold on to Ben.

That's what it feels like today, anyway.

As for tomorrow, that's TBD.

I change into something fresh at my apartment and pack a bag for overnight at his and then we decide to walk over the Brooklyn Bridge into Manhattan. Ben puts my backpack on his back and we hold hands and set out on our adventure.

"Will this heat ever die?" I ask Ben half an hour later.

Why do romantic things always start off sounding good but end up with me in a sweaty mess?

"Usually goes in the fall."

"When's that again?"

"Couple of months."

"I'm not built for this."

He brings my hand to his lips. "You look cute in shorts, though."

I look down at what I chose to wear. A pair of white linen shorts and a featherlight tank top. It's as close as I can get to being naked in public. "I wish there was somewhere we could go swimming."

"Like the river?"

"Pretty sure that would kill us. But what about a pool?"

"There are a couple."

"Have you never been?"

"When I was a kid, sure."

I laugh. "I can see you cannonballing into the water."

"That may have happened."

"We should rent a car and drive to the Adirondacks. I could go for a jump into a cold lake."

"Maybe next weekend? Depending on . . ."

"You need to stick around for your mom, I get it."

He'd called her this morning and she was still stable. His sister and dad were visiting. He's going to check in tomorrow and probably spend the day with her.

"We'll find something fun to do, though," he says.

"We will."

"Have you been for dim sum yet?"

"I haven't."

He rubs his hands together. "Excellent. I know a fantastic place. I'm warning you now that it's nothing to write home about in the décor department, but the food is perfect. I'm usually the only white guy there when I go."

"Why is that relevant?"

"That's how you know it's good." He has this boyish grin on his face that he gets when he's excited. It's weird, we've only been together a week and already it feels like I know so much about him, and vice versa.

And then there are these whole swaths of things that I have no idea about.

Better not to think about those.

"Where is this place?"

"Not too far. We can take the subway."

"Isn't it even hotter down there?"

"Good point. Hop-on hop-off bus?"

"Are we allowed on there if we live here?"

"Don't see why not." He takes my hand. "Come on, there's a stop not far from here."

"You know the schedule?"

"I do."

"Do I want to know why?"

"It was a perk of my mom's job. She got free passes to it all the time. In high school, my friends and I would use it to get around the city."

"And terrorize the tourists?"

"Probably."

"Someday we'll go to Cincy and I'll show you all the places where I was a brat when I was a kid."

"Will there be marionettes?"

"One can hope."

We walk to the hop-on hop-off stop and get on the next bus. The guide is an old-timer, with a thousand stories and a voice that sounds like cigarettes.

I listen to his patter, holding Ben's hand, seeing the city in a new way. There are many things I should've done when I got here, but instead I settled into work and my routine, and now I barely know anything about the place I live in except for what I've seen in movies or read in books.

When we get to Chinatown, Ben takes us to a restaurant that can only be described as a hole in the wall. The décor is from the '70s, and the air is full of the smell of fried things. But it also smells amazing, and, as promised, we're the only white people in here.

A waiter leads us to a table and we sit down.

"You trust me?" Ben asks.

"Is this a trick question?"

"I meant about the food."

"I like everything but chicken feet."

My grandfather loved dim sum and he used to take me to the one good place back home when I was a kid. When he was feeling playful he'd get a plate of fried chicken feet and make them walk across the table. I was never able to eat them; they looked too realistic.

"Noted." A woman pushes a cart full of steaming bamboo baskets over to us and Ben addresses her. "We'll have the har gow, shumai, and the peanut dumpling."

She plucks the containers off her cart and puts them on the table, marks what we ordered on our bill, then leaves. Another cart will be by shortly, but for now, this looks like we're off to a good start.

"Tell me something I don't know about you," I ask Ben as I grab a dumpling with my chopsticks.

"What category of thing?"

"Doesn't matter. Anything."

"I'm enjoying *Felicity*."

"It's good, right?" We've only made it five episodes in. TV Ben hasn't won Felicity back yet, but she's thawing.

"Ben makes some questionable choices, but I feel for the guy."

"This is really good," I say, pointing to the har gow.

"Right? Your turn."

"Hmmm. When I was eight or nine I had scarlet fever."

"For real? Like in the olden days?"

"I was pretty sick."

"Were you in the hospital?"

"Almost. And it was right after Sara died."

"What was she like?"

I smile at my memories of her. "She was fun. Like always in a good mood, I remember. Some people don't get along with their sisters, but we did. I'm glad about that."

"What's your best memory of her?"

"It's weird to say it, but that day. Right up until the end, it was this amazing day on the boat. Perfect weather. I got up on water skis for the first time. We had this awesome picnic. I remember thinking: this is a perfect day. Which is a weird thing for a little kid to think. Maybe I had a premonition." I shiver at the thought of it. I used to think that when I was kid if I'd said something, I might've saved her. But that's silly. No one would've listened to me. And my feeling wasn't specific. Just a generalized feeling of contentment.

I have a moment of insight—maybe that's why I don't trust being happy. Because it means something bad is about to happen?

Ben plays with his chopsticks. "The day my mom got diagnosed with MS, we'd gone to the park together. To the bridge I took you to. And we were standing there and she was telling me about meeting my dad for the first time or their date, maybe how he proposed, and she was happy and lit up, and I had a similar thought. Like, I'm the luckiest kid. My mom is great. And then she got this funny look on her face and her knees buckled. It turned out she'd been having symptoms for a while but brushed them off, and that was her first serious attack."

"That sounds scary."

"It was." He stares at the dumpling on his plate. "Sometimes I used to think I made it happen. Like somehow my thoughts had given it to her."

"Kids think stupid things sometimes."

"They do."

I squeeze his hand. "Tell me something funny you did as a kid. Something cute."

"I wet the bed until I was eight."

"Um."

"Too much?"

"No. I like it that you feel comfortable enough with me to tell me something like that."

"Your turn."

"No bedwetting stories, but I did use to make up songs when I was a kid and sing them to other people."

"Interesting."

"Embarrassing, you mean."

"It's cute. Do you still sing?"

"Only in the shower."

"I'd love to hear you."

"You really wouldn't. You're a professional. I'm not your next act."

A woman arrives with a new set of baskets. Fried squid and greens and some items I've never heard of. Ben fills up our table again with food.

"Everything is delicious, Ben. Thank you for bringing me here."

"I want to show you all the New York things."

"You love it here, don't you?"

"I do. You don't?"

"There are things I love for sure. But this city can be a lot."

"It can be, I get that."

"You'd never want to live anywhere else?"

He puts some fried squid on his plate. "I've never thought about it. My company is here, my connections. My family. That would be a lot to leave."

I nod. "It was easy for me to leave Cincinnati."

"Because of your parents?"

"My last boyfriend turned out to be a jerk. He got most of our friends in the breakup. And Kit had already moved to New York. When the chance to apply for my job came up, I was ready to go."

"No regrets?"

"Not really. It's a good job. Not right now, maybe, but in general."

"How come not right now?"

"I meant all that interpersonal stuff. That stupid story about us and the fight with Jameela. And Tabitha made me do this list . . . anyway, it doesn't matter."

"Matters to me."

"Thanks, Ben."

He smiles at me, then pats his stomach. "Do you think I'll ever need to eat again after this meal?"

"I bet you'll manage."

We slip through the rest of the weekend.

When it's the two of us, things are uncomplicated. We create this bubble together; it's something we've done from the very beginning. I don't know what it is—chemistry? We have that in spades, but it's more than that. It's like we've known each other for as long as I've known Kit, but there are still all these holes in our knowledge of each other.

I want to fill them, though, and we do a lot of that this weekend.

Oh dear, I heard how that sounds in my head.

Ahem.

Anyway, the weekend slips by and Ben leaves midmorning on Sunday to spend the day with his mom with a promise of telling her about the end of him and Rachel if she's up to the news, and I make my way to Kit and Theo's.

Kit answers the door in her pajamas—a pair of boxer shorts and a tank top with no bra underneath.

"I don't rate real clothes?"

She shrugs. "It's hot."

"It is."

"Theo's trying to fix the air-conditioning."

"He's dressed, I hope."

She cocks her head to the side. "Define dressed."

"I don't want to see parts I shouldn't."

Kit glances over her shoulder. "Should be safe."

"Phew."

She laughs and steps back, letting me in. They've done a good job of decorating the place in the few short weeks they've lived there. She's painted one of the walls a bright yellow and their furniture is soft and comfortable. If I can ever afford a bigger apartment, I'm hiring Kit to decorate it.

"Ever thought of a new career in decorating?"

Theo pops his head out of the kitchen. He's wearing a shirt, thank goodness, but it is hot in here. "I told her the same thing the other day!"

"Great minds."

"But I like my job," Kit says.

"They fired you."

"But theoretically. I like what I was doing before my boss became a jerk."

"You'll find a new job doing that, then. How was the rest of the party?"

"It was great. Though we did miss you. One week with a boyfriend and this girl drops her friends."

"Did I?"

"No."

"Phew. But you'll tell me if I do that, right?"

"I will. Are we sitting or what?"

I let her go. "Yes, we are sitting!"

As we move to the couch, my phone beeps. It's not a text; it's the sound I've assigned to my work email. I remember I got some other work email yesterday and I never checked that either.

I pull my phone out of my purse and open my inbox. There are three messages from Tabitha. The last one is marked URGENT.

What the hell is going on?

I open it.

Chloe,

I'm going to assume you have not seen my last two messages but regardless, do not come into the office tomorrow. You are hereby placed on administrative suspension for one week while I try to sort out this mess.

Tabitha

OMG, what?
What the fuck is happening?

Chapter Thirty-one

"What's going on?" Kit asks. "Are you okay?"

"I'm on suspension."

"What? Why?"

"I'm not sure, can I use your laptop?"

"Of course. But are you sure you're all right? You look pale."

I sink into the cushions. What could've happened to put me on suspension on a weekend when I didn't even check my email?

Kit brings me her laptop and I log into my work email. There are two other emails from Tabitha. I open the first one, which is in response to the list of rom-com titles I sent her on Friday as I was leaving the office.

Is this a joke? She wrote. *Because it's not funny.*

Okay, she didn't think my titles were funny. But why am I on suspension?

I open the second email.

Chloe,

I have been informed that this completely inappropriate list has been sent to the entire company. As such, I am consulting HR on next steps.

Oh shit, what?

I go into my sent emails and find the email I sent on Friday. It was the last thing I did before I left the office. I open it and immediately see the problem. Somehow, instead of sending it to Tabitha, I sent it to To-All, which is a function on our server that sends an email to everyone in the office—all fifty employees, including the corporate offices, which are on another floor. The email program autofills email addresses once you start typing the first letter, and this had happened to other people before, but never to me before now.

But what was the problem? No one else had been put on administrative leave for doing it. Usually, it led to a round of funny emails that continued until someone higher up told us all to go back to work, but it wasn't anything serious or problematic.

Why am I in trouble?

And then it hits me.

Oh no, I couldn't have.

I click on the attachment to my email To-All and open it. It's the list of porny titles I was supposed to send to Kit. Instead of the rom-com titles I'd made for Tabitha, I'd sent the wrong list to the entire office, including the president of the company.

"I'm going to get fired."

"Why?" Kit says, sitting next to me.

I show Kit the email and its attachment. Her eyes go wide when she sees the list. The title at the top is *GO DOWN ON ME*. It gets worse from there.

"How did that happen?"

I lean back on the couch, feeling dizzy. "I was doing too many things at the same time. I rushed out and sent it without checking. I'm so screwed."

"I'm sure you can explain to her what happened."

"Maybe," I say, but I doubt it. Not only does it look like I didn't do the work I was supposed to but it also means I was screwing around at the office working on personal things. And the president of the company is a conservative sixty-something guy who reminds me of my dad. No way he's going to be okay with this.

Kit pulls me into her arms. "It's going to be okay."

"What am I going to do if I get fired? I can't afford to stay here if I don't have a job."

"You'd go back to Cincy?"

"I don't want to. I had this massive fight with my mother yesterday."

"About?"

"I might have told her that I knew she wished it was me who died, not Sara."

"Yikes," Kit says, but with sympathy. She knows better than anyone what I've been through with my parents.

"You can always stay here," Theo says, coming fully into the room this time. He's wearing shorts and a T-shirt and holding a wrench. I'm not sure what that has to do with fixing the air-conditioning, but now is not the time to ask.

"That's sweet."

Kit smiles at him. "He means it. We have two bedrooms."

"That's nice, you guys."

"I bet you could stay at Ben's too."

My stomach tightens into a knot. "That's a lot for the beginning of a relationship." I stand up. "I need to go. I need to try to call or write to Tabitha and fix this."

"You sure?"

"I've got to handle this."

"Okay, but don't be afraid to reach out for help if you need to."

"I won't."

I hug her again and then stand and hug Theo too. "I forgot to say on Friday that if you hurt her I'll kill you."

"That was implied."

"Good."

"You're always welcome here."

I feel like I'm on the verge of tears. I need to go. "Thank you. I love you, guys."

I don't wait for the echoing response. I'm loved here, and they don't have to prove it.

I get outside in the hall, clutching my phone. I need to call Tabitha but I don't have her cell phone number. An email will have to do.

Hi Tabitha,

I am sorry for the delay in my response. I've been tied up all weekend and didn't have any reason to think I should be checking my work emails. I've learned I accidentally sent a joke list I was making for my friend who is getting married to you and the rest of the staff at BookBox. I did do the actual list you asked me for, which I'll send you when I return to my apartment.

I have no excuse for how this happened other than to say it was obviously in error and I am sorry for any embarrassment or other issues that it might've caused you or the other employees. I can send a general apology to the company if you think that's appropriate. I love my job at BookBox and don't want to do anything to jeopardize it. Would it be possible to come in and talk this through?

Again, I am sorry this happened.

Regards,
Chloe

I read it over three times to make sure there are no typos and that it's addressed to Tabitha alone, and then send it.

By the time I'm outside in the heat of the day, Tabitha has already responded.

Chloe,

  I will discuss this with HR but for now, the suspension stands. I have forwarded your email to the president and will discuss it with him this week. I understand mistakes happen, but you've been distracted at work, and coupled with the "missing campaign" that you ran without permission, I believe we have grounds to terminate you. This is not a decision I take lightly, but I need to be able to trust my team, and that trust has been violated. I suggest you take this week to think seriously about the choices you've been making lately.

Tabitha

I lean against the building, winded, my mind whirling.

I'm going to get fired.

I'm going to get fired and the thing is?

I understand why. Tabitha's right. I haven't been thinking straight.

Not since I met Ben.

"Can we talk about this?" Ben asks four hours later.

After I settled myself down by walking for hours, I texted him and then went to his apartment to collect the few things I'd left behind and to tell him face to face that I can't be in this relationship right now. He greeted me with a big hug and a bigger smile, which was immediately crushed when I said I was ending things.

Now, it feels like someone is squeezing my heart so hard it's going to burst.

"I can't, okay, Ben? My life is falling apart."

"I understand, I do. But running away from me isn't the way to fix it."

I turn around. His face right now is going to kill me. "It's not a good time for me, Ben. I thought you'd understand that."

"Of course I do. But you taught me that it's not about the timing, it's about the person."

This stops me. How can it not? "I don't know about that. I have to be realistic with my life right now."

"What does that mean?"

"It's been a mess ever since I met you. I'm making stupid decisions. That whole 'Missing' campaign I did to find you? I didn't even get permission to do that. That's not like me. And it's not like me to make mistakes at work. I'm going to get fired, Ben. *Fired.*"

"I apologize for anything I contributed to that. Please, let me help you."

"I think . . . I have to help myself."

"And that means moving on from me?"

"Yes, unfortunately, it does."

Ben takes my hands in his, and I feel it, that attraction between us that's been there from the beginning. "Do you think this happens every day?"

"I—"

"It doesn't. You know it doesn't."

I pull my hands away. "That's just attraction. Pheromones. It doesn't mean anything more than that. I was stupid for thinking it does."

Ben flinches but moves closer to me. "No, Chloe, no. *This* is what I was hoping I had with Rachel all those years. I know the difference. I get that the timing isn't right, or doesn't feel right. But what I realized was that you can't wait for the right moment to come along. Because life isn't like that. You have to make the moment."

"I'm not sure I believe that."

"What about the fact that we keep being pulled back together? We both tried to walk away but it didn't work."

"That's the Venn diagram."

"The what?"

"The law of averages. Like how you hear a word for the first time and then you see it everywhere. We don't live that far away from one another. We probably passed each other a bunch of times before and never noticed. It was only because I was looking for you that it felt like it was some big life-meaning coincidence when we ran into each other."

"I don't believe that." He takes my hand again and puts it to his heart. I can feel his heart beating as mine's breaking. "I know you feel what I feel."

"It doesn't matter what I feel."

"Of course it does. That's the only thing that matters."

I pull my hand away gently. "No, Ben. I'm sorry, but no. We aren't in a rom-com. The universe is not putting us together for a reason. Relationships that start with trust issues don't magically work out."

"You don't trust me?"

"I don't trust myself. Not with you. I walked out on my best friend's engagement party because you weren't there. And then there's Rachel."

"She's not a factor."

"Really? You told your mom you'd broken up then?"

He looks at the floor and I don't have to ask again to know the answer to my question.

"What can I do?" he says.

"There isn't anything either of us can do. It's the way it is."

"There must be something."

"There is."

"What? Name it."

"Let me go." I gulp, but I force myself to continue. "This is hard enough for me already. You don't even know how hard. Please let me walk away." My throat tightens. I have to get out of here or I'm going to start crying.

He takes a step back. "This isn't what I want."

"I wish things could be different, but they aren't. Please don't make this any harder than it already is."

"Okay, Chloe."

I reach up and kiss him quickly on his cheek, then bolt for the door before I change my mind and stay.

Chapter Thirty-two

There's this thing in movies called the dark night of the soul. Once you know about it, you always recognize it. It's that moment when all seems lost in the protagonist's life. When they hit rock bottom and can't see a way out. Everything they've tried to do has failed. Every path they want to take is blocked. But in the morning, there's a glimmer of light. Something shifts, and they realize something that they haven't thought of until then. They claw their way back and before you know it they're tackling that obstacle, or solving that crime, or finding the love that was elusive until then.

That's how life works in the movies.

But my life?

It's the morning now. I barely slept last night. I couldn't get the image of Ben's broken face out of my head. I couldn't help wondering if this was another one of the stupid decisions I keep making.

BookBox is a job. I can get another. I can move to some other city or back to Cincinnati. But if I do that, then I won't have Ben.

Ben.

I haven't known him for long, but it feels like he'll be imprinted in my life forever.

Am I in love with him?

That's what Anne Shirley realized in *Anne of the Island* in her dark night of the soul after she learned Gilbert was dying. That she'd loved him the whole time. But there I go again—looking to books to solve my very real problems.

Because it doesn't matter if I'm in love with Ben.

It doesn't change the reason I broke things off.

What I said was true. I can't trust myself around him. I can't trust that what I'm feeling is the best thing for me. And how are you supposed to build a relationship if you can't have that?

How are you supposed to build a life?

My phone beeps on the nightstand. I check it, half hoping it's Ben even though I told him not to contact me. I'm surprised by the time. It's after ten. I haven't slept this late in a while, but I guess I have nowhere to go. I still feel exhausted.

It's a text from Jameela. Only we've never texted before, so that's how her text starts. *This is Jameela. Are you okay?*

I'm okay, I write.

I can't believe they put you on suspension.

Before I can answer another text appears and I realize it's a group thread. The other person is another number I don't recognize.

There are a couple of old ladies who work in fulfillment who nearly had a heart attack after they read your list.

Addison? I ask.

Of course.

Jameela and Addison have made up. That's something. I picture them, sitting at their desks in the triangle with my empty one, messaging me on their phones. I guess they couldn't call me in case Tabitha heard.

I can't believe this is happening, I write, partly to them and partly to myself.

It'll blow over, Addison says.

I'm getting fired. Tabitha wants to fire me.

But sales have gone up month over month since you've been here, Jameela writes.

And that thing you did with that campaign made that book a bestseller, Addison adds.

Doesn't seem to matter.

You going to take this lying down?

I *am* in bed.

Ha-ha. No, girl. No, Addison writes. *Get up. Fight. This is bullshit.*

Agree, Jameela says. *You have to fight for the family you want.*

I can't help but laugh. *#Bridgertonquotes forever!*

Totally, ha-ha. But I mean it. This isn't like you. Just accepting this.

I broke up with Ben.

Why?

Because you were right, Addison. I was making stupid decisions.

When did I say that?

In your Wattpad story. You know, the one about me?

There's a pause, and I wonder how she's going to react.

That's fiction.

It's inspired by me, right?

Maybe.

I'm not mad. You made me see some things. Thank you.

My phone pings with a new text in a separate thread. It's Jameela.

I can't believe you brought that up!

Is she mad?

Nah, she seems fine. Someone contacted her about publishing it?

What?

An editor at Wattpad? Deanna something.

OMG.

The other thread pings and I toggle back.

I wasn't trying to teach anyone any lessons with that book.

It's fine, Addison. Whatever you were doing, it resonated with me. And lots of other readers too.

You sure you're not mad?

Nope.

Cool.

Ping!

OMG, Jameela writes in the other thread. *I can't believe she's not telling you about the book!*

I'm sure she will when the time is right.

Doesn't she need your permission or something?

For what?

To use your story?

I don't know.

She should give you a cut.

Ping!

What are you two texting about? Addison writes.

Does she have magical powers? But no, she's not dumb and Jameela's right next to her. She can see that Jameela is texting more than what appears in the thread.

Jameela mentioned you might have some interest in publishing your book?

The other thread goes. *!!!*

I can't lie to her again. I'm in enough trouble.

Ping!

That's true.

I think it's great, Addison.

Really?

Yeah, really. If it's your dream, go after it.

Good advice. You should take it.

Right.

I mean it, Chloe. What do you want out of your life? If BookBox is it, then go get it.

How?

Ask for a meeting. Make your case. If you don't try you'll never know. Same goes for Ben.

Ouch.

Why did you break up with him? Jameela writes.

Because ever since I started trying to find him my life has been a mess. I make stupid decisions. All that stuff with his phone number. How he lied to me on our first date. How he didn't want to be with me until we slept together. I don't feel like I can trust it or him or me.

Respect.

But true love is worth it, Jameela writes.

I wish I lived in the ton, but I don't.

That was a racist, misogynistic time, Addison says.

You know what I mean. A fairy tale. Where everything works out.

Happily Ever After.

No HEA for me.

You can get that, if you want it, Jameela says. *Don't you believe that?*

Honestly, if I get my job back that will be enough for me.

You need help with that? Addison says.

I'll take all the help I can get.

Okay, Addison writes. *Can you come to the office at 4?*

I'm not supposed to.

I'll make sure it's okay. Just come.

Thanks, guys. I appreciate the check-in.

Jameela puts a heart in the chat, but it's some sort of text effect, because it keeps growing and growing until it explodes, splattering all over the screen.

Sorry, Jameela writes. *Not what I was going for.*

No, I write. *It's perfect.*

I show up at BookBox fifteen minutes before four. Addison texted to say it was okay for me to come, and there's no way I'm showing up late for this meeting. I have a bad moment when my pass doesn't work, and I have to go to security to get a visitor's pass, but I shouldn't have been surprised.

I'm on suspension.

Suspended in time.

Not welcome here.

Gah.

It doesn't help that I could reach out to Ben right now and he'd be there for me, sending me encouragement, offering to make me dinner after. It hasn't even been a day, and if I keep thinking about him then I'm going to start crying and that's not the look I'm going for.

Instead, I've dressed like I'm going for an interview, and I have a printed package under my arm with the sales numbers and initiatives I've implemented since I got here. I ride the elevator up to the BookBox floor more nervous than I was for my first interview.

Tabitha is there to greet me when the doors ding open. I guess she can't trust me to even walk into the office without an escort. I feel a flash of annoyance; it's not like I stole anything.

"Hi, Tabitha. Thank you for meeting with me."

She nods and glances over her shoulder. Jameela and Addison are smiling at me encouragingly from our shared workspace.

"Come into my office."

I follow her into her office and sit down where she tells me to. She's got some of the best-selling book covers up on her wall—there's one waiting to be mounted. It's the book I worked on, *Most Wanted*.

"I'm listening. What did you want to tell me?"

I put my folder down on her desk and open it. I hand her a copy of the printout. I went to Kinko's to get it done in color, and it looks impressive if I do say so myself.

"First of all, I wanted to reiterate that I did prepare the list of titles you were asking for."

"You didn't email it to me."

"Here it is." I push a document across the table. I spent the rest of the morning preparing it and the rest of the presentation. There's nothing like fear to focus the brain, and the list is pretty good. "And I'm happy to produce content like that whenever you want. On Friday, I had a lot going on. The other list . . . I know it's not funny, but it's a long-standing joke between me and my best friend. It was her engagement party on Friday. It's not an excuse, but it's why I was keeping the list. I was frazzled and I sent it to you."

"You sent it To-All."

"You know how that happens. I started to write your name and it came up as an option. I was working too quickly. Others have made the same mistake."

"Not with pornographic material attached."

"I'm sorry. I can write an explanation or go apologize to anyone who was offended."

She folds her hands on the desk. "That's the bare minimum."

"I also wanted to show you this." I take out the second document and give it to her.

"What is this?"

"It's our sales figures since I started here. You'll see that we're up twenty-five percent overall and *Most Wanted* was the most requested book of the last year and is still going strong."

"You're taking credit for this?"

"Not credit—I wanted to underline my contribution."

She looks again at the paper. "Where did you get these statistics?"

Addison gave them to me but I'm not throwing her under the bus. "I got them off the server."

"While you were on suspension?"

"No, I mean, yes, but only to show them to you."

"This is highly irregular, Chloe."

"I wanted to demonstrate how much my job means to me and how I've been doing here at BookBox. I screwed up a couple of times; I'm human. But I'm good at this job."

"What about your interpersonal issues?"

Does she mean Ben? "What are you referring to?"

"You and Addison and Jameela."

"We're good."

"I'm not an idiot, Chloe. Addison wasn't sick the other day."

"You'll have to ask her about that."

"I'm asking you."

I bite my lip. "She *was* sick. And we're all friends. I'm not saying everything is always perfect between us. Sometimes there's going to be little flare-ups, but nothing serious."

"I have trouble believing that."

"Didn't Addison and Jameela convince you to take this meeting?"

She leans back in her chair. "That's true."

"Why would they do that if we were in a fight?"

"That's a good point."

"And nothing will happen like this again. I've taken care of the distractions in my life. I will be one hundred-percent focused on work."

She considers me. "What about this man you were searching for?"

"He's not a factor anymore."

"Are you sure?"

"Yes."

"After all that?"

"It wasn't working out."

"Why?"

Do I have to explain this to her to keep my job? "Um, that's private."

She smiles for the first time. "Good for you."

"I'm sorry?"

"That was an inappropriate question, and I'm glad you pushed back."

"Oh, okay. Thank you?"

She looks at the report again. "This is good data."

"Will it make a difference?"

"It might."

"Will you go to bat for me?"

She puts the report down. "I'm not sure, Chloe. I have my job to think about too."

I feel like a deflated balloon. "I understand."

"Give me a day."

"Of course." I guess I'll use that time to polish my CV. Ugh. I stand up. "Thank you for your time."

I turn to leave.

"I'm surprised," Tabitha says.

"About what?"

"That you're not with that man anymore. Ben?"

"Why?"

"Because he called here today to ask me to go easy on you. Said it was his fault that you were distracted at work. He seems nice."

I squeeze my hands together, shock enveloping me. "Sometimes nice isn't enough." I blow out a long breath. "Is it okay that he did that? It didn't hurt my chances did it?"

"Did you ask him to call?"

"No."

"Good. I like a woman who can save herself."

I give her a wan smile. "That's me."

Chapter Thirty-three

I leave Tabitha's office in a state of shock. My mind is swirling with possibilities. Should I be mad that Ben called? Happy. Why did he do it?

"How did it go?" Jameela asks. She's wearing a deep-red color that I've seen her using to alter photos of Kate. It suits her, though I still think it's weird to alter photos of some actress you don't know to see if you like her better in another color of dress.

"Give us the skinny," Addison adds. She's done her braids up in an intricate pattern on her head, like something that might've been worn in *Bridgerton*. Was this how she and Jameela made up? It seems out of character for Addison, but then again, she has many hidden parts of her, like everyone.

I glance back at Tabitha's office. The door is closed. "It went well."

"Why do you look like that, then?" Addison asks.

"Like what?"

"Like a scared chicken."

"Addison!" Jameela taps Addison on the arm. "We talked about this."

Addison shrugs with one shoulder. "Sorry."

"It's fine." I sigh. "It was something that happened in the meeting with Tabitha."

"What?"

"Ben called her."

They exchange a guilty glance.

"You knew this?"

Jameela's face flushes. "He called me earlier wanting to get Tabitha's number."

"How did he get *your* number?"

"The company directory? You've talked about me, I guess."

"Only good things. What did you tell him?"

"Just when the best time to reach her was."

"You sure that's all?"

"What else would I tell him?"

"Why, though?"

Jameela's confused. "What do you mean?"

"Why did you give him Tabitha's number?"

"Did he say something bad?"

"No."

"Then what's the problem?"

"I don't need my ex meddling in my affairs."

She uses her arms to hug herself. "But it's so romantic."

"Is it? What if he'd made things worse?"

Jameela looks down at the floor. "I didn't think of that."

I try to smooth out my tone. This isn't Jameela's fault, and I don't want to be in another fight. I'm angry, though I'm not even sure why or at who. "I know you meant well, Jameela, but I broke up with Ben for a reason."

"What's the reason?" Addison asks.

"Because I can't trust him."

She crosses her arms. "He cheated on you?"

"No."

"He lied to you?"

"A little."

"What about?"

"His sister knew about the contest. He could've found me."

"Why didn't he?"

"He wasn't ready."

Addison shrugs. "Doesn't seem like that big a deal to me in the grand scheme of things."

I swallow a bitter laugh. These women are my allies. "Zoey doesn't think so."

"I told you, that's just a story."

"It's close enough to reality to make me see my reality."

"So, change it."

"I can't rewrite my life."

"Can't you?"

If you'd told me a couple of weeks ago that I'd be arguing with Addison about my right to break up with Ben, I would've thought you were nuts. But instead, everyone around me thinks *I'm* nuts for ending things with him. I haven't even told Kit yet what happened. It doesn't take a genius to figure out that I'm scared that she's going to think I'm making a huge mistake.

That I'm scared I did.

"But it's my life," I say to Addison. "My decision. Isn't it?"

"Of course."

"I need to go."

Jameela pats me on the arm. "When will Tabitha let you know?"

"She said tomorrow."

"That's good."

"What if she fires me?"

"She won't."

"She might."

"There are other jobs," Addison says. "Have some confidence."

I smile at both of them. It's easy to speak about confidence when your head isn't on the chopping block. And it can't be easy to get a new job when you've been fired from your old one. I push those thoughts away. "Thank you for helping me. I truly appreciate it."

"Co-workers should stick up for one another," Addison says.

"I agree." I consider hugging Addison, but she's not a hugger. "Any news on your book deal?"

"Not sure. They seem excited."

"And you?"

"I'll believe it when I see it."

"You're cautious, I understand that."

"We've all been hurt before."

I meet her eyes. "Yeah."

"See you around."

"Thanks, Addison."

She goes back to her desk and it's just me and Jameela.

"You're not mad at me, are you?" she asks.

"No."

"At Ben?"

"I'm not sure. It was invasive."

"He was trying to show you how much he cares."

"It's a fine line between stalking and showing someone you care about them."

"You should know."

I start to laugh. "Touché."

"Are you going to call him?"

"Not sure."

"I'll stop pushing. But—"

I put up a hand. "Please do not quote Violet Bridgerton to me right now."

I have the line in my head anyway, something about how I shouldn't lose Ben. How even if it's hard, I shouldn't push love away. Or something like that. Maybe I'm filling in the blanks with a message I want to hear.

"I won't."

I hug her. "Thank you."

"I'll see you later this week."

"That would be nice."

"It'll happen."

I release her. "Then I'll believe it."

Outside, on the street, I hold my phone, unsure about what I want to do. Part of me wants to rip Ben a new one. To remind him I don't need saving, that I can save myself. Part of me wants to thank him for trying. Part of me wants him back, even though it's only been a day.

I don't feel like I've ever been this indecisive before, not knowing what to do or how to act. It's tempting to see this as a sign of something. A sign we're meant to be together, that I made a huge mistake. But didn't I just tell myself I'd stop looking for signs from the universe? Why would the universe be speaking to me anyway? Why would it even care?

Hi Ben, I had my meeting with Tabitha. She told me you called her. I appreciate you trying to help, but I got this on my own.

He answers like he was sitting there waiting for me to text him. And maybe he was.

Some backup never hurts.

I didn't ask for backup, tho.

I'm sorry. Did I make things worse?

No.

Is she going to give you your job back?

That's still being decided.

I hope it works out.

Thanks.

Are you mad?

I do feel angry, but it's mixed in with so many other things I don't know if I can recognize what I'm feeling. *I'm not sure.*

I shouldn't have said anything.

No.

I keep doing the wrong thing.

I don't write anything. I'll let my silence speak for me.

Any chance I can make this up to you?

I don't think so, Ben. Let me go, okay? Like I asked you to.

I don't want to do that.

I grip my phone harder. Am I really going to push away this man I worked so hard to find? Is that how my life is working now?

Yes. I've picked my path. I have to stick to it.

It's my choice, tho. Please respect it.

Okay, Chloe. Be well.

I shove my phone in my purse and start to walk in a direction, any direction. It doesn't matter where I go, as long as it's away from here.

But my questions chase me down the street.

Am I making the right decision? Everything in my body is screaming *no*. But that's the chemicals talking. The pheromones. I'm in withdrawal, like Ben was a drug.

It may hurt now, but I don't need a relationship to be happy. I was okay before.

And maybe, if I'm truly lucky, the universe will deliver me another Jack.

Chapter Thirty-four

"You did what?" Kit says that night.

"I broke up with Ben."

"Are you insane?"

"That's not helpful."

She picks up her glass of Chardonnay and tosses it back. We're in a restaurant equidistant between our apartments, an Italian place she brought me to when I first came to New York. I don't feel like eating. All I've had is wine. They sell a great house red by the liter.

"This isn't a joke?"

"No."

"Why?"

"It wasn't working out."

"Bullshit."

"Tell me how you really feel."

"Okay," she says, and clunks her empty glass down on the table. "You're being an idiot. You're afraid to be happy."

"I'm not."

"Yeah, you are. You and Ben are great together. You thought that so much you chased after him like, frankly, a crazy person, and now you've broken up with him after a week?"

I gulp down my wine. It's not having the effect I wanted.

"Was the sex bad?"

"No."

"It's just okay?"

"It was great. The best."

"You're nuts."

"There's more to a relationship than sex."

"Uh-huh."

"Come on, you're telling me that the reason you're marrying Theo is because the sex is great?"

She shrugs. "It's not not the reason."

"I thought it was because you loved him."

"Yeah, of course. But I'm not marrying someone who doesn't fulfill my needs."

I grip the stem of my glass. "I wasn't going to marry Ben."

"Sure, that's why you have a whole notebook with your name written as Chloe Hamilton."

"What? I do not."

"Uh-huh."

"Is this helpful?"

She touches my hand briefly. "I'm trying to knock some sense in you."

"Well, it hurts."

"It's supposed to."

"I meant, my heart hurts."

"Because it knows you're being an idiot."

"Kit."

"What?"

"Will you listen to me for a minute instead of judging my decision?"

She crosses her arms. "Okay."

"You like Ben, despite your reservations."

"*You* like Ben."

"Yeah, I do. I do like him. But that isn't the point. He's not good for me."

"Based on what evidence?"

I stare down into my glass. "Based on everything that's happened since the day we met. He lied to me, he disappeared, he had a chance to find me and didn't take it. Then when I found him, he lied to me again, and the only reason we got together is because I went to some concert with tickets *Jack* paid for, and we ended up in bed." Kit starts to speak and I raise my hand. "And that's another thing. Jack. Weren't you #teamjack?"

"That's before I saw you and Ben together."

"Just because he passed your weird test doesn't mean he's a good guy."

"Are you done?"

"No. He was with his last girlfriend for ten years, off and on, he hasn't told his mother about me, he wouldn't give me his phone number, he called my boss to try to get my job back—"

"What an asshole."

"It was invasive."

"He was trying to help you."

"I don't need his help," I say. "He's the reason I'm in trouble in the first place."

"He sent an email to your entire company with porny movie titles in it?"

"No, but—"

"He wrote that list for you?"

"Obviously, no, but—"

Kit picks up the decanter and pours herself a fresh glass of wine. "It's his fault you didn't ask your boss if you could run that 'Missing' campaign?"

"Are you done?"

"What do you want from me, Chloe?"

"I want you to support my decision."

"Even if I don't agree with it?"

"Yeah."

"That's not what friends do."

"Sure, it is."

Her mouth twists. "I'm sorry, Chloe, but no. This relationship is messy. I'll give you that. And I get that you think it should be easier than this. But that's not how life works. There isn't some magical creature looking out for us up there. If you meet someone you connect with, then you should hold on to that person because that might never happen again."

"That's depressing."

"It's true. Look how long it took me to find Theo."

"You're not that old."

"He's my first serious boyfriend, though. And you basically hadn't dated anyone in two years before you met Ben. Which is why I pushed you to go out with Jack. What if this is it? What if you don't find anyone else?"

"Then I'm alone forever, I guess. But I'm not even thirty. I have plenty of time to find someone."

"You think there are so many people out there who will take you as you are?"

That stings. "I'm so difficult to love?"

"That's not what I meant."

"What then?"

"Ben doesn't seem to care about any of that stuff. He's a relation-ship guy and he wants to be in a relationship with you. This city . . . there aren't that many guys like that."

What she's saying is true—those bad date stories I told Ben when we first met: The guys who did weird things. The guys who looked nothing like their profile pictures. The guys who made it clear that they weren't looking for a wife or even a girlfriend but only for a good time. Ben wasn't like that. But he had other downsides.

"What if he breaks my heart?"

"Ah, now we're getting to it."

"Maybe?"

"That's the risk you take for love, Chlo."

"Seems like a big risk."

She tips her glass at me. "One you'd both be taking."

"No one's said love. And he didn't even fight me that hard about the breakup. He hasn't texted me. Just answered when I texted him."

"You're mad at him because he did what you asked?"

"No."

"You're testing him?"

I slump down in my chair. "Would that be wrong? You did."

"That was a bit of fun. I was never going to tell you not to date him. So long as he wasn't a psycho."

"He's not a psycho."

"He could've been, though, that's my point."

"I feel dizzy."

She runs her hand up the side of my arm. "Hey, hey, this is a lot. And I get that you're scared. That you're looking for excuses not to be with him. I've been there okay?"

"With who?"

"Theo. I almost broke up with him six months after we started dating."

"You never told me that."

She looks grim. "I didn't do it."

"Why?"

"Because I was scared."

"Of Theo? He's a puppy."

"Of getting hurt. It all seemed too good to be true. I couldn't face it if it didn't work out. I decided to take things into my own hands and end it."

"What happened?"

"I chickened out."

"Why?"

"Because the thought of no Theo was scarier than the thought of taking a risk and having him leave me in the end."

"Same result."

"No, not the same. Because him leaving me was something I was scared about, it wasn't something that was going to happen. But if I broke things off, then it was happening for sure."

I speak slowly, absorbing her meaning. "Like me and Ben. That's happening for sure."

She squints at me. "And I have to say you're taking it way better than I thought you would."

"Honestly? Me too."

"Why?"

"Maybe I'm not as into him as I thought."

"I don't think that's it. You're clearly into him."

"Then why aren't I more upset?"

She considers me. "Because you don't think it's real."

"How could I not think it's real? I broke up with him, didn't I?"

"You don't think it's going to stick. I can tell. You think he's going to come back and convince you to try again."

I breathe out slowly. I have been doing that. All day, I've been waiting for him to do just that. "I'm not saying that's right, but if it is, is that so wrong?"

"It's risky."

"Maybe he should have to fight for me."

"Like in mortal combat?"

"Not literally. But I went to all this effort to find him and maybe he should show me that he wants to be with me as much as I want to be with him."

"Did you tell him that?"

"No."

She cocks her head to the side. "Planning to?"

"I doubt it."

"You're going to end up alone."

"Probably."

"Seems stupid to leave it to chance."

"I'm mostly stupid."

"Why aren't you acting like yourself?"

I eye the wine. I've lost track of how much I've had to drink, which is never a good thing. "How's that?"

"I would've expected tears and at least two cocktails plus pizza."

"I'm sure it will hit me in a minute."

"Don't wait too long."

"It's only been a day."

"Hey, you're the one acting nuts, not me."

"But you still love me, right?"

She smiles. "Of course. And so does Ben. For now."

Oof. Does Ben love me? I've been so wrapped up in how I was feeling that I've never even wondered. "He's never said he loves me."

"It's written all over his face."

"No, it's too soon for that. You can't love someone that quickly."

"Who says?"

I want to argue with her but she's right. About all of it. I haven't been acting like me. That's what I told Ben, wasn't it? That none of this was like me. And it isn't.

But maybe I've got the wrong part wrong?

My god, even in my head, I'm not making sense.

Maybe tomorrow I'll be able to figure this out. But for now, more wine.

At least I know how it will affect me.

And then, maybe then, I can recognize myself.

Chapter Thirty-five

I spend a night with weird dreams and when I wake in the early morning in a bed that still smells like Ben because I haven't changed the sheets since the last time he stayed over, I feel a wave of sadness.

This is the emotion I've been holding at bay, ever since I told Ben it was over. I don't know if it's regret or fear or sadness or a mix of all of them, but it's pinning me to the bed. It feels like I'm never going to get out of it. Like days might pass and I won't notice. Like this is the point in the movie of my life where a montage starts to play to some heart-kicking song and the pages turn over on a calendar and by the time I'm ready to get out of bed, it's a different season.

I hope it's fall.

Not only because I love fall, but because I can already feel the heat pushing at the windows, overcoming the air-conditioning.

If I stay in here, I won't have to face the day. I won't have to wonder if Ben will text me. I won't have to wonder if I'm ever getting my job back. I won't have to wonder if I'm in the middle of making the biggest mistake of my life.

Because I probably am, and that's so much pressure it's crushing me. I'm being crushed by my own stupid decisions. But how do you walk those back? How do I fix the mess I've made? I can't make a chart of all of the things I've accomplished with Ben, like I did for BookBox.

I'm not sure if I even want to. Because my heart hurts right now, but it could hurt worse.

I *am* afraid.

My head is such a mess. There are so many questions swirling around that I can't grab onto any of them. But the one that's there, front and center, is why hasn't Ben texted me? Why didn't he fight harder for me? He accepted it when I broke up with him and barely put up a fight. If he was in love with me, then he wouldn't have given up so easily. He would've tried harder for me. He would've—

I don't know what he would've done. Put up WANTED posters for me all over town? Gone searching for me when he already knew where I was?

Made some big romantic gesture so he could prove his love to me?

Do I want him to show up with a boom box? Is that what I'm waiting for? How could it be? We don't have a song. We weren't together long enough to find one.

What would be playing on the boom box, even?

I pull the covers up over my face. I've been living in a fantasy. I need to face reality.

But how does one do that, exactly?

I fall back asleep and when I wake my phone is ringing.

Ben!

But it's not Ben, it's Tabitha.

"Chloe?"

I sit up. My head feels woolly. I glance at the clock. It's mid-afternoon. "I'm here."

"Is this a good time?"

"Yes, of course."

"I've talked it over with the president and we've decided to give you one last chance. You'll be on probation for the next year, so you can't make any more mistakes, but—"

"Thank you."

"I wasn't finished talking."

"I'm sorry."

"That's all right. I was going to say you can come back in on Monday."

"Not today?"

"Why don't you take the rest of this week off? We think you can use some time before you get back into the thick of things."

Ugh. I need work. I need a distraction. "Okay."

"Did you have something you wanted to say?"

"I appreciate this. And you won't have to worry about me. I promise. I'll do a great job. I won't screw up again."

"I certainly hope not, Chloe."

"I won't. I appreciate this more than I can say."

"I'll see you on Monday."

"Yes, thank you."

We hang up and I hold the phone to my chest in relief. I kept my job. Despite everything, I still have a place to work.

I want to tell Ben.

But instead, I text Kit.

I still have my job.

Oh, thank goodness.

You didn't want me living with you?

Not really!

Ha, I knew it!

You could stay if you needed to.

I know.

I'm glad it worked out.

Me too.

Are you going to tell Ben?

Kit's always been able to see right into my brain. It's both annoying and sweet of her to make the effort. *Why would I?*

Since he helped you keep it.

Not sure if what he did could be considered help.

He tried.

He did.

Still on the fence, huh?

IDK.

Sounds like the definition of being on the fence.

Okay, I'm on the fence.

What would bring you off the fence?

IDK!

Why don't you talk to him?

It's hard.

You mean, you'd realize that you still wanted to be with him.

Get out of my head.

Call him already.

I don't text anything more, just throw the phone across the bed and pull the covers up again. I might as well catch up on sleep while I can. I'm going to have to put in some serious hours next week when I get back to work and the stress and nerves of it all will affect my sleep patterns.

I settle my mind and start to count backward. Amazingly, it works and I'm on the edge of sleep when it happens.

My phone pings again. I assume it's Kit. But when I look I see that it's a Facebook notification.

Ben Hamilton has been tagged in a new photo.

Every fiber of my being tells me not to check. But I'm not strong enough.

I open the app and go to the tag. It's a picture Rachel posted with her and Ben and Tyler and Tyler's moms. She has her arm around Ben's shoulder and looks like she's holding him possessively. And Ben's grinning as wide as can be. One of his genuine smiles, which he only does when he's happy, because I cataloged his smiles last week like I was learning him by heart.

Ben and Rachel are back together.

Fuck.

I hide in my bed for the rest of the day, but I don't fall back asleep. Instead, I torture myself with the Facebook photo, searching for clues.

Was that all it took? Two days apart and he was already back with her?

And though, eventually, I realize there are plenty of other potential explanations—it might be an old photo, or an innocent visit, or any number of other things—I can't keep the image of them together again out of my mind.

Because she's the one Ben was meant to be with. She's the one he couldn't quit. She's the one he kept breaking up with and going back to time and again.

I'm not the love of his life; I'm the blip that made him see who he should be with all along. And maybe that wouldn't have happened if I hadn't pushed him away. Maybe we'd be together right now if I'd let him in. If I'd let him stay. If I hadn't been so up in my head about whether it was right to be with him that I let it be.

But instead, I did the thing I was most afraid of. I was scared of something and then I made it happen. I'm an idiot of the highest order.

When I get up the sun is setting, and I sit in the nook in my window and look out at this city that felt alien to me when I arrived, and which is now starting to feel like home. Ben helped me with that. Showing me all the things around me I hadn't bothered to investigate. I can hold them to my heart and keep learning about this city. Or I can run away and go back to everything I know and am comfortable with.

I'm not sure what I'm going to do right now.

I need to get through this day and the next one and delete him from my life so I can't do something stupid like call him and tell him everything I'm feeling.

Yes. That's the first good idea I've had in a long time.

I do it before I have too long to think about it. I unfriend Ben on Facebook, and then block him for good measure. Then I go to our short text thread. I want to read through it to look for clues that there was something real between us. But that way lies madness, so instead, I block his number and delete him from my contacts. I wish I could erase the numbers from my mind, too, but they'll fade eventually.

All of this will fade eventually.

My heart will heal. The memories will become just that—things I can remember that don't hurt anymore. Like my memories of Sara. He can be dead to me but still with me. And all I can do is hope that in this city of millions of people we fall off each other's Venn diagrams.

The rest of the week goes by with me trying to do all the things I've promised myself. Not think about Ben, keep busy, discover new things about New York while avoiding any spot that might bring me too close to him.

And I succeed after a fashion.

I don't think about Ben every waking minute.

Only every other minute, which feels like a win.

But that happiness I'm searching for? That feeling of relative peace I had before all of this started? It feels far away. I have to give it time. I shouldn't give Ben such outsized importance in my life, but it's harder than I thought to get over him. To move on.

Kit's been giving me daily pep talks, and now it's Saturday and we've agreed to meet for brunch at a new place we haven't been to before. I get here early, because I can't help myself, and I'm sitting at a table in the sunshine, but it feels good because the air is on high.

While I wait for Kit to arrive I people watch the usual crowd—a couple having breakfast, another who look like they're on their first date, a family with a new baby in a carriage. So many lives, so many stories I'll never know.

I check the time. Kit is late. Five minutes, eight, ten.

I tap my foot against the tiled floor, fighting off the feeling of déjà vu, then text her.

WTF.

Hold your horses.

Do not goad me. I'm out of the porny movie title business.

You'll be back.

Where are you?

Don't worry, you won't be alone for long.

What does that—

"Chloe?"

I look up. It's Ben. My eyes travel back to my phone and my fingers move without thought.

What have you done?

Kit sends back a devil emoji in response.

"Can I sit?" Ben asks.

"Um, what?"

"Do you want me to go or can I join you?"

"No, I . . . please sit." My heart is hammering in my chest and it takes me a moment to realize Ben's wearing the same shirt he wore the day we met. Breakfast, the shirt, him being late. I've been here before, which means—

I swipe that thought away.

This isn't a sign from the universe. It's Kit. Kit is behind this, like she was the first time.

Ben sits across from me and puts his hands on the table.

"Kit sent you?" I ask.

"She didn't send me. She helped me set this up."

"Why?"

The corners of his mouth turn down. "You blocked me."

"Huh?"

"On Facebook? On your phone? I couldn't reach you."

"You tried to reach me? When?"

"Tuesday night."

Tuesday night. Right after I deleted him from my life. Because of course. "Why?"

"I wanted to talk to you."

"To tell me you're with Rachel?"

He pulls back. "What? No."

"I saw that photo of you on Facebook."

"That was from last summer."

"Why did she post it?"

"I have no idea. But when I saw that she'd done it, I told her to take it down. And then I tried to text you but it didn't go through. Same on Facebook. Then I knew you'd seen it."

"I did."

"I'm sorry."

"Okay."

"But that's not why I'm here."

"Why then?"

He picks up a fork off the table and fiddles with it. "I watched the rest of it. *Felicity*."

"The whole show?"

"Yeah."

"Wow."

"I had some time on my hands. Time trying to figure out what happened with us."

"You figure it out?" I ask.

"I think so."

"What was it?"

"You couldn't trust me. Like Ben. Like TV Ben. That's what you think. That I'm going to go away or leave you for Rachel or disappear. Right?"

I don't know what to say. It is what I've been thinking, though it isn't based on anything substantive. Having him say this is confirming my worst fears; it's making them come true.

"Something like that."

"The thing is you can. You can trust me. I'm not going anywhere."

"You can't promise me that."

"I can."

"Ben."

He leans forward. "I know why you wanted me to watch that

show. I can see the parallels. She ran after him and he pushed her away because he was scared of having something real with her. And that's what I did to you. And even though we ended up together for a while, you didn't trust that it wasn't all going to go away again."

"Okay, say that's true. What do we do about that?"

"I have an idea."

"What is it?"

"I tried to think back. To figure out what the moment was that I would do over if I could. Like TV Ben. What set us down the wrong path."

"What was it?"

He checks his watch. "It was right about now."

"What?"

"In our first meeting. This is when I knew I liked you."

"Ten minutes in?"

"Yeah. And that's when I should've done this." He holds out his hand.

"What am I supposed to do?"

"Take it."

I hesitate.

"Please."

I reach out my hand. Our fingers touch and I feel that spark. Something chemical that only seems to grow the more times we touch.

Ben grips my hand firmly. "I have something to tell you. I'm not Jack."

"Oh, I—" I almost laugh. "Are we doing this?"

"My name is Ben Hamilton. I don't know who Jack is but if he stood you up, he clearly sucks."

"He got stuck at work."

"He's going to regret it."

"Oh yeah?"

"Definitely."

Our eyes meet and I feel my cheeks start to flush.

"Are you going to let go of my hand?"

He lets it go and I wish I hadn't asked him to. Now and before.

"Why did you sit down?" I ask.

"Sorry?"

"If you're not Jack? Why lie to me?"

"I couldn't help it."

"You couldn't help lying to me?"

"No, I meant I couldn't help but sit down."

"Because?"

"Because you looked like you needed a friend."

I clear my throat. "Is that what we're going to be? Friends?"

"I hope so."

He wants to be friends. All of this was to tell me that?

"Chloe?"

"Yeah."

"I don't only want to be friends."

"What do you want, Ben?"

He reaches for me again, his fingers touching the ends of mine. "I want you. Right from the beginning. I could've turned you away politely when you rushed up to me, but I didn't. I sat down and I liked you and I wanted to see you again. I want to see you again."

"Are we still in the reenactment?"

"If you want to be."

"You think we can start over like that?"

"We can start *together* like that. That's what I want. To wipe away the mistake I made in not telling you who I was right away and asking to stay anyway."

I watch our fingers touch. "I might've told you to get lost."

"Why?"

"Because that would've been embarrassing. Everyone in the restaurant was watching us. That's why I made such a big show when you showed up. I was feeling judged."

"No one was judging you."

"Janie was."

"Janie?"

"The waitress."

He smiles. "She was judging *me*."

I smile back. "She was."

"So, what do you think the moment is?"

"The moment we should do over? I'd have to think about that."

"I wanted to show you that I get it. And I'm here. I'll wait until you're ready. Until you can trust me again. I'm not going anywhere."

"Why is it so important to you?"

"Because I'm in love with you."

My heart starts to race again. "You are?"

"I am. Maybe this is going to sound nuts, but it felt like I was from that first day. From the Met. I told you I've never felt this way before, and I meant it."

"I don't know what to say."

"If you don't feel the same way, I'll walk away. Just say the word."

"You'd give up that easily?"

"Is this a test?"

I smile again. "Pretend it is."

"I'm here because I believe that you *do* feel what I feel. But I'm not going to force you, Chloe. It'll be a bit of light stalking before I give up."

I start to laugh. "Light stalking, huh?"

"You'll barely notice me."

"Pretty sure I'd notice you anywhere."

He takes my hand properly this time, fingers intertwined. "You feel it, right?"

What's the point of denying it? We both know I'm in love with him. Everyone seems to know it. "I do."

He squeezes my hand and smiles. "That's a relief."

"You think it's enough?"

"Hell, yeah, I do."

"It doesn't erase everything else."

"That's why I was trying to build a time machine."

"I appreciate that."

"So." He picks up the menu. "What's good here?"

"You want to eat?"

"Isn't that what we're doing?"

"I guess."

"Hey, Chloe?"

"Yeah?"

He stands and walks to my side of the table. Then he kneels so we're eye to eye and takes my face gently in his hands. He kisses me slowly, and I feel the heat rise up my face.

"People are watching," I say against his lips.

"I don't care."

He kisses me again, and now I don't care either. My hands go up to his face and cradle it as our mouths explore each other. When he pulls away this time, we're both a little breathless.

"You have plans after this?" he asks.

"What did you have in mind?"

"You want to meet my mom?"

I lean my forehead against his. "That was it."

"What?"

"The moment I'd go back to."

"Meeting my mom?"

"Not meeting her, being kept a secret. I didn't like it."

"Then we're fixing this."

"You're sure?"

"I already told her about you."

"When?"

"On Monday."

"After I broke up with you?"

"Yep."

"That was bold."

He touches his nose to mine. "I realized I was being stupid about it. My mom isn't weak; she's sick. I shouldn't have confused the two."

"What did she say?"

"That she was happy for me. And to get you back."

I laugh. "Sounds like we'll get along great."

He kisses me again, then stands to go back to his seat.

I catch his hand. "Ben? I love you too."

His face breaks open. "You sure?"

"I'm sure."

"Still scared?"

"Definitely. You?"

"Nope."

"Confidence, I like it."

He kisses my hand. "You love it."

"I love it."

Epilogue

ONE YEAR LATER

"Are you sure you want to do this?" Ben asks me.

We're standing outside my parents' house, holding hands. It's the summer in Cincinnati, which isn't the same as the summer in Manhattan. Maybe it's because my parents live in the suburbs, and the air is full of the smell of freshly cut lawns and the laughter of the children down the street who are running through a sprinkler.

We arrived last night and stayed in a hotel downtown near the river. I showed him all the things I love about the city. The historic downtown, the Seven Hills, the best place to get Cincinnati chili, the Rookwood tile factory. We haven't seen a marionette yet, but Ben has high hopes.

And now, my parents.

I didn't talk to my mom for three months after our blowout, but then, one afternoon, she texted me. It was something benign about a girl from my high school she'd run into at the grocery store, but it was something. Maybe it was because it was a few weeks after Ben's mom died and I was feeling tender, but I took a deep breath and answered her back, and we had a normal conversation.

A few weeks later I saw that a movie she likes was on a streaming channel and let her know. She answered that text and again, we had a normal conversation without tension.

Over the next couple of months I told her about me and Ben. How he was doing after his mother died—sad, but stoic. How we were looking for an apartment. How he'd signed a band from Cincy. Sometimes I even called her and my dad got on the line too. It was slow and steady and now here we are, on the weekend that Kit and Theo are getting married a few blocks from here, staying with them for the night.

"Are you sure *you* want to do this?" I say back to Ben.

"I'm here for you."

"And this is why I love you."

"Right back at you," he says, squeezing my hand.

In my other hand I'm holding a bunch of flowers. They're not for my mom, they're for Sara. It was the only condition I imposed on coming here—that we had to go and visit her grave for the first time as a family since we put her in the ground.

I got the idea from Ben. A week after his mom's funeral he asked me if I wanted to come with him to visit her. I didn't understand what he meant until he explained. She was gone but she was still here, in a way. He could visit her when he wanted to. I went with him to the graveyard, and we sat at her graveside and he told her about his week while tears sprang to my eyes and my throat closed up.

I was sad for him, but I was sad for me too. I could've had this, this whole time. I could've kept my relationship with Sara. But it had never occurred to me. Maybe that wasn't my fault—at eight, I was too young to know about visiting gravesides. But once I was older and had access to a car, I could've done it. Instead, I packed her away like my parents had.

I wasn't so different from them.

Maybe I didn't have to be angry.

Maybe I could forgive myself *and* my parents.

I said some of these things to them. Others I kept to myself. But I said enough to get through to them, and here we are. Standing on the threshold.

"Thank you for being here, Ben," I say.

"I wouldn't want to be anywhere else."

"You say that, but what if I catch the bouquet tomorrow?"

His eyes dance. "What if you do?"

I gulp down what this means because I can worry about that later. Not that there's anything to worry about. I only see my life with Ben. He feels that way too.

But right now I have my past to attend to.

I squeeze Ben's hand again. "Ready?"

"Ready."

We begin.

Acknowledgments

A second book! A dream come true. Thank you, dear reader, for being here and making it this far.

Thank you also to Deanna McFadden for giving this book a home. And to the entire team at Wattpad Books for getting the book out there.

To Stephanie Kip Rostan, dream agent.

To my friends and family for their support.

To the writers of *Felicity* for inspiring me with the best get-back-together in TV.

To the *Bridgerton* megafans for having a sense of humor. #Kanthony supremacy forever.

Chloe and Ben make it. In case you were wondering.

About the Author

Katie Wicks was born and raised in Montreal, Canada, where she now lives and writes full time. An amateur guitar and tennis player, Katie's debut novel, *Hazel Fine Sings Along*, was set in a reality singing competition. She's never been stood up on a blind date, but then again, she met her husband when she was sixteen. How romantic is that?

Chloe Baker's Lost Date
DISCUSSION QUESTIONS

1. Part of the reason Chloe is hesitant to begin dating in New York is that she finds New York guys too forward re: apps. Do you think apps have improved the dating experience or opened up any positives for people of all sexes and genders?

2. After leaving "Jack" and Central Park, Chloe feels that it was her most perfect date ever. What's your idea of the perfect date?

3. Would you forgive "Jack" for not telling Chloe who he really was? How do you think his momentary action to go along with Chloe's assumption that he's her blind date colors their entire relationship? Are you pro "real" Jack or "fake" Jack (Ben)?

4. Chloe has recently moved to New York, but she still sometimes feels like a "tourist in the city [she] lived in." What are the advantages of being a tourist in your own city? If you could relocate to any city in the world, where would you go? And what would it take for you to truly feel like you belonged there?

5. Chloe loves the book *From the Mixed-Up Files of Mrs. Basil E. Frankweiler* because it helped her cope with her sister's death. Is there a particular book from your past that resonates? If so, what is it, and why is it special?

6. One of the most important relationships in Chloe's life is her friendship with Kit. Do you think Chloe is a good friend? Why or why not?

7. The book explores themes of fate and missed connections. Do you believe in fate? Or do you think we make our own luck? What are some of your own experiences that felt like fate intervening?

8. Both Chloe and Ben are dealing with huge, definable losses in their lives: Chloe's sister and Ben's mother's illness. Chloe describes the loss of her sister like this, "It was like someone took a bite out of us, one that wouldn't heal." How do you think life-changing events like this impact a relationship? Does a loss have a greater impact on a current or future relationship? Why is that?

9. "It's life. Not everyone has a happy family." Chloe says. Ben replies: "Everyone deserves one, though." How do you think Chloe's feelings about her mother in particular contribute to her insecurity about her new relationship with Ben?

10. There are complicated relationships in Chloe's world. Ben's ex Rachel. The fact that she's seeing Jack at the same time as she and Ben sleep together. How do you feel these were handled in the novel? Were they realistic?

11. How do you feel about Ben's grand gesture? Would you give him a second chance to make a first impression?

CHLOE'S TOP FIVE PLACES IN
New York

1. The Metropolitan Museum of Art—the architecture, the knights in shining armor, the Templer of Dendur. And let's not forget all the places in *From the Mixed-Up Files of Mrs. Basil E. Frankweiler*. What's not to love?

2. The High Line—a beautiful walk above the street. It's a little oasis in the middle of the city.

3. Central Park—the lakes, the bridges, the reservoir, the winding paths. It might be obvious, but that's for a reason. Rent a bike and ride it around the park. Get lost in one of the many fields. Sail a little boat. Have a picnic. Every day is different and there's always something to do.

4. The restaurants—okay, is this cheating? There are so many of them, but that's what's great. Eat whatever you want, whenever you want, at most price points. Have pizza, have sushi, have pasta, have whatever you like. It's NEW YORK, baby.

5. The streets—this might also be cheating, but who cares? One of the best things about New York is that you can walk everywhere and anywhere. Just pick a direction and go. Check out the neighborhoods, which change every twenty blocks (or less). The old

houses, the old buildings, the skyscrapers, the tree-lined streets. The honking cars, the way Times Square glows so bright you can probably see it from space. Downtown, Chinatown, Uptown, all the towns. Again, it's New York, baby. You can make it whatever you want to be. Or something like that.

LOVED CHLOE'S STORY?

CHECK OUT KATIE WICK'S DEBUT NOVEL!

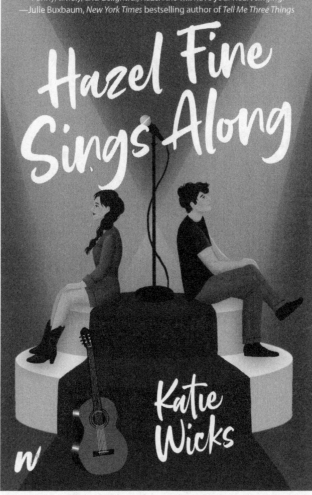

AVAILABLE NOW, WHEREVER BOOKS ARE SOLD.

Chapter One

"I'm so nervous!" Hazel said to Amber as she stared at every outfit she owned, all laid out on the uncomfortable bed of her long-stay motel. "What do you think I should wear to my audition?"

Amber cocked her head to the side. She was one of the sex workers who loitered by the fire escape of the Motel California every night, waiting for customers. Between jobs she loved to show Hazel pictures of her son, Theo, on her phone. They'd quickly become friends after Hazel had moved into the motel a year ago.

"What look are you going for?" Amber picked up a sparkly sequined bandeau top that Hazel's boss at the café where she worked had insisted she wear last Halloween. "This is sexy." Amber held the top against her body, checking her appearance in the grimy mirror. Tall and voluptuous, with platinum blond hair and almost black eyes, she was wearing an all-pleather outfit and five-inch heels. Hazel cringed at the thought of walking around in them.

"I don't think I pull off sexy. Plus, it's a singing competition, not *America's Next Top Model*."

Amber turned around. "Girl, no. They're casting parts, just like everyone else."

Hazel knew Amber was right. *The Sing Along*, now in its tenth season on Fox, was looking for a hundred men and women who could sing *and* fill a role. Hazel only had a couple of hours before she had to show up to the cattle call, where she'd line up all day and maybe, *maybe*, get a chance to sing in front of the judges—Georgia Hayes, the troubled country music star, and music producer Martin Taylor, who'd signed more acts than Hazel could count. They were intimidating and picky, and if she wanted a chance to impress them, Hazel knew she had to pick a lane. She just didn't know which lane would get her where she wanted to go.

"This would be a lot easier if you'd tell me what to do," Hazel said.

Amber laughed and stepped to the door, opening it and popping her head out. The sky was a dusky pink, the sun rising slowly over Venice Beach. Hazel had called Amber into her room for advice and moral support after she'd bolted awake at four knowing there was no way she'd go back to sleep. She didn't usually get to see the motel at this time of day. It was almost picturesque in the washed-out light. You couldn't tell that the sign had two letters that didn't light up anymore, and the cracks in the beige stucco faded into the background.

"Any customers?" Hazel asked.

"Nope. Slow night."

Hazel felt relief. She knew her friend was fine with what she did for a living, but that didn't mean Hazel didn't want more for Amber. That went for herself too. Her last year in this room had been depressing and demoralizing, eroding her hope to a thin flame.

With each passing day in this downtrodden life she felt further from her goals. When she'd been approached by a scout to audition for *The Sing Along*, it felt like her luck might be changing. But by the end of today her dream could also be shattered into a million pieces. If Hazel thought too much about it, she'd break out in hives. Definitely *not* the right look.

She picked up a green romper from the clothes pile. She looked cute in it, though it was a pain in the ass when she had to go to the bathroom. "How about this? I could do down-on-her-luck singer-songwriter with a plucky, can-do attitude, which is basically the truth."

"Love it." Amber reached down to the dirt-infused rug and came up with a pair of cowboy boots. "Wear these and do your hair in two braids. You won't look a day past eighteen."

"My ID says I'm twenty-two." When Hazel had obtained her new identity she'd subtracted six years from her real age and deleted her first and last names, leaving only her middle name and her mother's maiden name. Add in a new social security number, and *presto!*, she was an entirely new person. On paper, anyway.

"You get that from Vern?" Amber asked.

"Yeah." Vern was the sketchy front-desk man who always seemed to need access to Hazel's room to "check the plumbing." Hazel made sure to count her underwear every time he left. "He said it was guaranteed to work, and it better given the five hundred bucks I had to fork over for it."

"His IDs are legit, even if he isn't." Amber rummaged through the old makeup on Hazel's dresser, her bright-red nails clicking against the metal tubes. "This lip gloss should work. And just a hint of mascara."

"Thanks, Amber. I—" Hazel felt him before she saw him. Checkers, her rescue rabbit, was on the run, grazing past her leg as he hopped hopefully out of the room at a surprisingly fast pace. "Checkers!" Hazel called in vain. He never answered to his name. "Hold on!" she said to Amber as she sprinted past her to catch Checkers before he leaped into the scum-covered pool that took up most of the courtyard.

She ran down the rickety metal stairs to the concrete landing and caught up to him right as he was about to jump into the murky water. She gathered him to her chest. His heart thrummed against his rib cage, thrilled by his near escape.

Hazel walked him back to Amber, who was waiting for her by the stairs. A black Toyota Camry pulled up and idled near the bottom of the fire escape.

"Duty calls," Amber said, eyeing the Toyota.

"I could wave him off."

"Nah, that's all right. Break a leg today." Amber sauntered toward the driver's window, then tossed her head back and mouthed "Dad bod" in an exaggerated way.

Hazel laughed, feeling her body unclench around Checkers's soft brown-and-white fur. She watched Amber get into the Camry, then noted the license plate as it drove away, memorizing it like a piece of sheet music. She'd write it down when she got back to her room.

Checkers squirmed against her, and she brought him to her face. "Bad bunny."

Checkers didn't respond, only gave her his patented sad-eyed look with his round black eyes.

Hazel sighed. She only had Checkers because of this kid, Jessie, who'd stayed at the motel with his strung-out mom. She wasn't going to let him bring Checkers to their next stop, and they were going to release him into the wilds of Venice. He wouldn't have lasted a day.

"I'll take him!" Hazel had said, the words out of her mouth before her brain could catch up. Jessie's joyous smile had made it worth it at first, but she had no idea how to take care of a bunny. When she'd googled it, the first thing that came up was: *bunnies typically go to the bathroom two to three hundred times a day.* That, it turned out, was not even remotely an exaggeration.

She'd tried more than once to get rid of him, but she couldn't go through with it. Between the lingering memory of her promise to Jessie to keep him "forever and ever" and the fact that Checkers was her only company, she'd resigned herself to life with the rabbit.

When she got back to her room, she put Checkers in his cage, making sure the door was firmly shut. Then she coiled her chestnut hair into two braids, one on each side of her face, and let them flop over her shoulders. She applied a light coat of lip gloss and mascara. She picked up the romper and held it against her body, the way Amber had, checking herself in the mirror.

A young, down-on-her-luck singer-songwriter stared back at her. She cocked her hip to the side and gave her friendliest grin, trying to project a can-do attitude, then focused until the smile lit up her cornflower blue eyes. She almost didn't recognize herself, but that was the point.

Amber was right. *The Sing Along* was casting parts, and Hazel was determined to get one. She smiled at herself in the mirror again, trying to fill herself with confidence like she'd been taught to do before auditions. Her heart was beating nearly as quickly as Checkers's had been, churning out adrenaline in a way she hadn't felt in a long time.

She could do this. She *could* do this. She was *going* to do this.

Hazel reached for a memory and pulled out the right lingo. "Slate, please!" she said, then mimicked holding up a slate. She rotated through the other voices that would mark the start of filming. "Picture's up!

"Roll sound, roll camera.

"Rolling!"

She slapped the fake slate shut, the clap of her hands echoing off the walls. "Scene one, take one.

"And action!"

"So, Hazel, what are you going to sing for us today?"

Twelve hours later, Hazel stared directly into the camera lens as she stood in the hallway of the Sheraton Grand in downtown L.A. The hall was thick with other contestants waiting for their auditions and the friends and family they'd brought along for support. Only Hazel stood alone. "I'll be singing 'Titanium' by David Guetta."

Keshawn Jackson's mouth broke into an ultrawhite smile. He'd been the host of *The Sing Along* for ten seasons, and had a polished banter that he engaged in with the contestants before they went before the judges. "Excellent choice. A personal favorite."

He said this to most of the competitors, but Hazel pretended not to know that. Instead, she adjusted her guitar strap and said, "It's my theme song."

"Had a lot of adversity in your life, Hazel?"

A highlight reel of her worst moments flashed through her brain. "You bet."

Hazel knew that if she was one of the special contestants who didn't have to wait in line all day, the show would immediately cut to a prepackaged montage about her hardscrabble beginnings and everything she'd sacrificed to get there. But she'd only been approached by a scout after an open mic night. She didn't have a manager or a viral song on TikTok. No special montage for Hazel.

"But so has everyone here, right?" Hazel added, with a winning wink.

Keshawn laughed with delight. He could tell what she was doing, and he loved it. *Finally*, she could see him thinking. *Finally, someone who gets it.* "Where are you from, Hazel?"

"Austin, Texas." That was the truth. Hazel was juggling enough details about herself. She didn't need to add a fake hometown to the mix.

"And how old are you?"

"I'm twenty-two."

"You don't look a day over eighteen."

"I know, right? I get carded all the time."

"I'll bet you do," Keshawn said, his voice warm and deep. "Tell me, have you had a chance to check out the competition?"

"There was plenty of time to do so in that line!" Despite what was shown on TV, the auditions before the judges were the last in a series of steps that took place over the course of the day. Hazel had already sung her heart out in front of a junior producer and an assistant producer on the mean streets of downtown L.A. Then she'd had to sing in a small basement room that smelled like nicotine while they did her camera test. There weren't any windows, but at least a homeless guy wasn't screaming about an alien invasion while a police officer looked on passively as she tried to hit the high note in the chorus.

"We've had an incredible turnout today," Keshawn said. "We've already seen some fantastic talent."

The audition room doors opened and an Asian guy in his early twenties walked out with a well-used guitar slung over his back. He was holding a blue card and sporting a wide grin. He high-fived a couple of surfer dudes who'd been waiting for him, while two girls in slip dresses giggled.

"Oh, look, here's Benji Suzuki—I knew you'd make it!" Keshawn said, beckoning Benji over. They were a sharp contrast: Keshawn in a three-piece suit, his dark hair close-cropped, his nails manicured. Benji's black hair was straight, feathered, and highlighted. Five ten and well built, he was wearing a short-sleeved shirt and multicolored board shorts. "I'm sure you've seen Benji on TikTok, Hazel?"

"Of course!" Benji had mastered cutting his songs into viral videos that drove teen girls crazy and inspired imitation. There'd even been a Suzuki Challenge a few months back.

"Are you excited about making it through to Universal Week, Benji?" Keshawn asked, moving the mic toward him.

Benji tossed his head in a practiced gesture. "Fo sho."

Hazel hid a smile. Benji knew what he was doing, too, and his brush-off was a bit too casual. He wanted this as much as she did.

"That's fantastic. Benji, you want to wish Hazel luck? She's up next."

Benji rolled his eyes to Hazel's. As they locked in place, he gave her a slow smile. Hazel found herself responding to it, an answering smile on her lips and a fluttering she hadn't felt in a while in her stomach.

"Well, well, well. I'll have to keep my eye on you two." Keshawn gave them a knowing nod then pointed to the audition room. "You ready to go in, Hazel?"

Hazel threw her shoulders back. "Fo sho!" She winked at Benji, and he mouthed "Good luck!"

"Go on then, go!"

Hazel put her hand on the door handle, anticipating what came next. The adrenaline that had come and gone throughout the day was back, her heart stuttering, her palms sweaty.

"Let's watch Hazel's audition," Keshawn said, addressing the camera. "And remember to . . ."

". . . sing along if you know the words!" the crowd shouted with him.

The audition room was a standard-edition hotel conference room—thick multicolored carpet on the floor, beige walls, and track lighting. This room was an upgrade from the last one Hazel had been in, though, with a wall of windows letting in the bright California sunshine that always buoyed Hazel no matter how hard her day was, and freshly piped-in air. There were cameras and key lights set up around the perimeter, and three people sitting behind a long melamine folding table that was filled with an array of headshots and cola. *The Sing Along* logo was blown up on a large canvas behind them, as were the faces of several past winners, including Hazel's favorite, Kate Maple.

Hazel steadied herself and focused on giving the judges her most confident smile. When Georgia and Martin had taken a lap through the cattle call earlier that day, the air had buzzed with excitement. One woman, Zoey Johnson, a Black country music artist Hazel had stood in line with for half the day, had nearly passed out when she'd seen Georgia, who'd been a force in country music for most of Hazel's life.

From a distance, Georgia looked the same as she had when she'd become famous at twenty. But up close Hazel could see that Georgia wasn't aging well. Her bleached blond hair was brittle and split at the ends and her screen makeup sat in the deep lines around her watery green eyes. Rumor had it she had a drinking problem, which might be true or might be a vicious lie spread by the record company that was apparently trying to welch on the back end of a multi-album deal. Georgia was smiling at Hazel, though. She was the nice judge, the one who encouraged even those she sent home.

"What's your name, sweetheart?" Martin asked. British and in his midfifties, he'd manufactured a hundred hits and a dozen girl bands. He was wearing a tweed jacket with patches on the elbows, and his dark hair was bristle-cut, almost military-like. The winner of *The Sing Along* got a record deal with his label. Hazel knew it was important to stay on Martin's good side, which was easier said than done. Unlike Georgia, he'd made more than one contestant cry with his withering assessment of their talent.

"Hazel Fine," Hazel said, trying to keep the quake out of her voice. She'd been through auditions before. She could survive this one.

Martin scanned her body from her scalp to her cowboy boots. His eyes felt like fingers, probing her. "And are you fine, Hazel?"

Hazel slapped on a smile that made her face hurt and her soul die. "As fine as can be!"

"Ignore him," Georgia said in her Southern twang. "Tell us about yourself, darlin'."

"I'm twenty-two years old and from Austin, Texas. A waitress by day, I'm a singer-songwriter by night."

Georgia laughed and the man sitting to her left cracked a brief smile. In his early thirties, with chestnut hair that had a light curl to it and dark-green eyes, he was wearing a black T-shirt and had a stack of notes in front of him. Hazel didn't recognize him, and she thought briefly about asking who he was, but then thought better of it. She wasn't there to ask questions. She was in the witness box.

Instead, Hazel tracked her eyes back to Martin. He was scowling at her as if she was a puzzle he needed to figure out. Hazel could feel the heat of the lights on her neck. A bead of sweat trickled down her back.

"What made you audition for *The Sing Along*?" Georgia asked.

"Singing is my life."

Martin crossed his hairy arms and leaned back in his chair. "Is it now?"

"I want it to be."

"Do you think you have what it takes?"

Hazel lifted her chin. She met men like Martin every day when she was waitressing. Men who thought they could touch her like she was part of the furniture or tell her what to do like she was their child. The only way to deal with someone like that was to meet them with equal confidence. Manfidence, Hazel had taken to calling it. "I do."

Martin gave her a brief smile. "Show us, then, love."

Hazel moved her guitar into place, her fingers falling easily onto the frets. She loved this instrument. When she'd seen it in the pawn shop six months ago, it had beckoned to her like a lover. She'd worked a month of double shifts to pay for it, but it was worth it.

As she got ready to start, Hazel thought back to the seedy motel where she barely made rent. How tired she was when she came home from a shift. How often her sleep was interrupted by someone pounding on her door looking for their dealer. She was tired of living like that. She shouldn't feel this old at her age, whatever it was. Her life was supposed to be more than this. She deserved more than this. And here it was, her chance—her *last* chance it felt like—if she could reach out and seize it.

So, even though she hated it when singers did that, she closed her eyes, focused on the strings she was plucking and the form her mouth had to take to get that first chord right.

And then she sang as if her life depended on it.

Because it did.

© 2023 Catherine McKenzie